New Avalon Rangers

M.K. Martin

Published in the United States by
Not a Pipe Publishing Ink-Corporated L.L.C.,
www.NotAPipePublishing.com

Trade Paperback Edition

ISBN-13: 978-1-956892-68-0

Cover art by Aaron Smith

Dedication

To Annika
We love you. We will always miss you.

Content Warning

New Avalon Rangers includes content that may be difficult or unsuitable for some readers. I've included a list of elements here. If you have concerns, check it out so you can decide whether to continue reading. Please prioritize your mental health over my wallet. -M.K. Martin

- Antisemitism
- Attempted rape (reference to)
- Body horror
- Childbirth
- Child death
- Cult
- Gore
- Profanity
- Racism
- Sexism
- Sexually explicit scenes (hetero)
- Sexual assault
- Violence

Prologue

TDPA, Fort Carson, Colorado, USA – Spring, Year 2

Erica hitched up her jeans and picked her way across the muddy pathway that led to the shower trailers. No point even trying that road. The running water had stopped working sometime in the winter. Besides, if rumors were to be believed there were potatoes in the camp kitchen. Now that would be cause for celebration.

The last of the Colorado snow still huddled in the spaces beneath the C-huts and hugged their northern sides where the sun didn't quite reach even in April. The melted snow turned the ground into a bog and the footpaths that crisscrossed the camp into avenues of mud. Most days, Erica stayed in her hut. Since the other family had left, she had the place to herself. It was comfortable, as long as she buried herself in a mound of bedding. No heat to her hut since the big storm in December, but who could she complain to? No one. Where else could she go? Nowhere.

But today, there were potatoes.

The line outside the mess tent was already halfway back to the wall that separated the Temporarily Displaced Persons Accommodations from Fort Carson proper. When Erica arrived at the TDPA late in the fall, she believed that her stay would be short. A few weeks, months at most, for the government to get the situation under control and then she could return home. They had a vaccine and the unofficial word around her office was that they'd located that scientist, the handsome one, who'd invented the vaccine in the first place.

See how that had worked out.

Erica got in line behind a man with two teenagers. The boy was tall and thin, leaning against the man and breathing in gusty gasps. Asthma? Or some other respiratory infection that had gone untreated too long. Erica had had a cough for so long that she barely noticed it anymore. The girl in front of her watched everything with eyes that looked too big for her thin face.

Erica frowned at the girl before she could say anything. People seemed to think an older woman alone was a good target for whatever unfocused aggression they had. Well, not this old gal. The girl flinched at Erica's glare and turned around. She put an arm around the boy. Yeah, that's right. You have a family. La-dee-da. Erica turtled down into her puffy coat and three scarves. At least she wasn't stuck with any dead weight.

The line inched forward and Erica shuffled with it. She was nearly up to the mess tent when she heard that clatter and yells that she'd been bracing herself for.

The Petersons.

Over the winter, the number of soldiers and aid workers from Carson had dwindled. Sometime about a month ago, the general had called a meeting during which he'd formally handed over the camp governance to a civilian committee. That had lasted all of a week until two of the five committee members were found dead. Another committee member hadn't been found at all.

After that, the Petersons took over. Not that they solved any problems. The shower trailers still didn't work. The port-o-potties were a joke. Everyone continued doing their business over the shit trench, which was getting worse and worse with every warm day. The pallets of bottled water still arrived from Carson, but the Petersons took nearly half for themselves, so everyone else was dehydrated and dirty.

And now they were taking the potatoes, too.

Erica could have cried, but she didn't have the energy.

Someone in the mess tent screamed, someone else laughed. Ahead of Erica people turned away, drifted off back to their huts. They still had their MREs and other food they'd hoarded. Who cared about potatoes? It wasn't worth getting beaten up for. Or worse.

Erica shrugged and started to trudge away. She had enough nightmare fodder without staying to listen to the Petersons having their fun.

"Don't!" the man who'd been in line ahead of her said.

Erica looked back over her shoulder. The girl had broken away from the man and boy and was sprinting toward the mess hall. Stupid kid.

Erica shook her head. She took the long route back to avoid the port-o-potties. Her stomach growled the whole way. By the time she arrived back at her hut, the sounds from the mess hall faded into the generally low noise of the camp.

Although the interior of the hut was dim, made worse by the ragged quilts Erica had pinned over the windows to block the drafts, she didn't light her lantern. That was for emergencies only. She let her eyes adjust and moved through the little cubicles with their plywood walls by memory more than feel or sight.

Until she kicked something. It was heavy, but soft. And it grunted.

Erica fumbled in her pocket for the knife she carried, caught the hilt on her scarf and dropped it. As she scrambled to grab it, she kicked it away. It went spinning across the floor.

"Please," cried a muffled voice. "Don't hurt me."

The girl from the line sat up out of the pile of bedding she'd been hiding in. She raised her hands in surrender. In each hand, she held potatoes.

Dusk came slowly down the mountains. The wind fell silent. The camp was still.

Erica stuck her head out of the hut's door and scanned the area. No one was around.

"All clear," she said.

Cassy, the potato girl, took off the blankets she'd been wrapped in and rolled them up before putting them on

Erica's bed. It was a nice gesture but would make more work for Erica later. She frowned.

"Thanks again for letting me stay," the girl said. "You probably saved my life."

"I shouldn't have to tell you that potatoes aren't worth your life," Erica said.

"We're gonna need all the food we can get for the trip to Yellowstone," Cassy said.

Erica waved her off dismissively. She'd heard enough rumors of all the better places to not credit this latest one.

"Yellowstone is no different from that place in Montana or Kentucky or Detroit," the older woman said. She crossed her arms, tucked her hands into her pockets. When was the last time she'd been warm?

"Maybe," Cassy said. She adjusted her knit cap, tucking in her ratty curls. "You could come with us."

Erica snorted. "Leave food and safety to wander out there? No thanks."

"What if the Infected attack, like that camp in Washington?"

"That's rumors," Erica said. "This whole business is nothing but rumors and fear. Last time I listened to all that nonsense, I left a perfectly good apartment and ended up here, so again no thank you."

"If you'd stayed you probably would have gotten HHV," Cassy said.

"Or HHV doesn't exist and this was just a way for the government to clear and resettle a bunch of real estate without paying eminent domain money."

"That's stupid," Cassy said.

"Then get out of my stupid hut," Erica snapped. This

is what happened if you were nice. People treated you like a doormat, good for nothing but wiping their shitty shoes on.

"I'm sorry," Cassy started but Erica pushed her out and slammed the door.

For a moment, she feared that the girl would bang on the door, calling attention to her hut, but after a brief pause, she heard the slushy-crunchy sounds of Cassy's sneakers moving away through the half-frozen slop on the ground.

Good.

Then she heard the low male voices, the snicker, and the half-scream, cut off by the dull thud of impact. A fist to the stomach probably.

Not my circus, not my monkeys, Erica told herself.

More low voices and Cassy's higher pitched one quavering between defiance and terror.

Erica covered her ears but the sounds wormed their way in, digging into her brain. She wanted to believe that the Petersons would deliver a beating, take back their potatoes and go. She wanted to believe it because she knew it wasn't true.

In some other life when Erica had been a young, naïve, up-and-coming paralegal who got invited to all the firm's swanky office soirees, she had taken a friend's advice and gone to self-defense classes. For women her size, escape was the name of the game. But she'd also gotten a mini stun gun.

Against all her good judgment and reason, Erica crept out the back door of the hut, her trembling hands fumbling the stun gun out of the waistband of her long johns. When she rounded the corner of her hut, coming into view of the muddy track, she froze.

She expected a crowd of hulking, brutish men, the sort of nightmare creatures that her self-defense instructor had painted so vividly in her training scenarios. But there were only two and they were young, scrawny even. They looked like the kind of boys she used to yell at for skateboarding in the park.

"Go back inside, you old bitch," one of the boys said with a sneer.

The other was pinning Cassy's arms back, his hands inside her shirt. There were tears in the girl's eyes, but she looked furious not cowed. It was that expression that kept Erica from sensibly leaving.

She still remembered the drunken drag queen's triumphant whoop as the man who'd taken Erica out to an alley stumbled away clutching his well-kicked balls.

"We queens have to stick together, honey," the drag queen had slurred as he put his soft, sweaty arms around young Erica.

And they did.

Erica lunged, jabbed the mini stun gun and squeezed the trigger.

The boy dropped, the front of his pants darkening as the smell of pee filled the air. The other boy let go of Cassy and grabbed Erica's arm. She screamed and dropped the mini stun gun like it was on fire. Had she really just done that?

The boy hit her.

Erica staggered back, crashed into the wall of her hut, saw stars, slid down to sit on her butt, her feet out in front of her like a discarded doll.

The boy jerked and fell. Cassy stood over him, the

stun gun clutched in her hands.

"Are you okay?" she asked.

"No," Erica snapped. "Not by a gosh darn long shot I'm not okay."

"We gotta go," the girl said, as if Erica weren't sitting there trying not to have a heart attack.

"Go? Where?" the older woman demanded between gasps.

"We can't stay here," Cassy said. She squatted beside the still twitching men and rummaged through their clothes, pulling out a couple of knives and a small pistol. "My dad and brother know to meet us in Yellowstone as soon as they can safely get away."

"No sugar we can't stay here now. You and those ever-blessed potatoes," Erica grumbled. She pushed herself up using the hut for support.

"Yellowstone here we come!" Cassy said with far too much cheeriness for a girl standing between the semi-conscious bodies of men who would happily murder her.

"We'll talk about that on the road." Erica opened the hut's front door. Everything she could possibly want to take with her fit into a backpack, plus the quilts, but she couldn't take those. She left them folded neatly on the end of her bed. Maybe someone would find them. Maybe that person wouldn't be a Peterson. But probably it would be one of them. The wicked always managed to thrive.

"How long until Yellowstone?" Cassy asked with a

grin. Erica had tired of this particular game hours, if not days, ago. The pair trudged along a road that seemed to go on forever. Ahead, low hills striped red and tan scraped at the cloudy sky. The scrubby desert ran away to the east and to the west lay a lake. RVs and cars sat abandoned at campsites along the rocky shore. Cars sometimes had food or camping gear in them, especially out here in the back end of Wyoming. More importantly, unlike RVs, cars had big windows. Very little chance the Infected were hiding inside, the way they did sometimes in the RVs.

"Not soon, according to that." Erica pointed to a sign. WELCOME BOYSEN STATE PARK.

"But how long from here to there?" Cassy's tone was the whine of a tired toddler. Erica frowned. She'd never had nor wanted kids. Frankly, cats were too needy for her.

"Do I look like a flipping GPS to you?" Erica snapped.

"You have the map," Cassy snapped back.

"Which you looked at when we stopped for lunch." Erica's voice rose.

"Lunch? Is that what you call it?" Cassy's rose to match.

"Don't blame me." Erica was yelling for real now, heedless of the potential danger the unexplored RVs posed. "I wasn't the one who thought we could walk three hundred miles on six potatoes."

"I didn't have a choice!"

"So, you dragged me into your mess? I could have been safe and warm back in Carson," Erica said, lowering her voice to not-quite-shouting by an extreme act of will. She was cold, hungry, exhausted, and entirely at her limit.

"You could have been eaten." Cassy made no effort to be quiet. "At least then you'd have made something happy for a few minutes instead of poisoning every waking moment with all your doom and gloom. Have you ever had a good day in your whole life or were you born miserable?"

Erica stopped walking and tossed her backpack down. She yanked out the map and wadded it into a ball, which she threw in Cassy's face.

Or she tried to. The wind caught the map. Ahead, the rocks rose up on either side making the road into the bottom of a short canyon. The map sailed away, skipping and flipping through the narrow passage.

"You bitch." Cassy sprinted after the map.

"Fudge." Erica did, too.

The map skittered out the other end of the canyon where the wind off the lake sent it inland. Cassy raced after it, Erica puffing along behind her.

Cassy screamed. Erica froze.

A man was tied to a signpost. His arms were up over the back of the sign, pulling his shoulders tight around his ears. His feet were tied to the metal post. He looked dead. Then he lifted his head and peered at them through a squinted eye.

Cassy screamed again.

"Shut up." Erica whacked the girl's arm. "You want the Infected on us, too? Go get the map." It was caught in some scrubby shrubs, flapping in the wind like it still meant to make a run for it.

While Cassy hurried to get the map, Erica pulled out her knife. She looked around, trying to see if this was some kind of trap. There didn't seem to be anyone else. There was a big white cross spray-painted on the man's chest. On the rocks behind him, someone had spray-painted a pair of white birds facing each other and some kind of four-legged animal that could have been a lamb or a dog or a small horse.

"Help," the man muttered.

Erica inched closer, holding out the knife menacingly.

"They left me ..." The man's voice was raspy and hard to hear above the wind. Cassy returned, clutching the crumpled and torn map. She huddled behind Erica, practically climbing on her for a piggyback.

"Get off, girl." Erica waved her back.

"The herd is coming," the man said. "They left me here as bait."

"Who did?" Cassy whispered, still huddled behind Erica.

"The Children of the Restoration." The man coughed. His eyes focused on the knife Erica was still pointing in his general direction. "Lady, if you're not going to help me, please kill me. I don't want to be alive when the Infected get here."

Erica shook her head. Even tasering those boys back at Carson terrified her. She wasn't about to murder a helpless person.

"Grab his legs, Cassy," she said. "I'll cut you loose, but don't try anything."

It took nearly ten minutes of hard work to get the man down. His arms and legs barely moved. His hands and feet were swollen and nearly black from being tied up so tight. He moaned in pain but insisted that Cassy and

Erica help him lift and move his limbs to get the blood circulating again.

They sat in the lee of the rocky canyon wall, listening to the wind, which to Erica sounded more and more like the howls of the Infected by the minute.

"We gotta get moving," Cassy said, giving voice to Erica's thoughts.

"I can't," the man said. He reached into his shirt and pulled out a wallet. It was the kind of sleek, expensive Italian leather Erica associated with senior partners and important clients. The man took a key card out and handed it to Erica. He gave the wallet to Cassy.

"If I don't make it, you need to take this to Crossroads. It's a little town in central Montana. Find Marius Tenartier. Tell him this is from Isaac Mendelsen."

"Doctor Isaac Mendelsen," Cassy said, reading something in the wallet. "What's the G-O-A-R-N? The go arn?"

"It's a medical thing from Europe, like the CDC," Erica said. She'd done some work restructuring medical debt, which required learning about the various governing bodies around the world.

"Indeed," Isaac said.

"Why would anyone tie up a doctor?" Cassy jumped to her feet, glaring around as if she meant to give the Children of the Restoration a serious talking-to.

"They didn't take the time to discuss my medical credentials," Isaac struggled to his feet. He was not going to go anywhere fast. Erica searched the surrounding hills. No Infected that she could see, but usually by the time you saw them it was too late.

"All they cared about was that I was Jewish." Isaac said. He started limping down the road. "Apparently, my kind killed Christ and some of the Christians are still miffed about it."

"That's stupid," Cassy said.

"People are terrified." Isaac shrugged. "They cling to anything that even faintly resembles salvation."

"You're way more understanding than I would be," Erica said. She stopped, peering back into the hazy distance the way they had come. Was the horizon darker or was it only her imagination? No, it was moving. Not fast, but faster than they were walking.

Isaac caught her eye and nodded slightly. The Infected.

"We have to run," Erica said.

"Do you remember where to take the key and the coordinates?" Isaac asked.

"Crossroads," Cassy said. "Small town, central Montana. A guy named Marius Tenner. Or something like that."

"Close enough," Isaac gave a small smile. "I must thank you for giving me a fighting chance."

"Not going to do you a fudging lot of good when that herd catches up," Erica said. She held out her knife. It was a good knife and she was sorry to lose it, but Isaac would need a way to make sure the Infected didn't eat him alive.

"No, indeed it may not, but still, you have my gratitude." Isaac took the knife. "Tell Marius that the Chrysalis protocol is in Detroit. In the salt mine under the city. He'll need the key card to get access and there's a map in my wallet with the coordinates."

Cassy stood for a moment, her eyes flicking between Erica and Isaac. Then she threw her arms around Isaac and hugged him. She pulled away and said. "I'm sorry. It's really shitty."

"Yes," Isaac smiled again, then looked over his shoulder. "Now please, ladies, I must insist you be on your way. This isn't misguided chivalry. I simply cannot keep up in my current state."

"I know." Erica hated that he was right, that they were going to leave him to die so they could live, but that's exactly what they did.

In the days and weeks that followed, as she and Cassy traveled through northern Wyoming and into Montana, she reminded herself of all the logical reasons what they'd done was the right thing, the only thing they could have done.

She didn't convince herself. Not even a little.

Chapter 1 - Torres

Torres crouched in the brush blind, her focus tight on the grazing buck. A few more steps and he'd be clear of the saplings and into the small clearing. The former Marine drew a long, steady breath, counting slowly to four as she did. She held the air, feeling the regular bump of her heartbeat. Her finger tightened, taking the slack out of the trigger. With only three bullets, she couldn't afford to miss a shot.

The buck moved forward. His new antlers were still covered in velvety fuzz, nearly as soft as the half-curled yellow-green leaf buds that hazed the trees. Around the buck, birds cheeped and warbled a cacophony of come-hithers. Pollen drifted on the air, which also carried scents of wet earth and blossoms.

The whole thing was way too freaking naturey for Torres's liking. Give her a decent range with some pop-up targets or better yet, a mount site with moving targets and she would hit 20/20 every time. But here, in this overly idyllic woodsy wonderland, she was out of her element.

The buck stopped, head lifted as if sensing danger.

Too late, buddy.

Torres squeezed the trigger. The shot range across the clearing, the surrounding hills echoing the sound back so that it clashed like waves. The birds bolted away, leaving only a horrified silence. The buck stumbled a few steps. Torres shot him again and he fell forward, long delicate legs folding neatly under him.

Killing was not new to Torres. As a Marine, she'd seen combat even before she'd had to fight for her life during the Chrysalis outbreak. Since then, she'd killed plenty of Infected and a few non-Infected, but those had all been in self-defense or defense of others. Killing a harmless, fully healthy, non-HHV mutated deer felt different. It felt like murder.

Torres shook her head at the illogicality of emotions. The buck would feed a lot of people, including herself and her six-year-old niece and ward, Elfy. Gone were the days of buying meat in neat, clean packages from the grocery store. These days, if you wanted animal protein you had to be ready to get up to your elbows in blood and guts.

She pushed her short, dark hair away from her face. Over the winter she'd let it grow. The wispy hairs tickling at the back of her neck reminded her yet again why she hated longer hair. She slung her rifle across her back and stepped out of the blind.

"Freeze!" a man shouted.

It was hard to pinpoint exactly his position by sound alone, but given the density of the spring foliage, Torres estimated he was off to her right, probably hunkered under the clump of pine trees there. The heavy branches would give him concealment if not actual cover. She couldn't get to her rifle without tipping him off.

Best to let him think he had the upper hand while she figured out how to get out of this alive. She stood still and raised her hands, letting her adrenaline tremble show.

The pine branches thrashed and snapped as the man pushed his way into the clearing. He was white, mid-40s, wearing a ball cap and a stained set of coveralls under an open coat with a woodland camouflage pattern. He also wore a red armband. A large white star crossed with a blue bar on the armband identified him as a member of the People's Defense Force, a militia out of Great Falls.

Torres's narrowed her eyes, quickly assessing the man. The well-broken-in hiking boots and his ability to sneak up on her argued that he was a local, probably much more skilled at hunting than the former Marine. The way he let his rifle's muzzle drop, not pointing exactly at her told her he didn't have combat experience and didn't see her as a threat, an advantage for her.

"Please. Please, don't hurt me." She quavered her voice. *I'm just a weak woman, don't be afraid to get closer. I don't have a hunting knife with your name on it.* Amazing how quickly she could go from tearful regret at ending the deer's life to feeling very murdery. It wasn't enough that the PDF had harried the folks from New Avalon all the long winter. Their leader, the Irish mercenary Liam, had sold Marius to the Enlightened.

"Keep your hands where I can see em," the man said. He walked towards the buck, keeping her in sight, but not really watching her too closely. He stood over the body and looked down. "Nice shooting. Clean kill. Not bad for a city girl. Too bad we'll have to confiscate this one."

"But we need the meat." Torres let her frustration fill her voice.

The man shrugged as he took a knee, yanking the buck around for easier field butchering. "Not sure if you should file that under 'so sad' or 'too bad'. Either way, that's a you problem, honey." He chuckled and went to work, slicing open the belly with a long, practiced stroke.

Torres crouched, slow and careful, her fingers finding the holdout knife she kept strapped to her ankle for just such occasions. It took the count of five full, steady breaths to stand up again. The man checked over his shoulder and waved with his elbow.

"Go wait over there. Want you where I can see you," he said.

"Why? Can't you just let me go?" Torres wondered if she was laying on the damsel-in-distress too thick. The man didn't seem to mind. He waved again with his elbow, giving Torres an excuse to start moving.

The second before her knife was at his throat he started to turn as if some deep instinct had finally rustled to life. Too late.

"Gah!" The man froze, his hands splayed out, dripping fresh blood onto the buck's soft fur.

"If I was you, son," Torres said, "I'd file this under 'so sad'. Toss your weapon away and put your hands up.

Interlace your fingers behind your head. Cross your ankles and sit back on them." The former Marine did a quick, thorough pat down, coming up with another knife and a walkie-talkie. She stuffed both into her pack.

A branch snapped and Torres spun, dropping into a low-ready stance. Two figures moved between the trees. As soon as Torres turned in their direction, the people held up their hands.

"Don't shoot!" a woman called, despite the fact that Torres's rifle was still across her back, annoyingly.

"Come out where I can see you," Torres said. Her voice was loud, commanding, but not yelling. She put a hand on the kneeling man's shoulder and muttered to him, "Don't get any smart ideas."

Two women emerged from the thin cover of the trees. One was a pale, skinny teenager, the other an older Black woman who glowered at Torres from several layers of parka. The former Marine blinked. One prisoner she could handle, but three?

"We surrender," the girl shouted.

Torres waved a hand, signaling her to quiet down. The forest was still. Even the wind had died down. No birds, no animals. Nothing but the heavy breathing of the kneeling man beside her. But there was something. A primitive survival sense Torres had learned to listen to from the first moment her boots hit a combat zone.

Slowly, the former Marine reached over her shoulder. The scar from a gunshot wound pulled as she twisted, sliding the rifle around. She hooked the sling over her elbow for added stability as she sheathed her knife.

"We already surrendered. You can't shoot us!" The girl's voice shrilled, but Torres wasn't listening to her.

There. A faint rustle in the underbrush behind her.

Torres spun on her heel, as pretty an about-face as any Drill Instructor could ever dream off. The rifle was up, butt in the pocket of her shoulder, cheek along the barrel, and the sight-post faintly blurred as she looked past it.

An Infected scuttled through the fuzzy green plants. It was some kind of furry creature, or it had been before the HHV infection had mutated it. Maybe a beaver? Torres didn't know a lot about animals, but living out in the armpit of Montana, she'd been learning quick.

She took the shot, quick and clean, started to turn back when something slammed into her legs. One leg flew up in the air while the other buckled. She fell forward, catching herself with one hand, but hanging onto the rifle, the sling still wound around her upper arm.

The man grabbed the barrel and yanked, trying to disarm her.

She squeezed the trigger.

She didn't even think about it, didn't stop to debate the pros and cons of killing an uninfected man or a fellow human being.

But nothing happened. Two shots for the buck and one for the Infected. Shit!

The man jumped on her, pinning her down with one arm under his leg and the other still clutching the rifle. Torres could hear the woman and the girl yelling, but beyond that sound, was something worse.

Infected. A pack. Drawn by the noise in the clearing, they charged through the forest.

"Run!" Torres tried to warn the others.

The Infected hit the man on top of her so hard that the bottom half of him stayed put while the top half vanished in a spray of blood and the Infected's flailing tentacles.

She kicked and clawed her way out from under the dead man, rolled to the side in time to dodge another Infected. She didn't see it clearly. Something with hoofs and fangs — that wasn't right.

Torres scrambled up. The girl huddled in the clearing. The woman clutched a small knife in one hand and tried to pull the girl back with the other. Two Infected were flanking the pair, moving in for the kill. Torres's useless rifle flapped from its sling, still wrapped around her arm. She grabbed the barrel like a ball bat and started toward the Infected.

Something caught her ankle, yanked her back. She kicked out, her boot crunching into her attacker.

"Feck's sake, woman, stop."

Torres recognized the Irish accent even though Liam's voice had a soggy, nasal sound. She whirled to glare at the mercenary. His ginger hair was tucked under a wool beanie cap. Like the PDF man, he wore mostly civilian camouflage hunting gear with a few military accents.

Liam cupped a hand over his nose, blood covering his chin. She'd broken his nose or nearly.

"You want rescued or not?" A fine mist of blood and snot accompanied the mercenary's question.

"You and what army?" Torres stood up, scanning for the woman and girl. They had retreated back into the trees, the Infected following them.

"Lads." Liam waved his arm over his head. Four PDF

members broke cover, advancing toward Torres. She pointed the rifle at Liam.

"Back off."

"Whist." He smirked. "You're out of bullets, love."

"So, this is more of a capture than a rescue?"

"Beggars, choosers." Liam winced as a fresh gout of blood leaked from his nose.

"At least go get those two." Torres waved toward the trees where the woman and girl had disappeared.

"What's in it for me?"

"I'm not gonna beg you to do the right thing," Torres crossed her arms.

"Eh, go on with ya." Liam motioned for three of the PDF members to go after the woman and girl. A woman stayed behind, keeping a compound bow pointed at Torres. "I'm not an utter shite, despite what you seem to think of me."

"You sold *him* to the Enlightened." Torres's fury was instantaneous. She barely kept herself from flying at Liam to rip his smug throat out. The guard's bow creaked as if she sensed Torres's intent.

"He went of his own will like." Liam snorted and tipped his head back, pinched the bridge of his nose. "I'm sure Bambi told you what happened."

"Bailey," Torres snapped.

"Him."

Gunfire barked from the clump of trees where the PDF had gone. The Infected's shrieks and cries shifted from hunting to rage.

"So, don't be blaming me if your man went off like the blessed lamb to the slaughter," Liam said.

"He didn't have a choice." Torres clenched her fists.

"Needs must," Liam said.

The girl and woman came out of the trees across the clearing, a pair of camo-clad warriors behind them.

"Now what?" Torres demanded.

"Now we see how much the Captain is willing to trade for his favorite little leftenant."

"A lot," a low voice spoke from behind them. Both Liam and Torres spun to find themselves face to face with Captain John Courage and a whole squad of the New Avalon Rangers.

Afternoon rolled in with bank of grey clouds, which was more of what Torres expected. Ever since the Portland Flash the weather had been weird. Lots of clouds, but not a lot of rain or snow. Marius's dad, Philippe, had explained something about how high-altitude particles might be keeping the moisture in the stratosphere. It sounded reasonable at the time. All Torres knew was the weather was crap most of the time. She planned accordingly.

What she hadn't planned for was a standoff.

Captain John Courage, former head of Chrysalis Biopharmaceuticals security team and current head of the New Avalon security team, barely spared a glance for Liam before looking Torres over. She spread the fingers of her left hand, signing that she was all right and not being coerced. Courage scratched the stubble on his face, tapping his nose three times as he did so. That meant there were three hidden team members, probably covering the other PDF members.

"I don't want to waste time, so here's my offer," John said. "Torres comes with us and we let the rest of you head home to Great Falls, no questions asked."

"Counteroffer," Liam said. "You give us those horses we've been asking about and we'll let this one go." With a smirk, he added. "No questions asked."

"Counter-counteroffer," Torres said. "Try to take me back to Great Falls and see how many of your weekend-warrior rejects I castrate before we get there."

"I never imagined you were so interested in my balls."

"What can I say? I'm into microbiology." Torres grinned wickedly.

Liam mimed being shot in the heart.

"Captain!" one of the New Avalon Rangers, Andy, ran up to John. "They cleared the Infected but Dawn says there's a pretty clear trail. Permission to investigate further, sir?"

John looked at Torres. She ran the Rangers' day-to-day operations and knew the roster better than he did. Torres nodded. Andy trotted off.

"Seriously?" Liam dabbed at his nose and studied the congealing blood on his sleeve. "You're a prisoner. Stop giving orders."

"Kiss my —"

"We should go," John interrupted. "C'mon, Torres." He started walking away. Torres was impressed with how steady he was. Over the long winter, his knee injury from Harrow Hall had gotten worse. Rajiv, an immunologist Marius had known from his university days, suspected a serious case of osteoarthritis, but without proper equipment, he couldn't confirm it.

Ursula, the local veterinarian, who was the closest thing they had to a general practitioner, concurred. She predicted eventually the knee would lock up completely.

Until then, John did most of his commanding from a recliner in the office in the barn of the Morning Star ranch. Occasionally, he rode, although even that was getting harder for him. Torres knew what it had cost him to be out here, this far from the ranch.

She fell into step beside him, ignoring the PDF's yells that she stop and come back. John had decided to call their bluff and she followed his lead. As usual, he turned out to be right. The PDF followed them out of the glade but fell back to reinforce Liam. The woman and girl stood awkwardly off to one side, not exactly prisoners, but not going anywhere either.

Briefly, Torres considered fighting for them, but she didn't even know they would want to go with her. Maybe they were headed to Great Falls all along. Much as she hated to leave them, she wasn't prepared to risk the lives of her friends for a pair of strangers.

As Torres started to turn away the woman gave her a small wave. She pointed to her back and then behind her. When Torres had first seen the pair, they'd both had backpacks on. The girl still wore hers, but not the woman. Was she signaling Torres where to find it? Why?

No chance to look now with the Infected so close and the PDF in the area. Torres had to hope Liam wouldn't find the pack before she got the chance to retrieve it.

Once out of sight of the PDF, John's limp returned with a vengeance. He stumbled and nearly fell to one knee. Torres caught him and hooked his arm over her shoulder.

"I'm thinking now's not the time to point out they stole my kill," Torres said. John's already tightly clenched jaw muscle jumped. "Got it, jefe." Back at the horses, she helped him mount up. Amazingly, her horse Ganymede hadn't wandered off or been stolen.

On the ride back to the ranch, Torres told John and the other Rangers what had happened in the clearing. Most were in favor of turning right around and going after the PDF, but John reminded them they still had to deal with the Infected in the area.

Torres detailed a couple of the younger Ranger scouts Helen and Diego to circle back to look for the woman's pack. Hopefully, they could follow the PDF enough to see that the woman and girl were traveling with them of their own free will.

As they crested the last ridge, coming at the ranch from the north, Torres marveled at how much had changed in less than a year. The ranch house itself was the only structure that hadn't undergone some major work. The barn was now the NAR headquarters. The bunkhouse had been expanded to serve as the NAR barracks. Three new greenhouses stood on the sunniest part of the south-facing rise in the front yard. Behind the ranch house, a shed had been converted into a laboratory and a plastic tunnel connected it to a newly dug cellar where molds and fungi of all kinds grew.

Most of the livestock had been moved to the new barn, although with the warming weather, a lot of the animals were out to pasture under tight security. Between the Infected, the PDF, and random strangers passing through the area, rustling of all kinds was a major concern.

The Rangers scattered from the barn. Torres sent one off to the radio shack, which sat in the foothills of the Rocky Mountains, boasting a clear line of sight for miles in all directions. She would let the radio operator know to alert the rest of the communities within the New Avalon collective about the Infected in the area and the PDF's movements.

The rest of the Rangers set about re-fitting their gear and updating their maps. Torres and John had drilled them hard on this point. Always pass all their information to all the other Rangers. It was part of the Ranger creed.

John lowered himself into his chair with a wince and a sigh. Torres leaned against the counter where Philippe used to keep various animal medicines. These days it was full of half-finished tactical gear. Everything had to be made of locally sourced, renewable materials. Lots of leather, linen, and wool. If Torres never smelled lanolin again it would be too soon.

"Let's talk about leadership," John said.

"Is this a conversation or am I getting yelled at?" Torres ruffled her hands through her hair and crossed her arms over her chest.

"Do you think you should get yelled at?" John picked up his coffee mug, sipped it, made a face and set it down.

"Torres, why did you go out alone?" The former Marine dropped her voice to imitate John's Midwestern baritone. "You know protocol states buddy teams." She resumed her normal register. "I know, John, but I needed to get out and clear my head and we needed fresh meat."

"You're pretty good at this," John said. "Maybe you

should be in charge of the Rangers.”

"Not a chance in Hell, jefe,” Torres said. “You're stuck with the job.”

"Then why'd you go out like that?”

Torres half-shrugged. "I needed to do something. To actually make a difference, not just wait around for the next thing to go wrong or fall apart or ...”

"Or the next person to die?”

"He's not dead!” Torres pushed off the shelf and stalked around the small room that served as John's office.

John nodded, not like he agreed with her, but like he was humoring her.

She yanked open the door and glared at the soldier.

"He's not. I'm gonna find him.” She slammed the door behind her, rattling the flimsy plastic sheets that served as the barn's windowpanes.

The roster was up to date. The maps had all the latest information. The radio was working fine. All Torres's gear was repaired. Her go-bag was fully stocked. Her ammunition was sorted back into the proper bins. She even disassembled and cleaned her rifle before returning it to the armory.

Whether she liked it or not, the former Marine had to face the fact that it was a full five hours until she could reasonably go to bed. She thought about dropping in at the school to visit Elfy. But that would disrupt the class and worry the teachers. Soraya and Phineas had enough on their hands trying to get ye olde one-room schoolhouse up and running during the collapse of Western civilization and the on-going threat of attack by everything from Infected to the PDF to roving bands of marauders.

Unable to face the hours, Torres walked. She came, as she often did, to the back of the ranch house. From here she could look up at the window. Marius's window. They'd only ever spent one night there together, but Torres treasured the memory.

His mother, Annette, lit a candle on the windowsill at night to guide his way home. In daylight, Torres could see the ever-growing tower of wax as one candle melted down and was replaced by the next.

She could also see the curtains were closed in the middle bedroom. That room used to be Marius's sister Percy's room. These days, Percy bunked with John and no one said boo to either of them about it. Once Torres had asked Percy if she wanted the Rangers to find some birth control pills on their scouting missions, but the other woman laughed her off, thanking her for her concern.

"We can't stop living. Hoping for the future is part of that," Percy said with a smile that showed her dimples. "Que sera, sera, right?"

"Venga lo que venga," Torres agreed with a grin.

After Percy moved in with John, Miranda moved into the empty room in the ranch house. Ever since Dawn brought Miranda back from the quarry, more dead than alive, the young woman had been different. Even after she'd physically recovered, she was withdrawn, spending most of her time alone in the room with the curtains drawn.

Torres went inside, passing through the mudroom into the kitchen. A huge pot of stew simmered on the stove. She could barely glimpse the ceiling with all the drying herbs hanging from strings there. A pile of new potatoes sat on the counter, waiting to be scrubbed and sorted. Lentils soaked in a bucket next to the massive, heavy oak table over which was spread fabric scraps. It looked like they were being sorted into pieces big enough for quilting patches and those that would get used for rag rugs or stuffing. Never before had folks taken the motto Reduce, Reuse, and Recycle so seriously.

Anatole, Marius's younger brother, was sleeping on the couch in the living room. Around him was a clutter of milk crates filled with printed pages. Before the internet vanished, the folks of New Avalon had spent days printing as much information as they could. Anatole was experimenting with different book binding techniques. As things stood, all that knowledge was one gusty day away from being gone.

Upstairs the Tenartier house still maintained some of its pre-HHV appearance. The main bedroom was at the end of the hall. Next to that was Anatole's room, then Percy's, which was now Miranda's, and then Marius's. His window overlooked the flat porch roof. He'd told Torres that as a kid he used to climb out on the roof to watch the storms come over the mountains.

"I always felt like there was this power or connection between them and the rest of the world," Marius had said as they sat on the roof that last night together. His body shielded her from the chill breeze of late autumn.

The clouds covered most of the sky, but occasionally they could see the blaze of the Milky Way wheeling above them. The only light for miles around was the lamps and candles in the barn and bunkhouse. In the darkness, his jade green eyes were nearly black, his olive skin taupe, his dark hair the midnight of a black cat's fur.

"Where did this hippie woo woo come from?" Torres teased. "I thought you were a serious scientist, Mister I graduated university at age twelve with eight Ph.D.'s."

"That's doctor." Although Torres couldn't see his smile, she could hear it in his voice. "But I didn't get my first degree until I was seventeen. Basically, ancient."

"Hmmm, you sound about as sharp as the leading edge on a bowling ball. I don't know if I can date someone who doesn't even know which crayons are the tastiest."

"Red?"

"Okay, yes, but everyone picks red, so that doesn't count." Torres started to push away, but Marius pulled her close. He buried his face in her hair and she snuggled into him, pressed her ear against his chest, listening to the beautiful, strong rhythm of his heart and the calm, steady sighing of his breathing. *I could stay here forever,* she thought.

But that forever had been only a few more hours. Then the trip to Great Falls.

She tried to remember the last thing she'd ever said to him. The last time they'd kissed. Had she said goodbye before leaving to go rescue the pilots from Liam's PDF? Probably not. She'd expected to be the one in danger. He would be safe with the Air Force. She didn't want to worry him by making a grand farewell.

Probably she had waved and walked off like any other mission on any other day.

Standing in the empty hall, facing the door to his empty room, Torres fought to keep back a sudden attack of sobbing. Even now if she went into Marius's room, she would find his half-packed ruck, the satchel Philippe had given him filled with documents about Marius's true origins, and his hastily made bed. Would his pillow still hold his scent, clean and spicy with an undernote of something smokey like old wood?

Instead of giving in to the temptation to yank open his door and fling herself wailing onto his bed like a high schooler with a crush, Torres went to Miranda's door and knocked.

No answer.

She opened the door.

The smell wasn't bad, exactly, just full. The room was full of the smell of shut-in. A few dishes sat on top of the dresser. A platoon of mugs, with bits of dried tea clinging to their insides, surrounded the bed.

Torres picked her way across the semi-dark room and opened the curtains with a loud *whoosh*.

"Gah!" The lump in the bed moaned.

"Yeah," Torres said. She unlocked the window and lifted it a few inches, letting in the cool spring air.

"Stop." Miranda poked her head out from under her pillow. "It's freezing."

"It's not freezing." Torres collected the mugs and set them in the hall. "You should get up and get a shower. Maybe a couple."

Miranda squinted at her, then her eyes flicked toward the window as if she heard something.

"What?" Torres stopped, watching the younger woman closely. "Is it the Infected?"

Ever since she'd infiltrated the Infected hive at the Starling Union Quarry and destroyed it, Miranda had lost her ability to communicate with the Infected. Or so she claimed. Torres wasn't convinced, but she respected Miranda's need for time to recover, not only physically, but mentally. If she wanted to shut out the Infected, who was Torres to say otherwise? Besides, Miranda's heroics had saved them all from the hive, which had planned to destroy the ranch. They owed her.

"N-no. Not the Infected."

"Good. Get out of bed. This malingering stops today." Torres stacked the rest of the dishes in the hall.

"I'm not malingering or whatever." Miranda wrapped one of the quilts around herself, peeping out like a kid at a sleepover scared of the ghost stories. "I'm depressed. Have you found any Xanax or Prozac?"

"Xanax is a tranquilizer," Torres said. "We're all depressed. Get up."

"This is super unhealthy. You can't bully people out of depression."

"You're right." Torres held out a relatively clean set of clothes. "We don't have any shrinks in New Avalon, but if you get up and get a shower, get dressed, and go eat at the actual table with other humans," she shrugged, "you might feel a little better."

"I won't." Miranda fell over sideways onto the bed.

"I can't make you." Torres set the clothes on the bedside table.

"Good. Get out."

"No."

Another stare calibrated to strip skin and cut to the bone.

"I'm not letting you do this," Torres said. I'm not letting someone else go without a fight. But she didn't say that. Her baggage was her baggage and Miranda had enough to deal with.

"I'm tired. I'll get up tomorrow."

"Cool. I'll stay here until then."

Miranda groaned loudly and rolled over, facing away.

Torres started whistling cadences. She made it through *I Wanna be a Drill Instructor*, *Baby Marine*, and *Jump Boots* before Miranda threw a pillow at her.

"Fine!" Miranda rolled out of bed and grabbed the clothes Torres set out for her. "I hate you," she called from the hall as she headed for the bathroom.

"Don't use all the hot water. Takes two hours to boil more," Torres shouted.

Chapter 2 – Marius

The Hive, Mammoth Cave, KY, USA – Spring, Year 2

For a long time, there had been nothing. Not a complete nothing, a dreamy nothing, or more accurately a nightmare nothing. A nothing filled with fear and regret and rage.

But even nothing comes to an end.

Sensation. Cool liquid moving against skin. Against his skin, between his limbs, around his face.

Water over his face. He thrashed in instinctive panic, but he wasn't drowning. There was something over his face, a rubbery mask covering his nose and mouth. If he calmed his breathing, he could pull air through the mask, could feel the warm moisture of his own exhalations in the mask.

His eyes were next, flickering open by millimeters. The world was a bluish blur seen through his gummy lashes. Darker shapes moved across his field of view.

They were talking. The muffled sounds rose and fell, like pressing his ear to a wall.

The light brightened.

The blue goo was draining away. He shivered both from the cold air and the shock of it against his tender skin after all this while.

Something around his chest and under his arms held him up as the last of the viscous liquid swirled down the drain under his feet. The tube opened from the front and he was pulled out, wrapped in towels, laid on his side on a cot.

That's when the vomiting started. Not so much vomiting as pouring out. It felt like gallons of blue bile-laced liquid rushed out of him. His stomach heaved and clenched, muscles tightening around the empty core of him.

A dozen bursts of sharp, snapping pain from his back, his sides, his chest, even his groin. His arms were too weak or uncoordinated to do more than flop around uselessly. He twisted his fingers around one of the tentacles as it withdrew from his brachial artery. He squeezed until someone caught his hand, tried to pry it open.

A hand, warm, human, touched his shoulder. It was small.

"Let go, Marius." The voice was soft, just starting to drop from the piping treble of childhood into something deeper. The boy had large, brown eyes. His skin was light brown, his hair a mass of loose black curls that had been inexpertly sheared at some point in the recent past.

"Let go," the boy said again. He patted Marius's hand until it opened finger-by-finger and released the tentacle. A trail of blood oozed down his arm. The boy pressed a wade of gauze against the puncture wound. His gaze moved to follow something behind Marius.

Someone grabbed Marius's chin and held his head still while they took his temperature with a forehead thermometer.

"He'll live."

Marius recognized the voice. Carmine Anino. They had worked together at the adjoining genetics and virology laboratories at Chrysalis Biopharmaceuticals. That was before the outbreak, before Harrow Hall even.

"Get him cleaned up and fed. Viers wants to talk to him," Anino said.

"Yes, Revered." The boy ducked his head.

After Carmine left, the boy brought more towels to dry Marius. When he started patting Marius's stomach, the scientist took the cloth and spread it over his waist.

"I'll do that," he said. His throat felt like it was being slashed while gravel was dumped on the cuts, but he had to start talking sooner or later. As the brain fog lifted, he looked around.

The room was small, and not exactly a room. Chamber might be a better word for it. The walls were natural rock formations. Stalactites dangled from the ceiling and lumpy stalagmites reached from the floor, which was slick with a thin layer of milky liquid.

"We're in a cave," Marius said. The boy nodded. He held out a pile of folded clothes that turned out to be a set of medical style scrubs. It took all Marius's strength to lever himself up and pull on the pants. He let the boy help pull the shirt over his head and lift his heavy arms through the sleeves.

"How long …?" He wasn't sure what he wanted to ask. How long have I been here? How long have I been in the tube? How long has it been since Great Falls?

The last thing he remembered was being in the helicopter, watching the burning city pass below him. He'd searched the river for kayaks, desperate from some sign that Torres had made it to either one side or the other alive. She was a survivor. Tough, determined, resourceful. She would be all right. She had to be all right. If not, then what had all this been for, whatever *this* was?

"I don't know," the boy said. "I've been here for almost a half a year. I think you were here first. The Enlightened started to get sick but after they put you in there they got better." The boy tipped his chin towards the empty tube. Shriveled pipes and slender tentacles hung down from the top or lay coiled in the bottom. They were inside me, Marius realized. They used me to process their blood like a dialysis machine, kept me breathing, fed, and took away the waste matter.

Why?

His scientific brain was already engaged even as a more primitive part of his lizard brain screamed at him to escape. He could easily overpower the boy and make a run for it. Well, no. Not at the moment. His body was weak, hungry. His limbs were sluggish and uncoordinated. Atrophied.

Besides, what would happen to the boy if he tried to escape? Would he be punished? Executed?

Marius bit his lip. He needed more information before he could act. And food. His very empty stomach grumbled.

"What's your name, kid?"

"Akeem, Revered," the boy said. He kept his head ducked, his eyes downcast.

"I'm not revered anything. Marius is fine," the scientist said. "Can we eat?"

"Oh, yes." A smile flickered over the boy's face. "There is soup today, with meat not just mushrooms." Akeem lowered his voice. "They don't like mushrooms. The mold scares them."

"That's a bit of good news, at least," Marius said. He stood, waited for the wave of dizziness to pass, and trailed Akeem out of the chamber into the winding passages of the larger cave system.

Marius followed the gently swaying light of Akeem's oil lantern. The boy explained that he usually didn't have any light when navigating the cave's numerous, winding passages.

"Revered Carmine said to bring one because you would need it," he added, looking at Marius over his shoulder.

Overhead, the ceiling rippled and moved in a constant, unnerving display of peristalsis. Tentacles, tubes, and vessels clung to the cracks and stalactites as they wound through the tunnels, networking the cave complex together more efficiently than any cable company could ever have managed.

For most of the short journey the only sounds, aside from their footsteps, were the faint gurgling from above and the equally faint dripping of water. The air was cool, dry, although not as stale as Marius expected. He'd been to a few caves while working as Chrysalis's field epidemiologist. He'd even been cave diving in the cenotes of the Yucatan. There the air had been hot and humid, filled with the sweet smells of flowers and the earthier ones of fungi and cave vegetation.

Thinking back, Marius couldn't remember what they'd been looking for, only that he'd been excited to go on the trip. The rest of the team had gone ahead, leaving Torres to keep an eye on him as he gathered the last of his samples and recorded his observations. She swam lazily in the turquoise water while he worked. When he announced he was finished, she climbed out of the pool. She swept her short, dark hair back from her forehead. The muscles of her shoulders and arms stood out. Water beaded on her skin, rolled down her body. One of her bathing suit straps had slipped, revealing the rim of a red floral tattoo. Months later, as they spooned on the twin bed in his childhood room, he traced the image with his finger.

"It's Belize sage," she said. "For protection and healing. I got it right out of Boot. Practically mandatory. Got all your gear? Sir, yes, sir. Got your tattoo? Sir, yes, sir."

"Shhh." He covered her lips with kisses until she groaned and wriggled under him.

After, they drowsed, tangled together that last night, listening to the wind around the house and each other's heart beats. He had wanted to stay in that dark, safe place forever with her. But when he woke in the chilly pre-dawn light, she was already gone. He never got the chance to tell her all the things that could only be said under the cover of night.

Akeem stopped. Ahead of them was an Infected. Parts of it were still recognizable. It had once been a dog. Its overly large head was mostly bare of fur. It had several extra eyes on the sides of its skull. Sensory tentacles, barely the diameter of drinking straws, clustered around its chin and shoulders, waving like a sea anemone's arms.

At seeing them, the Infected lifted one of its thick shoulder tentacles and growled. Akeem ducked his head and reached out to the wall, where a node of the bioformation that crawled across the ceilings ran up from the floor. The boy pressed his hand into the node and waited. The Infected reared up. Marius grabbed the lantern and brandished it.

"No," Akeem hissed. "Don't resist. Never resist them."

The Infected reached for Marius. He swung the lantern, shattering it across the Infected's face. The creature bellowed and stumbled back. But Marius had dealt with too many Infected to assume they were in the clear. His fumbling fingers searched the cave floor, until he found a shard of glass from the lantern. Without hesitation, he sliced across his palm and squeezed. His hand filled with blood.

The Infected wrapped its shoulder tentacles around his wrist and pulled him forward.

Good. Exactly what he expected it to do.

Marius smeared his blood directly into the Infected's face. It screamed and let go of him, pawing at itself.

The destruction was satisfyingly swift, but Marius

didn't wait to see the whole process. Besides, the last thing the boy needed to do was watch the creature dissolve as its own DNA rebelled against the virus that had been holding it together.

"C'mon," Marius said. "You said you don't need light to get around down here?"

Silence.

"Akeem?" Marius could hear the boy's breathing — short, panicky gasps — he was there. The scientist reached out, feeling his way toward Akeem.

"Listen, we don't have a lot of time before more show up," he said, his hand on Akeem's arm. "I know it's awful, but we have to go. We might not get another chance."

"No." Akeem sounded like he was crying. "They're gonna put you back in the tube. They'll kill me."

"Not if we escape. You saw what my blood does to them."

Footsteps echoed down the passageway. Akeem flinched against Marius. A light shown out, illuminating Carmine's face and the upper half of his body. He played the beam over Marius and Akeem then the dying Infected. Behind Carmine, the hulking shapes of Infected moving in the gloom.

"Bro, I told Viers this was a bad idea," Carmine said. "The good news is now we get to do things the fun way."

The Infected pushed forward. Marius held up his cut hand in a STOP gesture.

"You can't bleed on all of them," Carmine said. "But you can try. Then I'll tell Viers how you killed yourself. Problem solved."

"Please don't, Revered," Akeem said. "He didn't

understand. The Enlightened need him, remember?"

Carmine sighed loudly. "Fine, if he wraps up his hand. Live to fight another day, bro." He offered a strip of fabric.

"Please." Akeem tugged at Marius's arm. "You can't save anyone if you're dead."

But if I'm dead, they can't use me either, Marius thought. This wasn't the first time the Enlightened had tried to force his cooperation. Last time, it had been only himself in the Veterans Affairs hospital in Portland, Oregon. This time there was the kid to consider.

Wordlessly he snatched the cloth from Carmine. The moment the bandage was tied, the Infected grabbed him. They half-dragged, half-carried him down the passageway. Carmine trotted along behind. The last he saw of Akeem, the boy was heading back the way they'd come toward the tube chamber.

Marius wasn't able to see much of the cave system as the Infected escorted him to Dr. Viers's office. What he did see was that the walls and ceilings were covered with the bioformations. A few Infected moved through other passageways. He saw several uninfected people and one Enlightened, the still mostly human Infected.

Even back at Chrysalis, he'd observed that not every mammal infected with HHV reacted in the same way. Most became animalistic, driven by aggression and hunger. Some retained higher thought processes. His later research supported his initial hypothesis. There were two stains of HHV. Any mammal infected with the FOX-H strain would devolve into the Infected, while humans infected with the SAM-D strain became the Enlightened. They kept some of their higher reasoning and controlled the lower Infected, using the bioformations as a communication network.

Dr. Viers was still recognizable from his days as the CEO of one of the premier biopharmaceutical corporations in the world. His most obvious mutations were below the waist, where multiple thick tentacles that acted as legs. His sallow skin looked slightly damp like a frog's. He had gone bald and dark veins pulsed just below his skin, which was marred by small ulcerous sores and dry patches of flaky eczema.

Even his chamber had been fitted out to look like his Chrysalis office, minus the framed photographs and awards. There was a desk, and a specially designed chair that accounted for Viers's additional limbs. He leaned back, his hand starting to reach to adjust the glasses he no longer wore. Old habits.

"Marius," Viers said as the Infected let go of their prisoner's arms. Marius flexed his hands, feeling the tingling rush of blood flow return.

"There was no need to attack anyone," Viers said, eyeing the bandage around Marius's hand.

"There was no need for a lot of what happened, but here we are," Marius said.

"On the contrary." Viers shifted his weight, his lower tentacles rearranging themselves as he leaned forward. "I knew what you did in Portland."

"I blew up your lab."

"If that had been your only treachery, you wouldn't

have to be here," said Viers. "Let's talk about the mold."

There was no point lying about it. Marius had created a genetic inhibitor to HHV's DNA. It prevented future mutations, which was fatal to creatures infected with the highly mutagenic virus. Once the inhibitor started working in the Infected, their mutations stopped working together. They started self-cannibalizing as the virus tried to find energy to fuel its never-ending quest to be better.

Marius had used mold as a vector to spread the inhibitor as certain molds were virophages naturally. It didn't hurt that mold was also incredibly tenacious and adaptive, making it easy to tailor for different environments.

"As things stand, we have maintained our side of the arrangement," Viers continued. "We have not moved any additional assets into the preserve around Great Falls."

"So, my family is safe?"

"I have no way of knowing that. There are plenty of other dangers aside from our concerns," Viers said. "Let's return to the topic at hand."

"Why am I here?" Marius stepped forward. Immediately, both of the Infected lunged at him, but froze as Viers lifted a hand.

"You see how we are all connected?" Viers waved around the room, taking in the bioformations, the Infected, himself, Carmine, and Marius. "The Enlightened are the heart and soul of the hive. The Infected are our eyes, ears, arms, legs, mouths and so on. When you first arrived, Carmine was good enough to assist me with the finer virological points of using your body to purify our tainted members from the effects of the mold you created."

The idea of being used against his will to provide life support to the Infected made Marius's still empty stomach churn.

"That doesn't explain why I'm here now, not in a tube of blue goo." Marius bit his lip. "What's changed? If it was working, why not keep doing it?"

"The situation has escalated. We are in need of a better, more permanent solution to your little Portland prank," Viers said.

"You've been using my organs, you could have taken as much blood as you wanted, and if killing me would have fixed things, we wouldn't be having this conversation, so what do you actually need from me that you can't take?"

"Oh, bro, we can take it," Carmine said. "And we will if we have to. Dr. Viers still thinks you can be reasoned with or bribed or threatened."

Marius shrugged, suddenly exhausted. He had no idea when he'd last had real food in his stomach, and the adrenaline rush from fighting off the Infected in the passageway was waning.

"Which are you going to try? Reason, bribe, or threaten?"

"All three," Viers said. "I'll explain why you must help us, offer you an enticement, and detail the consequences of refusal."

"Plus, if you don't do it, we'll just stick you back in the tube," Carmine said. "Forever."

Viers waved again. "But that is an unwanted last resort, especially as the tube is not completely functional at the moment. What we prefer is for this to be a win-win situation. There's no reason for you to be uncomfortable here. You already agreed to help us."

"I never agreed to help you!" Marius growled. "I agreed to turn myself over as a prisoner in exchange for the lives of the humans who would have been infected or killed in Great Falls."

"Well, you're here now," Viers shrugged. "There's no ethical review board, so we can do whatever we believe will most expeditiously solve our problem."

"You still haven't told me what the problem is," Marius said. The fatigue was worsening. All he wanted to do was lie down and sleep. Whatever they were going to demand, he hoped they would be quick about it.

"The problem is the Enlightened," Viers said. "For the past few months, we've been able to use you to filter out the mold, but we're seeing signs of de-evolution in some of the Enlightened, especially those further from our hive. Whatever you did is starting to affect them."

Marius grinned.

Viers narrowed his eyes. "Don't look so smug. What do you suppose will happen to your precious human preserve when the Enlightened lose their control over the Infected?"

That was a sobering thought.

"You, Dr. Tenartier, are going to stabilize the SAM-D strain. If you don't, there's no chance Great Falls will survive the five or ten years it will take for the mold to kill off all the Infected."

Chapter 3 - Miranda

New Avalon, Montana, USA — Spring, Year 2

The yard was abuzz with activity. After days - weeks? - in her room, Miranda was overwhelmed.

There had been a lot of refugees coming to the ranch, but John sent most of them into Crossroads. Even so, there were a bunch of people who all seemed to be hurrying here and there.

Miranda took a mug of stew and her quilt to the front porch. She cocooned herself and sat on the porch swing. From here, the view was largely unchanged. The yard sloped gently down into a shallow depression then rose up toward the front pasture. Beyond that, the high wooden fence, with watchtowers every several hundred yards, was new. But from the porch, over a mile away from the perimeter fence, she could barely see it.

The front door opened and Bailey stepped out onto the porch. He had a full beard and his hair had grown out from the Air Force high-and-tight that he'd sported when they'd first met. His black, horn-rimmed glasses remained the same.

"Oh," he said when he saw Miranda. He stood awkwardly, looking over the front yard, rocking slightly back and forth.

"Do you wanna sit?" Miranda scooted over, making room on the swing's bench seat.

"Okay." Bailey sat down stiffly. His back was straight, hands on his thighs, fingers flat and together like he was posing for an old timey photograph or something.

"Relax or at ease or whatever," Miranda said. She sipped at her stew and found she was surprisingly hungry. A few cattle wandered across the pasture. A breeze ruffled the new grass. A pair of birds darted and swooped across the sky, chattering to each other.

"It's too loud," Bailey said.

"The birds?"

"Inside. Everyone's busy. It's loud."

"Yeah, I get that." Miranda nodded.

The door swung open and Torres came out, pack slung over one shoulder, pistol in a hip holster.

"There you are, Zoomy. We need the call signs," she said to Bailey. To Miranda, "Nice to see you up, even if you did take bed with you."

"I'm here. I have pants on." Miranda rolled her eyes. "What more do you want from me?"

"You could go with us," Torres said. "There's a herd of Infected in the area. Would be nice not to have to watch our backs while we're worrying about Liam and his pack of wannabe weekend warriors."

"What now?"

"We found this." Torres handed Miranda a key card. It was similar to the ones they'd had at Chrysalis. "And this."

The last time Miranda had seen that access badge, it had been hanging around Dr. Mendelsen's neck, flapping wildly as everyone ran for the last plane escaping the Wiltz firestorm.

"Where did you find this?" Miranda set down her stew bowl and pushed back her quilt.

"The women Liam captured had it. One hid her backpack and I sent some Rangers back for it."

Miranda twirled the badge back and forth. The plastic felt so clean and perfect under her fingertips. It was hard to remember that things used to be like that, not rough and ready, wired together from whatever scraps the Rangers could bring back.

"What's the plan?" Miranda asked, still mesmerized by the badge's simple lines and exact edges. It was an artifact from another world.

Miranda shifted in the saddle. It had been at least two years since her last riding lesson, probably longer. Still, some of it was coming back to her. Enough to know that her butt was going to be deeply sore the next day. And her thighs.

They rode for hours, through the morning and afternoon, stopping occasionally so one or another of the Rangers could hop down and stare at the ground for way too long. How hard could it be to find the PDF? They were going mostly north toward Great Falls but veered east to avoid riding through the foothills. It was safer in the flat lands.

Miranda regretted she didn't have her camera or access to her social media accounts. The area was ridiculously picturesque. Bright green shoots of grass poked through the matts of last year's growth. Wildflowers scattered across the fields in swaths of pink, yellow, and white. From near the line of aspen trees that marked out a stream, a doe watched their progress, chewing thoughtfully. Even the air was ridiculously good; clean and fresh with a hint of chill but warmed by gentle breezes that set the new leaves of the trees fluttering as they sighed contentedly.

Much as Miranda hated to admit it, Torres was right. She did feel a little better. Not great. Not even good. But she didn't feel like she had never left the quarry, which was how she'd felt lying in the dark in her room. Alone, abandoned, unloved. Everyone else had moved on after that day. Torres had the Rangers, John had New Avalon and Percy. Marius ... well, Marius was gone. For all anyone knew at the ranch, he was dead.

For most of the day, Dawn rode near Miranda. She had her long, blue-black hair braided back into the kind of French-inside-out braids any cheerleader would envy. She smiled at Miranda but didn't say much. No one said much. They all seemed to know what to do and if there was ever a question, Torres would do a bunch of hand signals and off they went as if that was totally clear.

Miranda amused herself by giving the gestures illustrative names.

The crow flies at midnight. Barking dogs hate

pudding. Get up, no just kidding, stay there LOL.

Hello, Miranda.

She nearly fell off her horse.

Did you think we abandoned you, like you abandoned us?

"Are you still with us?"

"No!" Miranda shouted. "Leave me alone."

Dead silence. All the Rangers turned to look at her. High school nightmare stuff from back when the worst thing she could imagine was a socially awkward situation, not gruesome, gory death.

Torres tugged at her horse's reins. The animal turned his head to gaze back at her reproachfully. Torres pulled harder, lifting the reins. Wrong answer. All the horse knew now was that she was putting pressure on the halter. She finally leaned to the side and the gelding headed over, but not before breathing out a deep whiffling sigh to let the other horses know he was just humoring his ineffective rider.

"What's going on?" The older woman scanned Miranda quickly, then the surrounding area. "Is it the Infected?"

Don't tell her anything.

A surge of resentment followed, pushed from the Infected to Miranda. They, too, remembered Torres. The former Marine had cost them dearly in the past.

Go away! Miranda pushed the command at the Infected. Deep within the slimy hive in the quarry she had taken control of the Infected, held their attention and directed them. She called up that feeling now, the way the Infected's minds felt like a part of hers or she a part of theirs.

Welcome back. Welcome. We missed you. Welcome home. They were glad to see her. She wasn't a burden, a princess to watch over or stick in a tower somewhere. No. They were the enemy.

Are we?

"Don't touch her." Torres held out her arm, blocking Dawn, who'd moved her horse over next to Miranda's mare.

"Her face," Dawn said.

Miranda touched her face. Her nose was bleeding. Again.

"It's them," she said. A couple of the Rangers gasped as if they were surprised there might be Infected out here.

"So much for the great truce of Year One," said one of the younger ones. If Miranda's memory wasn't totally scrambled, her name was Helen.

"Technically, this is New Avalon territory, so not covered by the truce," Dawn said.

"Irregardless-"

Torres held up a hand and everyone shut up.

They had stopped near a sycamore grove. Other than the horses moving and the leaves rustling, Miranda couldn't hear anything.

Let us listen.

But if she opened her mind to the Infected, it would be harder and harder to get rid of them. She'd almost lost herself to the hive mind before.

But she was stronger than last time. She knew what to watch out for. She wouldn't make the same mistakes again.

While Torres waved hand signals, sending several of

the Rangers off from the rest of the group, Miranda tried to relax and ready herself. Opening her mind while limiting the Infected's access was tricky, like doing one of those hand-held little mazes with the tiny ball bearings. John used to get her one from every far-flung place he visited.

Her favorite had been the one from Caacupé, in Paraguay. It was shaped like the cathedral. There were two ends to the maze. One was a beatifically beaming Madonna and Christ child, the other a cartoonish devil, skipping and holding hands with a hairy little Pombéro.

The first Infected Miranda found was a Little, one of the small creatures that served as scouts and messengers for the hives. They gathered information and food when they could. They also showed the other, larger Infected where prey was.

Initially, it was hard to get into the Little's mind, but it was all coming back to Miranda, like trying to move an arm that had gone to sleep. She could do it, just a few more seconds, and *pop*! She was inside; she had control.

Around the Little the world was mostly scents and sounds. Whatever it used to be it had terrible eyesight. Miranda could feel that as it mutated, it kept growing more and more eyes, but still didn't have good vision. But not to worry, next time the Little got enough meat, it would grow another set of eyes and this time they would work.

By smell, Miranda knew the Little was in the hills, overlooking their position. It knew where they were - the horses, the humans, their soaps and sweat and other body odors. North of them were more humans, but no horses. These humans had something with them that smelled like saltpeter and urine.

Miranda opened her eyes, pointed towards the other humans. "That way." She wiped the blood away from her nose.

"How many?" Torres asked.

"More than us, but no horses." Miranda shrugged.

Torres pointed to two of the remaining six Rangers and sent them to go get the scouts. Miranda didn't know what she was planning, but it would probably involve some kind of silly heroic charge. Torres was a shoot first, assess later kind of person.

Bring the rest, Miranda commanded the Little. She filled its tiny brain with the smells of carnage and the sounds of crunching and munching. Why should the New Avalon Rangers risk themselves when the Infected could fight that fight for them?

While the Rangers waited for the scouts to return, they repacked and secured their gear. They also pulled out what body armor they had. Most of it was BMX jackets, but a couple had sets of bulletproof plates salvaged from military or law enforcement sites.

Miranda felt the tugging, tapping of the Infected. They wanted her to be with them as they attacked.

It'll be fun!

She kept her mind shut. She'd given them enough access for one day.

The Rangers' scouts arrived and huddled up with the rest while Torres outlined their tactics. Miranda zoned out. No need for all that. By the time the Rangers got there, the Infected would have been and gone. Funny to think that she was more dangerous than all the Rangers put together.

"What are you grinning about?" Dawn nudged Miranda's elbow.

"Just enjoying being OP," Miranda said.

"Huh?"

"Never mind. Oh, looks like we're moving."

They mounted and set out in two files, going quickly, but quietly. The late afternoon sun sent their shadows reaching out over the prairie.

The crows found the bodies before they arrived.

Five people were scattered across a field near a clump of pines. Ropes of intestines wound up the tree trunks and laced through the branches like disgusting holiday streamers. What the Littles hadn't been able to eat, they ripped apart and scattered.

"Shit," Torres said. "Freaking Infected got them first."

Helen gagged and turned away. Dawn and Andy dismounted while the rest kept a lookout. Miranda could sense the Littles were headed back to their hive. No other Infected in the area. She didn't know if any of the PDF members had escaped.

"Liam's not here," Dawn reported to Torres. "I don't see either of the women from before but it's, ah, hard to tell. Don't have my CSI team or anything."

Torres frowned. Her gaze traveled from the corpses to the lowering sun in the west, to the other Rangers, to Miranda.

Before Torres could ask, Miranda said, "They're gone."

Torres made a gather-round hand sign and the Rangers huddled up.

"It's too far to get back before dark. We're gonna head

over to the Jenkins' place and see if we can stay there for the night. Tomorrow we'll divide up and see if we can figure out what happened."

A couple of the Rangers glanced from Miranda to the bodies. They knew what had happened.

"Is she okay?" A woman's voice - Percy's.

Miranda sat in the back office, a little room tucked away behind the mudroom off the living room. It used to be Annette's office, where she did most of the ranch's paperwork. Since the HHV pandemic, it was a radio room and a storage closet for medical supplies. A stack of boxes along one wall held all the family photos and mementoes cleared out of the rest of the house. An album on top of the stack contained a collection of pictures from various science fairs, all featuring young Marius.

The first was a downward shot of him standing near a table in an event hall. The picture caught his long, thick eyelashes, chubby little kid cheeks, and his signature lower lip bite as he pulled out what looked like a strand of frozen snot on a popsicle stick from a mini freezer. In Annette's looping cursive, the caption read: Marius, age 6, Junior Science Explorers' Symposium, Seattle. Under that in a childish scrawl: DNA extraction.

Miranda softly set the photo album down, listening to the clunk of footsteps in the mudroom. A brief whoosh and slop of water in the washing up buckets, then the footsteps moved into the kitchen.

"I don't know," John's voice was a low rumble, but carried easily through the wall. Everyone else was still out, hot on the trail of the PDF or the Infected. After spending the night in the Jenkin's barn, Miranda returned to the ranch. She wanted to go alone, but Dawn insisted on going with. As chaperone, friend, or guard?

The way the Rangers side-eyed her set Miranda on edge. Torres asked her to go with them, encouraged her to 'help' with the Infected, but when she did, when she used her connection with them to keep the Rangers safe, they acted like she was the problem. The problem was the PDF. And the Infected. But the Infected could be controlled, plus if they stayed out of the Infected's territory, they'd be fine.

"Nice to see her out of bed, at least," John said.

"It's weird, though," Percy said. "Because you always try to get me to stay in bed."

"Hey now," John said with a low chuckle that turned into the muffled sound of kissing.

Miranda rolled her eyes. She absolutely was not going to sit in the office like some sad peeper and listen to a guy who was basically her adopted dad make out with someone only a few years older than her. Granted John wasn't as old as her dad, but still, it was weird and uncomfortable.

The only way out of the office was through the kitchen. Or through the window, but it was sealed with plastic to keep the heat in.

No way to avoid it.

Miranda opened the door into the kitchen. Percy was half-sitting on the counter, her legs around John's hips, arms around his neck. John's shirt was half off and his sandy blond hair was a tousled mess.

"Gross," Miranda said.

"Miranda!" John took a couple limping steps away from Percy, hastily tucking his shirt back in. Percy also tucked in her shirt. She grinned, not embarrassed at all; more that 'Oh yes I did!' look that Miranda had seen on Percy's brother's face when Marius had made some breakthrough or other in his research.

"Hi, Miranda," Percy said. "It's good to see you. There's coffee."

"That's not coffee," Miranda snapped, irrationally irritated with Percy's chirpy attitude. So easy for her to be happy with her picture-perfect family and now John, the ultimate soldier, there to protect her. What did Miranda have? A weird co-dependent relationship with a bunch of mutants who would be equally happy to rip her to shreds and eat her.

"It's mostly chicory, you're right." Undeterred, Percy shrugged. "It's got recycled coffee grounds in it. Torres said the Rangers are always on the lookout for real coffee. Maybe now you're helping them, they can expand our territory and start trading with other communities."

"Neat," Miranda said. She sounded like a grumpy toddler and she didn't care. So there.

"I bet there's tons of coffee still in Seattle," Percy continued brightly.

"Oh, yeah, totes," Miranda muttered. She slunk out of the kitchen, ashamed of herself and also annoyed. No one was in the living room, although she could hear people moving around upstairs. She returned to the porch swing.

Mistake.

Soraya and Phineas were doing some kind of obstacle course with the ranch kids. The children ran and tumbled, squealing and giggling, while the adults shouted encouragement, mediated squabbles, and tended to scrapes, bumps, and owies both real and imaginary.

Soraya's oldest daughter, Mirzha sat on a blanket, reading. Washington, the boy Phineas had found, sat near her, pretending to read while gazing at her.

Even with everything that was going on, the kids got on with the business of growing up. For the younger ones, like Elfy and Wahida, Soraya's younger daughter, that meant going to the lessons Soraya and Phineas taught and playing with each other. For the young teens like Mirzha and Washington, nothing was more important than that first awkward crush.

Just thinking of awkward crushes made Miranda cringe. She had thrown herself at Marius. To be fair, who could blame her, with his brainiac nerd demeanor and his movie star perfect looks? Still, the rejection hurt. After Harrow Hall, she'd been so lonely, isolated literally and figuratively at Chrysalis while everyone waited to see if she'd turn into an Infected. Marius had been there for her, always ready to get a midnight macchiato and listen to her talk about nothing.

The door opened and Percy poked her head out.

"Hey, they found something," she said.

Miranda raised an eyebrow, the unspoken 'So?' loud between them.

"Torres says she thinks she knows where the Infected are coming from. There's a hive between us and Great Falls."

Chapter 4 - Marius

The Hive, Mammoth Cave, KY, USA — Summer, Year 2

They called it the Dome, the humans who were still human. They were mostly young, too young to be elevated. That's what they told those kids. That if they worked hard enough, they would be given the opportunity to be infected with HHV. If they survived the initial infection the lucky ones would become Enlightened. The truth was most of them wouldn't make it through the first mutation. They would die in agony, their young bodies torn apart as the virus struggled to hijack their DNA.

The Dome was a huge open area, extending several floors up. Half of the Dome had been covered with bioformations to make a series of small rooms. Marius wasn't allowed in there, but he peeked in the openings whenever he passed by. They seemed to be nurseries, filled with fresh meat and lined with thick veins to help the newly infected survive their first mutations.

Marius's lab was cobbled together with a variety of gear, ranging from folding card tables to state-of-the-art microscopes and laptops that could spit out DNA sequences at astonishing speeds.

"Anything you want, you let the Enlightened know and they'll send the Infected to get it," Carmine said as he supervised Marius setting up the lab on that first day.

It was hard to keep track of how many days had passed since. The light never changed. The Infected didn't care about maintaining normal human circadian rhythms. Meals were sporadic, depending on availability of food, so sometimes it was a day or more between. Other times, there was too much fresh food and it had to be consumed before it spoiled.

During his waking hours, Marius focused on solving the devolution problem. The first order of business was determining the rate and frequency of the devolution. How many Enlightened had been affected? To what degree? Why were some breaking down faster than others? Proximity to the inhibitor he'd spread when he'd been in Portland? Or some other factor?

Against his will, Marius found himself sincerely engaged. He told himself that he only acted to save the humans. But it was easy for him to fall back into the work as he had in Portland. Even the routine was similar, except this time Carmine was his jailer, not Reyka.

"What does it all mean?" Akeem slipped in and poked at the test tubes, Petri dishes, and agar plates.

"It means that Carmine's data is correct," Marius said. He had re-run the calculations enough to know that the inhibitor he'd created was having a cumulative effect on the Enlightened. Viers and Carmine using him to filter the affected blood only delayed the inevitable. And the inevitable was that the Enlightened would devolve, which would free the Infected to follow their most aggressive instincts.

"Carmine's a good scientist," Akeem said.

"He's a scientist," Marius agreed.

"Are you going to fix them?" Akeem nodded toward the other rooms.

Marius bit his lip, searching for the right answer. Or any answer. If he did nothing, the Enlightened would devolve. Eventually, the inhibitor would spread to all the Infected, ending HHV. The problem was that in the meantime, the Infected would be able to wipe out the surviving humans.

"I don't know," Marius admitted reluctantly.

Akeem looked over his shoulder and all around. He scooted close to Marius and whispered, "You're the only one that can kill them all. Viers told me. That's why I broke the tube. So they would have to wake you up."

Marius stared at the boy. He couldn't be older than twelve or thirteen, dark curly hair, light brown skin, dark brown eyes. Although his voice occasionally broke, he still had a bit of baby fat in his cheeks. He was just a kid. Marius could hardly imagine the weight of responsibility Akeem must have felt at such a young age.

"Are you mad?" Akeem's eyes darted up to the ceiling where the hive's network of veins and tubes writhed and twisted.

"Mad? No, why would I be mad?" Marius put a hand on Akeem's thin shoulder.

Akeem picked at his shirt sleeve. It was threadbare. Who was looking after this kid? Who was looking after any of the kids who scurried and skulked around the hive?

"Akeem," Marius tried again. "I'm not mad. I'm grateful. This way I have a chance to do something. To fix this. Maybe."

Akeem nodded jerkily, peeked up at Marius and gave a small smile. Marius wished it were true. He wished he was grateful for being woken from the blue dream of nothingness. But as it stood, he couldn't see how his being awake could do an ounce of good.

"I can help." Akeem's smile broadened. "I know all the tunnels, even the ones They don't know about. I know where the Pit goes. They keep away because the river has mold in it. They're afraid of the mold."

"Good to know." Marius forced a cheerful tone. Let the kid hope. "I better get back to work."

Akeem saluted and darted out of the lab. Marius listened to the soft slap of the boy's feet until it vanished among all the other overly organic noises the hive made.

Over the next few days or waking times, as Marius thought of them, Akeem kept busy stealing and stashing supplies and gear.

"For our escape," he whispered, showing Marius a tin of sardines he kept back while inventorying a newly elevated person's pack. Akeem didn't mention if the person survived the initial mutation, and Marius was glad. He knew the mortality rate: nearly seventy percent.

"Why do they do it?" the scientist asked. He wanted to head off Akeem's questions about when they would be ready to escape. The answer was never. There was no gain in that. The Infected would recapture him. They would kill Akeem. They might kill him, but at that point wouldn't it be a mercy?

"Do what?" Akeem returned the tin to his pocket.

"Why do people agree to be elevated. Or don't they have a choice?"

Akeem gave a half shrug, hands up in a 'you got me' gesture. "People were scared. The Infected were everywhere. The government wasn't doing anything. The Enlightened offered a solution. You can be safe. You'll never need anything again. You'll always be with your loved ones, a part of them even. It sounded like Paradise. My sister…" He winced and shook his head.

"I don't want to end up like Them. You can make sure that doesn't happen. Your blood, right?" The boy reached out to touch one of the slides Marius was working on but stopped short.

It was Marius's turn to glance around. There were no surveillance cameras here like there had been in the Chrysalis quarantine facility, but the feeling of being watched was the same. How much could the hive understand of what he and Akeem said and did? The Infected had barely more than animalistic intelligence. It was the Enlightened he had to worry about. But they gained information through the bioformation network and from the Infected's reports. So, if the hive didn't know and the Infected didn't know, the Enlightened wouldn't know. Right?

"Yes," Marius said, kept his voice low, barely more than a whisper. "There's a way to do it with my blood."

Akeem dropped his head, fidgeted with his shirt, his dark eyes flicking to Marius as he asked, "Would you?"

"It could be dangerous," Marius said.

"Even if it kills me," Akeem said. "Please. I don't want to be like them."

Marius hesitated. If Carmine or the Enlightened knew or even suspected that he was spreading his immunity around in the heart of their hive … killing him and Akeem would definitely be a mercy.

"Please. I can get you anything you want. I know where there's alcohol or coffee."

"Canned peaches?" Marius said with a small smile.

"Anything. Truly," Akeem said.

Marius waved him off. "Don't worry about the peaches. I was joking."

"But please." The boy's eyes brimmed with tears.

"Oh, hey," Marius held Akeem's shoulders, turned the boy to face him and looked into his eyes. "I will do whatever I can to help you. You saved me. I owe you. Okay? You don't ever need to offer me anything. Just ask and if I can do it, I will. I promise."

Akeem sniffed, swiped his sleeve across his face, and smiled. "Deal."

Over the next few waking times, Marius plagued Carmine. He needed hypodermic needles, medical tubing, and a means to store and ideally warm his blood before the transfusion. He also needed for Carmine to not know what he was going to use so he concealed his true aims in a mass of requests for equipment.

Once the scientist had what he needed to perform the

transfusion, the next problem was deciding when, where, and how. A direct transfusion would take too long and be risky. Carmine could walk in any time and he would know exactly what was going on.

The solution was for Marius to extract his blood a little at a time. If Carmine asked, he could easily lie and say that he needed it as a control against the other strains of HHV. Once Marius had a least a pint, a process that took four working waking periods, he was ready to start Akeem's transfusion.

Akeem slipped in, looking excited. He pulled the bioformation as closed as it would go behind him. Marius hated touching the thing. It was feverishly hot and softly pulsating. And it smelled of partially digested rot, the nutritional medium the Infected needed to make their transformation and power their subsequent mutations.

"Ready?" Marius muttered after the boy had given the 'All Clear' sign.

"Ready." Akeem rolled up his sleeve.

Marius handed him a small mesh bag. Inside the bag was a pint of his blood, the IV tubing already in place. He explained to Akeem how to attach the IV to the luer connector.

"Aren't you going to do that?" Akeem looked worried.

"I can't." Marius swabbed the boy's inner elbow with disinfectant. "I'll put in the IV needle and tape it down, but then you have to go hide. Remember you said it was safe in the Pit by the river? Go there until all the blood is out of the bag. When it's empty, throw everything in the river. Far out so it floats away."

"Why?"

"The Infected know my blood. If they smell it on you or in the hive, they'll know what I did. They won't be happy." Marius selected a small needle. It would take longer for the transfusion, but the boy's veins weren't big enough for anything larger.

Akeem winced as the needle went in. Marius taped down the IV and disposed of the needle. Even here, he missed his sharps container.

"All set," he said with a bright smile. Akeem pulled down his sleeve and clutched the mesh bag to his chest. "Get going, kid." Marius shooed him out of the lab.

He tried to keep busy over the next few hours, but the longer the boy was absent, the more he worried. What if the Infected caught Akeem? What if Carmine suspected something? What if Akeem had fallen or gotten lost or couldn't manage the IV or ...?

"Where's the kid?" Carmine swaggered into the lab, wearing his favorite headlamp, which he liked to shine in Marius's eyes.

"This is a lab, not a daycare," Marius said, turning away to rearrange perfectly arranged test tubs. Carmine doesn't know, Marius told himself. He can't know. It's coincidence he's here asking for Akeem at this moment.

"If you see him, tell him Viers is looking for him." Carmine strolled along the worktable, poking at and disorganizing things.

"Why?"

"Because you work for us, bro."

Marius was not violent by nature, but Carmine possessed an inexplicable ability to bring out Marius's most aggressive instincts with only a few words. He clenched his fists. Carmine wouldn't tell him anything if he was whining about a bloody nose.

"Okay," the scientist said in his most reasonable voice. "I was wondering why Viers wanted him. Unless you don't know."

"Nice try," Carmine said with a snort. "I'll send some of the Infected to find him. Let me know if he comes back here. Thanks, bro. You're a regular employee of the month."

After Carmine left, Marius squatted in a corner, letting the panic run through him. Once his breathing and heart rate returned to normal range, he went through possible scenarios of what Viers wanted Akeem for. The most likely reason was that Viers had decided to elevate the boy. How would that work if Akeem was immune to HHV?

It wouldn't.

Then what would happen to Akeem?

From what Marius knew of the hive, anyone who didn't survive HHV infection was used as nesting material for the newly mutated Infected. A few people were partially immune to HHV or at least resistant to it, like Reyka. They could be infected and would even start mutating, but they never joined the hive mind or went through significant physiological or anatomical changes.

Best case scenario was that Viers would write Akeem off as naturally resistant and allow him to stay on, serving the hive as he'd been doing. But more likely was that the boy would die horribly.

Marius almost didn't realize he was running until the darkness of the tunnels leading away from the Dome closed in around him. He stopped and took out the little LED flashlight Akeem gave him. For a moment, he hesitated. The air was cool and dry in the tunnel, chilling his body and bringing him back to reality.

If he went after Akeem, he would be giving up any chance to interfere with the hive. Viers would decide he was too dangerous, too unpredictable to be left in a lab where he could alter his own base strain of HHV.

Saving Akeem meant letting the inhibitor take its course. It meant devolution for the Enlightened and free rein for the Infected. It meant everyone he loved in New Avalon would be in more danger. What would it mean beyond that one small community in central Montana? What about the rest of the US? The rest of the world?

Once, John had told him, "We save the ones we can." Marius had been furious and horrified at the soldier's callous attitude. Pragmatism had never been Marius's style.

But there was no John here, no Torres. No, don't think about her.

There was no backup. No one would lift a finger to save Akeem if he didn't. If he stood aside and did nothing, the boy would vanish like millions of other victims of HHV. Marius would have a chance to make a difference. He might be able to find a solution to HHV, something quicker than the inhibitor. He might ...

But he'd promised Akeem. He owed the boy.

Turning into a tentacled mutant wasn't the only way someone could become monstrous. Refusing to do everything he could to save Akeem would be surrendering to the Enlightened in a way Marius refused to even consider.

He clicked on the flashlight and headed down the tunnel, listening for the distant sound of water and hoping he wasn't too late.

Marius traced his left hand along the cave wall. When in a maze, keep turning left. John told him that. Maybe it would work in a topiary labyrinth, but did it also hold in a natural maze like a cave system? Regardless, it was the best heuristic available.

After abandoning the lab, Marius passed the mess hall, a wide, low-ceilinged room filled with mismatched camping chairs, as well as several hand-carved rocking chairs of the kind sold outside Cracker Barrel restaurants across the southeastern US. A few adolescents lingered in the mess hall, carefully sorting the food into piles that could be used in later meals for the humans, piles for the Enlightened, or slop for the Infected. Akeem had explained the system.

Marius hoped to find the boy in the mess hall. His post-transfusion instructions included getting something to eat.

No sign of Akeem in the mess hall, or in the cells - the long, narrow rooms where the postulates awaited their calling from on-high.

Where else would Akeem go? How long before Carmine noticed Marius's absence from the lab?

There were plenty of Infected with enhanced physical characteristics - sometimes only one sense, sometimes all of them. Marius had no doubt that tracking him down wouldn't present a problem once Carmine decided to do so.

A clatter of footsteps from a side tunnel. Marius pressed himself against the wall, listening. The steps were quick, rhythmic and clipped. Not the random, organic scurry of the Infected.

Carmine dashed past. Apart from the night of the Chrysalis outbreak, Marius had never seen Carmine run. Whatever it was, it must be critical.

It only took a few minutes for Marius to deduce where Carmine was going. Viers.

The bioformation curtain outside Viers's quarters/office was tattered. Necrotic patches bloomed and spread across it, like embers falling on dry grass. Marius immediately recognized the effect. Nothing caused that kind of systemic damage to the Infected the way his blood did.

The only person who had his blood, other than him, was Akeem.

Marius pushed aside the shredded remains of the bioformation and peered around the corner. Viers slumped over his desk. His lower tentacles looked unharmed, but the upper half of his body was a mass of oozing sores and ulcerating wounds.

Akeem cowered against the back wall. In one shaking hand, he clutched a nearly empty IV bag of blood. In the other, he had a knife. On either side of him, an Infected raged. They burst forward but shrank back as Akeem waved the blood bag at them. Between the Infected shrieking, Viers's wailing, and Carmine's shouting, no one seemed to notice Marius at all.

The chaos had a dream-like quality, like a movie. Like watching an actor dressed in his clothes as they calmly crossed the room, moved behind Carmine, and reached an arm out, slowly, almost lazily, to wrap around the other man's neck.

He remembered John's voice perfectly. Quiet, patient, like he was telling Miranda how to boil an egg or what the network password was.

"Hook your arm under the chin and pull into you. Use your other arm to control the head. They'll lose consciousness in less than a minute."

John was right. As usual.

Carmine sagged against him. The acrid stench of piss joined the rotten meat smell of the Infected.

Marius let go of Carmine, let him slither to the floor into his own urine. The Infected whirled to face this new threat. One reached out, brushing the other with its tentacle. They were coordinating.

Akeem jumped forward and splashed the Infected with the remainder of the blood from his bag. They shrieked and pawed at themselves, tentacles whipping out in a vain attempt to catch the boy. Akeem scrambled back behind Viers's desk.

From the ceiling, hundreds of tendrils unspooled, reaching for the bodies below. Marius knew the kind of wracking pain they would inflict if they caught either him or Akeem. Crouching low, he scuttled over to the boy.

"Don't let them touch you," he yelled to be heard above the roars of the Infected and Viers inarticulate shouting.

One of the tendrils bit into Akeem's shoulder. The boy screamed, twisting away from Marius as he slapped at it. Another landed on Marius's forearm. Its needle-sharp teeth pierced his skin, but almost before he could register the pain of the bite, the tendril withdrew. The same rapidly spreading narcotization Marius had seen earlier raced up the tendril. If it got into the hive proper, what would happen? If a hive the size of the one filling Mammoth Cave went up in a Flash like the one he'd caused in Portland, how much destruction would result? Would it be contained underground?

Akeem mentioned a river running out of the cave. That could spread contamination to the surrounding area and downstream. Would it also spread his blood? No, it would be too diluted.

Marius watched the black rot of his blood eat its way up toward the throbbing ropes of veins, tubes, and nerves that covered the ceiling of Viers's office. Whatever happened with the Flash, it would be dangerous to stay. He had to take Akeem and get out while they still could.

He grabbed the bite wound on his arm and squeezed, letting the blood pool in his cupped hand. He caught Akeem's arm and smeared his blood on the tendrils attached to the sobbing boy. They snapped away, flailing through the air like a dropped garden hose turned on full.

Above a white ring formed around the base of the tendril Marius first contaminated with his blood. It cauterized the organ, which broke away from the ceiling and fell to floor where it flopped and twitched as it rotted away.

"Fool," Viers rasped. He hunched over his desk, his face streaked with white lines. Marius could see the scars forming as his former employer's flesh knit itself back together. "We're not as simple as you think."

Akeem whimpered.

Marius didn't wait for Viers to call reinforcements. He half-dragged the boy out of the office and away through the tunnels. By the time he calmed down enough to stop running, he was completely lost.

"Rest," Marius said. He leaned against the wall, which was blessedly devoid of bioformations in this tunnel. Overhead a thin rope of twisted tendrils burbled and gurgled, moving nutrients and information through the hive.

"I'm sorry." Akeem wiped a sleeve across his face. "I'm sorry I lied to you. I wanted to save everyone."

"What do you think I was doing?" Marius was too tired to be angry.

"Nothing." The boy's chin stuck out. "Worse than nothing. You were cooperating. You were working for them." He glared furiously at Marius, even as tears rimmed his eyes.

"I was trying to fix the virus so the mutations would stabilize. If the Enlightened devolved there would be nothing to control the Infected."

"It should matter to people if they get murdered by Enlightened or by Infected?" Akeem hugged himself tightly.

"No, that's not ... no." Marius sagged against the wall. The bite in his arm had stopped bleeding for the most part. Had he been leaving a blood trail? Would Carmine and his Infected enforcers even need one to find them?

"They're going to kill us when they catch us," Akeem said.

"Yep." Marius raked his fingers through his hair. Maybe he could make a deal to save the boy. But Viers held all the cards and they both knew it. Marius had already traded his only bargaining chip. Viers was not likely to trust him again, no matter how much the hive might need his understanding of genetics and virology, his strain or his antigens. He was too great a risk, too little reward. Bad ROI as the suits at Chrysalis would have said.

"We can run away." Akeem's words interrupted the scientist's train of thought.

"I thought you said no one can escape. They've got all the exits covered."

"But not the Pit."

"The Pit?"

Akeem smiled.

Chapter 5 - Miranda

Miranda couldn't believe the Rangers did this every day. Up before dawn, quick breakfast eaten while they listened to their mission briefing, gathered their gear, checked it, repaired it, packed it, double-checked their buddy's gear and all that before they even started getting their horses ready.

The ranch's 4x4s were still functional, but stashed in the far reaches of the barn, in case. In case of what Miranda didn't know. What could be worse than what had already happened? They were cut off from anything resembling civilization. Just four small towns in the middle of the foothills of the Rocky Mountains that had barely made it through the winter.

But here came Torres, looking like the results of an image search for 'badass female warrior', and acting like this next mission would be the one to fix everything. If

Miranda didn't know better, she would have guessed that the former Marine was overcompensating for losing Marius in Great Falls. Or maybe she didn't feel responsible for that. Maybe she was so used to being busy all the time she couldn't be still for a minute.

Whatever her deal was, it had the annoying effect of getting Miranda up in the dead of night to stumble out to the freezing cold barn for a lecture on small unit tactics for a unit she wasn't even a part of.

Rolling one's eyes while they were all droopy with sleep was a trick, but Miranda was a pro.

Eye roll completed she lifted her mug, enjoying the warmth in her mittened hands, if not the smell of weak coffee and much chicory.

Briefing completed and the teams hurried away. Miranda got Thebe ready. She was the same mare from last trip, a misty grey with patches of charcoal on her withers and rump as if she was always sweat-soaked. Clouds of steam rose around the Rangers as they moved out into the cooler air of the barnyard. Several barn cats watched the riders with levels of interest ranging from meh to food? to whatev-er as they got their horses into a straggly line and headed north again.

They stopped around noon. The horses delighted in the new spring grasses while the humans ate a quick, cold lunch. Torres, Dawn, and Nestor, the Morning Star ranch's foreman before the HHV pandemic, gathered around a map, discussing and updating it.

Miranda wandered away from the rest of the Rangers. She refused to hang around the edge of their little group like the unpopular kid. Besides, it was easier to get a sense for the Infected without a bunch of people jabbering. It should be, anyway.

Nothing.

Miranda frowned and focused harder. They were there. She could barely sense them, like sitting near someone who was listening to loud music on expensive headphones with noise cancelling. It was as if she was getting more the vibrations than the actual sounds of the Infected.

That wasn't right.

When she and Dawn went to the quarry hive, she had to fight the whole time to keep the Infected out. A hive should be easy to find. It should be loud or bright or whatever sense she was using to notice them. But instead, it was fuzzy or muffled or ...

Hiding.

A shiver crawled down her body. Why would the Infected be hiding from her? They'd ignored her before, but this was different — deliberate.

"Hold it right there," Torres said.

Miranda jumped and whirled, but the former Marine wasn't looking at her. A man was standing in the field. He held up a white T-shirt. Behind him, up the rise a short way, near the access road that paralleled I-15, a group of PDF members clustered around Liam. He gave Miranda a wink and a little wave like they were buddies. She glared at him.

"We come in peace." The spokesman waved his T-shirt flag.

"What happy horse shit is this?" Torres walked out into the open field. Liam met her at the spokesman, who tucked the shirt away and rejoined the rest of the PDF.

Liam held out a hand, which Torres ignored with cat-like aplomb.

"And here's me, hoping for once we can set aside past misunderstandings for the greater good." Liam pulled a hand-rolled cigarette from behind his ear and lit it.

"And here's me, not shooting you on sight," Torres said. "See, we're practically best friends."

"Sure, what could be better?" Liam drew deeply. "I'm thinking you're out here for the same reason we are." He pointed toward the huddled mass of low buildings that was their destination. According to the scouts, Helen and Diego, the hive was in a prepper compound. No sign of the preppers. Probably among the Infected by now.

"It's got to be dealt with," Torres said, not agreeing, but not not agreeing.

"Mold must be working out then, eh?"

"Don't worry about our capabilities," Torres said. "Why are you here, anyway? Great Falls is in the preserve."

"We've been having troubles with our boundaries of late." Liam held up his and waved. A woman jogged over from the PDF group. From Torres's description, Miranda guessed she must be the younger one from the confrontation a few days ago. She looked fine, no bruises or anything like that from what Miranda could see.

"You remember Cassy, our newest recruit?" Liam put an arm around the girl's shoulders.

"Where's the other one?" Torres demanded, peering past Liam, like the older woman might be crouching behind him.

"Erica wanted to stay back at the base," Cassy chirped, smiling worshipfully up at Liam. Was that how Miranda used to look at Marius? Gross.

"The PDF's not in the business of holding any against their will," Liam said, looking very serious for a change.

"Still doesn't explain what you're doing out here," Torres said.

"Got word there was a nest of them and thought you might need help rooting them out."

"Hive," Miranda said. They all looked at her. She walked over. "The big groups are hives, like network nodes, or whatever on the internet. They collect information from the Littles and the hive's Enlightened passes it to the Infected so they know where to hunt."

"That sounds like bollux." Liam looked at Torres for confirmation.

"Feel free to ignore her," Torres said. "We've got a hive to deal with. I don't trust you or your happy hooligans," she waved at the cluster of PDF folks, "but I do believe that you're not stupid enough to work against us with the Infected at your gate."

"Partners?" Liam held out his hand.

"Allies of necessity." Torres shook it.

The plan was to draw most of the Infected out of the hive, where the Rangers, joined by the PDF, could fend them off. While that was happening Dawn and Miranda would go in and dump the mold and get out. Torres would go with them for security, while Arnaldo coordinated the Rangers outside the hive.

Things would be a lot safer, if not easier, with the PDF to pad their numbers. Miranda didn't like admitting that

Liam was doing something helpful for once, but there it was.

And there was the hive. The smell was unmistakable - sweet rot like being stuck in traffic behind an overloaded garbage truck on a hot day. The compound was walled in. There was a chain link fence around part of it, and the rest was metal sheeting or a concrete wall, topped with shards of glass. The gate, a rolling panel of metal with a rectangular cut out at eye level, was half open.

Bioformations grew up the inside of the fence and over the top in some places. Miranda could sense the low hum of energy moving through the network. It wasn't dead or offline or anything like that.

The Rangers and the PDF divided into their fireteams, moving to take their positions. Dawn fell in beside Miranda and Torres joined them. She double checked the bag of mold she carried.

"One for you." She handed Miranda a plastic baggie full of squishy black mold, oozy like all-natural honey from the farmers' markets. Miranda smiled to herself remembering how much people used to go out of their way to get home-grown vegetables.

"Y uno para ti." Torres handed Dawn another baggie and unslung her rifle. "Let's do this."

The women stalked forward, Dawn and Miranda hanging back to give Torres a clear field of fire. Okay, so not all the tactic drills were totally pointless.

"Anything?" Dawn muttered.

"Nothing," Miranda said. Other than the low buzz of the bioformations and the wispy touches of a few Littles leaving the hive, there wasn't any sign the place was connected to the larger Infected network.

"The hive was active two days ago when Helen and Diego found it," Dawn said. "No way they up and left the whole thing overnight."

"I'm telling you, I don't feel them here." Miranda fought to keep the frustration out of her voice. It wasn't her fault the Infected vanished. She wasn't Queen of the Infected.

"Do you just not feel them or are they not here?" Torres asked.

"What?" Dawn looked confused.

"I don't feel them ..." Miranda trailed off, "here." She turned to stare at Torres, watching the former Marine have the same realization. They're not here, which means they have to be somewhere else.

"Can you find them?" Torres looked around at the ground like she was some kind of wilderness survival expert.

Miranda closed her eyes and reached out with her mind. Only a few Littles and they were all heading in the same direction. Miranda spun slowly like a compass needle pointing the way where the rest of the Infected had gone. Even the Enlightened had left the hive. Did they mean to come back? Was this like the nature shows where the queen bee flew away and the rest went with her? Or was that ants? It was definitely some kind of bug.

Hungry. Hive is hungry.

Miranda stumbled a little as she caught the mind of one of the Littles.

Attack the ranch. Eat them all.

"They're going to the ranch!"

The pillar of smoke rolled up over the ridges, visible even before the ranch came into sight. The shed where the mold was grown was on fire. So was the barn and the house. Animals and people were running around like crazy. The Infected picked off any that strayed too far from the huddle of armed people by the bunk house.

Some of the Rangers started to charge down the hillside, but Torres called them back.

"We're outnumbered. We need to be smarter." She looked at Liam.

"Ah, for fuck's sake," he said. "Yes. We'll help."

"Give us a minute," Torres said to Liam. She beckoned Miranda away from the group a short way.

From the ridge, the fire looked pretty, festive even. The smoke danced up the wind. The people, animals, and Infected might have been doing some kind of complicated musical act.

"You got anything now?" Torres asked in a low voice.

Miranda signed and closed her eyes. She fumbled trying to connect with the Infected below. They were deliberately trying to hide from her. That pissed her off. She pushed harder, smashing through their feeble defenses like she had in the quarry.

Oh no, you useful little idiots. You don't get to lock me out. Not me.

Pushing through into their minds was easier than Miranda remembered. Had she gotten stronger since the quarry? No time to wonder now. She followed the network as it flickered and jumped between Infected. Each individual Infected was its own creature, but they were also part of the hive mind, especially when they touched each other or the bioformations. It was like up- and downloading information.

The signal got stronger as it got closer to the Enlightened.

There it was.

Hello, Miranda. The Enlightened wasn't surprised.

What are you doing here? Why now? She tried to get a better grip on the Enlightened's mind, but it was busy, so busy. A million impressions flooded in from the Infected, threatening to wash her away like hair down a shower drain. There were the sounds, feet rushing, tentacles failing. The wet smack as they hit skin. Screams, grunts, whimpers. All the sounds the uninfected made as they fought to keep apart from the Enlightened.

"Miranda!" Dawn grabbed her arm, breaking her concentration. "We need you. Can you get them away from the house? Annette went back inside."

She pointed up to the back porch's flat roof. The window of Marius's room overlooked the roof. It was open and Annette climbed out. She looped a satchel over her head and one arm and edged towards the lip of the roof. Below an Infected that had once been a deer checked itself mid-charge to the burning barn. It raised its head on a long thin, snake-like neck and growled. Annette jerked back. A wisp of smoke drifted out the open window. She couldn't go back inside. The deer Infected clambered up the porch support, tearing the morning glories off their trellis.

Another Infected charged Dawn and Miranda. This one still had parts of a cow sticking out in places. Dawn shot it twice, which slowed it but didn't stop it. She shot again, missing completely as she pushed Miranda back.

"Go!" she yelled.

Someone dashed from the bunk house across the open yard, dodging two Littles and kicking a third so hard it launched into the air and bounced when it landed.

The cow Infected in front of them reached out for Dawn, but it was Miranda's turn to yank. She stepped in as the thick, tentacle, covered in short, patchy fur, struck.

It hit her shoulder and she staggered, but dug her feet in.

BACK OFF!

The cow Infected froze.

No eating? The tentacle moved more slowly, feeling around her face and neck. It was looking for her communication tentacles. She'd seen these, usually near the necks or shoulders of the Infected. They were smaller, thinner tentacles and they twisted together to make the Infected's mind-meld easier or more complete.

No eating. Miranda imprinted the command, adding the revolted feeling the Infected got when they smelled Marius's blood, which gave her an idea.

That one is corrupted. She directed the cow Infected's attention at the deer Infected climbing onto the porch roof. Annette stomped on its tentacles and limbs as they reached up, but there were too many. She risked getting dragged off the roof if she got too close to the edge.

Kill it. Save the hive.

The cow Infected backed away, turned and lumbered hesitantly toward the house. Miranda pushed a sense of urgency at it. The Enlightened was busy directing everything, reacting to the arrival of the Rangers and the PDF. It didn't notice when she took control of one Infected.

The cow Infected picked up speed and slammed into the deer Infected at full speed. The two tumbled into the yard. As they fought, the communication tentacles touched. Miranda used the opportunity to seize control of the deer Infected. So much easier when they were touching. She could understand why the hives set up bioformations.

Stop. It's fine now. She commanded the cow Infected. Slowly, the two untangled themselves.

But they aren't. They're contaminated! She pointed her two Infected towards a group near the back of the barn. As long as she kept her Infected away from the Enlightened, it wouldn't try to stop her. She felt like just another part of the hive to it.

"Are you okay?" Bailey sprinted up the low rise. He looked terrified but determined. Dawn hugged him quickly.

"You should have stayed in the bunkhouse. We talked about this, remember. Any idiot can ride a horse and shoot. You're our radio operator. We need you to be safe."

"I need you to be safe," Bailey said.

"Do you mind?" Miranda said with an eye roll. "I'm trying to stealth turn the Infected against the Enlightened."

"Of course," Bailey said, nearly nodding his head off.

"We got your back. Do your thing," Dawn said.

Miranda shook out her hands and took a deep cleansing breath, then dove into the frantic chaos that was the Infected's group mind. She used her two to get two more then four more then ten. By then most of the Infected had either been killed by the uninfected or by her Infected. She sent her forces against the Enlightened.

It was risky. Once an Infected she controlled touched the Enlightened, it seemed to wake up and turn against her. She only used very injured Infected to attack the Enlightened. That way they were easier for the Rangers and PDF to pick off when they switched back.

Something hit the side of her head. Her whole body jerked. Her limbs coiled up, shock and pain paralyzing her. She fell to the ground, her one good eye blinking furiously to keep the sludgy blood out. She was lying near the smoldering remains of the shed. She knew because Miranda knew that inside the shed was the mold. Some of it might have survived the fire. She crawled, dragging her mostly useless lower body. Something was wrong with her spine. Two of her legs weren't working.

The ground was still hot. Her skin sizzled, the remaining fur burning off in stinking clouds. Over the threshold and into the shed. Embers glowed. A deep, earthy smell infused the smoke. She could feel it tickling in her nose as she inhaled the spores. She coughed. Coughed again. They were rooting in the delicate, wet, pink membranes of her lungs.

She didn't have much time. Already the virus was

rushing to incorporate this new life form. She would be dead soon, killed by the hungry fungus.

She filled her paws and her mouth with the smoldering mold. It burned into her tongue and her cheeks.

Only a few yards to get from the shed to the Enlightened.

What are you doing? The Enlightened was confused, angry. A part of its body — the burning, dying Infected — wasn't doing what it expected.

Abomination. She lurched, lunged, stuffed handfuls of mold into the Enlightened, even as she felt the teeth and claws of her other Infected selves sinking into her.

Miranda screamed.

Chapter 6 - Torres

New Avalon, Montana, USA – Summer, Year 2

The house was still sound but the fire had damaged the front and side. Torres handed a bucket to Percy, who passed it to Philippe. The last of the fires in the barn were almost out. Everyone who could lift a bucket was in line from the cistern to the barn.

John collected the kids and the elderly and set them to combing through the wreckage for anything salvageable: food, medicine, ammunition. Fortunately, nothing had cooked off in the fire, but knowing how easily it could have gave Torres stomach cramps. Especially when she looked at Elfy.

Her niece was running bandages to the injured. She and Wahida made of game of it, racing each other. Their faces were smeared with soot and grime, but they barely seemed to notice. Torres was constantly amazed by how resilient kids were. Until they weren't. They were more fragile than adults — they just didn't know how to gauge when they were close to their limits.

But Torres couldn't take time to check on Elfy. The barn needed to be saved. The bodies of the Infected needed disposed of. The bodies would be covered with what mold they had and burned. They would need to be taken somewhere they wouldn't contaminate the watershed or disrupt the herds' grazing areas.

So much of their survival depended on others' lives. Or deaths, in the case of the Infected.

Dawn joined the line, handing Torres a watering can.

"Miranda's still asleep," the younger woman reported.

"How many did we lose?" Torres handed off the watering can and stepped out of line, pulling Dawn with her.

"Two Rangers, three civilians, and a townie — Mrs. Kawzinski," Dawn said.

Torres's first thought was "How?" They survived the winter with fewer casualties. Now on her watch, she'd lost six in one afternoon. Going after the hive was her call and it was a bad one. She didn't even know how the fires had started. Knocked over lamps? That she knew of, the Infected never used fire as a tool. Small freaking favors ...

"Torres?"

"Yeah, uh, have the bodies moved over there, near the family plot." The former Marine pointed. "Away from the Infected," she added before returning to the bucket brigade.

About an hour later, the clouds were back and the wind whipping up a shuddering, grumbling squall. Even

Torres could see the roiling thunderheads coming down south, aimed at the ranch as if Nature were in on it.

John beckoned Torres over to a small gathering of the ranch's leadership. Percy and her parents were already there, as was Soraya. Everyone else was crowded around an impromptu cookout. Phineas was supervising the children as they ate.

Some of the injured livestock had to be put down. No sense wasting the fresh meat. Anatole and some of the original ranch hands set up a drying rack for what couldn't be eaten right away. Torres squinted at the clouds but gave up trying to guess if they would dump rain or not. Even Philippe admitted that ever since the Portland Flash, the weather had been too chaotic to get a good read on.

As Torres joined the leaders' meeting, Percy held up her notebook. It was one of the hardback olive-green Army notebooks John preferred.

"We lost Sierra and Nick. From the Rangers, Gus, Viggo, and Helen," Percy said.

"Shit," Torres said. Helen was barely eighteen, the minimum age John and Torres had set as the standard to conduct off-the-ranch Ranger missions. Kids were allowed to apprentice to the Rangers at sixteen with the permission of a parent or guardian.

"How did this happen?" Soraya asked. She tucked strands of her thick, dark hair back under her hijab. It had grown out a bit since Torres cut it in the ICE camp back in the autumn.

Annette and Philippe exchanged a look, as did John and Percy. No one looked at Torres.

"It was my call," she said. "I thought we could handle

the hive. We underestimated them. Even with the PDF, we," she swept her arm toward the smoldering ranch house, the barn, the skeleton of the mold shed. "We barely survived."

"That's not how I see it," Annette said. Her face was bruised and her arm was wrapped in bandages, but she was alive and upright. Torres tried to count that as a win.

"I'm just glad you're okay," Philippe said. "Nothing in that house was worth getting killed for."

Annette nodded but hugged her satchel tighter. Philippe frowned and kissed the top of her head, looking both relieved and exasperated.

"Talk us through what happened," John said.

Torres recounted how the scouts had found the hive, alerted them, and she'd decided to conduct a preemptive strike mission.

"I thought with Miranda there to help control the Infected and the mold, we'd be in and out," she said. "The hive either knew we were coming, or it was shit luck that they moved when we did."

"Is it possible that Liam set us up?" Philippe asked.

Torres started to shake her head — Liam had been there, his militia members had been in just as much danger as they had, except that wouldn't be true if he'd set them up. If he'd known the hive would be empty, the PDF risked nothing by going with them.

"How many did they lose?" John asked the question that was on Torres's mind.

Percy checked her notebook. "One and an injury, plus a bite that we treated from the emergency stock."

"Which leaves us how many attested doses?" Torres wished she'd never heard words like that, let alone had to use them in casual conversation.

"Seventeen," Percy said.

They all stood silent for a long moment, watching the smoke drift up. The wind brought them the petrichor scent of incoming rain. People were hurrying to set up tents and awnings before the storm hit.

If this had happened even a month ago, they would be in serious danger of hypothermia, not just a soaking. Regardless of the time of year, they would need shelter and soon. The Rule of Threes still applied: Humans can survive three minutes without air, three hours without shelter, three days without water, three weeks without food.

"Let's talk about where we go from here," John said.

Annette gave one gasping sob but didn't cry. Philippe blinked back some tears. He and Annette hugged each other. This had been their home for decades. Their kids had grown up here. In the middle of the collapsing world, the Morning Star ranch had seemed like the last safe place on Earth. Against all odds, their missing son had come home to this place.

If Marius was still alive, where would he go but here?

Torres had one job: protect the people of New Avalon, especially the folks on the ranch. She'd failed. Failed them and failed him.

But she couldn't let the crush of grief and self-doubt bury her. Elfy needed her. Marius's family needed her. The Rangers needed her.

So, she said what needed to be said: "We have to leave."

"It won't be fun." Elfy pouted on her cot. Around them, the canvas sides of the hut billowed and snapped with the wind.

Torres added sandbags to her mental checklist. They would hold down the edges of the tent she and Elfy shared with Soraya, Mirzha, and Wahida. Moving to town had not been easy. Even after a week, they were only half settled. The folks from the Morning Star ranch mostly stuck together, setting up a temporary tent and RV city on the high school's athletic field. The plan was to rebuild the ranch house, the barn, and the shed and then move back.

It was a good plan, except that people had started moving out of the tents and into the town. There were a number of empty houses to choose from. Some had been abandoned by people going to the designated evacuation sites in Great Falls or Helena. Others were left when their owners were killed either by the Infected or any number of other things since the HHV pandemic arrived in central Montana half a year ago.

Torres worried that once people settled into life in town they wouldn't want to go back out to the ranch. Not that living in Crossroads was the lap of luxury or convenience. Still, it had a school, a market, and a clinic.

If people settled in town, life would get a lot harder for Marius's family. Without the protection and labor pool of a larger community, how long could the Tenartiers stay out on an exposed piece of land?

From a strategic standpoint, the Morning Star ranch and others like it served as LP/OPs for New Avalon's towns. Without the ranches, there would be less warning about threats to the whole area. Keeping the ranches up and running not only benefited the ranchers, but everyone in New Avalon.

"School's not meant to be fun," Torres said. She strapped on her holster and checked her gear. Her go-bag contained the survival basics that every Ranger carried on every mission, no matter how short. A fire starter and tinder in a waterproof baggie, iodine tablets, bandages and antibiotic cream, a camp knife, a flare, a compass, fishing line that could also be used to make snares, and most precious, a vial of attested HHV vaccine. Torres didn't have to worry about getting infected, like some of the Rangers, but if she met someone within the first few hours of infection, she might be able to save them.

"I want to go with you," Elfy slid bonelessly off the cot and onto the blanket that served as their floor. Torres didn't want to think of how mucky the place would get if they couldn't get proper flooring in before the next big storm.

"You can't go with me." Torres checked her niece's school bag. It, too, had some survival basics. Warm, waterproof jacket, mittens, a fuzzy hat that looked like a bunny with big lop ears hanging down on either side of Elfy's face, and always at least a day's worth of food and water.

"I wanna," whined the puddle of kid.

"Tough," Torres snapped. She didn't have time for another tantrum.

Predictably Elfy began to wail.

"Fine," Torres said. She had to raise her voice to be heard. "Stay here. I'll let Soraya know you won't be at school."

She left the tent, ignoring the muffled sobs as best she could. The world wasn't a soft place and coddling Elfy wouldn't be doing her any favors long term. The sooner the girl learned to stand on her own, the better. Torres couldn't carry her and the whole rest of the ranch, the Rangers, and New Avalon.

Anatole and Dawn were waiting for her at the makeshift horse corral. The townies were a lot more accepting of livestock in the city limits these days, especially if it meant keeping the Rangers close. Travel was difficult and dangerous. They were back to the days of Pony Express riders to get messages and supplies from one town to another. The Rangers kept the towns of New Avalon connected with each other.

Before the hive shit storm, Torres had brought up expanding their patrols.

"We need to reach out to others, pool our resources, get things up and running again," Torres had said. She sat on the floor of the barn's office, putting the final coat of polish on her boots. Waterproofing was serious business.

"Agreed," John said. He half leaned on the table, studying the area maps. One of the most vital duties the Rangers performed was area reconnaissance. Updating the maps was one of the first tasks for anyone coming in off patrol. It was even in the Ranger Creed: "I will share information about the terrain, people, and hazards I encountered. I will be honest with my fellow Rangers, keeping nothing back. I will never judge my fellow Ranger's decisions — I was not there; I did not have to make their choices."

The last was John's idea. In order to create an atmosphere of absolute honesty among the Rangers, they needed to be able to trust each other. No one made it this far into the HHV pandemic without seeing or doing awful things in the name of survival.

"Ready, Freddy?" Dawn asked as she vaulted into the saddle. Anatole also made it look as easy as rolling off a log. Torres sighed. Ganymede, her trusty steed, rolled a liquid brown eye and stamped a hoof. Torres clambered into the saddle like a hungover private back from their first weekend pass.

"Ready," she said, fighting to keep from sucking wind at the minor task of climbing onto a horse's back.

Anatole and Dawn were pretending to study something off on the horizon while not noticing the former Marine's difficulties.

"Let's do this," Torres said.

The ride back to the ranch was nearly two hours. Not hard going. The roads were still in pretty good shape, even if the gravel needed filled and graded. Problems for another day.

The ranch buildings weren't smoking, but the char smell lingered over everything. The watch towers were undamaged and as they rode up, the sentries radioed up to the bunk house to let Arnaldo know friendlies were inbound.

Rain started in scattered bursts as the trio rode up the dirt driveway. The red maple still stood in the center of the turnaround. The front porch and even the freaking porch swing were fine. The lumpy dog bed still sat in the corner of the porch, beside the swing. Buddy, the family's mutt, had gone with Philippe and Annette into Crossroads. They were staying with Eugenia and Ernest Crowchilde above E & E's Grocery.

Anatole and Dawn hopped nimbly off their horses. Torres clambered down, grateful for solid grown beneath her boots.

"We bring gifts!" Dawn held up a bag of pasties donated from the bakery. The work crew dropped their equipment and rushed her. Torres was pleased to see that those on guard duty resisted the temptation and stayed focused on watching the perimeter. She was even more please to see that the ones she'd assigned to keep an eye on Liam and Cassy were doing their jobs.

While Dawn and Anatole supervised the lunch break, Torres beckoned Liam over.

"Why are you still here?" she asked as she handed the mercenary a pastie.

He took a big bite and chewed thoughtfully before answering. "Why haven't you asked me what you really want to ask me?"

"Why do you have to make everything so hard?" Torres nibbled her own pastie. The crust was still flaky. Inside the meat was either lamb or goat, seasoned and stewed with onions, carrots, and some kind of chewy root vegetable. She didn't think it was a potato, too stringy.

"Why don't you just come out with it?"

"Is this what you do for fun?"

"Sometimes. You?" Liam smirked.

"No." Torres narrowed her eyes. "Are you willing to

trade or not?"

"Depends. What are you looking for, exactly?"

"A crane."

"What happened here?" Torres shifted. The saddle creaked under her. Ganymede flicked an ear.

The last time the former Marine had seen Great Falls it was from the bed of an Air Force Humvee. She barely remembered the trip. Between escaping the Infected swarming the city, organizing a bombing run with Captain McCormick's pilots, and trying to get the full story about what happened to Marius from Bailey, she'd been too busy to focus on the city itself.

Still, she knew that the Air Force had been in control of the west side, with the PDF hunkered down across the Missouri River to the east. The militia used the Malmstrom Air Base as their headquarters.

Torres wasn't sure what she expected to find six months after the collapse of civilization, but squalor wasn't it. No way McCormick would allow open sewer trenches in the median strips of major roads. Especially not so close to the river. The risk of cholera alone was enough to stop that kind of nonsense.

"Oh, this?" Liam waved at the crowd of sullen-looking folks gathering in their wake. Some were wrapped in blankets or tattered coats. They looked skinny, sickly, and angry.

Torres regretted her decision to come to Great Falls. Strategically, it was the right move. New Avalon couldn't afford to leave any chance at contact with the wider world unexplored. Plus, they really needed a crane. The main beam of the ranch house was damaged. No one was sure how badly, but it didn't seem like the kind of thing to take chances with. Philippe found a beam that would work at an abandoned housing development construction site. But they needed something that could lift in up two stories. Hopefully, this trip would be worth leaving Elfy with Soraya. Hopefully, her niece would ever speak to her again.

Besides, Torres reminded herself, the kid needed to be around others her own age. And Torres couldn't watch her all the time. Not if she wanted to get anything else accomplished.

"Hardly a grand welcome," Liam said, lighting a cigarette. "They're a might cautious, is all. Need to warm up to you. Maybe tell us a joke or something."

"I'm not your freaking monkey," Torres said. "Your morale problems are yours to deal with. I'm here for the crane."

"That'll be over here, then," Liam said. As they left the main street, the crowd drifted away. Here and there, Torres saw small gardens, but most looked as if they'd been abandoned. Piles of trash and debris mounded against buildings or drifted along the streets. Most of the homes looked empty, some with broken windows, or doors left open to the weather.

"Ta-DA!" Liam waved at a crane parked in a lot filled with a variety of heavy machinery and construction equipment.

"Does it run?" Torres circled the crane slowly. During her time in the Marines, she'd done all kinds of vehicle inspections. She wasn't familiar with cranes, but she knew in general what to look for. Other than a hearty crop of weeds under and through the tires, and some rust patches, the crane looked serviceable.

"Might do," Liam said. "You said you wanted a crane."

"It's no good to us if it doesn't work," Torres said. She leaned a hip against one of the huge, knobby tires and folded her arms across her chest, eyeing Liam. "Did you drag me all the way up here to punk me?"

"I enjoy your company the way a cat enjoys a soaking, so yeah, let's set up together then."

Torres pushed herself up and started walking back toward the strip of grass where Ganymede nosed happily for new clover.

"Oy!" Liam caught her arm, but wisely dropped it as she spun to face him.

"It works," said a woman's voice. The older woman, Erica, stood at the edge of the lot. She looked cleaner and Torres didn't see anyone guarding her. That was a relief. It had bothered Torres, thinking that she'd left the other woman to some horrible captivity. Even with Cassy's assurances that everything was fine, Torres had been cautious. Cassy was young, naïve, and very eager to feel safe and secure even if she wasn't.

"There you are." Liam waved at Erica. "Call it a deal, then? The supplies we talked about for the crane? We'll even throw in enough diesel to get her to Crossroads."

Torres didn't want to agree too quickly. Ever since leaving the ranch, the anxiety had grown inside her. They were out in the open, exposed in soft-sided tents. Theoretically, the hive had been eliminated. The Ranger patrols had dealt with a few Littles, but the area seemed mostly Infected free. Probably staying clear of the mold that the Rangers dispersed with every scouting mission.

"Let me talk to Erica," she said.

"She can talk to anyone she blinking well pleases," Liam said. "No one's here who doesn't want to be, love."

Torres glared at him, but he sauntered off, tapping his empty cigarette pack as if it might magically refill.

"You can come to New Avalon with me," Torres said as soon as Liam was out of earshot.

Erica pulled her sweater tighter around her shoulders and smoothed back her hair. Torres could see the line at the tips where she used to use relaxer. That along with the large, pink pearl drop earrings said 'corporate'. How the woman had made it so far was one of the many mysteries of the HHV pandemic. Sometimes the strongest, most prepared died for the dumbest reasons, while the massively unfittest evaded every danger, blissfully unaware of how freaking lucky they were.

"Thanks, but no," Erica said. "Cassy and I are done traveling. Besides, Liam says you're not in the Preserve."

"Fair enough," Torres said. "But know the invitation is open. We don't have some of the resources that Great Falls has, but we've got the basics. We're rebuilding and expanding."

"How, with the Infected everywhere?"

Torres briefly explain the mold, which had been infused with Marius's inhibitor.

"We don't know how long it'll take to clear the Infected, but it's a start." She finished with a shrug.

"Did you find my pack?" Erica asked.

"I did," Torres said. "Where did you meet

Mendelsen?"

It was Erica's turn to recount what had happened. Torres waited until the end of the other woman's story to ask her questions. "How long ago was that? Where exactly did you meet Mendelsen? How did you know to give me the key card?"

"I didn't know you knew who Marius was, but I didn't know who Liam was and you seemed," she waved her hands at Torres, "capable. I'm glad we have a chance to talk now. We heard about you and Marius. Mendelsen also wanted me to give you these coordinates."

It took a few minutes, but Torres committed the coordinates to memory. She would need to look at a map to figure out where that was. From the look of the key card, she guessed a top-secret government facility of some kind. If they were still there and still had any capabilities, they might be interested in helping her find Marius. She felt the first flickers of a real plan forming.

"I can't thank you enough for this," Torres said. "We'll send your pack up with the supplies. Come visit Crossroads any time. Let us know if there's anything you need that you can't get in Great Falls. The Rangers are out scouting for other communities and we find the weirdest stuff sometimes."

"Have you had any contact with Yellowstone?" Erica asked.

"Yellowstone? Like the national park?"

Erica recounted the rumors from the refugee camp about a safe and thriving community based out of Yellowstone National Park.

"Good to know," Torres said, adding Yellowstone to the list of scouting missions. She and Erica shook hands and she went to find Liam. Moving the crane down to Crossroads and then to the ranch would be a few days' work, not to mention the actual rebuilding, but knowing there might be other people helping look for Marius put a spring in her step and a smile on her face.

Chapter 7 - Marius

On the Road, Kentucky, USA — Summer, Year 2

The Pit yawned, the entrance into the void, as far as Marius could tell. The mouth of the Pit was at least a hundred yards across. A very questionable looking plank bridge lay across the Pit. A set of even more questionable rope handrails accompanied the plank. Even if Marius had been a tightrope walker, he would have had serious doubts about getting across the Pit.

But they didn't have to get across the Pit, not completely. The trip through the tunnels left Marius disoriented and tired, but now wasn't the time to go back for supplies.

"Do you hear them?" Akeem trembled beside Marius. The boy was exhausted and terrified. Marius could relate. For the past few minutes, the scientist kept thinking he was hearing something pursuing them. He tried to convince himself that it was his imagination.

No, the scuffling, shuffling sounds grew louder. Marius pressed himself back against the tunnel wall. The noise echoed, making it hard for him to estimate how close behind them the Infected were. He assumed Infected. Carmine would have been gloating or threatening if it were him.

"Let's go," Marius said. He tried to sound confident. This could work. He stepped onto the plank, testing its strength under the weight of one foot. It groaned. A shower of dust fell away.

"You go first," he said. Akeem gaped at him.

"It might break under my weight. You're lighter. You go first and I'll follow."

Akeem visibly swallowed. Marius grabbed his shoulder and squeezed it. "You can do this. You're the bravest kid I've ever met."

The boy edged out onto the plank. He had to turn sideways and shuffle to keep completely on the wood. His shoes scraped dust and small stones off the plank, sent a shower down. Marius strained to hear it hit the water below.

Nothing. Only eerie silence.

Soon, Akeem was lost in the shadows, his form a darker silhouette against the gloom.

From the hall, Marius heard a grunting snuffle. He turned, knowing what he would see.

Three Infected. The one in the lead looked like it had been a Dalmatian once. The ones behind it were devolved humans, so former Enlightened. The Dalmatian Infected lunged into the open chamber that surrounded the Pit, its low growl bouncing and echoing off the walls.

"Marius?" Akeem's voice drifted back from the dark.

Marius waved at him to go on, but the boy couldn't see him.

"Keep going," Marius whisper-yelled. "I'm fine."

"F-f-fine?" gurgled the bigger of the devolved Enlightened.

"Fine," Marius muttered. He glanced over his shoulder at the lip of the Pit. If he got a running start, he could probably get enough momentum to clear the sides. Assuming they were straight down, which he had no way of knowing.

If he did make a run for it, that would leave Akeem alone with the Infected.

He needed to stall them until he knew the boy was safe. He couldn't help laughing at the idea. Safe? They were about to jump into a hole that was more than a hundred feet deep, in the dark, with monsters at their heels.

The Infected spread out, the devolved off to either side, the Dalmatian coming at him from the front. Did they know his blood would kill them? Did they care? Speaking of his blood — Marius dug at the barely closed bite on his arm, reopening it. He smeared the blood on his hands, let it trickle down his forearm, and waited.

The Dalmatian charged but veered off at the last second. That was when the devolved on his right rammed into him, knocking him off his feet. He skidded along the ground on his hip. As the devolved reached for his feet, he twisted and slammed it full in the face with both hands. The blood spattered across its head, scattering pinpricks of rot wherever it fell.

The devolved tried to pull away, but the second one

piled on from behind it. They crushed him under their combined weight. Marius kicked and bucked, fighting to free his hands.

The Dalmatian surged out of nowhere from his left. It sank its teeth into his shoulder, growling loudly. It shook its head back and forth, worrying the wound even as Marius's deadly blood filled its mouth. The necrotic effect swept over its face, stripping what remained of the fur and skin. Even as its flesh sloughed off, the Infected kept its jaws locked.

The devolved on top of Marius slumped sideways, entangling the other for long enough that Marius could claw free of the pile of bodies. Dragging the Dalmatian by its disintegrating muzzle, he crawled for the edge of the Pit.

"Marius?" Akeem sounded further away. That was good. He must be near the middle of the plank by now.

"Jump," Marius yelled. "I'm right behind you."

"Promise?"

For a moment it wasn't Akeem and they weren't in stale cave. It was Otto and they were on the flight line in Wiltz.

"C'mon, we have to get to the plane." Marius had reached out to shepherd the boy through the frantic press of evacuees. "We'll be safe. I won't leave you."

"Promise?"

The security team had taken Marius away. For his own good. The last time he saw Otto was the boy standing alone as the chaos of the crowd surged around them.

"Promise?" Akeem was louder, more frightened sounding.

Marius dug his toes into the ground and pushed with his knees. Somehow the Dalmatian was still growling. Its head was a tatter of skin, tendons, and muscles, jaws still locked. Marius caught flashes of white bone. His or the Infected's?

"I promise."

His fingers found the edge of the Pit. Behind him the remaining devolved was up again. He could hear the moist smack of its tentacles as it tried to push its way past other Infected. If it got to him …

But it wouldn't. This time he would keep his promise.

Marius hooked his elbows over the edge.

The devolved wrapped a tentacle around his ankle.

He stretched and strained. The Dalmatian gave a wheezing growl as it slipped over the edge.

And that was enough.

The weight of the beast yanked Marius forward into the Pit with a devolved coiled around his ankle.

In *The Fellowship of the Ring,* Gandalf stood against the Balrog, a demon that dwelled in the deepness of the mines of Moria. The Balrog had taken the wizard with it when it fell to its doom. But did Gandalf let a little thing like inevitable death deter him from fighting the ancient evil every second? Not hardly.

Marius wished he were that focused, that coordinated. After slithering headfirst into the Pit, he lost all sense of up or down. His righting reflex failed profoundly.

After what seemed like a ridiculously long time to be tumbling through silence and darkness, Marius realized that the Dalmatian Infected was still attached to his shoulder by its remaining few teeth. It was pulling on him, which meant that way was down.

He twisted as best he could, trying for feet first. As a kid, he used to go to the Starling Union Quarry with the other locals and jump off Lunatic's Launch. It was a twenty-foot drop to the icy water below.

Marius had learned to point his toes up and take the smack of the water's impact on the soles of his shoes. Keep his arms in, folded across his chest like a cinematic vampire.

About a nanosecond after he oriented himself and assumed crash position, he impacted. In the near total darkness, he didn't see the water, so he didn't have the chance to take a deep inhalation before he was submerged.

It wouldn't have mattered; the impact of hitting the water at what he was pretty sure was terminal velocity, drove all the air out his lungs.

He sank.

For once, he was grateful for the Infected. Not them, in general, but the Dalmatian, still doggedly clinging to his shoulder. His anchor and his point of reference for up and down.

Marius pried the last bits of the Infected off him and kicked away. If he had miscalculated and was swimming down, the chances of having enough oxygen in his system to keep his brain functional long enough to reorient and swim in the right direction were minuscule.

But he wasn't wrong.

Red and white phosphenes were bursting in his vision as his head broke the surface. He gasped.

The current wasn't overwhelming but it was definitely moving him downstream.

He reached out with his hands and down with his feet, seeking the bank, the bed, some solid part of the river's anatomy. His right arm barely moved. No chance to inspect the damage. He had to hope it was just punctures, not some spurting arterial laceration that would exsanguinate him in minutes.

Far behind him, upriver, there was a high-pitched cry, followed shortly by a splash.

Was that Akeem or the remaining devolved?

The current picked up. Marius couldn't have swum upstream to investigate even if he wanted to.

But he didn't.

A heavy, hazy feeling was seeping through his body.

I'm not bleeding to death, he told himself. It's the crash after an adrenaline spike. That's all. Definitely not feeling sleepy and cold like I did at Chrysalis.

At Chrysalis, where he'd nearly died of organ failure after bleeding out well over the advisable, sensible, or even slightly risky amount of blood.

Had it been worth it? At the time he thought so. He believed his sacrifice would quell the outbreak, keep HHV forever confined to Chrysalis and the annals of *This was Almost a Pandemic*.

Something nudged him. Why was Miranda trying to wake him up? He had just gotten comfortable on the couch in the day room.

Another jostle. His eyes opened. It was dark. Mostly, dark. Ahead, a dim, greenish light. Was he still underwater? Had he drowned?

Someone tugged at the collar of his shirt, pulled his head up and out of the water. Oh. There was the water.

"Swim," a voice hissed in his ear. "You're too heavy."

He paddled lazily. The light was brightening, the current strengthening as the river narrowed. His feet bumped something, dragged through layers of silt, bumped over deep lying rocks and driftwood so saturated it broke apart at the slightest pressure. How long had this part of the river been undisturbed?

"Swim!"

He didn't have to. The riverbed rose up beneath him and he walked. He put out his left hand and parted the curtain. It wasn't a fleshy membrane. It was vines and moss. Along the waterline, it was mold, trailing black tendrils downriver like a drowning victim's hair.

Akeem sloshed along next to him, pushing him past the cave's mouth and toward a sandbar. Around them, the world was filled with color and light and sound. So much sound. Birds twittering, insects rattling, a falcon's shrill call, the leaves rustling and shushing as the wind set the tree limbs moaning and groaning.

Under his knees and then his hands, Marius felt dry sand. The sun-warmed, river-smoothed stones gave him their heat. The air was fresh and filled with the newly released scents of a forest after a rain. He half-crawled, half-walked out of the river, the mud of the bank trying to steal his shoes to no avail.

Above the river, the grass was long and sharp, the kind that had never lived in fear of a lawn mower's blades. Marius slumped against a pine tree, the bark itchy and warm against his back, the needles tickling at the top of his head. Akeem sat next to him, legs splayed out, chest heaving. He pushed his dark hair back with both hands and looked around.

"I haven't been outside for almost a year," he said. He pulled his knees up, curled into them, and sobbed.

Marius rubbed the boy's back. He felt slow and blinky. The chill was coming back, crowding out the good warmth of the sunbaked forest.

Okay, shoulder time.

Marius craned his neck as far as he could. Punctures from the Dalmatian Infected's canines. The other teeth had left minor cuts and scrapes. He gingerly palpated the area, feeling for injures he couldn't see. The blood was bright red, which was good. Nothing major had been nicked.

"How is it?" Akeem asked. His voice was raw from crying, but he sounded resolved.

"It needs to be cleaned and stitched." Marius let his head fall back against the tree trunk. "You don't happen to have a sewing kit handy?"

"No, I'm sorry."

Marius ruffled the boy's hair. "It's a joke. Here, help me take off this shirt. We can tear it up for bandages."

It was night. Not the artificial night that was a lull in the rhythm of life in the Mammoth Cave hive. True night. The kind that came with a breathless calm of the wind and stars overhead dancing between the clouds and the forest canopy.

Marius lay on his back in a glade and stared and stared and stared. Akeem lay next to him. Neither had moved in a long time, so Marius assumed the boy was equally entranced. The ground was slightly damp. Water seeping up, gathering gradually under Marius's body. From the river? He didn't know and he refused to let his science brain go on its usual wild hunt for associations.

For the moment, they were free. They were safe, as safe as anyone could be in a world where the dominant life form was a virus. All they had to do was nothing. No Infected watched their every move. No Carmine coming around with demands to complete this or that test.

"I'm hungry," Akeem said. And just like that, they were back in the real world.

Marius sat up gingerly, trying not to put any unnecessary strain on the bandages around his shoulder. The pain was a constant gnawing at the back of his brain, but in the scope of everything else, it seemed trivial. He was out. He was free. He was ... in Kentucky?

That was a long way from Montana, even before the planes all crashed and the trains stopped and the buses were abandoned to rust on the interstates. But before he could even start worrying about trying to cross most of the US on foot, he needed to find food, shelter, and medical supplies. That meant a town. Marius didn't know much about the surrounding area, but most national parks had small towns or at least outfitters around their perimeters. They catered to tourists, specializing in sunblock, bug spray, snacks, and first aid kits.

"Let's walk," Marius said, climbing carefully to his feet. His ankle was sore, abraded from where the devolved's tentacle wrapped around it. His whole body was sore from hitting the water after a hundred-foot fall. And his shoulder throbbed and blazed by turns.

By dawn, they were far down the gravel road. The eastern sky was banded in pink and orange, pale blue vanishing in the clouds. The grass was heavy with dew, and if it hadn't been for his rumbling stomach and aching body, it would have been the most perfect morning.

They found a general store that had been only lightly looted. Nothing to eat, but they did get some wet wipes, bug spray, and a first aid kit that still had antibiotic cream, gauze, and tape in it. Marius took a couple of aspirins and, with Akeem's help, re-bandaged his shoulder.

In the clear light of day, he could see that there were several chunks of tissue missing. The scar would be ugly and deep. He didn't want to risk moving his arm too much, so he couldn't rule out the possibility that the bite might leave him unable to fully use that limb.

It took most of the afternoon to walk into town from the little store. Marius and Akeem were both jumpy, turning at any sound in the forest around them. No Infected. Yet. But Marius couldn't believe that Viers would let them go so easily. They needed to put as much distance between themselves and the cave as possible. They also had to avoid all Infected because any of them could report back to the hive.

But first, food.

The town was small, quaint, charming even, if it had been alive. Several of the homes and businesses along the main street were wrapped and draped in bioformations. No animals wandered the empty streets. Only last year's leaves, moldering away in piles and drifts along the edges of the road.

"Ready to do some breaking and entering?" Marius said as cheerfully as he could. Akeem nodded mutely. He looked exhausted, head dropping, dark hollows under his eyes.

The first two houses had been picked clean. The third yielded some canned spaghetti hidden in the living room, but no can opener. The electric one on the counter mocked their hunger. They finally found a can opener in an abandoned rucksack behind a mechanic shop. They sat in the middle of the street, eating spaghetti by the fingerful and watching the cloud shadows pass over.

The rest of the afternoon they slept. Marius didn't mean to. He knew they needed to get on the road, to get away, but his body was done. They went inside a house looking for clean clothes and blankets. The upstairs master bedroom had a picture window and the bed was sun warmed. Marius lay down, feeling like a cat. He rolled onto his side, baking himself. He closed his eyes.

"Hey, look what I found."

Akeem's voice drifted through the layers of sleep that mounded over Marius.

He pushed off the quilt that covered him, winced as his shoulder reminded him that sort of thing would not be tolerated, and sat up.

It was dark. The room was fill of shadows. The house was filled with breathing.

The Infected had found them. Marius lurched out of the bed, flinging away the quilt. Where was Akeem?

A light blazed from outside. Marius half-jumped,

half-ran down the stairs. Without breaking stride, he snatched one of the knives out of the block on the kitchen counter and hit the screen door taking him out into the narrow side yard. He pressed his back against the wall and inched to the corner.

Okay, on three, he told himself, trying to give his internal monologue Torres's authoritative ring of competent command.

He eeled around the house and froze.

Akeem stood beside a blue and silver smart car. The lights Marius had seen were its headlights.

"Electric. She doesn't need petrol." The boy grinned and patted the roof. "Let's go!"

Chapter 8 - Miranda

Miranda stood at the edge of the market and pondered her options. She needed a new pair of gloves. Or she could go back to her room at the school gym. 'Room' was a very misleading term. It was some plywood boards slapped together over 2x4s. She could see through the cracks into her neighbors' rooms. Plus, there was zero privacy. Every cough, every snore or fart was known to everyone in the gym. And yet, people still thought their private business was private?

Either they didn't know or they didn't care who heard them doing what. Miranda wasn't a prude. She didn't care about the suspicious rustling and grunting noises late at night. What did bother her was the gossip.

"I heard she's infected, but asymptomatic."

"Why does Torres keep her around?"

"She has to. Courage basically raised her."

"As if having a useless rich brat hanging around wasn't bad enough, she's probably working for the Infected."

"All I'm saying is that it was very coincidental how Marius got grabbed when she was gone, and how the hive knew to attack us when the Rangers were gone."

It didn't matter that during the day they were all polite as punch or pie or whatever these yahoos liked to have at their annual cowpoke festivals. Miranda knew how they really felt about her. They weren't even bothering to hide it.

Well, she was not going to be intimidated by their ignorant, nasty comments.

She lifted her chin, tossed her hair, and strode into the market like she owned the place. All the better to ignore the stares and whispers, my dear.

The market looked like any of the dozens of cute hippie farmers' markets Miranda had frequented, except for the stalls trading weapons and armor or the ones trading gas and car parts. There were the usual stands with honey and soap, goat's milk body lotion and beeswax candles. The knitters were in high demand. No one cared much if the mittens matched or the hats were a little lumpy and lopsided.

Miranda strolled through the other shoppers, or traders more accurately now that money didn't have much value other than as tinder. The first time Miranda watched Torres start a fire with a wade of crumpled twenties, she'd teared up at the horrible finality of it. The world she'd known was never ever coming back.

"We're closed," said the man sitting behind the little table filled with leather gloves and boots. The gloves were lined with lamb's wool. Miranda had been eyeing them for days. Ever since they moved from the Morning Star ranch into Crossroads.

"What?" Miranda blinked. The booth was clearly open. All the stuff was on the table. The man's lunch was in a box next to his camp stool. He clearly wasn't packing up any time soon.

"We're closed." He made a shooing motion, like she was a dog. "Go on."

"You're totally not closed." Miranda put her hands on her hips and leaned forward, getting in his face and in his space. It was a trick she'd seen Torres use to intimidate guys way bigger and meaner than this one.

The man put his hands on the table and half stood, glaring at Miranda. Was he going to hit her? In public? In front of all these people? What if he did and no one did anything to help?

Miranda knew she should back down. It was the safe thing to do, the smart thing.

The man shooed her again, a smirk on his stupid face, and that settled it.

"I will literally die and turn to dust on this spot," Miranda said. "Or you can sell me those gloves."

"It's a free country," the man said. His voice rose as he added. "I reserve the right to refuse service to anyone. Including you."

"Why?" Miranda snapped. Her own voice was getting louder, but she didn't care. They wanted a scene? Let them have one with sprinkles on top.

"We all know what you are," the man said.

"What do you think that is, exactly?"

"One of them Enlightened or whatever they call 'em."

The man looked less certain with all eyes on him. No one was even pretending to shop anymore. "A collaborator. A spy for the Infected. You been working for 'em the whole dang time."

"Hey!" A man pushed past the gawkers. Bailey. She had never seen him confront anyone before. She glanced around, hoping Dawn was back. That would mean Torres and John were probably close by.

Such a big girl, hoping to be rescued.

Miranda didn't need the Infected to sneer at her. In fact, it was hard to tell if that was them or her because she was having the same thought. It made her annoyance flare into something white-hot. She reached out and pulled the Infected. Any survivors of the hive, the scattered Littles, the rovers between hives. She was surprised how far her ability extended. She could feel it being received and passed on in a hive south in Wyoming and west in Idaho. It was a little scary but also thrilling. Power surged through her.

"Hey what?" The man turned to Bailey. "You got something to say, boy?"

Bailey stood mutely next to Miranda, his cheeks bright red, fist clenched at his sides.

The man stepped around his table and pushed Bailey. Not hard. Barely more than a tap, but Bailey launched himself at the man, screaming. The man stumbled back, slapping at Bailey like a toddler. Miranda covered her mouth to suppress a bark of laughter.

The man tripped and fell back, landing hard on his butt. His nose gushed blood.

Two other men grabbed Bailey, pulled him away.

"Don't touch me!" Bailey thrashed against them.

"Get off him." Miranda knew how much the Airman hated being touched.

"Calm down," one of the men holding Bailey said, but it was no use. He twisted and jerked, frantic to escape.

"He can't calm down," Miranda said. "Let him go!"

"Don't let him go," the seller on the ground said from behind his bloody hands, his voice nasally. "He's gonna attack me again. He busted my nose."

Percy stepped through the gathered onlookers into the small opening around the seller's table. Miranda looked around and spotted Torres and John at the edge of the market area. Torres started to push her way into the crowd, but John put a hand on her shoulder and said something. She nodded, and stopped, frowning with her arms crossed over her chest.

"Now, Harlow, Cooper, we can see Mr. Nolan isn't seriously injured, can't we?" Percy said. The man holding Bailey nodded. "You let this fellow go and I'll keep an eye on him, all right?"

"He attacked me!" Mr. Noland got up, with the help of a woman from a nearby stall. "I want him thrown out. We got enough troubles without being attacked in our own town."

"That's BS!" Miranda glared at Nolan, her hands clenched tight.

Should we find him and chew out his eyes?

That would be satisfying, but no. Miranda pushed the Infected away. It had been easy to find them, to let them back in, but now she wasn't sure she wanted them with her. They could be intrusive.

"You all saw him." Nolan waved a hand at the other shoppers and sellers. He squinted at Miranda, who didn't miss the smug smile on his face behind his hands.

"You want to get rid of me, but you can't so you're trying to hurt Bailey. All he did was try to help." Miranda fought to keep the tremor of rage out of her voice, the tears of fury from her eyes. She knew what they would say. "She's too emotional. She's hysterical."

"Mr. Nolan, I agree we can't let this matter drop, but we're not gonna engage in mob justice as a means to right our wrongs," Percy said. She turned to Bailey, still thrashing in Cooper and Harlow's grip. "Will you agree to stay with me under my parole until we can have a hearing about this?"

Bailey nodded.

"Good. You can ease up now, gents," Percy said. Her tone reminded Miranda of the way Philippe spoke to his ranch hands. The quiet assurance of unquestionable authority.

And it seemed to work. The men let Bailey go. Miranda wanted to hug him but knew he wouldn't like that. She handed him his glasses, which had fallen off at some point in the kerfuffle.

The hearing began at dusk. From the size of the crowd packing into the town hall, everyone from Crossroads and its outlying area turned up to spectate and speculate. Bailey perched on a wooden chair at the front left of the conference room. The town council, headed by Mayor June Flynn, settled into their chairs behind a long table.

June called the hearing to order. A few of the rowdies in the back didn't quiet fast enough for her liking, so she stood to her full 5'2" height and squinted her most orneriest granny glare at the offenders, who shut up with a quickness. June summed up the events at the market and ended by calling Mr. Nolan to the stand.

He walked up to the lectern that until about six months ago had been used to call out Bingo balls, organize local bake sales and blood drives, and host high school debate teams. He seemed to be limping. Miranda was sure if he could have found one, he'd have been wearing a comically large neck brace.

To hear Nolan tell it, Bailey was a hulking brute with advanced ninja assassin fighting skills.

Then it was Bailey's turn. He shuffled over to the podium and mumbled his version of events, eyes downcast and shoulders hunched.

"We've heard from both parties," June said. "Normally, this kind of simple assault would be a small fine, maybe some community service. I'm of a mind that's fair. Lord knows we need all hands on deck these days."

"I object!" yelled a woman. Miranda remembered her from the market. She had helped Nolan up.

"Mrs. Fenster, come on up and say your piece." June waved to the podium.

Mrs. Fenster stomped to the front of the room. She grabbed the podium like she meant to wrench it apart. "The thing is, he's not a member of the community. Neither is she. They think they can just push us around because they're friends with the Rangers."

There was a low murmur from the crowd. Miranda

felt their eyes on her back like pinpricks.

We told you. You're one of us, not them.

She couldn't think of a compelling counterargument.

"I don't see any of the Rangers interfering here," June said.

"She did." Mrs. Fenster pointed at Percy.

Miranda snorted loudly and Mrs. Fenster whirled to glare at her. "What? You got something to say to me?"

"Not to you, hon," Miranda said.

Mrs. Fenster's face reddened.

"Ms. Viers, why don't you come up here?" June said. "Mrs. Fenster, please have a seat. Let's keep this civil, folks."

"Kay." Miranda took her time getting up, tossing her hair over her shoulder, and sashaying up to the podium. She set her hands on it and looked over the crowd. There were friendly faces like John, Torres, Percy, and the rest of the folks from the Morning Star ranch. There were angry faces like Nolan and Fenster. Most people looked either confused or worried. A few of the kids looked bored.

You're not one of them.

I know. She could feel the Infected's satisfaction. It was a relief to admit she shared it. A relief to know that after this she didn't have to see these people again. They had made it plain that she wasn't welcome. She would never in a million billion years beg for acceptance.

"Bailey was trying to protect me," Miranda said. "Not that any of you fine people care about that. You spend all your time gossiping and whining about how no one's saved you yet. You wanna know why?" She leaned forward over the podium. "Because anyone who tries to help you gets shit on. Marius tried to help you and look what that got him." She paused, letting them grumble and mutter before raising her voice to not quite a shout. "He could have been safe in a government bunker, treated like a king, but he came here. And when the Infected threatened you, he traded himself to protect you."

"Ms. Viers," June cut in. "Do you have anything to say about what happened at the market?"

"Oh, sure thing, Ms. Flynn," Miranda said sweetly. "Mr. Nolan was being a nasty, small-minded bigot who wanted to discriminate against me because of my condition. Bailey tried to defend me since no one else was gonna say, 'Boo,' to keep me safe, but sure, I'm the problem, right?"

"Miranda." John made his way up the side aisle to stand next to the front row of seats. His face wore an expression that was part anger, part disappointment, and the long-suffering look he'd had since she'd first known him as a kid.

"It's fine, John." She grinned at her audience. "I've said all I care to say to these good people."

She stalked down the central aisle, knowing full well John wouldn't be able to hobble fast enough to catch her.

Leaving was easier than Miranda expected. Being Ranger-adjacent had its benefits. She knew where all the good gear and supplies were stashed. She also knew where Torres kept the keys to all the still functioning cars. She picked a Forester out of nostalgia for the one they had used to travel up the Pacific coast. Miranda felt a twinge of guilt taking a car, knowing that Torres kept them fueled up and in good repair in case Soraya ever needed one to take the kids and run for it, but there were other cars. Plus, she really needed it.

It was Miranda's turn to run for it. She packed the necessities: sleeping bag, tent, tarp, food, water and water filter, a pistol with ammo, a first aid kit, warm clothes, and extra boots. She even stopped by the market, broke open the cabinet under Mr. Nolan's stand and took the gloves.

The Forester had a full tank of gas and she took four of the five-gallon Army gas cans that John kept carefully locked up in the bunkhouse. She smothered the sadness and regret that pinged through her as she lifted John's trusty clipboard. Somehow it had survived everything. She remembered him letting her carry it as they checked his security team, back when she'd wanted nothing more than to be his big helper.

But she grew out of that innocent child and John found a place to make a family of his own rather than guard other people's.

"If you think about it, I'm doing him a favor," she confided to the Forester. "I'm holding him back. With me gone, he can marry Percy or whatever."

She followed the Forester's headlights out of Crossroads, south and onto the interstate. By morning, she was almost to South Dakota. She stopped by the side of the road and slept. It was weird, the silence. The last time she was alone had been ... she couldn't really remember. Maybe in Los Angeles? How long ago was that? Back in the era of endless hot water and electricity that didn't come from a generator or solar panels or a wind turbine. When makeup mattered and lattes were a given.

Miranda ate a cold breakfast of cheese and apples sitting cross-legged on the Forester's hood. By noon, she needed to stop and fill the tank. She drove on into Minnesota, barely noticing the wrecks along the highway. There were a few places she had to leave the highway proper, but the Forester was a sturdy ole gal who could be coaxed through a lot of off-roading. She didn't have to worry about humans because the Infected let her know if any were in the area.

In a suburb of Minneapolis, she finally ran out of gas entirely. All through the outskirts of the cities, as the plains gave way to farms and then to homes, businesses, and institutions, there had been hastily set up billboards and signs: Evacuation Point is at the Mall of America!

And they'd gone. All the people who wanted to evacuate. Where did they think they would go? How bad had things gotten to convince nearly four million people to abandon their homes?

Miranda set up camp in the Bakken Museum. She liked the glass fronted tower, the Lantern of the Lake, the visitor's brochure told her. From there she could watch the heat lightning dance through the thunderheads at night. The place was half castle, half fancy British country estate. It also had power, thanks to the numerous solar panels still happily doing their job in the absence of humans.

Most humans. There were the Infected, some of whom used to be human, were humanish still. Miranda could hide her presence from them or distract them, or tell them to leave her alone, if she had to. She didn't like confronting them because their Enlightened might see it as a challenge. Frankly, she just wanted to be left alone.

"If you're going to be lonely, you might as well be alone." She wrote in big letters across the visitors' registry near the defunct information counter at the main entrance.

Being lonely wasn't a problem for the busy. Miranda spent three days fixing up a suite of rooms. It rained twice in the afternoons, the only break to the humidity. Wasn't it supposed to be cold in Minnesota? But no, the days were long, and hot, the nights sticky with sweaty dreams and not the sexy kind.

Miranda found a powered dolly used to move big exhibits and spent hours lugging the most expensive memory foam mattress from the show room of a nearby bedding store. After that, she decorated her rooms, raiding IKEA a few times. Prints on the walls, cute hand towels outside her favorite port-o-potty, and a desk that took her a day to build, which she never used, but stocked with paper, pens, notepads, and even a dead laptop.

After a few days of setting up her living space at the Bakken, she ventured to the University of Minnesota's campus. She wandered the halls, peeping into dark and echoey auditoriums, cozy coffee nooks, and professors' offices. She like the College of Life Sciences best — the professors' walls and shelves were filled with mementoes of far-flung research trips to places like Papua New Guinea, the Amazon, the Arctic. She went to the Registrar's office and signed herself up for Fall semester, spending a wonderful rainy afternoon devising a schedule for all her classes, including Beginning Aikido and Rock Climbing 101.

"I need better clothes," she said, staring at her reflection in the fountain's pool outside the Coffman Memorial Union building. She had twisted her hair into a French braid. She wore a short sleeve T-shirt over a long sleeve T-shirt, a fashion she picked up from the folks at the Morning Star ranch. Her jeans were grubby and worn, but not in any sort of high fashion pre-made holes kind of way.

"I look like the Before girl," she said. She didn't remember when she started talking to herself, but at least the conversation was pleasant enough.

"Get thee to a clothing boutiquery," her reflection commanded and she obeyed.

Fall fashion was on full display in the shops, sleek cardigans and fuzzy sweaters, scarves running the gamut from fat, wooly ones to cashmere nearly as smooth as silk. Miranda tired of trying on floppy berets and lumpy knit caps and wandered into the bargain basement, looking for hiking boots and maybe waterproof pants or sports bras with half-decent elastic.

Among the racks of puffy coats and flannel shirts, capri and cargo pants, was a summer display. A beach chair with white and yellow plastic straps, a wide umbrella on a stand, potted plastic palm trees, and a mannequin reclining in a pair of teal hibiscus print surfboard shorts. He was holding up a metallic sun catcher to the UV lights rigged above.

It was refreshing to see a darker skinned mannequin. Here at the end of the world, big business had finally found diversity profitable.

The mannequin hooked a finger in his Ray-Bans and lowered them to peer at Miranda. She screamed and jumped back, yanked out her hunting knife and pointed it at him.

The man raised his hands.

"You got me," he said, and winked.

Chapter 9 - Torres

Torres tucked her thick fleece into her pack. She glanced around the bunkhouse's kitchen/living room area, which had been turned into the Rangers' headquarters. Nothing left but Jimmy's HK. She strapped on her hand-made leather hip holster and secured the small pistol.

John sat in his favorite chair, leg extended stiffly toward the fire as he massaged balm into it, working the muscle to keep the limb functional as long as possible. They both knew how that story ended, but neither of them mentioned it. Easier to pretend that John wouldn't become a cripple and that Torres wasn't running off like an idiot with a schoolhouse crush.

She had to go. There was a chance that whoever Mendelsen had been working with had resources not available to a bunch of ranchers in the middle of nowhere Montana. What if they had a satellite or drones? What if they knew where Marius was or could track him?

Even after nearly half a year, she felt his absence as a physical ache. She could no more ignore the pull to look for him than a compass needle could ignore true north.

But Detroit?

"Why would anyone ever go to Detroit?" Torres double-checked the coordinates against the USGS map tacked on the bunkhouse's wall. There were no military bases nearby.

"Lots of infrastructure that no one's using," John said. "Great place for a bunker you really don't want on anyone's radar."

"I'll be back in a couple weeks."

"You keep telling me that," John said. "Which one of us are you trying to convince?"

"I know it's a really bad time is all," Torres said. "I can stay until the house gets rebuilt." She didn't need John's blessing or his permission, but she also couldn't quite bring herself to leave him, to leave Elfy and Soraya and everyone who depended on her. She more than half wanted him to talk her out of this. Give her an iron-clad reason to stay so the decision wouldn't be hers, the responsibility wouldn't be hers.

"I didn't know you were a Sea Breeze." John rubbed his shiny hands clean on a rag and rolled down the leg of his sweatpants.

"You mean a SeaBee and those are Navy, not Marines," Torres said.

"You could keep an eye out for Miranda while you're on the road," John said.

"Still can't believe she took the Forester," Torres

grumbled, her anger covering her fear for Miranda and her sadness that the other woman had felt that running away was her best option.

"I'm glad she has something reliable," John said. "We can always find more cars."

Torres nodded. She should have taken better care of Miranda, should have been alert to her worsening isolation.

John sat back with a deep sigh and studied her for a long moment. She refused to fidget.

"We will miss you. We definitely could use you here," he said, but when Torres opened her mouth to agree, he held up a hand. "But you need to go and honestly, we all want to know what happened to him, to both of them if possible. You're not just doing this for yourself. You're going for all of us."

"I know what you're doing," Torres said.

John didn't even look ashamed to be caught.

"Fine," she said. "I'll go." Impulsively she bent to wrap an arm around John's shoulders. She kissed the crown of his sandy blond head in blessing and left before either of them could get any redder of face at the physical contact.

Elfy took the news of Torres's scouting mission as well as the former Marine expected. After counting to a slow and measured thirty, Torres left the tent, letting the cloth door fall to slightly muffle the shrieks, punctuated by kicks at the cots' legs or at the trunk filled with Elfy's clothes, a few toys, and some books. Somehow Claudia had gotten the library up and running again, not that Elfy seemed to appreciate the literacy program or anything else the adults were killing themselves to get for her.

Soraya waited outside the tent, a bundle in her arm. It smelled wonderfully of curry. She hugged Torres and they walked away from the tents to where Ganymede and the pack horse waited.

"She will miss you," Soraya said.

"She hides it well," Torres said as she tucked away the food. She would savor it that night before it went bad. After that it would be cold rations and whatever she could scrounge or scavenge.

"I will miss you," Soraya said.

"That I believe." Torres smiled to cover the unexpected knot in her chest. Even before she left home at eighteen to join the Corps, she'd always been restless. It felt strange and a little scary to realize she had roots, had a place to come back to and people who were more than temporary friends or deployment lovers.

Soraya hugged her again and stepped back and smiled reassuringly.

"Well," Torres said, adopting a lazy drawl, "it's burnin' daylight and I better light on outta here like."

"Indeed. Safe travels." Soraya smoothed her hijab as she walked back to the tents, stopping to wave at the door to hers. Mirzha and Washington were seated on a rough-hewn bench outside, strenuously ignoring each other and blushing.

Elfy burst out of the tent, her school bag half on one shoulder, her bunny hat askew, and one shoe untied. She stomped up to Torres and stopped, pudgy hands on her hips, her lower lip thrust out.

"I'm ready to go," she said.

"You're staying with Soraya," Torres said. She did not need this drama.

"I'm going with you." Elfy dodged around her and grabbed Ganymede's stirrup. The gelding looked over and flicked his tail in annoyance but held steady as the child tried to haul herself up into the saddle.

"Elfy, stop it." Torres caught her niece under the arms and pulled her away. Gany sidestepped and snorted, clearly nearing his limit. Torres could relate.

"You stop it." Elfy noodled, but this time Torres was ready and scooped her up before she could slither to the ground. She heaved the child over her shoulder like a duffel bag and trudged back to the tent. By the time she arrived, Elfy was sobbing in great, breathless heaves.

Torres set the child down on her butt and she huddled into herself, clutching her backpack.

This was the moment, Torres knew. She should leave. There was nothing to be gained by dragging this out or entertaining Elfy's tantrums.

"I practiced," Elfy mumbled, her voice clotted with snot and tears.

Go now. Don't get involved, Torres's inner voice urged her.

But she paused. She remembered huddling in just that position, heartbroken over some stupid school fight that she didn't even remember all these year later. What she did remember was the pressure, as if her whole body would burst with rage and sadness. More than anything, she had wanted Mamá to hold her, to tell her that she was good and loved and it was going to be okay. But Mamá had been out; at work or visiting friends or just gone to the corner store. It didn't matter. What Torres remembered were the long hours of watching the stripes of shadows and light from the blinds crawl down the wall and fade into darkness. When her legs went numb, she got up and wobbled to the bathroom. She scrubbed her face and stared at herself in the mirror. She promised she would never ever sit around waiting for someone to come for her again. No one would because no one cared.

If she walked away from Elfy, she would be teaching her niece the same thing. Sure, she was tough and self-reliant. But she was also desperately lonely. She didn't want that for Elfy.

Torres sat down next to the girl. She tried to find the right thing to say, but what did you tell an irrational six-year-old to calm them down?

She put a hand on Elfy's. The girl yanked away and curled tighter into herself.

Torres sighed and tried for a light tone. "What did you practice?"

"You don't care! You just want to leave me because I'm stupid."

"Elfy, I don't want to leave you and you're not stupid."

"Ya-huh."

Torres looked at Soraya, who was loitering just outside the tent. The other woman shrugged but smiled sympathetically.

"I have to go. I can't take you with because it's really dangerous."

Elfy sat up and smeared her sleeve across her face. "I could help you," she whispered. "I practiced the survival stuff Mr. Phineas taught us. Be quiet, keep low, run away from the Infected. And I know how to poop in the woods. You have to make a little hole and bury it like a kitty."

"Wow, that's a lot," Torres said.

Elfy's face brightened.

"I really need you to stay here."

Elfy's lip trembled.

Torres hurried on. "I need people who can handle themselves, like the Rangers, like you. Can you help keep Soraya and the other kids safe while I'm gone?"

Elfy narrowed her eyes, not entirely sold.

Torres lowered her voice and leaned in. "I know I can trust you. You're a tough kid, right?"

"Uh-huh."

"Can you be tough for me now?"

"Uh-huh." But this time with a rising quiver of tears.

"Good. Because I need you." Torres's own throat closed up and she struggled to force out the words. "I need you to be strong and brave for me."

"I love you, Tia Lourdie." Elfy launched herself into Torres's arms.

The former Marine buried her face in the child's soft hair. She smelled like the raspberry shampoo Torres found a few weeks ago.

"I love you, too, mi sobrina favorita," Torres whispered and squeezed her niece tight.

Morning fog draped the river valley. Water pattered softly down onto the tarp, either light rain or dew collecting in the trees. Torres rubbed her eyes and blinked up from her bed of pine needles. Her sleeping bag was snugged up to her chin. From the light, it must be late morning. How had she slept so long?

Jimmy's HK was still safe under the wad of shirt she used as a pillow. The pack horse dozed while Ganymede cropped grass from along the riverbank, unconcerned about the human's lazing in bed when they had another hard day of riding to get to. How many days was it now? Sixteen or seventeen? Torres rolled onto her elbow and pulled out her map and logbook. Seventeen. She checked the day's route. She'd made better time than expected. Another week or so and she'd be in Detroit.

She lay back, watching the light play among the branches, trying to remember the last time she'd felt so relaxed.

A rumble. An engine. A car? For a wild moment she imagined Miranda had changed her mind and come back from wherever she'd gone with the Forester. But no. Torres couldn't afford to think like that. Anyone she met had to be treated as a likely hostile until they proved otherwise.

Torres scrambled out of her fart sack, managing to keep from getting it twisted around her stocking feet. Her boots were upside down beside the remains of last night's little fire. She stuffed her feet in, no time to tie them. She snatched up Jimmy's HK and Gany's picket line and pulled the horse away from the fire. There was no smoke, only a few banked embers, slowly choking under the weight of their own ash. Hopefully, she would be able to return for the pack horse.

The car was getting closer. Torres cursed herself for

camping so close to the road. She had been tired and hadn't scouted the area. She was using the interstate highways as guidelines, although she didn't ride right on them. Usually, she tried to find a good spot to sleep away from the road in case ... well, in case.

With only her go-bag, the pistol, and one of the horses, she scuttled back along the riverbank until she found some cover behind a blowdown tree. The car stopped. One, two doors opened and shut. Shit freaking shit freaking shit. There were at least two people and they weren't worried about noise discipline, which meant they were probably armed.

Torres looked around, assessing her situation. Never make a decision out of panic. Act, don't react. Okay, what could she leave? The food, the pot she'd set to soak in river water last night, meaning to scrub it with sand today, and her sleeping bag. She would regret losing the pack horse, but it wasn't the end of the freaking world. She smiled to herself at the phrase.

The one thing she couldn't do without was the map. The whole point of this little adventure was to get to Detroit and find the coordinates Mendelsen had given them. Torres curled her fingers into the seams of her jeans and squeezed out her frustration.

Okay, first she needed to secure Ganymede. He stared at her, clearly annoyed that she'd disrupted his breakfast.

"Sorry, big guy," she mouthed as she hooked his lead over a tree limb.

The wind carried the low murmur of voices. They scratched at her ears after so long with only herself for company. A lower-pitched voice, probably a man, and one that had the cracking quality of a teenage boy.

Torres edged closer, crouched and quiet. The dewy grass soon soaked her pants to the mid-thighs.

On the highway, the boy laughed. The man said something and the boy responded. He was walking along the edge of the road, so close, Torres could have reached through the juniper bush she was hiding behind and touched his neck.

"There's a horse over there," the boy said, standing up on his tiptoes.

"What?" said the man.

Torres yanked the boy backward and pressed the muzzle of Jimmy's HK under his chin.

"Tell him to back off," she hissed into the boy's ear. She kept ducked mostly behind him, trying to peer over his shoulder to see the man. All she saw was the car, a little blue Kia.

"She's got a gun," the boy called. "She says back off."

Torres listened, straining to place where the man had gone. He wasn't talking, which meant he wasn't a panicky civilian. That made things worse for her.

"Akeem, stay calm. She hasn't shot you so she probably doesn't want to hurt you. Do you?"

Torres had never been struck by lightning, but she was sure in that instant that she knew exactly how it felt. Her whole being froze, tingled, and went weak. If she hadn't had an arm around the boy to keep him under control, she might have fallen to her knees.

As it was, her fingers went limp and the gun slipped, rolled, and clattered down the boy's body to land with a faint plop on the highway's dirt shoulder. The boy dodged away as soon as she let go of him. He didn't go for the gun or even look back, just ran.

There was nothing between them. Only air.

Marius was thin. His hair was longer, brushing his shoulders and tied into a tail at the nape of his neck. His arm was in a sling. He stared at her, his bright green eyes practically glowing in his deeply tanned face.

She took a step and her mouth moved. She didn't know if she said his name, but like a whispering a spell, he was there.

Their arms were around each other, squeezing tight together. They both sobbed. They both talked. They took turns looking each other over and commenting on scars new and old. They kissed. They laughed. They kissed some more.

Marius introduced his traveling companion, Akeem. The boy lounged around the Kia and let Torres and Marius have what privacy they could beside her campfire's ashes.

"I can't believe …" Torres started but didn't finish. There was no point questioning what had happened or how they had found each other.

"Me neither," Marius said. He pressed his face into her hair, pulled her closer to his side.

"How are you even here?" Torres asked. Marius told her about Viers and the hive in Mammoth Cave, about how he and Akeem had escaped down the river and found a car.

"When we ran out of gas, we walked until we could find another car to steal. I've committed approximately a dozen counts of grand theft auto in the past few days," Marius said. "We were following the interstates to Montana. Why are you here?"

Torres hesitated. What if she explained about Mendelsen's information and rather than going back the Montana, Marius wanted to continue on to Detroit? What would they find there? It was fine for her to go on a wild goose chase after a secret government vault. If it wasn't there, she wouldn't be heartbroken. But Marius took disappointment and failure so hard, so personally. She knew he still blamed himself for HHV, no matter how many times and in how many ways everyone rationally explained it wasn't his fault. He always agreed. Of course not. That was silly. Yet, his shoulders still sagged under the constant weight of responsibility and guilt he either couldn't or wouldn't set down.

"Looking for you," she hedged. She lifted her head to scan the road. The Kia was still there. Akeem was sprawled over the hood, asleep in the sun like a cat.

Marius watched her intently, not rushing her, but waiting for the rest. It annoyed her that he knew her silences so well. Not annoyed. It freaking scared her the way he could see all the way to the foundations of her. No one had ever understood her that way. But for all that it made her feel vulnerable, it also made her feel intensely interesting, desirable. It was flattering to be so fascinating.

If she loved him, she had to trust him, had to let him make his own choices. That meant giving him all the relevant information. She scooted back a little to better study his face, to try to read him as he so clearly read her.

Torres told Marius about the keycard and Mendelsen's coordinates, waited, watching his face while he digested the news.

"A bunker or a lab or some kind of facility under Detroit?" He bit his lower lip the way he did when he was thinking or worried. She had missed that so much. She pressed her ear to his chest, listened to the thump of his heart. It sounded strong, everlasting, but she knew what a massive lie that was.

"If we keep going that way," Torres pointed northeast, "we'll run into Detroit."

"If we go that way," Marius pointed west, "Montana."

"Yeah." Torres moved his hand so he was pointing northwest. He was still terrible about directions.

"I want to check out Detroit," Marius said. Torres's shoulders hunched. She looked away, out past the gently swaying tree branches and innocently burbling river. This didn't look like a war zone, but she'd never felt more afraid. Could she keep him safe all the way to Detroit and back?

Marius touched her cheek, bringing her attention back to him. He searched her face for a moment then squared his shoulders.

"We'll go to Detroit," he said. "But not yet. I'm less than keen to escape Viers and then hop right back into being a someone's lab rat. When we go, we'll go with a few more reinforcements."

Chapter 10 - Miranda

On the Road, Minnesota, USA — Summer, Year 2

He was shorter than Miranda with loose dark curls that brushed his shoulders. In board shorts and sweating under the artificial UV lights, he hardly looked like a threat. His cocky smile looked like a different kind of threat — one Miranda was not only willing but eager to be at the mercy of.

"I'm Eli," he said. "Pleased to meet you." His accent was something throaty, either Arabic or Hebrew, if Miranda had to guess.

For a moment, Miranda was so shocked, surprised by the sound of another human voice, that she stood staring wordlessly.

"I didn't know anyone was still alive in this city," Eli said. He slowly lowered his hands, still keeping them in plain sight, out beside his body. "We looked for those," he waved a hand, "plague nests, but didn't see any around here."

"We?" Miranda said, her voice husky and creaky by turns.

"Him and me," said a woman's voice behind Miranda, who remembered enough of John's combat training lessons to move sideways before turning. She wasn't going to end up caught between the two if she could help it.

The woman was also shorter than Miranda, with long dark hair pulled back into a high ponytail. She was shockingly pretty, heart-shaped face with full lips and big, wide eyes. She wore a close-fitting coat, which made it easy for Miranda to spot the bulge from a shoulder holster. The woman held her hands out, near the holster but not touching it.

"I think most people evacuated," Miranda said. "There's not a lot of bodies or whatever."

"You've been canvasing the city?" the woman asked.

"Not long, but I've been through enough places," Miranda said. No point in telling these people that the Infected gave her updates on the number and density of humans in her vicinity. "You can tell when someplace is empty."

"Romi and I have also been observing," Eli said, his smile still warm and welcoming.

"What?" Miranda started. "Why? What? What are you doing here?"

"Probably the same thing you're doing." Romi gave a half shrug and waved her hand around. "We were looking for a way out, then a place to be safe, and now just trying to find other survivors."

"We heard some places have a cure," Eli said. "Like

Yellowstone or New Avalon."

Miranda felt a lurching thrill like being on that amusement park ride that dropped from a tall tower. They knew about New Avalon or had at least heard the name. But how?

"We heard there was, like, a government bunker or something in Detroit," she blurted.

"We?" Romi asked.

"I used to be with a group." Miranda felt suddenly exhausted. She didn't want to get into it. Not with a pair of strangers. 'Yeah, I was part of a nice community, but some of the people were mean to me so I ran away.' It sounded so stupid and high school, but she still didn't regret it. She wasn't going to grovel to anyone for acceptance. Let them deal with the next hive or nest or whatever without her and then see how much they missed her.

Romi and Eli watched her silently. She had trailed off and was now standing there like she needed someone to prompt her with her next line.

"It didn't work out," Miranda finished awkwardly. Gah, when did she lose her social skills?

"Lots of things haven't been working out," Eli said, throwing her a much-needed lifeline.

"Are you vaccinated?" Romi said.

Miranda almost laughed out loud. Of all the things she had to worry about in the world, the Infected didn't make the list. She managed to keep a straight face and said, "Yeah, you?"

"He is," Romi said, pointing at Eli. "I'm not. Missed it by an hour. Stupid line."

"So, we have to try to avoid the Infected as much as

possible," Eli said. "We heard it was maybe airborne?"

"It's not," Miranda said.

"You seem very confident," Romi said.

"I've been around," Miranda said. She liked the powerful feeling of having more knowledge than they did. Was that how Marius felt all the time? No. She wasn't thinking about him. Or John. Or the way John would be disappointed that she'd left and worried about her while she was gone. She wasn't John's little girl anymore. Not that she'd ever been, but ... they were staring at her again.

"Ah, yeah, and I've been on my own for a while. Not used to having actual conversations with people who answer back," she said.

"Well, you're in luck because we are both tired of each other's jokes and it would be great to have some new stories," Eli said.

"Are we, like, hooking up now?" Miranda fluttered her eyelashes. Eli smiled, eyeing her with a gentlemanly amount of obvious interest.

"Unless you prefer the coatracks for company." Romi turned a slow circle, waving at the mannequins dressed in the very latest of pre-outbreak Midwestern fashion.

A low rumble sounded overhead. They all froze, listening.

"Is that a car?" Romi whispered, tiptoeing toward the stairs out of the basement.

"Too quiet." Eli yanked on a pair of trousers over his shorts and pulled on a T-shirt that only emphasized his broad shoulders.

"Could be military." Miranda tore her eyes away a second before Eli's head cleared the T-shirt's neck hole.

"They have heavier trucks and stuff." She joined Romi on the stairs and they crept up, pausing to listen every few steps. The boutique was darker than Miranda remembered. Was something blocking the display windows, parked outside? Miranda squatted behind a clothes rack and peeped out.

Nothing. The street looked the same as it had when she came in. Except it was definitely darker.

Lightning flashed.

"It was just thunder," Miranda said, standing to her full height. Romi joined her, leaning out to look around. She was a half a head shorter than Miranda, with a compact body and very toned muscles. She looked like she could be one of those bodybuilders.

Eli and Romi exchanged a look and carefully walked around, checking everything in the shop. Another rumble of thunder sounded, louder this time. Or maybe the other one had sounded quieter because they were in the basement.

"We should get back to our camp," Eli said, poking his head out to look at the churning clouds. A huge white cloud charged towards them, attended by a swirling mass of darker clouds. Lighting flashed inside the thunderhead and sometimes down towards the ground.

"I'm at the Bakken," Miranda said. She wasn't totally sure she wanted to travel with Romi and Eli, but she wanted more time to make her choice. After a few days on her own, she knew being solitary forever wasn't for her. Better human company than the Infected.

By the time Miranda gathered the few things she'd unpacked, the wind was gusting. She could see trees leaning, their branches reaching out as if they were all doing the wave at a ball game. No rain yet, so she went outside to see if she could spot Romi and Eli. What if they didn't come?

Lighting flashed and she flinched. The wind dropped and the air felt heavy and still. Miranda adjusted her pack and looked around again. She wasn't going to wait outside in a thunderstorm forever. What if they didn't know where the Bakken was? They couldn't pull up their GPS and put it in or anything.

"Miranda," Eli called from about a block away as he and Romi rounded a corner. They jogged over. Eli carried some kind of hunting rifle.

As they arrived the wind started up again, slow at first rising up in fits and starts. A rattle sounded from the roof and something hit Miranda's shoulder and bounced off. She looked down to see a small chunk of ice, about the size of a pea. Hail.

"Those are very strange clouds," Romi said.

The clouds looked like someone had stuck a bunch of fat marshmallows into the sky. Instead of being pink or white, they were yellowish and even a bit green.

"Tornado," Miranda said. She remembered those weird clouds from a class on weather in 10th grade. Or was it 11th? Didn't matter. What did matter was that she knew those kinds of clouds came with really big storms, like tornadoes.

"What?" Eli held up his hand to shield his face as more tiny hail bounced off them.

"We should get inside," Romi said.

"Not in there." Miranda pointed to the Bakken with its multi-story windows. She could imagine all that glass shattering and flying around like ice in a blender. "We need somewhere with a basement."

Rain started in a sudden downpour, but at least the hail let up.

"Somewhere close," Eli said.

"This way." Romi took off at a lope. Miranda and Eli followed. They wove between the stately buildings surrounding the museum, passing a small pond filled with duck weed on one side and a row of houses on the other. Romi stopped in an intersection, looking right and left. They were in a residential area.

"That one." She pointed to an older house and the sprinted for it. The thunder was louder and more frequent. Lightning lit the clouds, which were either greenish or grey or black. A strike behind them hit a tree near the Bakken, which burst into flame. Luckily, the pouring rain doused it almost immediately.

Romi sprinted up the house's front steps and across the narrow porch, hit the front door and bounced off it.

"Locked," she yelled to be heard above the wind and rain.

"Move." Eli darted past her and kicked the door right above the doorknob. It was that motion, something Miranda had seen John's security team practicing probably hundreds of times over the years, that made everything click into place for her. The easy way they carried their weapons, their obvious fitness, the calm, confident way they'd dealt with a stranger barging in on them. They were military, maybe even from some kind of special operations unit.

The door cracked and popped open. Eli went in, looking around — clearing the room — as he did. Romi followed, automatically moving to a different part of the room. Yep. Military. Miranda smiled to herself. She knew how to deal with military types.

"This way," Eli called from the kitchen. He held open the door leading to a big dark nothing. Miranda's mind flashed back to the quarry, to fumbling blindly in the dark with the heat and the stench of the Infected all around her, trying to hide herself and Dawn from the Enlightened's perception as they stumbled through pools of sludgy blood and tripped over twisted ropes of nerve bundles and blood vessels wrapped in a fibrous fleshy sheath.

I can't, she thought. I can't go back there.

Can't betray us again. The thought was so clear and sharp Miranda knew without a doubt that it must be an Enlightened. None of the Infected had thoughts beyond attack, kill, eat or shelter.

"Come on," Romi said. She clicked on a flashlight and handed it to Miranda, who took it with a surge of gratitude. Outside, the wind was making a weird rushing sound like an approaching train. Miranda looked back and froze.

It was nearly pitch dark outside, but the flashes of lightning illuminated the twisting spiraling column of air reaching down from the clouds. A burst of debris jumped from the ground to meet it. The tornado danced and skipped toward them, whisking up small trees, cars, even buildings, which it spat out quickly as if they were too heavy.

Someone grabbed Miranda's shoulders and pulled her back. Eli. His face was near hers, his lips almost brushing her ear, but she could barely hear him above the roar of the wind and the crash and clatter of whatever the tornado had picked up.

She allowed Eli to guide her, even though she could feel the wind drawing at her, the tornado hungry for something soft and alive to complement all the houses and cars it was consuming.

Down the stairs. They were carpeted. The basement was finished, although it had that musty cellar smell. The flashlight beams jittered and jumped around. Romi stood in the doorway of a bathroom, barely big enough for a toilet and sink, waving her arm in big, looping 'come here' gestures.

Eli and Miranda wedged into the bathroom. Miranda had to perch on the closed toilet's lid. Eli yanked the mirror off the wall and pushed it out of the room before closing the door. Romi locked it, which nearly made Miranda burst out laughing. A little bathroom lock that a five-year-old could pick with a butter knife wasn't going to keep them any safer.

Then the wind was screaming right above them. Miranda clamped her hands over her ears and tucked her head between her knees. Brace for impact. Something smashed against the bathroom door, nearly battering it open. Eli and Romi braced themselves against it, her on one knee with her foot against the opposite wall, him with his shoulder at the door, his arm reaching out to push off the far wall.

I don't want to die here, Miranda thought.

Come to us. We can keep you safe. The Enlightened was back, calm, serene, but behind it, Miranda could sense other Infected. She pushed past the Enlightened's mind and dove into the hive itself, reaching into the network that connected the lesser Infected in the area. It was like having a map overlay to the city with little points or clusters of visibility wherever the Infected were. Visibility wasn't quite the right word. Perception. The Infected didn't always see. They sensed, sometimes with hearing or vision, taste, smell or touch outside of Miranda's human senses. But when she was with them in the hive network, she could understand as they understood, know what they knew.

"... okay?" Romi's voice. Miranda could hear the other woman's voice. The wind was still screaming, but quieter now. Eli still leaned against the door but wasn't putting his full weight against it.

The tornado moved on. They lived.

"I'm okay," Miranda answered the question she guessed Romi had asked. "We're okay."

The house was gone. There were stairs leading up to nothing but a patch of linoleum about the size of a card table. Miranda, Romi, and Eli picked their way through the tangle of exposed pipes and broken wires until they found a relatively clear patch of sidewalk. The houses on either side were smashed in as if a giant had punched each one.

The rain still poured down, but looked like it might taper off soon. Looking west, Miranda could see the rim of the dark clouds and a strip of blue sky underneath. East, the tornado thinned, lifting itself back up to the clouds before reaching down to brush the ground, then back up again.

They found a house with an intact front porch and stood in its shelter, dripping and shivering. The day, which started so hot and humid, turned chilly, the wind pebbling Miranda's arms and legs with goose bumps. She sorted through her pack to find her jacket but hesitated to put it on. She could dry a lot faster than her clothes.

"We should get out of town," Romi said.

"Where are you going?" Eli held out a hand towel to Miranda, who accepted it gratefully.

Drying her face gave her time to think about her answer. She hadn't planned much in the way of where she was going *to*, more where she was going *from*. Minneapolis seemed nice. No crazy militias and only a few Infected. Since most of the human population evacuated before the Infected arrived, there had been little for them to use for nests. Weirdly, the government's plan to move people out of the path of the Infected seemed to have worked. Except Miranda had no idea where all those people had gone. They might have been moved directly into the path of a bigger wave of Infected.

"It's fine," Romi said.

"What?" Miranda had totally space-cadetted.

"It's fine if you don't want to tell us where you're

going. We're not trying to threaten whatever group you're with," Eli said. "We were only hoping that we might have the pleasure of your company for a few more miles."

"It's smart to stay together at least until we get out of all this." Romi spun in a small circle, waving at the destruction all around them.

"The river's that way and we can follow it south out of the cities," Eli said.

Look out! Run! The Infected burst into Miranda's brain in a frenzy. She frowned as she focused on pushing them out and actively ignoring them: the mental equivalent of plugging her ears and singing la-la-la-lah.

"Yeah," she said, determined to hold a normal conversation like a normal human. "Let's do that."

The Infected's panic battered around her, every bit as insistent and nearly as distracting as the storm had been.

She walked with Romi and Eli, frustrated that most of her mental energy, which should have gone to learning more about them, who they were, where they came from, where they were going, how they got to Minneapolis, instead was taken up by telepathically shushing the multitude of tiny voices in her head.

They passed the Mall of America, roads in all directions lined with abandoned cars, and crossed the Minnesota River.

Fire! Fire! Go back! A particularly strong Infected's warning broke through Miranda's mental block.

What? Show me. She stopped, closed her eyes and let her mind move with the Infected, experience what it experienced. There was a wall of fire moving out in all directions from a fuel tanker truck that was parked on a flight line. Miranda could see long banks of windows that overlooked movable gangways intended to connect planes to the terminal. The airport was on fire. Jet fuel was on fire and there were no firefighters.

"Miranda?" Eli's warm brown eyes were locked on her face. "What's wrong?"

"Fire," she blurted out.

Romi stopped walking and looked around. The rain had mostly tapered off to a drizzle. The sky was still overcast with the darker clouds hurrying away as if trying to catch up with the rest of the storm. North, across the river, a column of black smoke rose. The gusty wind tore tatters from it, but it was thickening by the moment.

"The airport?" Romi asked and Eli pulled a plastic bag out of his pack and withdrew a paper map from inside. He quickly unfolded and re-folded it to show the part of the cities where they were. The Minneapolis–Saint Paul international airport was on the other side of the river from them, right at junction of the Minnesota and Mississippi Rivers.

"What's the chance of the fire jumping the river?" Miranda wondered out loud.

"Everything's wet from the storm. Maybe that will help," Eli said.

"We should hurry," Romi said.

Miranda didn't know how long they'd been walking at as fast a pace as they could without actually jogging. Her hips hurt and her knees throbbed. Her shoulders were sore from the weight of her pack and her lower back felt bruised from the constant small impacts of the pack banging gently against her.

"Shit," said Romi. She pointed off to left. A dozen small plumes of white and grey smoke rose into the air. "It's catching up."

"We could go back to the river," Eli said.

"The water was pretty low. I don't know if that would help," Miranda said. Fear sizzled through her, making her stomach clenched and her palms sweaty. She rubbed them on her still damp jeans. They needed a path out, not something that would end with them being surrounded and crisped. She remembered stories of famous city-wide fires, like the Great Chicago fire. How much worse would a fire be with no one even trying to put it out and modern fuels instead of just wood to burn?

This way. The Infected tugged at her and without thinking she turned west.

"This way," she said. Romi and Eli exchanged their special look but didn't question her.

The next few hours were a hectic blur of trying to get information from all the Infected, stay away from the areas that were on fire, get out of the cities, and figure out what she was going to tell Romi and Eli when eventually they demanded answers.

You should leave them. It's better on your own.

Not happening, she sent back grimly. She'd let one community run her off, she wasn't about to leave two capable, reasonable people just because they might think she was weird. Everyone was weird now. That's what made them survivors. All the not-weird people were either in government camps, Infected, or dead.

As evening fell, the storm disappeared completely, but the reddish-orange glow over the cities was unmistakable. From time to time, they heard explosions. Once they saw a fireball lift into the air before exploding in a shower of molten pieces and embers. That couldn't be a good sign.

Even when it was truly dark, they could keep going, their way illuminated by the fires that flickered behind and sometimes alongside them. It was getting harder for Miranda to get information from the Infected as more and more of the Littles and Scouts succumbed to the inferno they weren't fast or lucky enough to escape. Miranda refused to think about them broiling or burning or choking on smoke and fumes as they relayed their final positions to the rest of the Infected in the area. She used the information to keep herself, Romi, and Eli away from the worst of the fire.

Sometime well into the dead of night they stumbled to a halt on a country road by a sign that said: VERMILLION HIGHLANDS — A Research Recreation & Wildlife Management Area.

"I'm done," Miranda said. She pulled off her pack and let it slither down her leg to the ground before falling onto her butt. She leaned back against her pack and stared up at the sky. Only a few clouds looking west and south. To the north, the glow of the fires raged on, but for now, they seemed safe enough. She barely had the energy to dig out her sleeping mat and bag and kick off her hiking boots before she was asleep.

Chapter 11 - Torres

On the Road, Iowa, USA – Summer, Year 2

They left the Kia parked at a roadside rest stop in western Iowa. With Ganymede and the pack horse, they were forced to drive slowly anyway. Without the car, they took turns walking and riding. They kept a constant lookout for signs of the Infected. The way had been mostly clear when Torres came east, but that didn't mean it would stay that way.

"Luckily, I brought this," Torres said, carefully pulling out the little plastic baggy filled with black mold from what had survived the fire at the ranch. She had told Marius about the fire and that Miranda had left New Avalon. Neither speculated out loud that she might go to her father in Kentucky. But where else would she go? Where else were there people?

Around them, the corn fields of Nebraska spread out in wide, untilled patches, bounded by windbreaks and punctuated by farmhouses and outbuildings. Despite not having been plowed or planted, many of the fields already were nearly ankle deep in corn, and the ones that weren't boasted an impressive crop of weeds.

Ahead a sign proclaimed: Valentine, Nebraska–Small Town, Big Adventure–WELCOME.

"We should stay over here," Torres said. "It's a sign, don't you think, Marius Valentine Tenartier?" She grinned at Marius and flashed her eyebrows.

"My parents are the worst namers." He rolled his eyes, but she could see the corners of his mouth fighting to smile.

"Que romantico!" Torres did her best impression of a swooning damsel, wilting over backwards. Marius caught her and leaned down, his lips hovering centimeters above hers.

"I should let you fall," he said, but kissed her instead and helped her stumble back to her feet. She glanced over at Akeem, who was riding Gany as the adults walked the pack horse. He gave her a thumbs up, his cheeks flushing at their ridiculous public display of affection.

"We could all use a good night's sleep in a bed," Marius said.

"What makes you think we'll sleep?" Torres swatted Marius's butt.

They stopped at a farmhouse, and after clearing the barn and the house, they set up a bag shower outside in the bright sunlight, taking turns showering while the other two scoured the house for anything useful. Akeem found some canned vegetables and homemade pickles that were still good. Marius found some first aid supplies to add to his kit. Torres found clean socks and boy's underwear in the dryer, which fit Akeem. They spent about an hour coaxing the half-feral chickens back to the yard and then another half-hour trying to catch one, but in the end, they had roast chicken for dinner.

As sunset streaked the sky with reds, oranges, and pinks, they sat on the porch, drinking the last of their tea and enjoying their full bellies.

"HTS," Marius said, patting his stomach. "Happy Tummy Syndrome."

"How about no more syndromes from you?" Torres teased. If she hadn't been watching his face, she might have missed the pain that flashed in his eyes, but he quickly hid it with an amiable grin.

"Fair enough." He pointed his mug out at a white puffy cloud that was reaching higher than all the surrounding ones. "Bet we're going to get a storm tonight."

"I'll check on the horses," Torres said. She hadn't meant to hurt him, but she had. She felt awkward around him. She knew how to treat him as a friend, but they were more than that now, weren't they? They'd said they loved each other, but that had been nearly a year and many miles ago. Did Marius still love her? Or was she assuming intimacy where he had none to give? They'd both been through a lot since last they'd seen each other.

In the barn, she fussed around the horses, wasting time, delaying so she wouldn't have to go back into the house and face the question of 'Do we sleep in the same bed or not?'. On the road, they each had their own sleeping bags, and there was Akeem to consider. Plus, as sweaty and smelly as they both were, the question of sex hadn't really come up.

But now ...

Torres stood in the dim barn, looking at the house, with the two small lanterns lighting it. Against all the broad nothing of the falling night, the lights seemed magnificent signs of civilization. Oh, how her standards had changed.

With a deep breath and a squaring of her shoulders she left the barn and headed for the house, following the faint trail of Marius's light.

The rain started just as Torres reached the back door. She took her time closing up the house, checking the windows were shut and the curtains drawn. She moved the collection of things they meant to add to the pack horse's burden near the back door where they would be harder to forget. She paused in the living room to peer at the pictures on the walls and photographs on the mantel. What a happily boring family these people had been. Blandly white in the kind of way that made her imagine maybe the photos had come with the frames. A trip to the beach, probably to Hawai'i judging from the leis they all wore as they squinted, grinning at the camera. A high school graduation with tassels for the tall, plain-faced daughter. An action shot of the tall, plain-faced son throwing a baseball from the pitcher's mound on a day of piercing blue skies and idyllically lush grass. The parents slow dancing under a banner that read: Happy 20th Anniversary, Freddy & Sally!

Twenty years. And where were they now? Were they alive? Were they with their children? Or had the daughter gone away to some out-of-state college, never to return?

Torres wished them well wherever they were and turned to soft light coming from the open door of the ground-floor bedroom. Akeem had taken the boy's room upstairs, which Torres thought was very tactful of him. She and Marius hadn't discussed sleeping together in the same room and she felt uncertain of her welcome, uncertain of her desire to be with him. She'd fantasized so many times about how they would be together and not once had her imagination included feeling awkward or anxious.

What do I want? she asked herself, lingering in the shadow of the half-closed door. I want to be with him. I want to have sex. I want to let go and feel alive and free and safe.

There was no chance of that happening if she stood in the hallway, so she went in.

Marius was asleep.

Torres let her jeans drop to the floor. She slipped into the empty side of the bed in her T-shirt and panties, feeling both relieved and disappointed that he'd fallen asleep. He stirred but didn't wake. She reached out and lightly brushed his cheek. It settled him. She smoothed the hair out of his face and let her fingers linger. Now clean, his hair had the sheen of a black cat's fur, not blue or brown or any color other than itself.

Not opening his eyes, Marius took her hand and pulled it to his chest. She wanted to be close, to know he was safe and they were together. She tugged him to her and he nestled his head into the hollow between her head and shoulder, drew a deep breath and mumbled something that sounded like, "Smell good." Then he was out. She could feel his weight shift as sleep well and truly took him.

Torres propped herself up on and elbow and looked him over. The scars on his back from his time in Portland were slightly raised. They were threaded through with fractal patterns of dark ink. It looked like someone had taken a felt tip pen and pressed it to a sheet of rough grain paper. The dark ink spread under his skin in delicate, fern-like fans.

The wound between his neck and shoulder was still raw looking, what she could see peeping out from the gauze bandage over it.

He was very thin, collarbones, hips, ribs standing out against his taut skin. He was tanned, and even where the sun hadn't touched him, his skin was darker than most white people's. Considering what he'd told her about the circumstances of his birth, it seemed likely he was Mediterranean. Philippe had found him in Spain, after all. Maybe he was part Spanish. Or Arabic. Or Romani. It didn't matter. He was there, against all odds, alive, whole if scarred.

Torres pulled the blanket over them and luxuriated in the feel of his body next to hers. The rain beat out a slow, low rhythm. Far away, thunder grumbled back and forth like giants rolling boulders between them. Marius breathed deep and steady. Torres closed her eyes and gave in to sleep.

The first thing Torres noted upon waking was how warm she was. The body next to hers was a furnace. She opened her eyes and found Marius lying awake on the pillow next to her.

"Hi," she said.

"Hi." Marius smiled a slow, sleepy smile that banished most of her remaining doubts about his feelings.

She brushed his cheek, and he kissed her fingertip. His lips were warm, moist, and silky soft. She gasped. He looked at her quizzically. She blushed at how sensitive she was to his touch and his smile broadened, turning mischievous.

"It's been awhile," she said, putting a hand on his chest, feeling the strong *thump* of his heart.

"I'd take 'No' for an answer," he said.

"So would I," Torres said, sitting up to search his face for any hesitancy.

"I know." Marius grinned up at her as he lay back on the pillows. "Have your way with me."

She pulled her T-shirt off and tossed it on the floor. Marius reached for her breasts, but she caught his wrists and pinned him down. She leaned in and buried her face in his neck, drew in the scent of him. Soap and woodsmoke and something that was just him. Spicy, with a note that reminded her of the sharp clean scent of an aspen grove after a rain. She kissed his neck. He kissed hers, his warm lips sending tremors down her body. Her nipples hardened and he grinned, clearly pleased with her response.

Torres ran her hands down his sides, caressed his hips and then took him in her mouth. Marius groaned and arched toward her. It was only minutes, but she judged by his rapid, ragged breathing and reddened face that he would soon reach the point of no return. She sat up and looked at the beautiful man writhing in the bed with her.

"Oh no fair," Marius panted. He sat up and motioned for her to lie down. Since Ramon, her sister's boyfriend, had tried to rape her, Torres had difficulty with any kind of rough or forceful sex, something she used to enjoy on occasion. Marius tried to never push her into anything. She appreciated how he let her set the pace.

She lay back, watching him, reminding herself that he was not Ramon, that she was safe with him. He started with her neck, torturing her with kisses, licks, and nibbles, working his way down. He slid his hands between her thighs, and she eagerly let him spread her. Last time he had started to go down on her, it had been too much and she'd stopped him. This time, she felt ready and willing for him to explore. In fact, she wanted him to do more than that. She twisted her hips suggestively, moaning out a wordless plea for him.

"Two can play the teasing game," he said. His voice was low and the feel of his hot breath against the tender skin of her inner thighs sent a fresh wash of shivers up her body. Torres sighed and grabbed the headboard for support.

"Do your worst," she groaned.

"I'll do my best."

Between his delicate tongue, his silky lips, and his long, agile fingers, Torres was soon bucking her hips in wild abandon. Just as she was about to come, he paused.

"Oh God! Please," she wailed. Marius laughed and returned to his work. Torres came in a trembling, shuddering mess, gasping and grabbing his hair. To hold him where he was or push him away, she didn't know.

She wriggled and moaned, afterglowing for a few seconds. Marius sat watching her, a proud smirk on his face.

"You think you're so good?" she gasped.

"Yeah." He lifted a shoulder in a half shrug.

"Fuck me, you are," she said.

Marius crawled up her, and never breaking eye contact, reached down to guide himself into her. She lifted her hips. He was hot and hard and eager. She wrapped her legs around him and pulled him in.

"You're so sexy when you cum," he groaned, thrusting deeply into her. "It's been a really long time,"

"Then don't make me wait." Torres grabbed his hips and pulled him tighter to her body. That was all the encouragement Marius needed.

His excitement, the intense look of concentration on his face, the feel of him inside her after so long with only her own hand for comfort. She came again and then so did he. After, he rolled off and she handed him a towel.

"Wouldn't want to waste the shower," Marius said as he wiped himself clean. Torres cleaned up as well and turned back to him. He held out his arms in wordless invitation and she laid her head on his chest, tucking herself against him. He wrapped his arms around her and pressed his nose into her hair. He sniffed rapidly, sounding like a dog. Torres giggled.

"What? Your hair smells good," Marius said. "Your everything smells good." He sounded sleepy again.

Torres lifted her head to look at him. His eyes were green slits.

"Typical," she teased him. "Guy shows up, eats all the food —"

"And you," Marius interjected.

"Has sex," she continued, "and then falls asleep."

"In defense of said guy," Marius mumbled, pulling her back to him, "a full tummy and empty balls is about as close to true happiness anyone's getting these days. If I had peaches and toilet paper ..." He snugged his arms around her, as if she might try to escape while he slept. Nothing could have been further from the truth. She had been so lonely; it was more likely she would tie him down.

"I found toilet paper in the basement," she cooed, in her best sex kitten voice.

"If you have peaches too ..."

"In the kitchen, by the door." She smiled. Among the food Akeem had found was a jar of canned peaches.

"She's a witch," Marius muttered, this time eyes closed.

They fell asleep together like that, a tangle of limbs, warm and safe as the thunder rolled away across the plain, leaving a fresh washed prairie and quiet night.

In the week since leaving Valentine, they had seen

Infected four times. Twice from a distance, and once close enough that Torres was considering shooting when the three Littles turned around and left the area. The fourth time was the tiny town of Decker.

"It's official," Marius said, when he saw the sign. "We're in Montana."

"Practically home," Torres said. It was her turn to ride, and she patted Gany's flank to let him know he'd soon get a nice long break from her.

"Marius," Akeem said nervously, pointing at the tiny cluster of buildings that seemed to be the entirety of the town. Bundles of fleshy tubes stretched across from roof to roof as if the inhabitants of Decker were trying to steal cable from each other. The sides of the buildings gleamed slightly pinkish red and not just from the setting sun.

"Let's go around," Marius said.

"Way around," Torres added. "Why don't you come up here, kiddo?" She kicked her foot out of the stirrup and Akeem climbed into the saddle, while she slid back to give him room. Marius mounted the pack horse, finding a perch among the backpacks and sleeping bags. They turned hard east, going until they came to a river, and then turning north along it.

The long dusk of midsummer finally died as true night came on. Ahead, Torres spotted a sign for a campground. Mercifully, this one seemed to be Infected free. They picked out a campsite with a fire pit that had the shore at their backs. Torres was beginning to really understand Medieval Europeans' obsession with building their castles on islands or the edges of cliffs. Having at least one side of your defenses handled for you was a big help.

While Torres did a quick perimeter sweep, Marius and Akeem got their camp set up. By the time the former Marine returned, Marius had a pot of stew going and Akeem had finished tending the horses.

"We didn't see any of the Infected in that town," Torres said. "Maybe they all left or died off."

"They were probably hiding," Akeem said, squatting in front of their campfire. "The Infected don't like him." He waved at Marius.

"I know," Torres said. "It's one of the reasons we do like him."

Even as the words left her lips, Torres wanted to take them back, wanted to assure Marius that he was worth far more than his blood. She had meant it comfortingly, but it ended up sounding overly pragmatic, utilitarian, even.

Marius stirred the stew, which was mostly scrounged tubers, wild onions, and a chunk of ham steak from an MRE. Torres longed for the days of greasy fast food, burgers so tall she had to unhinge her jaw like a snake to eat, and milkshakes so thick she could barely slurp them up the straw and so cold that when she did, she got brain freeze.

"Do you think the Infected followed us?" Akeem asked.

"I think we should assume they did," Torres said. Something splashed in the river to the east of them and they all froze, straining to hear more. Silence. After a few tense moments, Marius stirred the stew again, then moved the pot onto a couple of rocks nearby to cool.

"Should we put out the fire?" Akeem stood up and

looked out into the night. The moon was half full, so it wasn't completely dark, but still not enough light to do them any real good.

"The Infected already know where we are," Torres said. She took the baggy full of mold out and considered it. "We could use this. I've been hanging onto it for just such an occasion."

"That's the inhibitor mold?" Akeem poked at the still steaming stew.

"Yep," Torres said. "The Infected like it about as much as they like Marius's blood."

"So, not at all," Marius said. He settled in a cross-legged seat next to Torres and leaned his elbow on her knee. She loved the way he seemed to want to always be in physical contact with her if they were close. She felt the same about him, but didn't want to appear needy, which her more rational self found ridiculous. If she couldn't be honest about what she wanted and who she wanted to be with here at the end of civilization, then when?

"The advantage is anyone can grow the mold," Torres said. "Plus, you get to keep your magic blood on the inside, which is — "

She stopped.

Something was coming down the road. She held up a hand, and turned her head, closing her eyes to listen. Yes, those were definitely footsteps. She set down her bowl and stood, moving to the side, so Marius wasn't between her and whoever or whatever was coming. She drew Jimmy's HK, mentally counting the rounds as she always did nowadays. Ten. She had started the trip with a full fifteen, but a few of the Infected hadn't accepted

'No' for an answer.

"Hello," said a quiet voice. It was low, most likely a man's voice.

Torres toed Marius, who was also on his feet, his camp knife out and ready.

"What do you want?" Marius asked. As he talked, Torres stepped back further from the fire, moving out to look and listen for others.

"It's only me," said the man. "Can I come to your fire?"

Marius glanced at Torres. So far, she hadn't been able to detect anyone else, but that didn't mean there wasn't anyone else out there. They might be just keeping very, very quiet while hunting wabbits.

Torres nodded. She kept from looking directly into the campfire, letting her eyes adjust to the darkness. She didn't see anyone else, but she couldn't afford to assume the stranger was alone.

The man walked up the edge of the firelight. He kept his hands out where they could be seen.

"I'm Doug," he said. "I'm not infected or anything like that." He had a gentle drawl to his speech, something from Texas or Oklahoma if Torres had to guess. "I saw you pass by the town back there, if you can call it a town, and thought I'd introduce myself."

"On whose behalf?" Torres asked. She watched Doug out of the corner of her eye as she stalked slowly around the fire, maneuvering herself behind the newcomer.

"Y'all might have heard of us," Doug said, sounding not at all bothered. "We've got a little piece of civilization going down Yellowstone way."

"I've heard of Yellowstone," Akeem said.

"Did you now? Where abouts are you from? You're not an American, are you?" Doug jutted his head forward as he studied the boy.

"I don't see how that would matter," Marius said, putting a hand on the boy's shoulder.

"Don't matter to me none who y'all travel with." Doug started to put his hands in his pocket, but Torres cleared her throat and he stopped.

"What kind of civilization?" Marius asked. "Do you have communication with anyone else? Is it a big community? How many are vaccinated?"

"Well, the thing is, I wouldn't want the wrong kind of people coming into Yellowstone, but y'all seem mostly harmless," Doug said. "My job here is to make first contact with new potential citizens and let y'all know we're there and there's an open invite. Whenever you've a mind, head on down."

"To Yellowstone?" Torres asked. She'd nearly completed her circuit and still hadn't seen or heard anything to indicate Doug had backup.

"Just a mite south of there, actually, miss," Doug said. "But if you make it to Yellowstone one of our outriders can show you the rest of the way."

"That's tempting, but it's also a really long way to go these days," Marius said.

"So, what's in it for you besides my fine company?" Doug asked. "Not gonna give away all our secrets, but our founder, Mr. Sebald, saw all this coming. He'd been out there on vacation a few times and knew it would be a good place to set up. No big population centers, not near any international borders, lots of geothermal energy like they use in Iceland, and all the buffalo burgers you can shake a stick at." He paused and then said ruefully, "Although some of those did get pretty nasty when there was a breach. We dealt with it though and now buffalo's back on the menu."

"Do you have anything to trade other than information?" Torres asked.

"No, miss, I surely do not. Think of me as an apostle for Sebald, a voice crying in the wilderness. We need all the capable people we can get to put civilization back on its feet." Doug took a deep sniff. "Although, I wouldn't say no to some stew. Come to think of it, I got some toothpaste I'd trade for it. Got three tubes and only the one set of teeth."

"Deal," Torres said. Hygiene items were getting harder and harder to find.

While Doug ate a bowl of stew, Marius quizzed him on the route he'd come by and the countryside he'd passed through. Doug was careful to only talk in generalities about where his group's headquarters was located, but happy to tell them which communities he'd come across were empty of humans and which had Infected in them. In exchange, Marius and Torres told him about their route east as far as the Mississippi River.

When Doug left, Torres tailed him until he crossed the river. At least that way, they would have a good chance of hearing him if he came back.

"What do you think?" was Marius's first question when she returned to the camp.

"I think we need to keep an extra good watch tonight," Torres said. She picked up her now very cool bowl of soup and dug in. Hunger was still the best seasoning.

Chapter 12 - Miranda

On the Road, Illinois, USA – Summer, Year 2

The morning had started easy. Miranda woke in a bed, an actual bed. They had found a little cottage in the woods somewhere in western Illinois. It seemed to have been part of a hippie commune or art center. Whatever it had been before, it had its own well water and a note on the kitchen table:

Dear Travelers,
  Blessed be all who enter here.
  Please take what you need and leave what you can.
  With Love & Peace,
                              Stan & Eliza Worley

Beside the note were three cans of condensed soup and a pile of individually wrapped sanitary wipe packets. Miranda left one of her two tubes of ChapStick and two watch batteries she picked up in Minneapolis, but never found a use for.

After clearing and securing the house, they heated water over a campfire and filled the tub for baths, a process that took most of the day.

While Miranda was enjoying her turn, lazing in the steam, enjoying the last capful of bubble bath, and staring at the ceiling as if it was just another day, like she might get up and go watch some TV or call her friends or go shopping, there was a tapping on the bathroom door.

"I have a surprise for you," Eli said. His voice was soft, and Miranda could practically hear the smile on his face. "May I come in, fair maiden?"

"Awfully rude, don't you think?" Miranda said, flicking some suds across the water in the door's direction.

"Wait until you see what I have," Eli crooned.

"Come in, but no peeking," Miranda slid back into the water until only her knees, head and shoulders, and the tops of her breasts were out of the bubbles.

Eli opened the door wide enough to step through and closed it quietly. Did Romi know where he was and what he was doing? Did it matter to her? Miranda hadn't noticed any kind of sexual tension or intimacy between them, only friendship.

Eli kept his head ducked as he walked to the middle of the bathroom. From behind his back, he pulled out a magnum of champagne. It wasn't an expensive one, probably not even real champagne, but Miranda squealed and clapped with delight nonetheless. Eli held out his other hand, in which he had two teacups by their delicate little handles.

"Et voilà!"

"Bravo, bravo." Miranda leaned her elbows on the edge of the bathtub and smiled up at Eli. "But what are we celebrating?"

"Us," Eli said and popped the cork, causing Miranda to jump at the loud noise in the small room.

"Us?" Miranda raised an eyebrow.

"Us who are surviving," Eli said. "Every day we don't die or get infected is a miracle, don't you think?"

"Fair," Miranda said, watching as Eli poured the pale amber bubbly into the cups. Without looking directly at her, he held one out.

"Ugh, no. No, sir," Miranda said primly.

"Sorry?"

"One adores drinking champagne in one's bath," she said in her best posh British accent. "But for such an occasion, we need a proper toast. Now, you go wait outside and I'll be out in a minute."

Eli tucked the bottle under his arm, careful to keep it upright and not spill a precious drop of champagne as he left. Miranda toweled off quickly and pulled on the tank top and cotton shorts she used as pajamas. She ran her fingers through her long hair and stepped out of the bathroom.

Eli stood in the center of the living room. He had moved aside the coffee table and spread out a checkered tablecloth. The indoor picnic scene was completed by a wicker basket with wildflowers poked through the open weave and a plate with cracker sandwiches. The teacups and bottle of champagne waited on the coffee table. Eli lifted a plate of small strawberries and offered it, his smile charming and confident.

Miranda took a tiny berry and brought it to her lips, feeling its soft, plump flesh. It was hardly bigger than her thumb and deep red, the kind that would taste far better than any of the giant GMO fruits from corporate farms. But there were no more corporate farms. No more corporations. No more Chrysalis. No more Chrysalis CEO father - only a monster who had left her in Oregon.

Miranda, your father —

No. She cut the Infected off before they could get any further. She willed herself into the now, into this room with this man and his simple desires.

"If I didn't know better, I'd imagine you were hitting on me." She nibbled the strawberry and smiled at Eli.

"How do you imagine you'd feel about that?" Eli moved closer, reached out to brush back a lock of Miranda's damp hair, his eyes gentle, hopeful as he searched her face. She admired his self-control that his gaze didn't drop below her shoulders, at least while she was watching him.

"I imagine anyone brave enough to set up something like this would be brave enough to come right out and tell me what they wanted." Miranda popped the strawberry into her mouth, let the juices fill her senses.

"I want you." Eli's hand moved from her hair to trace along her cheek, his thumb stroking her lips.

"What about Romi?" Miranda asked, catching his wrist and moving his hand away from her face. She didn't like the proprietary way he touched her, as if he already owned her.

"This has nothing to do with Romi," Eli said.

"Are you sure?" Miranda didn't owe Romi anything, but she wasn't going to be Eli's 'other' woman. Marius could have Torres if that was who he wanted. Miranda was determined to never be someone's second choice.

"Believe me," Eli said. "She can handle herself. She made that crystal clear."

Miranda turned Eli's hand over in hers, tracing her fingernail across his palm as if she was reading his future. "And believe you me, if you fuck me over instead of just fucking me, I will end you." She lifted her gaze to meet his. "Clear?"

"Crystal." He leaned in, his lips nearly touching hers, but waiting, letting her cross the final distance between them. She kissed him hard, and jumped up, wrapping her legs around his hips as he stumbled slightly back. He caught her under the thighs and carried her, kissing her face, her neck, her shoulders, to his room.

They stayed at the cabin for three days, scavenging the nearby small town for supplies. Miranda and Eli found plenty of chances to make out and more. Romi seemed contented to read while sunning herself in a hammock in the cabin's back yard. By some unspoken agreement, they all were acting as if they were on vacation. Soon, they would pack up their things, and return to their real lives in lands far, far away that HHV had never touched, let alone ruined.

The Infected arrived in the night, their presence rousing Miranda from a deep sleep with a sensation like a million ants with stabby little feet were running over her. She gasped, bolting up in bed. Romi's room was down the hall, and Eli's down the stairs.

Disoriented, Miranda kicked off the sheet and stumbled to the window, expecting to see a horde of Infected in the yard. It was empty. The waning moon hung low in the sky, casting the yard in silver shadows and black pools of darkness.

"What is it?" Romi stood in Miranda's doorway. She was wearing a slip and holding her gun, her hair loose and tousled around her face.

Miranda glanced back at the yard. She'd been so sure the Infected were close, but there was nothing there.

Romi crossed the room to look out the window herself. After a long, searching moment, she turned to study Miranda.

"What's going on with you?"

"Nothing." Miranda braced her hands against the windowsill. The night was sticky and still. She felt feverish and longed for the next storm. Far away to the north, summer heat lightning danced pointlessly in the clouds.

"We're all messed up." Romi set the gun down on the bedside table and lifted her hair off her neck. "But you're messed up in a way I don't understand."

"Is this about Eli?" Miranda hoped to deflect attention. The last thing she needed was Romi prying up her armor and poking her wounds.

"I don't care what men do with their dicks as long as they keep them away from me," Romi said.

"Oh. Ooooh." Miranda blushed as she understood what Romi was telling her.

"So, why are you up in the middle of the night?" Romi said.

"Bad dreams?" Miranda fidgeted.

"That's bullshit, darling," Romi said. "You knew there was a fire, but no one else noticed. You knew how to get out of Minneapolis, and you said you were never there before. Let's assume that both of us are smart, okay? So, what's going on with you?"

Miranda studied the other woman. How would Romi react if she found out Miranda was a collaborator, to use Torres's word? The worst part was, Miranda didn't even know if Torres was wrong. She did communicate with the Infected. She benefitted from their information, used them to scout for her, even to kill for her if the need arose, which it did a lot more these days than she ever would have imagined. Miranda of Harrow Hall Preparatory School would never have dreamed of killing someone. Miranda of many long days on the road would hardly hesitate. What a difference an apocalypse could make.

In the end, it was that knowledge, that no matter how Romi reacted, no matter what Eli might do, Miranda wouldn't be truly alone, that settled her mind.

We are always here for you.

I know.

Aloud, she said, "My father's name was Albert Viers."

"This is not okay." Eli paced around the kitchen, circling the table where Romi and Miranda sat. Ever since Miranda had told him about herself, about the Infected, and the Enlightened, and her father, he hadn't made eye contact with her, certainly hadn't touched her. It was as if she was contaminated. Well, maybe she was, but he'd been happy enough to have all kinds of contact only a day ago.

"It's not her fault," Romi said for the tenth or hundredth time. Miranda sipped her sun tea and watched. She felt detached, like the other two were an interesting sit-com.

"She should have told us," Eli said. "Don't we deserve to make an informed choice?"

Miranda cleared her throat and set her glass down with a click.

"Speaking of informed choices," she said. Eli folded his arms across his chest and stared out the kitchen window. Romi's eyes flicked from him to Miranda. She didn't look worried, only amused and a little exasperated, as if she was tired of Eli's whining.

"What military are you from?" Miranda asked. "Are you from the same unit or whatever?"

"Military?" Romi said too innocently.

"Yeah, military," Miranda said. "Like that's at all worse than what's going on with me."

"We're Israeli special forces," Romi said. Eli heaved a huge, aggrieved sigh. "What? Like any of our mission perimeters are still intact. When was the last time we had any kind of contact with anyone?"

"That doesn't change our objective," Eli said through gritted teeth. "Our objective is still the same."

"And what's that?" Miranda asked sweetly. "Besides seducing the locals, obviously."

"I really liked you," Eli snapped. "You were sexy as hell."

"Great," Miranda said. "So, I'll see you in the bedroom in five?"

Eli glared at her. She smirked. Better to be feared than loved. Love was weak, temporary, easily distracted with new people. Love left her alone again and again; first her mother, then her father, then Marius and John, Torres, the rest of the New Avalon people who didn't even see her as human anymore. No, love was as permanent as a tissue and about as useful. Fear, on the other hand. Fear settled deep in people's bones. Fear kept their hands off her throat when they wanted to strangle her. Fear protected her.

"I'm going to Detroit," Eli said to Romi. "If they've got a cure, maybe he's there already."

"He's not," Miranda said. She sipped her tea and watched Eli from under her lashes. His eyelids were kind of droopy and his hair was a little thin at his temples. Amazing the things she had avoided noticing before.

"You don't even know who we're talking about," Eli said dismissively.

"Yeah, I actually do." Miranda met his angry look with one of distain.

"Who do you think we're talking about?" Romi asked, leaning forward so she was between Eli and Miranda.

"Marius," Miranda said. She gave her head a little shake and laughed. "It's always about him, isn't it? I traveled thousands of miles and it's still about him. Well, you know what, you can all have him. I'm done. I'm out. Go to Detroit. I'm sure he'll be there with a parade or whatever and all the vaccines you could ever want. He's gonna single-handedly unfuck the world, you stupid assholes."

Without meaning to, she was on her feet, tears of rage pricking her eyes. Even here, even after everything she'd been through, everything she'd lost, he was taking these people from her.

Not that you want them. The Infected reminded her. They were closer now and so many voices all together. A hive? *They don't want you. You don't need them. Come with us.*

Miranda remembered the Infected scout that had come to the Morning Star ranch right after she'd destroyed the hive in the quarry. Unlike all the other Infected, who'd been afraid of her, this one had brought a message. *Come to Kentucky. Your father's waiting for you.*

Why not? Miranda thought as she stormed out of the kitchen. Why not join the Infected for real since everyone already thought she was a part of them?

You are a part of us. You never have to be lonely again.

She grabbed her pack from under her bed and started to fill it. *Tell my father I'm on my way.*

Another storm threatened, but Miranda would rather die than stay a minute longer in the house with those judgy commandos. She hitched up her pack and stomped down the road, sweating in the humidity. Rain would be nice. She would find a car with gas, or, more likely, a bike that worked. Maybe a horse. She could put the expensive riding lessons, which her mother insisted should be a part of a young lady's formal education, to use. As if it were the nineteen century and she was going to go fox hunting or some other ridiculous bourgeoisie thing like that.

She could sense the clamor of the Infected, getting stronger as she walked. It was hard to pick out a single mind, so there probably wasn't an Enlightened with them. But why were there so many together? Where were they going? Usually, the Infected moved only short distances from wherever they started. They kept close to the hives, which in turn were connected by bioformation and occasionally roaming scouts.

"Miranda!"

She stopped and turned.

Romi hurried down the road, waving for her to stop. When she caught up, Miranda could see the other woman had all her gear. She hadn't simply come after her to say goodbye or get in some final little dig at Miranda's siding with the enemy.

"I'm going with you," Romi announced, which was probably the most surprising thing she could have said.

"Like hell you are."

"I am. Where you go, I will go." Romi smiled.

"Why? You don't even know where I'm going. I'm going to Kentucky, to a cave full of Infected." There, that should scare her off.

"Great." More smiling. It was annoying. And confusing.

"Great?" Miranda blew a puff of air up to flick her bangs out of her face. "They'll kill you."

"Not if I'm with you, right?"

"Why would you want to go with me?" Miranda

regretted asking as soon as she said it. She sounded so pathetic. Lonely and pathetic. Well, she was alone, at least as far as any of the non-Infected could tell, but she wasn't lonely. She could never be alone with the ever-present scritching and scraping of their millions of tiny minds in the back of her brain.

"Two reasons," Romi said. She started walking on in the direction Miranda had been going before she stopped. "Number the first, my mission — our mission — is to find a way to protect our people from the virus. We're very good at closing our borders and keeping out human threats. We've been fighting for survival since ... ever. But HHV, that's new even to us. So, Eli goes to Detroit to see if there is any such cure there and can they share. And I go with you to learn about the Infected from the person who knows more about them than any other human being. Even Doctor Tenartier doesn't know as much about them as you. How could he? To him, they are the enemy. He will never try to understand them, only try to understand how to kill them."

She's trying to flatter you. The Infected were not impressed.

It's working. Miranda shot back. She was tired of everyone else thinking they knew better than she did. Besides, let the Infected worry about her commitment. She was also tired of being taken for granted.

"What's your other reason?" she asked Romi.

Romi turned to glance over her shoulder at Miranda. "I'm looking at her."

"Awfully presumptuous," Miranda said. She started walking, too.

"Maybe," Romi said with a shrug to adjust her pack.

"But Eli said you don't like to play games. Besides, who's got that kind of time? We might all be dead tomorrow. When I was in secondary school, I had the biggest crush on this girl, but I never told her. About ten years later, I found out she was married to one of my friends. One of my lady friends. What if I had told her how I felt? I might be in Tel Aviv right now helping her raise our three kids."

"What if I'm not into women?" Miranda said.

"Are you?" Romi seemed utterly undaunted. "Have you ever been with a woman?"

Miranda had kissed a few girls in high school, but she'd never really decided if she was one way or the other. It just seemed easier to find guys to hook up with. Well, not easier, exactly — more like unavoidable. She didn't even have to look. She'd been young, rich, popular, and attractive. Guys seemed to take that like she was carrying around a sign reading: Hit on me IMMEDIATELY.

"I don't like to put labels on things," Miranda hedged.

"That's not a no," Romi said. She stopped and turned to look at Miranda fully. "I like you. I think you are cute and funny and fierce as all the fucks. I want to get to know you more. Maybe that will become a friendship. Maybe more. Could you agree to give me a chance to be your friend?"

"But if that's all it ever is, no whining about being 'friend-zoned,' okay?"

"How would being your friend be worse than nothing?" Romi held out a hand. "Truce?"

Miranda shook. "Truce," she said with a slow smile. She really hadn't wanted to go all the way to Kentucky with only the gibbering horde for company.

Chapter 13 - Marius

Marius had never thought much of Crossroads. The most exciting events in years had been the opening of a franchise fast food restaurant and the high school replacing the bleachers at the football field. To his younger self, it was a small, boring town, a place to be from, never a destination. But that had been before the pandemic, before the world had fallen apart, and before Kentucky.

He paused as they turned off the main highway onto the state road leading to Crossroads, waiting for the rush of nostalgia or homecoming to hit. This spot looked exactly as it had since he could remember. A slight rise as the elevation gradually increased from the prairies to the east into the Rockies to the west. Grass bowed before the breeze while fat bumble bees droned their slow circuit among the bluebells, goldenrod, shooting stars, and yarrow. If he closed his eyes, he could be back in time five, ten, even twenty years ago. Whatever was going on with the rest of the world, this piece of Montana was getting on with the business of being alive. Here, at least, some of his efforts to fix the colossal disaster that his immunity ushered into the world seemed to be paying off.

"Should I ride ahead and tell them to roll out the welcome wagon?" Torres asked. It was her turn on Gany with Akeem leading the pack horse.

"It's okay," Marius said. "I don't want to make a big fuss." He felt oddly shy and even a little ashamed. He had gone with the Infected willingly, trading himself for their safety, but he'd failed to secure that. Worse, he'd been helping the Infected, first while they used his body as a kind of life-support system for the Enlightened, and later actively trying to undo the inhibitor's effects on the Enlightened. Miranda had left Crossroads because people believed she was working with the Infected. But Marius actually had worked with the Infected. How could he face them, knowing he was not only the cause of the pandemic, but also had a hand in helping the enemy?

Before he could ponder the matter further, a rider came galloping down the road. His brother, Anatole, pulled Pickles into a stop, the mare rearing back and dancing a little before settling to shake her mane and touch noses with Ganymede. If only coming back into the fold could be so easy for humans.

"Marius!" Anatole launched himself at his brother. Even as Marius hugged him, he noted how much Anatole had changed in the time he'd been away. He was leaner, his face a little sun- and windburned, with a comfort on Pickles that Marius would never have imagined, given that in high school, Anatole was lord of the D&D nerds and a self-described 'avid indoorsman'. Anatole, who dreamed of studying at MIT or starting his own MMORPG company, now turned scout and forager.

As they walked into town, Anatole tried to tell them everything that had happened while they'd been gone. Who'd left, who'd died, two babies had been born, one of the ranches to the east had burned down after the barn was struck by lightning. The main house at the Morning Star ranch was nearly fully repaired and so were the outbuildings, including the mold shed. And they'd added another shed.

"Good thing someone around here knows how to run a good growing operation," Anatole finished with a self-congratulatory smile.

"And mold's all you're growing?" Marius asked, hearing the older brother tone creep into his voice.

"Maybe." Anatole didn't look a bit worried as he waved to the crowd gathering on Main Street.

Crossroads looked like a poorly staged Wild West re-enactment with people wearing anachronistic combinations of handmade items and patched, mismatched machine-made ones. Solar panels gleamed under the summer sun. Backyards had been turned into kitchen gardens or livestock pens. The number of sheep, goats, horses, chickens, and geese in town was shocking.

"Make a hole," someone yelled, and Philippe stepped out of the crowd. He caught Marius in a bearhug and, with no apparent shame at all, cried on his son's shoulder. After a moment, when both men had gotten themselves under control, he said, "Your mom's at the ranch with Percy. C'mon. Almost home, son."

The reunion at the ranch was both better and worse than the one in town. Better because there were fewer people. Marius didn't have the sense of being constantly center stage under a spotlight. Worse because there were fewer distractions, more questions. Most shocking had been seeing the house. It was nearly the same but with clearly new, roughly finished siding and a new roof. There were still scorch marks on the upper parts of some windows and under the eaves, but in general the reconstruction was nearly finished.

"Amazing how much work gets done when I'm not around," Torres joked. She and Akeem disappeared into the barn to get Gany and the pack horse all the oats and apples their horsey hearts could desire.

When Marius had drunk all the tea he could hold and answered all the questions he could stand, he excused himself to go see his old room. The closet was the same, complete with the poorly hung door that never stayed shut. His bed was gone, replaced by a queen-size blow-up mattress on a collapsible frame. His papers, notebooks, and drawings, normally scattered over his desk, the floor, and tacked to the walls, were collected into a neat pile on the desk. He didn't check to see what had survived the fire.

The satchel his parents had given him with all the documents about his true identity hung from a hook behind the door. A Coleman lantern stood on his bedside table and a small bucket was tucked discreetly under the bed, telling him the ranch still hadn't figured out how to re-establish indoor plumbing.

He crossed to the window and opened it. The wooden frame and glass were new. He climbed out onto the roof of the back porch and sat, looking out over the yard that rolled away into the foothills of the mountains, already blue with the coming night.

He was home.

He put his head down onto his knees and sobbed.

"It's a bad idea." Torres had her ready-for-a-fight look; arms crossed and chin tucked as she studied Marius across the table. Around them in the barn, the sounds of Rangers coming and going petered off as folks stopped to watch the unfolding drama.

"How is it a bad idea?" Marius tried to ignore the weight of everyone's eyes on him. They kept thinking he was going to save them, despite how anything he did only seemed to make things worse.

"Because," Torres said and stopped, her mouth half open.

"I have more experience out there than just about anyone else," Marius said. "I'm immune, so don't have to worry about the Infected." Torres snorted, but he continued. "Summer's nearly over and we need to use all the good weather to expand our communications. Trading with the folks in Great Falls and Helena is a good start, but we need to find where everyone went. Where are all the people from Seattle or Denver or Salt Lake City? Those are pretty big population centers, and we don't know if they're hives or empty or what."

"I agree summer is the best time for long range missions," John said. He was sitting in Philippe's old recliner, carefully unpicking the damaged leather lacing from a saddle.

Torres shot him a narrow-eyed glare.

Unruffled, he said, "What did you have in mind for Marius to do around here, Torres?"

"Not get kidnapped or killed," Torres said. "You're all acting like he's just a Ranger like anyone else, but we all know he's not. The Infected have gone out of their way, way out of their way, to capture him. Twice. Third time, I'm betting Viers will finally decide he's more trouble than he's worth. We know from Miranda they can communicate at high speeds over long distances, so they've got a significant advantage on us in intelligence gathering and information dissemination."

"I'm not at any greater risk than anyone else who goes out there," Marius said. Two weeks back and he almost couldn't stand the ranch a minute longer. Everyone treated him like he was simultaneously made of the most delicate crystal and utterly bulletproof. He knew they meant well, that they loved him, that they wanted him to be all right, to get over or through whatever had happened, to be the charming and scatterbrained genius they remembered him as. But he wasn't that person. He barely even knew that Marius anymore and trying to be him was exhausting. Some days, getting out of bed was exhausting. He couldn't face the mold sheds again. They were dark and musty. They were too much like Mammoth Cave. Besides, there was nothing for him to do there. The mold would grow for anyone. That was the great thing about mold; it was hardy and adaptable.

"Bullshit," Torres said, pulling him back to the present. That happened a lot, too. People would be talking, and he'd be gone, not daydreaming or working over some scientific theory, but mentally gone, like his mind shut down. All his life, the one thing he'd relied on most was his intellect. It was terrifying.

Marius glanced at John, hoping for a sign of what he'd missed. John was watching Torres, who was watching him. Clearly it was his turn to talk.

"It's not and you know it." There. That was broad enough to cover anything she'd said.

"You are at greater risk. I'm not arguing facts."

Ah, okay, that he could concede.

"Yes, the Infected would be extra happy if they killed me. That doesn't make my life worth more than Dawn's or Andy's. If I stay here and they go out and get killed, they would be just as dead, even if the Infected weren't expressly looking for them."

Torres took a deep breath, her nostrils flaring with irritation.

"We've got two priorities for the Rangers," John said evenly, as if Torres wasn't going into full pissed-off wolverine mode. "We need to secure the area around New Avalon, keep presence patrols up for any of the Infected scouts or Littles passing through the area. That's a search and destroy mission with a high likelihood of direct combat. The other mission is long-range recon, recruiting folks to come to our community and establishing communication with potential trading partners."

"They need Marius." Torres pointed in the direction of the mold sheds.

"I'm not doing that anymore," Marius said.

Torres's face went from surprised to suspicious to something like sadness or regret. Marius looked away. On the road with Akeem and later with Torres, it had been easier. Simply surviving from one day to the next had been a challenge that engaged his mind and kept him tired enough to sleep at night. Since coming back — he couldn't even think of it as coming home — he'd existed in a strange limbo world where everyone had crafted lives that didn't involve him, not as a real person, anyway. He might as well be a saint, someone they invoked when they sent their wishful thoughts for protection from the Infected out into the uncaring universe. Saint Marius of the Useless Immunity.

"Marius wants to be a Ranger," John said. "We accept any adult who can perform the basic functions. Don't we?"

Torres looked at Marius again, her shoulders slumping.

"We've been planning to send a team to Minot," she said, speaking to John as if there'd been no discussion, just another mission. "Bailey says there's a small Air Force base there. If it hasn't been entirely picked clean, we might find something useful."

"I'll leave in the morning," Marius said.

Torres had been quiet most of the last night and at first Marius thought she was sulking, but after they lay down in the darkened room, listening to the rustles and creaks of the newly built sections of the house fitting into the old, she heaved a deep sigh and rolled toward him.

"I'm not mad," she said in a near whisper, which made it hard for him to gauge her tone.

He rolled toward her, propped himself on his elbow and stared at the mostly blank silhouette of her. He was failing her, as he was failing everyone else. He didn't know how to even discover what the problem was, let alone how to make things better.

"I'm ... sad." Her voice dropped even lower. "I'm lonely. I feel —" She stopped and sniffed, wiping at her face with an irritated motion, like shooing away a fly.

"Lourdes, I'm not leaving because of you," Marius said. Her sorrow scraped at him. He loved her. She had traveled halfway across a continent looking for him, at no small personal risk. How to explain that she was one of the few good things left? She loved him. How to explain that her love wasn't enough to fill the hollow inside him, that place where hope and joy and even anger went to die, leaving only a tired despair?

"It feels like you are." Torres laid her head down on the pillow of her arm.

"I'm not," he said helplessly.

"Stay with me." She put a hand on his bare chest.

"I can't."

She stroked her thumb along his collarbone, ran her palm over the nearly healed scar between his shoulder and neck, up the column of his throat, and traced his jawline before brushing his cheek. She lay back down flat and breathed, one, two, three deep breaths, then she got up and left the room.

They left at dawn without saying goodbye to anyone.

Marius rode Chaldene and the other Ranger, a Canadian named Emile, rode Honey-Spice. They took a pack horse and expected to be gone two or three weeks. Emile was a short, slender man who didn't seem to have any desire to chat, which suited Marius's mood perfectly. Apart from a few necessary exchanges about the route or the terrain or possible Infected signs, they said very little to each other.

The first night, they camped in an empty RV park. They ate the fresh food that would spoil quickest and didn't bother with a fire, which was dangerous both because it might start a grassfire and because it would announce their presence far and wide.

"We usually stay near the roads," Emile said, breaking a silence of nearly three hours. Marius looked up from the paperback he'd brought. He'd never been much of a fiction reader growing up, always more interested in pouring over *Scientific American*, *Cell*, *The Journal of Genetics*, and *Xenobiotica*. Since coming back to New Avalon, fiction had been a way to spend his time when he couldn't bear the mold shed any longer.

"Mmm," Marius said, and they both returned to silence for the rest of the night.

On the fifth day out, they crossed the state line into North Dakota. None of the horses were impressed. They did enjoy the plentiful grass, yellowing under the late summer sun. They had seen three groups of Infected and several towns covered in bioformations, which they noted on their map, but in general the roads themselves seemed mostly clear. There were a few places where accidents had happened, the vehicles and sometimes their occupants simply rotting away wherever they had come to a stop.

Marius and Emile were skirting a particularly big pileup where a semi had jack-knifed across into oncoming traffic, effectively damming the road in both directions, when they heard a scream.

When the Rangers left New Avalon territory, they carried at least one rifle and one handgun. They usually also carried a bow and knives. Quiet weapons could be vital. When they heard the scream, Marius was carrying the bow, looped over his back, with the quiver over the horn of his saddle. He also had the pistol in a holster on his thigh. Emile had the rifle.

Both Rangers dismounted and loosely tied the horses to wing mirrors of the wrecked vehicles. Since Emile had the rifle, he moved to get a good overwatch position. Marius skirted the remains of the accident, trying to get closer to the source of the noise.

A hatchback car was parked on the shoulder. Bags and suitcases were piled around the back of it. Both the tailgate and rear window were open, as were both back doors. Whoever had been in that car had gotten out in a hurry. But why remove the luggage?

"You're doing so, so good, sweetheart," said a woman's voice and Marius froze behind a neighboring car. He peeped over and saw three women in the back of a station wagon. The rear seat was down, providing them space. One woman lay on her back, propped up on her elbows with her knees up, legs spread. The second woman knelt behind the first one's upper back, her hands gently messaging and stroking the first woman's shoulders. The third woman squatted between the first's knees, starring fixedly towards her groin and the very large, clearly pregnant belly above it.

"Hold it right there," said another woman's voice. Marius looked around and then up. The woman stood on the side of the overturned semi-trailer, pointing a shotgun at him.

"I know how to use this and I will," she said. The tremble in her hands and the quaver in her voice made Marius doubtful, but far be it from him to make someone else feel more helpless and out of control than they already did. He slowly lifted his hands.

"Are you alone?" the woman with the shotgun demanded. At least she was asking the right questions.

"No," Marius said. "My friend Emile is around here, but I don't know where exactly."

"Should I tie him up?" shotgun woman asked.

"Annie, we're all a bit busy just at the moment," the woman between the pregnant woman's knees said.

"Do we have anything to tie him up with?" Annie asked.

"Figure it out," the other woman snapped as the pregnant woman gave another shriek. "Fuck, I think she's stuck. Navi, I'm gonna have to reach in, so please don't push or you'll break my wrist, okay, sweetie? You're doing great. Just hold off." The woman half lay down, while Navi moaned and whimpered in pain.

"Breathe, honey, breathe," the woman holding Navi's shoulders reminded her.

"Can I help?" Marius asked, stepping forward.

"Hey!" Annie yelled and he stopped, hands back in the air.

"I'm a doctor," he said.

"So am I," the woman between Navi's legs said.

"Oh."

"What kind of doctor?"

"Not an OB," Marius admitted.

"Come here," the doctor said. "Annie, don't shoot him."

Marius walked towards the car. If Annie freaked out and killed him, it would certainly simplify a lot of things, he thought.

But she didn't.

He stopped near Navi's shoulder. "Hi, Navi," he said. "My name's Marius. I'm going help your friend and we're going to help you and your baby, okay?"

"Yep, great," Navi said, then panted through a contraction. "Get her out."

Marius joined the doctor. He had a basic medical training that included a round in obstetrics and gynecology, but it had never been a passionate interest of his, so he waited for the doctor's directions.

"I'm Reggie," she said. "I need you to get me her vitals. I'm worried about blood loss. Got it?"

"Got it."

While Marius checked Navi's vitals, Reggie sat back on her heels and wiped her brow with the back of her wrist.

"Is she stuck?" Marius said softly, after telling Reggie Navi's vitals.

"Yep," Reggie said, and he could see the defeat in her.

There was no way to operate to widen Navi's pelvic opening. They didn't have any tools or any painkillers stronger than aspirin. "She's turned. I can feel where her shoulder's stuck, but I can't reach it to turn her." Reggie held up her hand. "Big Norwegian hands."

Marius held up his own hand, wider and with longer fingers. "I'm no help either, but I might know someone who can be. Emile!" he called. "Come here."

Her name was Asha, which meant hope in Hindi. She had ten tiny perfect fingers and ten tiny perfect toes. Her eyes were brown, and her fuzz of hair was dark. After she was born, while Reggie and Marius tended to Navi, Emile sat cradling Asha, beaming as widely as if she were his own daughter. Annie sat on one side of Emile and the other woman, who Marius learned was Navi's sister Veda, sat on the other side. The three of them chorused soft coos and high-pitched nothings, until Navi was ready to take Asha. She nestled against her mother's bare breast and went immediately to sleep, much to the oh-ing and ah-ing of the adults.

After, Marius and Emile put some of their supplies in to make a dinner. Reggie told them that the women had been heading for Navi and Veda's family lodge somewhere in western Montana.

"As soon as Navi and Asha are fit to travel, we should get going," Veda said and everyone agreed. No one wanted to camp on the highway.

While the women watched over Navi and Asha, and

repacked their luggage, Marius and Emile scouted the area.

It would be possible to unload the hatchback and drive it over the grass and around the multi-car pileup, but no one was suggesting they do that with a brand-new baby and an exhausted postpartum woman.

Emile found a roadside motel they could drive back east to that was free of signs of the Infected. Reggie soon had Navi and Asha installed in the wedding suite, with her in the next room. Annie and Veda stood guard so the others could sleep. Marius told them about New Avalon, explained about the mold, how it deterred and even killed the Infected, and gave them some. He also showed them where Crossroads was on their paper road atlas. It seemed like a good idea not to mark the Morning Star ranch itself. Doug, from Yellowstone, had the right idea: get people close enough that outriders and scouts could pick them up.

The next morning, Reggie announced that Navi needed more time to recover and asked for the others to look for clothes, towels, sheets, really anything that could be made into diapers.

At breakfast Emile hummed softly to himself while waiting for his porridge to finish cooking.

"Why don't you stay here for a few days?" Marius said. Emile looked up, started to speak, but stopped by the sound of Asha's shrill cry.

Instead of arguing, Emile nodded. "Where are you going?"

"Well, we still need to check out Minot," Marius said.

"You shouldn't go by yourself," Emile said.

"I can go with you," Annie said. She stood in the

doorway to the dining room, twisting her hair into a bun. "We can also look for baby clothes and udder balm and pads. Navi will need lots of pads." Annie raised her eyebrows as Emile wriggled uncomfortably at the mention of pads.

Veda came in and sat down, helping herself to a bowl of porridge from the pot. She watched the men carefully while she ate. Annie sat next to her, munching on a cold campfire biscuit.

"You can come if you like," Marius said. "I'm not in the business of telling anyone what to do these days."

"Plus, if Emile stays with us, it gives you a good reason to bring Annie back, alive and unharmed," Veda said.

"There's that," Marius agreed easily. A little hostage-taking made sense with the current state of the world.

Before they left, Marius checked in with Reggie and Navi. Reggie was concerned that Navi was still bleeding more than the doctor was comfortable with. Marius explained about his immunity and that his blood type was the universal donor. Reggie had misgivings about transfusing Navi with untested blood. For her part, Navi was eager for anything that might help her recover faster and the potential to pass immunity to Asha via her colostrum. In the end, Reggie grudgingly agreed that it was Navi's choice. She also seemed more comfortable with sending Annie out with Marius if he was down a pint of blood.

Once on the road, Marius and Annie found a quiet companionship. Annie was neither chatty nor overly anxious. She had been a Girl Scout as a child and had been on a few camping trips as an adult.

It took two days for them to arrive at Minot. Before they even got into the town, Marius knew they were in for disappointment. The boxy government buildings were festooned in bioformations with fleshy membranes covering doors and windows and twisting tubes of veins and nerve bundles roped from place to place.

"Let's try the mall," Annie said, as they sat on their horses. She pointed back the way they had come. "Maybe some diapers or something?"

There was evidence that the Infected had been in the mall. Some of the shops had that last stand look, as if people had retreated there, trying to hide from or fight off the Infected. The bloodstains were a rusty brown and the streaks of gore mostly unidentifiable. Whatever had happened here, it had been over for some time. As Marius and Annie stalked through the mall, they saw evidence of recent scavenging. A pile of skirts that had been on a display table was scattered across the floor, some of the garments overlaying the dried pools of blood.

"What's the diagnosis, doctor?" Annie said, her tone quiet but echoing against the high ceilings and abandoned shops. "I'm thinking there aren't any Infected here now, but there were some before. Maybe that means more stuff got left behind."

"I concur," Marius said, doing his best TV doctor impression. "Let's stick together and get what we can in the next hour or so. Don't want to be here after dark." He couldn't rationally explain it, but the whole place gave him the sense of being watched, as if the ghosts of shoppers past still roamed halls and loitered in the food courts, arcades, and movie theater.

"No." Annie shuddered as if she shared his feelings.

There were also footprints in the soil from an overturned potted palm. Marius pointed them out to Annie, who started to follow them.

"That's far enough," said a man's voice.

Marius stopped and looked up. Three men stood along the railing on the second floor. Two had rifles pointed at him and Annie. The third was clearly their leader. He was an older man with a salt and pepper beard that fell to nearly his stomach. Each man wore a small badge with a pair of white birds embroidered on it.

Hands tied in front, sacks over their heads, but at least they were together and on their own horses. A little light filtered through the loose weave of the pillowcase over Marius's head. He focused on it, fought against the panicky feeling that kept insisting he throw himself off Chaldene and make a run for it. He squeezed his fists, pressing each nail deeply into his palm while he counted to five, then moving on to the next digit as a means of keeping his brain focused and busy.

The horses stopped. He could hear the rustle and murmur of a crowd around them. Someone took his arm and guided him off Chaldene, then walked him into a building. Their footsteps on the hard wood flooring echoed around the space, giving Marius the impression of a big room. He was seated on a bench and soon felt someone sitting next to him.

When the pillowcase was removed, Marius saw he was in a church. It was the kind that had a stage, probably for Christmas and Easter pageants. The bearded man stood at a lectern on the stage. A thick book was spread open before him as he surveyed the gathering. Marius turned to look around. He and Annie were seated in the front row of pews. Next to them was one of the men from the mall and behind them sat the other. There were no weapons that he could see, but it seemed unlikely they would be totally disarmed. They hadn't searched him or Annie, that he knew of, so he still had his small camp knife in a sheath at the small of his back. That did him exactly no good with his hands tied in front of him.

The first two rows were filled with men. They all had a similar look to the bearded man. Even the teenagers were trying to sport facial hair. Behind the men and older boys sat the women and children. All the women had long hair done up in buns or braids and covered with loose scarves or caps.

Marius's gaze met Annie's and she had the same 'what kind of cult is this?' look on her face as he must have on his.

"Brethren," the man on the stage said, and what little movement and sound there had been in the church stopped. "The Lord has seen fit to bless our community with two new members. Let us pray and give thanks." He led the congregation through a prayer and then three hymns, which everyone seemed to know by heart as there were no hymnals that Marius could see.

After the service, the women and children got up and left wordlessly. Marius and Annie exchanged another worried look.

"I'm Pastor Jerry Heyes." The bearded man came to stand in front of them. "We are the Remnant." He took out a small pocketknife and cut Marius's bonds then turned the knife, handle first, and offered it to him. "As a general rule, we don't put our hands on another man's wife."

"I'm not his wife," Annie said.

"Is she your sister?" Jerry didn't even look at her.

Marius cut Annie free. Whatever else was going on in this place, being tied up wouldn't make it better. He started to nod, but Annie shook her head.

"I'm not his anything," she said. "We're just traveling together."

"Frank, it'll be best to bunk her in with the Tillis sisters," Jerry said to one of the men from the mall. Up close, Marius could see the other man was a younger version of Jerry, his beard brown, but otherwise nearly identical.

"You can't keep us prisoners here," Annie snapped.

"Your ..." Jerry paused, still not acknowledging Annie's presence. "Acquaintance must have been very sheltered. Have you seen many of the Damned on your travels?"

"We call them the Infected," Marius said. "Yes, we've seen some. We're always happy to share information with uninfected people. We're a little startled to find anyone out here. I had thought most people evacuated."

"The government did try to round us up and put us in their camps, but we knew that during the time of tribulation, being around so many of the unredeemed would be dangerous." Jerry turned and held out a hand to usher Marius down the aisle and out the door. When Annie started to go with him, Frank stepped in the way and blocked her, letting her follow a few paces behind once Marius and Jerry started walking.

From the look of the community surrounding the church, Marius guessed they were still in or near Minot. The houses had the same prefab look as some of the neighborhoods he and Annie had passed through on their way to the Air Force base. Lines for hanging laundry stretched between some buildings. Down the street, in a cul-de-sac, three woman and several older teen girls were leading a group of children in reciting Bible verses.

"Of course, we don't have women teaching in church or instructing the older boys," Jerry said, noting Marius's curious look. "But helping to bring up children to follow the right path is something some of them are called to do, even outside the home. And it's good for the younger ones to practice for when they have their own children."

Marius fought to keep from rolling his eyes. For whatever reason, Jerry assumed that he could grab people off the street and simply add them to his flock, as if anyone would be overjoyed at the prospect of joining a society with the sensibilities of the Puritanical era.

He hoped, for her sake, that Annie could keep her temper in check long enough for them to escape. He'd never imagined seeing a witch burning, but he felt with absolute certainty that these people would delight in one.

Marius had been allotted a house near the mouth of the cul-de-sac. He didn't know where his gear was, where the horses were, or where Annie was. With the Tillis sisters, wherever that was.

Jerry escorted him to the house, said a prayer to bless the house and asked that God quicken Marius's loins to seed many healthy children who would be pleasing in the sight of the Lord.

"Since you're not married yet," Jerry said, standing in the doorway as Marius stood in the empty space that was probably supposed to be a living room. "I'll talk to the elders and once you've been here long enough to earn your place, we'll get you fixed up. Shouldn't be too long. You seem whole and healthy enough to do an honest day's work."

"How long —" Marius started to ask how long until they would let him go out alone, but that seemed too obvious.

"Shouldn't be that long. Not like Jacob trying to get a wife or anything." Jerry patted Marius's shoulder. "You've come to one of the only good places left. You'll see after a few days. I'll have some food and clothes brought over." He looked around as if noticing the house was empty apart from the built-in and likely useless appliances. "And a cot."

A boy arrived shortly, carrying a fold-up cot over one shoulder and sack with other supplies in it. He introduced himself as Seth. After he helped Marius set up the cot in the empty bedroom, he offered to stock the kitchen.

"Thanks, but I can manage," Marius said. Seth fidgeted with his patchy beard, loitering in the doorway between the kitchen and living room. "Here." Marius handed him a wad of clothes to sort and fold. The boy clearly had something on his mind and Marius needed any potential ally he could find.

After a few minutes of aimless folding and smoothing, Seth asked, "So's it true you're a doctor? Frank was telling us about how they found you."

"Yes." Marius watched the boy out of the corner of his eye, waiting for whatever he was working up to.

"Would you." Seth stopped folding and glanced around, lowered his voice. "Would you take a look at my sister's baby? We've been doing everything: praying, anointing with holy oils, some fasting, but ..."

"Was the baby premature?" Marius asked.

"I don't know about things like that." Seth lifted a bony shoulder. "They get born when they're ready, don't they?"

"Not always," Marius said. "A lot of times, especially when the mother's stressed, like not getting enough to eat or working too hard or worrying about Infected attacking, the baby might come early. Then they need extra help."

Seth shoved his hands deep into his pockets and stared at the floor between his boots. Marius waited, trying to figure out what was going on in this place. He'd heard of various religious sects that rejected modern medicine, believing that whether a patient recovered or died was up to divine will and it was a sin to interfere.

"The baby's really small," Seth said.

"Why don't you show me?" Marius said. "If anyone asks, tell them I asked for a tour of the community." It would give him a chance to try to find Annie and maybe even their horses. Marius had no intention of staying with the Remnant no matter how soon they might find him a bride.

The golden light of sunset gilded the community. From the streets, as they walked, it might as well have been Mayberry or Pleasantville or any other 1950's fantasy of white suburban utopia. Women, all dressed in long flowing skirts and modest blouses, called children and men in for supper. The children, who had been playing together in several clusters, broke apart and raced home. The men, all dressed in earth toned clothes with their badges displayed on their breast pockets, stopped whatever chore they were doing and walked home, waving and calling to each other as they went.

People watched Marius and Seth, but no one tried to stop them. Either they didn't believe anyone would be so foolish as to try to leave the community alone, or they had perimeter guards. Or both.

"In here," Seth opened a door to one of the smaller houses a few blocks from the cul-de-sac. Marius stepped inside, blinking against the gloom. All the windows were closed, the curtains drawn. The room smelled vaguely of sickness and sweat and cloyingly sweet essential oils. The scent was a muddle of lavender, orange, mint, eucalyptus, and something woody-smokey like frankincense. The walls were hung with religious paintings and symbols, some very ornate and others woven from twigs or bits of half-spun yarn.

A cradle stood in the middle of the room and beside it a chair. In the cradle, a tiny baby, so small that at first glance, Marius mistook it for a doll. He went to the cradle and put a hand on the baby's cheek. Unlike baby Asha, this one didn't turn her head or start instinctively sucking. He lifted the thin blanket that covered the infant. Her limbs were so thin. She had a fuzz of dusky hair over her shoulders and down her back. Her stomach looked swollen. He delicately touched it, feeling for masses or bubbles.

"What are you doing?" A woman's voice hissed. Marius looked up, startled. For a moment, his brain had been completely engaged, trying to figure out what was wrong with the baby.

A young woman, barely older than Seth, stood with her back to the door, hands behind her as if to keep it shut.

"Ida, I asked him to come and look at the baby," Seth said. "He's a doctor. Maybe he can help."

He couldn't. Whatever was wrong with the baby, likely something stemming from an underdeveloped digestive tract, needed a hospital. The baby needed scans, blood tests, probably a surgery, maybe more than one. Things that might as well not exist any longer.

"We're supposed to leave her in God's care," Ida said, not looking at the cradle. "He has a plan. All things work together for His glory."

"Ida, I'm sorry," Marius said. She had to know already, because she was nodding as he spoke, but still he had to say it out loud, as if it was the only way to release them all from the terrible in-between place where the baby was forever dying but never dead.

"I'm sorry, but I can't help your daughter. She needs a hospital and there aren't any."

"See?" Ida said, her word so harsh that Seth actually ducked away. "This is what happens when you question God's plan. You bring a doctor in here, you get your hopes up for nothing. Now it's worse." Tears started and she turned away, shrugging off Seth's tentative hand on her shoulder. "There's nothing can be done for her. I'm her mother and I can't do anything for her."

Seth looked at Marius, his eyes pleading.

"You can do something for her," Marius said, forcing the words past the lump in his throat. "You can hold her close, talk to her, tell her you love her so she's not alone in the dark."

Ida shuffled to the cradle, moving slowly and woodenly. She stared at her hands gripping the sides of the cradle and then reached out a finger to touch the baby's tiny fist. The baby wrapped her fingers around her mother's and gave a strangled little cough.

Ida touched the top of her daughter's head and whispered something too low for Marius to hear. She gently spun her finger, pulled away from the baby's grasp, and turned her back to the cradle.

"The Lord is testing us. If we keep our faith strong, we'll be rewarded," she said. "In this life or the next."

She pushed past Marius and Seth and out the door, which banged shut.

"Ida," Seth said and hurried after her.

Marius went to the cradle, feeling a million years old. He could do nothing for the baby except be with her, see her, know that she had been, and carry her memory when she was gone.

He wrapped the blanket around her, noting her cool skin temperature even in the overly warm room. As he picked her up, he could feel the hitch and rattle as her tiny lungs fought for air, the flutter and pause of her struggling heart.

He put his head down, lifting the baby so she was cradled to his chest, sheltered by his face.

"I'm so sorry, little one," he whispered. "No matter what happens, I promise, you won't be alone." There was nothing else he could do for her. He settled back into the chair and he told her about the world, about the sky and the clouds, about how the air was made up of different gas molecules and how molecules were made up of atoms. He told her about auroras, energy from the sun dancing across the Earth's magnetic shielding. He told her about music and art, admitted he didn't really know how to appreciate either properly, but added that there were people who did. There were people who were transported beyond themselves by poems or paintings, by songs, and by stories.

When the baby had longer and longer pauses between each little breath, he stood up and walked with her, rocking her back and forth. He told her about the oceans and tides, about the abyssal trenches more alien to humans than the Moon.

"Marius." Annie stood in the open door. Behind her were their horses, complete with all their tack and even a few bundles of supplies he didn't recognize. Seth waited next to Annie.

"Ida is keeping Jerry busy, and I'm supposed to be chaperoning Annie," Seth said. "She's to be back at the Tillis house by dark." He glanced at the sky. The last of the sunlight was gone. Dusk claimed the land. The first few stars took their places. "It won't be long before they come looking, so you should go."

"Will you stay with her?" Marius couldn't bear the idea of the baby dying alone.

"I can't," Seth said. "I have to trust and believe."

"I don't," Marius said. "And I won't leave her. She doesn't have long now."

"Take her with you," Seth said. He stared back at the Remnant community, his throat bobbing, eyes blinking away tears.

"You should say goodbye to her," Marius said. He held the baby out to Seth, who looked surprised, but then took his niece while Marius mounted Chaldene. Seth kissed the crown of the baby's head and passed her up to Marius, who tied his jacket around himself to make a sling over his chest. He tucked the baby in, steadying her with one hand as they rode out of the Remnant community.

It wasn't long and when the time came, Marius and Annie dismounted. Annie led the horses away a little distance and then came back. They sat, shoulder to shoulder, stroking the baby, and whispering what comforting phrases they could think of.

When she finally stopped breathing, neither moved.

They sat together until both felt as cold as the baby had grown.

In the morning, they buried her under a willow tree by a stream.

Chapter 14 - Miranda

On the Road, Kentucky, USA — Autumn, Year 2

The Infected were moving in herds. No. Herd was the wrong word. Herd was what a bunch of cattle or horses was called. Nice animals that were generally useful and rarely tried to kill people.

The Infected were moving in packs.

Miranda and Romi saw the first pack only from a distance as they left the house in the hippie commune. To Miranda's sense, they seemed like a swarm. Maybe that was a better word than pack. She settled on swarm. They gathered by some signal that nothing else noticed and headed to some destination that nothing else knew about. Even Miranda couldn't get a clear idea from the swarm because none of the individual Infected seemed to know for sure, but they all moved together.

"They're like those big flocks of birds that all swoop around together," Miranda said, shading her eyes as she looked west, watching the swarm of Infected disappear into the sunset.

"You're sure they won't bother us?" Romi set up their tent and hung out some laundry to dry overnight.

"Not from over there." Miranda waved at the faint low cloud of dust that marked the swarm's passage.

"Good. Come eat," Romi said. She and Miranda ate the last of the bread they baked in a pizza place's brick oven with some fried fish Romi caught and three packets of horseradish sauce Miranda found in an Arby's lobby.

That night, they crawled into their tent, leaving the sides open to catch what breeze they could.

Miranda was half asleep when Romi said, "What did you want to be when you were a kid?"

"A race car driver," Miranda said without hesitation. "When I got older, a TV newscaster."

"Huh," Romi said. Miranda waited for more questions. She was experienced at giving interviews. She'd done her first at ten. But Romi didn't say anything else that night.

Over the next few days, Romi quizzed Miranda about all sorts of odd topics. Did she prefer leggings or tights? What was her favorite color and why? How many pets had she had? What were their names? Which did she like the best and why? Favorite perfume? Least favorite scent? Most over-rated celebrity pre-collapse of civilization as they knew it? Favorite and least favorite subjects in school? First crush? First heartbreak?

By the time that question came up, they were in southern Indiana, only a few days from Kentucky. They had seen two more swarms, one heading northwest and the other west. Thanks to the Infected's warnings, they had avoided three groups of the non-Infected. Both women agreed that they were probably better off on their own.

It was hard to notice if the seasons were changing as they traveled south and east. The heat and humidity seemed about the same. Miranda kept track of daylight, checking sunset and sunrise times against a watch she picked up. With the satellites down and no way to charge phones or other wearable tech, she was back to an analog watch that could be wound. How long until that was too high tech for the world, she wondered.

"So," Romi sat cross-legged, braiding her hair into a complicated rope. "Heartbreak. Who was it?"

"You assume I've had my heart broken." Miranda stretched out, wriggling her toes to air them out. Her socks were drying on one of the tent's grounding lines. Her boots sagged with their laces out, the tongues lolling, and the insoles covered in a light scattering of freshly plucked pine needles in an effort to freshen them up a little.

"It has been," Romi said. "Otherwise, you would just say so or you'd make up something, like some embarrassing breakup and think that was the worst thing ever."

"Or maybe I've just had a lot of shitty things happen to me. We all have." Miranda studied her toes. Oh, her queendom for a pedicure.

"If you don't want to tell me, I'll respect that," Romi said.

"There's nothing to tell."

Romi picked a long-stemmed blade of grass and tickled Miranda's nose with the head of it.

"Quit." Miranda caught the grass and took it away. She sat up and put the stem in her mouth, chewing it in an imitation of movie yokels.

"Are you saying quit poking you?" Romi smiled at her. "Or asking questions? I want to get to know you."

"I'll make you a deal," Miranda said. "You get me some nail polish and I'll answer your heartbreak question."

The scent was fresh and easy to follow. With her extra limbs, she was able to move along the steep side of the hill. Some of the limbs weren't useful, and she kept those clamped to her side. She knew that they had been, but now they weren't. There was something wrong deep within her and it was reaching out, causing her to twitch and jerk. It made her hair fall off in clumps and her skin was mottled in dry, itchy patches, and oily ones that hosted pimples and sores.

Her mind, which might once have worried about such things, was focused on the prey. They were a small band, moving cautiously in the dark. She knew the Littles were flanking them and that the other one like her, the other one who used to live in a hive, like her, was waiting at the far end of the shallow gully in case the food turned back before it got to her.

It didn't.

She launched herself, spreading her mantle to catch the air and glide the last few yards from the hill to the head of the tallest one. When she sank her two rows of teeth into its jugular vein, Miranda woke up.

She scrambled out of the tent, half-panicked, half-crazed with the desire to *feed*.

She grabbed handfuls of hair, pulling them tight to her skull, feeling that they were secure, that her head was round and smooth, not lumpy. She wasn't the Infected.

Feed with us.

And she was so very hungry.

"Romi," she croaked. She needed an anchor, something to remind her where she ended. She wasn't part of them, no matter how much their hunger and desire roiled through her.

"Romi?" She pushed open the tent flap and peered in. Even in the near total dark of night, she could see Romi's sleeping bag was flat. Her boots were missing from their spot under the rain screen. Had she needed to go dig a hole?

Miranda squinted around.

Should we find her? We are good at hunting. Warm blood and crunchy bone bursting with sweet marrow.

No, she'll be back soon. Miranda took a few more steps out from the tent, the dewy grass chilling her bare feet. A wind flickered across the trees and whispered through the grasses, sending goose bumps climbing up her arms and legs.

She'll be back soon, Miranda told herself again, straining to hear anything under the gentle sighing of the trees as they swayed together in their night dance.

How much time had passed? Miranda counted slowly. One-Mississippi, two-Mississippi, three-Mississippi ... When she got to one hundred and thirty-something she lost track of how many Mississippis that was.

She left you. If you're alone, you can come to us. We can help you go to your father's hive.

No. She didn't leave me.

Oh. The Infected didn't believe her and they weren't even trying to hide that fact. But she couldn't very well argue. Even if Romi hadn't meant to leave her, she might already be gone for good, taken by marauders or something as silly as slipping and falling.

We found her.

Where? And a moment later, just to be on the safe side: *Don't hurt her.*

We have to hurt her. Viers said to clear this area.

Miranda clenched her fists and pushed her command. *Leave her alone.*

The Infected seemed to fragment, some minds cowering while others bristled angrily. A few submitted to her will, but more ignored her, chorusing: *Viers's orders. Viers's orders. Viers's orders.* It effectively drowned her out.

They didn't want to listen to her? Thought they could ignore her? Ha!

She whirled and retraced her steps to the tent. She lit one of the stubby candles, setting it on a rock outside the tent. She could find her socks and boots without the light but it would take longer. She grabbed her go-bag. John had taught her that when she'd been a kid.

It took nearly a half hour for her to pick her way to where she felt the strongest concentration of Infected in the near area. It turned out to be a strip mall, the kind of place that had probably already closed down long before the first outbreak nearly two years ago at Miranda's school.

In the light of the half moon, she could see the irregular shapes of the Infected, mostly Littles, but a few larger shapes. They used to be big dogs, cows, horses, even people. Here and there were exotic animals. HHV had gotten into zoos and private animal parks. The Infected moved with a slow deliberation that looked almost lazy.

Except for a cluster near the base of a billboard.

Romi sat on the walkway, leaning back on her elbows, her feet dangling over the edge. As Miranda watched, the other woman threw something. A couple of Littles ran after it, like dogs playing fetch. They snarled and grappled over whatever she had thrown, then separated.

It's nothing.

Miranda could sense their frustration and disappointment. They wanted to eat the warm body up in the air, but they couldn't figure out how to get to her.

Carefully, Miranda began filtering that sensation — the warm body for eating sensation — to the Infected near the edge of the group at the base of the billboard. She directed their attention away, down the street, around the corner, somewhere inside the strip mall. She worked her way inward and as the ones closer to the center caught her idea, they reached out to their fellows, who agreed, *Yes, we feel it too.*

Soon the Infected peeled off to lope away into the night in search of someone who wasn't there.

As soon as the last one turned the corner around a building, Miranda rushed to the base of the billboard.

"Romi!" She waved her red LED click light. "Hurry. I

can't keep them distracted for long."

Romi shimmied off the billboard's walkway and hung at the full length of her arms. It would still be a long drop, but she let go, hit, bounced, and rolled. She winced and grabbed her ankle.

"Just a sprain," she whispered. "Help me up." Miranda pulled her up.

"C'mon," Miranda said. She pulled Romi's arm around her shoulder and put hers around the other woman's waist, taking some of the weight off her injured leg. Together they hobbled away. It was a long, slow way back to their campsite, but finally, as the first light of morning feathered the sky with pale blue and pink, they arrived.

Miranda heated some water for tea and oatmeal while Romi wrapped and elevated her ankle.

"Okay, what the actual fuck?" Miranda handed Romi her mug and settled down next to her, facing the opposite way so she could look at Romi. She was a little dirtier than usual, with some scrapes and bruises, but otherwise looked like she escaped mostly unharmed.

"You sound like you were worried about me." Romi smiled at her.

"Obviously." Miranda tried to glare, but Romi crossed her eyes and stuck out her tongue like a kid, making her snicker despite herself.

"For real, though," Miranda said, determined to get some good grumping in. "Why did you take off in the middle of the night? Why didn't you wake me up?"

"That would have ruined the surprise," Romi said. She pushed herself up from her elbows, braced on one arm as she held out her upturned and closed hand. "Ta-da." In her palm was a bottle of sparkly teal nail polish.

It took two days for Miranda, with the help of the Infected, to find a car that both ran and had gas. Romi insisted that she would be able to travel soon, but Miranda didn't want to take any chances. Sometimes, when she was out by herself, scouting out different parking lots, she took her shoes off and looked at her teal toes and smiled.

When she found a car, it was only a few hours' drive to Mammoth Cave. Miranda cursed the car's lack of a CD player. What good did it do to have streaming music if it didn't stream? Romi sang snatches of songs she remembered, some in English, some in Hebrew, and one in Russian that she said Eli taught her.

They drove through a little town, more like a village, more like two streets with a general store and a gas station on it. The general store was the kind of place to get essentials for the park, and they stopped to pick up a paper map. The place was mostly covered in bioformations.

"I'll go see if there's anything still good," Miranda said. It was weird knowing she could move through the Infected unmolested. She was probably the only person who could actually travel freely around the country.

Well, not the only one. Marius didn't have to worry about the Infected, either, but he wasn't exactly moving around. Miranda didn't know what her dad had done with the scientist, but she was sure he wouldn't be allowed to run loose. Viers was nothing but compulsively controlling about anything he considered to be his asset. One of the reasons her mom had left him. Not that Miranda blamed Cecilia. She wouldn't have stayed with her father either if she'd been her mother. She did resent that her mom had left her behind, at least she had for years. Now that loss was just one of many and the pain was deep and dull like a sliver, hardly worth worrying about in comparison with the world falling apart around her.

The light was dimly pink inside the general store, filtered through the fleshy membranes covering the windows, walls, floor, and ceiling. Tubes ran across the ceiling, sensory tentacles writhing with information. A few detected and reached down to brush the top of her head and her shoulders. When they reached for her face, she swatted them away, sending out a feeling of annoyance. *Leave me alone.*

Miranda! Her name shivered through the Infected. Was Albert aware of how close she was? Probably. But she didn't want to deal with her father yet. Still didn't know how she would deal with him. Still wasn't sure why she had come except where else would she go? And maybe, deep in some pathetic place in her heart, she wanted to know what had happened to Marius. He'd been a good friend, even if never a lover.

On the counter was pile of rags, stained with old blood. Around the rags, the counter was clean - ish. It was clear of any sign of bioformation. Weird. She started to reach for the rags, but a sensation of terror shot through her. It was so strong and sudden she nearly pissed her shorts.

What is it?

Abomination.

But how?

The Infected could give no clear answer. They were afraid. They wanted her to leave. *Get far, far away. Don't bring it here. Don't touch it. Get away!*

In the end, she took a map of the park and some bug spray and went back to the car. She got into the driver's seat and looked at Romi.

"Are you sure about this?"

"Are you?" Romi's eyes danced across her face, measuring her in some way that made Miranda both excited and a little annoyed. She didn't like to be judged, didn't need to be accountable to anyone.

"I'll be fine," she said. "They don't want to eat me."

"But you'll protect me, right?" Romi said.

Miranda studied her hands on the steering wheel. They were very tan thanks to all the walking she'd done this summer. Her fingernails were short and chipped. They hadn't seen a nail file in months, maybe a year. Her forearms were lean and when she turned her arm, the muscles glided under the skin. She was strong. She wasn't a child anymore, not that softly pretty schoolgirl John and Marius had rescued from Harrow Hall. She was a survivor. She was a killer. Why not use her powers for good, or at least to protect Romi? She'd been able to protect Dawn in the quarry hive.

"I'll protect you," she said, resolving to mean it in a way John and Marius and Torres and her parents never had.

She put the car in Drive and turned onto the access road leading to the visitors' center.

WELCOME TO MAMMOTH CAVES NATIONAL PARK

The parking lot was nearly empty. Abandoned backpacks and luggage huddled near the main building. Miranda could see the Infected hovering inside the stairway leading into the cave system. They were arranged in a ragged line, like old fashioned servants at some fancy British manor estate.

Wordlessly, the women got out of the car and put on their packs. Romi took Miranda's hand and squeezed. Miranda squeezed back. They walked to the entrance.

The cave was cool. At first, the air was filled with the mossy, moldy scent of life, but as they descended the stairs, that fell away. It smelled like nothing until Miranda caught the first whiffs of the warm, moist, biological mess that was the hive's bioformations. They covered nearly every horizontal surface and twisted along the ceilings in thin streamers, knotting up at passage junctions.

Romi clicked on her flashlight and they continued inward. Miranda knew where her father would be. She moved through the cave system, trailing one hand along the wall to make it easier to find her way.

Here.

She stopped in front of a heavy curtain of the bioformation.

"Move," she said. It shivered and parted. She let go of Romi's hand. She needed to do this on her own.

She stalked into Viers office, shaking her head. He actually had a desk, like he was still a CEO. The last time she'd seen him had been in the VA hospital in Portland. Since then, he'd gained a spiderweb of white scars that practically glowed against the dusky grey of his skin.

"Daddy," she said. "I'm home."

Chapter 15 - Torres

New Avalon, Montana, USA – Autumn, Year 2

Torres studied the map on the wall in the Rangers' headquarters in the barn. The Rangers' missions had taken them as far west as Washington state, north into Canada, and east to the Dakotas, assuming Marius and Emile came back alive. She refused to consider any other possibility, even though they were on the outside edge of their three-week estimated date of return.

A few extra days didn't mean disaster. Besides, she needed the time to figure out what she wanted to do about Marius. While he was away, she stayed in his room. There wasn't a lot of bunk space elsewhere and she didn't want the gossip. But she didn't know how things would be between them when he came back.

They had said they loved each other, had made out like teenagers and more. When he was gone, she missed him, spent more time than was reasonable staring east in hopes of seeing him come back. Her body ached for his touch. She wanted to see him, to know he was all right, even if he didn't want to be with her.

It had probably been too much, too soon. He had been through a lot and he'd needed more space. But there she was, assuming that because she was ready for a fully committed relationship, and he was ready for sex, that they were on the same page.

No. She wasn't going to think about it that way. He hadn't used her for sex any more than she'd used him. They'd both wanted it and they'd both enjoyed it.

So, sex wasn't the problem. Maybe they could be friends with benefits. It would be better than the huge, screaming lack of him that bored through her when he was gone.

Admit it, she commanded herself, you want him more than you care about your pride.

But that wasn't strictly true, either. She did have pride. A lot of pride. She didn't want to be with someone who didn't want to be with her. She didn't want pity sex or even friend sex; maybe from someone else, but not from Marius. With him, she didn't think it could ever be just sex. It wouldn't be fair to either of them to lie and say she was fine with it.

"Ah-hem."

Torres looked over her shoulder. John stood in the doorway. He gave her a look with too much understanding and limped to his recliner.

"I've got the Yellowstone mission prepped," she said before he could say anything nice.

"Good." He lowered himself carefully into his chair and picked up one of the wooden pegs he was whittling to help with the fence building efforts. "Who are you sending out?"

"I'm going," Torres said.

"Hmmm," John said. "Who are you taking with you?"

Ranger protocol dictated at least two per mission, sometimes more depending on what might be needed.

Torres re-checked the roster. Dawn and Horace were back from a trading mission to Great Falls. Dawn she trusted, but Horace was still fairly new, having barely survived the trip to New Avalon from Utah. She planned to give Dawn some time off, which would be good for her. And for Bailey. He'd been spending a lot of time out in the radio shack alone and it wasn't good for him.

Nestor and Keith were on perimeter patrol and Seung was recovering from an Infected attack. Even with Marius's attested vaccines, being bitten was still terrifying and usually caused all sorts of immune responses, like high fevers, muscle pain, and fatigue.

Torres was saved from answering by the crackle of John's walkie-talkie announcing that riders were at the gate. Marius, Emile, and four newcomers.

"Duty calls," Torres said. She offered John a hand to help him out of the recliner. For a moment, he frowned then with a sigh of resignation, let her pull him up.

"Duty, is it?" John said after catching his breath. "Are you still mad at him for going out? Sometimes men just need to prove to themselves that they're still strong and capable."

"Are you seriously giving me a 'boys will be boys' speech?"

"No." John pulled on his wide-brimmed sunhat, which made him look like a granny about to enter a gardening contest in the Shrupshires of North Hazelton Glen.

"I am saying that he's been knocked down a lot. He needs a chance to get his feet under him, to test if he can stand on his own."

"That's freaking BS," Torres said. "I've gotten knocked down a bunch and I didn't take the fuck off from the people who cared about me and were trying to freaking help me."

"Oh, right," John said. "I forgot about how you joined the Marines and after that, instead of going home, you signed up to work private security, and then how you went to Iowa by yourself."

"That's different," Torres said. "I was a kid when I joined the Corps. Plus, I didn't have anyone who cared about me waiting back home."

"Are you mad that he left or are you mad that you're the one waiting at home?" John said.

"Both," Torres admitted. "It feels like shit that he didn't want —" She stopped and the unsaid "me" hung in the air between them. "He didn't want to stay and help out here. We need all the help we can get."

John put a hand on her arm and she stopped. They were across the barnyard area, nearly to the back door of the main house. Inside, people hurried around, eager to go to the gate and see the returning Rangers and their new recruits.

"It's not about you," John said. "You are enough." He smiled. "You're plenty enough for anyone, Torres."

She fake scowled at his backhanded compliment. "I know it's not about me, but that's kind of worse. I want to help him, but he doesn't even want me around."

"One of the things we learned about was Maslow's hierarchy of needs. Right now, Marius needs to meet his 'Love and Social Belonging' needs. He's been cut off not just from his friends and family, but from the entire rest of humanity. No wonder he's depressed."

"What do you mean? And when did you learn about all that psychological stuff?" Torres asked. Her mind was whirling. Was Marius depressed? He seemed cheerful and determined, especially when it came to leaving her … okay, cheap shot. Especially when it came to going out on a mission for the Rangers.

"We studied a lot of psychology at West Point," John said. "Yes, I think Marius is depressed. Considering what he's been through, I'd be surprised if he wasn't. He feels like he's not a part of our community, so he's going out on missions to try to earn a place for himself."

"That's ridiculous! We wouldn't even be here, probably wouldn't be alive, without him."

John scrubbed a hand over his face and shrugged. "Funny thing about mental health issues, not a lot of them go away because they have no rational basis. If feelings were logical, they'd be called thoughts."

Everyone acted like they had never seen a baby before. The way Emile hovered around, Torres would have been willing to believe Asha was his, which was clearly impossible. She had to practically drag him away to give his report and update the map, despite the fact that should have been his first stop after coming in.

It was easy to make sure she and Marius weren't alone together with all the excitement. Torres still didn't know how she wanted to address the rift between them. She wanted to help Marius, but she was also hurting from his abandonment. Was that how Miranda felt? Torres didn't like to think of herself in the category of 'People whose hearts Marius broke'.

While most people played Pass the Baby, Torres took Annie and Veda out to the bunkhouse to find a space for them. She told them about Crossroads, explained they might have more space there.

"Reggie's going to set up in town," Annie said. "I'd like to join the Rangers."

"Great. We always need more," Torres said. "Ursula will be glad to have a human doctor so she can get back to her furry patients. What about you and your sister?"

"I'm not sure," Veda said. "I think for now, Navi wants a safe place to stop moving. We saw the mold rings as we came in."

"Yeah, Rajiv's been experimenting with trying to make the mold hardier so it doesn't dry out in the wind, can survive the frost, and the spores will travel farther." She didn't mention the scientist's frustration at his own limited understanding of Marius's work. As he said, "I'm an immunologist, not a geneticist."

Rajiv also missed Marius, but probably not to the same degree. Or maybe he did. They had been roommates at John's Hopkins and Marius had mentioned male lovers. Rajiv had traveled all the way from Washington D.C. during the height of the collapse to find Marius. Well, he had come to Crossroads to get vaccinated, anyway. Torres gave herself an inward shake. Because she felt hurt and rejected, her mind was creating rivals out of everyone and anything that had ever interested Marius. She was better than that.

Wasn't she?

"Hey there." His voice still caused her heart to stutter and heat to rush through her body.

Torres turned to look at him. Marius stood just outside the doorway of the bunkhouse as if afraid to enter, as if this space wasn't his, hadn't been a part of his childhood, as if he had no claim on it, on the people inside, or on her.

"Hey." She made her voice casual, but not casual enough to avoid the knowing looks and small smiles Annie and Veda exchanged. To them, this moment was lovers sweetly reuniting.

"C'mon," Torres said, slipping past the other women and out as Marius stepped back, giving her space. "Let's get that map updated, Ranger. Annie's thinking of joining up, so you need to set a good example."

They walked in silence to the barn, close enough to touch, but not quite brushing hands.

"There was another baby," Marius said as Torres took out the logbook. She stopped and looked at him. His face was still, his eyes focused on some faraway thing.

"Tell me," she said.

He did, his voice low and flat, a careful recitation of the facts with enough scientific detachment to drown a platoon of elephants. She didn't interrupt him, wrote a description of the Remnant community in the logbook, and added Minot to the map as a potential trading partner with caveats. Their recruiting methods dictated that any Rangers venturing out that way should go in force and well-armed, make it clear they were only there to trade information and resources, not become part of the congregation.

When she ran out of mission-related questions and Marius ran out of mission-related information, they stared at the map together, the silence between them filled with unspoken fears, disappointments, and insecurities.

Wordlessly, Marius reached out, touching her pinky with his. She almost sobbed, but she got a hold of herself. She stroked her finger along his, a tiny echo of the way at night he would touch her foot with his and she would rub his leg with hers. A wordless call and response of "Are you there? I want you." "Yes, I'm here. I want you, too."

"Lourdes, I'm sorry," he said, still studying the map as if he meant to memorize it.

"I'm sorry, too," she said. She wasn't sure what she was apologizing for exactly; for not noticing that he was struggling, for not understanding, for resenting his leaving, for needing him because she was struggling, too.

"I'm not sorry I went," he clarified, and she smiled a little. Marius couldn't abide imprecision. "I'm sorry because I know it hurt you. I never want to hurt you. I — " He stopped and took her hand, still not looking at her.

"I know." She squeezed his hand.

The door burst open and Elfy skipped in. "Hi, Marius." She waved and he waved back.

"Aunty Nette wants you to come to the house," the girl announced before skipping away.

"You you or you me?" Torres asked.

"Damn English pronouns," Marius said, with a ghost

of his former ornery grin. "We should both go."

They crossed the barn yard, hand in hand. Torres still felt raw, but at least whatever was hurt between them had been cleaned and bandaged. It would heal in time if they could ever find the time to just be together.

"We're pregnant," Percy announced.

The Tenartier family, which now included John, Torres, Elfy, Soraya, Wahida, Mirzha, and Washington was gathered around the big, well-loved kitchen table. Percy sat, as was her habit, on a stool, but this time she didn't have her usual notebook or whiteboard to keep everything organized. John stood next to her, a huge smile on his face.

Annette gave a little shriek and clapped her hands to her mouth. She burst into tears and Percy hurried to hug her. Philippe shook John's hand and said, "Good work."

"Hey," said Percy, peeking over her mother's shoulder. "It's not like he did that on his own."

"Well, good work to you, too," Philippe said, a blush spreading up his neck and over his cheeks.

"We agreed to wait to tell everyone until things were a little further along," Percy said. "But someone," she poked John, "told Emile to have Norma make two cradles. Some head of security this one." John put an arm around Percy's shoulders, not the least chagrined.

"Oh, this is such good news," Annette said with a sniff. She wiped her eyes as she looked around the room. Her gaze settled on Marius and Torres, who stood together at the edge of the gathering. "Maybe more good news soon?"

"No," Torres said, her voice pitched louder than she intended. Everyone turned to look at her, their expectations like a physical presence pushing her down, hemming her, forcing her into a box where motherhood was not only inexorable, but highly desirable.

"I don't want kids," Torres said. "Not everyone wants kids." She didn't point out that given the current state of the world, having kids seemed like, if not the worst idea, than a close second.

She and Marius had never talked about having kids. Her long-term birth control had been working fine so far. But what if he wanted children? His immunity might be inheritable. It would make sense he might want to pass that on to his own offspring.

"I'm sorry," Annette said. "I shouldn't have assumed." She glanced at Marius and Torres's joined hands. Torres started to pull away, but Marius tightened his hold, not squeezing, but enough to make it clear that he was holding onto her.

"Thanks for your apology, Mom," he said.

"You don't want kids?" Elfy stared at her aunt from across the table, her lower lip quivering.

"Elfy, I don't mean you," Torres let go of Marius's hand to hurry around the table, but Elfy jumped up and dodged out of the kitchen through the mudroom, slamming the door behind her.

"Excuse me." Torres wedged her way between John, Percy, and the kitchen sink. "Congratulations, you two. Seriously. You're freaking brave as all hell." She made her escape into the barn yard and looked around for any sign of a distraught six-year-old.

No Elfy in the half-finished schoolhouse. No Elfy in the barn or the bunkhouse. She was about to get both very worried and very angry when she spied a pair of small feet dangling down from the maple that stood in the grassy circle in the middle of the gravel turnaround in front of the house.

Torres pushed past the wide, purplish leaves, trying not to think how much like the color of Infected blood they were, and looked up. The sun dappled down and inside the shelter of the leaves the air was cool and still.

"Elfy, I'm sorry," she said.

"Go away."

"It's not you," Torres said. "I just never expected to have kids."

"I don't care if you don't want me," Elfy said. "I can live with Wahida and her mama and she likes kids."

Torres didn't think pointing out that Elfy already lived with Soraya most of the time would help calm the girl. She leaned on the lower branches and reached up to gently tug at Elfy's foot. Elfy kicked at her and she let go.

"I don't like most kids, that's true," Torres said. "But I do like you, mi sobrina favorita. I couldn't ask for a better kid."

"I'm not your kid," Elfy said, her voice muffled as she buried her face in her arms.

"I know, Elfreda, but we're all we've got left." Torres had been wondering when the subject of her missing and likely dead sister, Cynthia, would come up. After the first few days, when they had been on the run from the outbreak in Los Angeles, Elfy hadn't mentioned Cynty again. She acted as if she was on a very long vacation with her Tia Lourdie and at the end, she would return home to her mamá and her abuela.

"My mamá wanted kids," Elfy said into the crook of her elbow.

"Your mamá was lucky to have you and I'm lucky to get to be your tia," Torres said.

"Did my mamá stay in Los Angeles so she could have other kids instead of me?"

"Elfy!" Torres was so shocked she pushed herself up in the branches, keeping close to the trunk, but scrambling up to the level where her niece huddled. She wrapped her arms awkwardly around Elfy.

"No, no, kiddo. Your mamá didn't stay in LA because she wanted to. She was sick and she had to stay in the hospital. Abuela stayed with her to take care of her. You and me, we take care of each other."

"But you don't want kids," Elfy said, but she relaxed against Torres.

"Sometimes things that we didn't think we wanted turn out to be really great, like you," Torres said.

"So, maybe you'll have some other kids?" Elfy snuggled.

"No. Not a chance," Torres said. "Nunca."

The Yellowstone mission was a good excuse for a lot of things. It gave Torres and Marius cover to leave the ranch, which both of them appreciated for different reasons. It also gave them about a week or two of time alone together. Torres couldn't help but feel that this was some sort of final test — either they would cleave together or they would cleave apart. She liked the ambivalence of the word; it fit the way she felt about her and Marius's relationship.

She suspected that Marius's family had tried to convince him to stay. He'd only just returned. He should rest. Rajiv and the other scientists could really use his help. So, they delayed leaving by three days while Marius worked in the mold sheds, finalizing a waterproof sheath for the spores to be added to a strain of mold used in swampy areas. The idea was that the spores would be able to travel farther, protected in a thin film until they landed somewhere they could dry out, at which point the film would crack open and the mold would take root.

Marius explained this as they packed their gear, collected their horses, and rode down the gravel drive. In addition to the new, aquatic mold, he brought along three types of mold samples to share with the Yellowstone community: the base strain, one that was resistant to drought, and one resistant to cold.

They swung east for the first two days so Marius could deploy the aquatic mold in the Yellowstone River.

"Ideally, some will make it as far as the Missouri, maybe even the Mississippi," he said, as they stood on the riverbank, watching the squishy looking mats of yellowish-green slime drift away on the lazy late summer current. "If this works, we won't have to travel all over the country passing out mold to everyone we meet. It'll be in the water and where it washes up, it can start new colonies."

"Have we considered that a world covered in mold might not be that great, either?" Torres shaded her eyes, turning slowly to survey the prairie that stretched out as far as she could see except for the mountains in the west.

"A little," Marius said. "But one of the things we humans are pretty good at is mold control. Plus, the mold isn't actively hostile to us as a species." He bent to carefully wipe a strand of mold off his fingers into the water. "Mostly, it's just yucky." He smiled up at her and she appreciated the effort he was making. His eyes were still haunted and distant, but he was trying. She wished she could be certain that would be enough, wished she could accept whatever he could offer instead of wanting, needing more.

They weren't even having sex, although that was probably smart while they were out in potentially hostile territory. Three days in and they had seen only a few Infected off to the east, well outside of New Avalon territory. Still, it was smart to stay focused.

On the first night, Marius had said he was very tired and went into his tent. Torres's dignity kept her from following, from trying to weasel or bargain for something he was clearly not interested in. She told herself it wasn't about her. If John was right and Marius was depressed, he probably really didn't have the energy or the desire for sex. It's not me, it's him, she told herself, sitting in her tent, watching the stars fighting with the clouds for their place in the night sky.

As the days passed, they fell into a quiet routine. Torres had never known Marius to not be bubbling over with random scientific knowledge. She had never been a huge talker, believing that you learned more with your ears open and your mouth shut. Miranda was the social butterfly of their group. But it had never seemed like a challenge to coax Marius into a conversation before. It was like she was riding next to his ghost, as if his body was a husk, but the spirit that had been Marius was missing.

On the fourth day they came to a canyon with a series of spectacular waterfalls. After consulting the map and her navigating tools, Torres announced that this was most likely Seven Mile Hole. They followed the river west where it would curve south into Yellowstone Lake.

Torres saw the rider first. He was on a ridge ahead of them and when she told Marius to look, the rider raised a hand. He kneed his horse, who ambled toward them. Torres maneuvered Ganymede out ahead of Marius and he moved Chaldene off to the side. No point in clustering together to make things easier for potential ambushers.

The rider stopped a few paces away and Marius stopped behind Torres, covering her back and watching the hills around them, while she focused on the rider. He was a middle-aged white man wearing a baseball cap, a sports jersey, and jeans. A bow was slung over the horse's withers with the quiver on the man's back.

"Hi there," he said. "Where you folks coming from? We had some reports about a pair coming in from the north."

"That was probably us," Torres said. "We're from New Avalon. It's up in Montana. We met one of your long-range scouts a while back — Doug — and he said we should pay you a visit."

"I'm Layton," the rider said. "We're always looking to add healthy people to the community,"

"We've got our own place," Torres said, the specter of the Remnant community looming large in her mind. "We're open to establishing communications and some trade. Not looking to move in here."

"Sounds good to me," Layton said. "Follow me, folks."

Chapter 16 - Miranda

Mammoth Cave, KY, USA – Autumn, Year 2

Miranda didn't need her father to tell her there was a problem in the Mammoth Cave hive. She could feel the instability throughout the network of bioformations. After a short meeting, Albert had shooed her and Romi out like they were little kids. "Go exploring. Find some rooms you like. The cave is yours. Let me know if you need anything. Carmine's around here somewhere. You can let him know, too."

Romi's brow furrowed as she looked first at Albert, then at Miranda, who gave her head a little shake. Not now. We'll talk later. Romi ducked her chin in a quick Got it gesture.

"Okay. Will do." Miranda stood, giving her father the chance to call her back, but he didn't. His eyes were focused on some middle distance, his communication tentacles entangled in the numerous ones that hung from the ceiling or reached out from the wall behind his chair.

Miranda led the way out. She didn't need to know the cave layout; the Infected network was present and so easy to access it was like having a video game mini map in the back of her brain. Romi took her hand and for a second Miranda thought the other woman needed her guidance. But no, Romi pulled her into an alcove.

"What is going on here?" Romi demanded, wrinkling her nose at the bioformations that covered the walls from rocky floor to rocky ceiling.

"I don't know, but it's messed up." Miranda sorted through the network, looking for Marius. Wherever he was, the Infected would know to keep a careful distance from his blood. If he was still alive. She hadn't even considered that they might have killed him, but the longer she searched through the hive without finding him, the more likely that seemed.

"Miranda?" Romi patted her arm, bringing her back from the flood of sensations and information whirling through the hive's network.

"He's not here," she said.

"Who?"

"Marius."

"Didn't the Infected take him from Great Falls? Where else would they have gone with him?" Romi asked the questions that Miranda was thinking.

"They must have brought him here," she said. She understood the hierarchy of the hives. Just like John and Torres and the rest of the security types, the Infected had a chain of command. The Infected reported to the networks, which were controlled by the Enlightened in their hives. Each hive had at least one Enlightened, sometimes more. The hives all sent information and resources to this hive, to her father, the first of the Enlightened.

"But he's gone?" Romi looked around as if for a place to set her pack. There wasn't a lot of clean space in the narrow passage they stood in. She settled for readjusting the straps instead. "Should we go ask your father what happened?" She didn't look eager to return to Viers's office, which Miranda couldn't help thinking of as his lair.

"Nah," she said. "I have a better idea."

It was easy for her to find a path through the tunnels and rooms. She avoided the noninfected humans. Too many weird questions from them. Plus, she didn't want to have to explain to Romi why those kids, and most of them were still kids, were there and what would probably happen to them.

Miranda stopped outside a hanging curtain of biofilm. She put her hand on it and told it to retract. It lifted away as easily as if she was brushing hair out of her own face. Inside was a very strange laboratory. She recognized a lot of the equipment from the Chrysalis labs and later the one Marius worked in at the UCLA campus. But also, there were things she could only describe as 'organic'.

Carmine was sitting in a folding chair, his feet up on a table. He was reading a magazine. The cover featured a young woman in a bikini and beach wrap holding out a green smoothie to a muscley man as he flexed for the camera. On The Hunt: Get the Girl of Your Dreams TODAY! was one of the articles listed on the cover.

Carmine dropped the magazine and stumbled to his feet, knocking the chair into the wall behind him.

"Miranda!"

"Hi Carmine," she said, managing to keep the condescending smirk off her face as she strolled between the rows of tables.

"Who's your friend?" He leered at Romi.

"Where's Marius?" Miranda stepped in front of him. She was used to his behavior. Back at Chrysalis, even though she'd been underage, he'd always checked her out and usually not very subtly.

"That fucker," Carmine rubbed his hands over his face and tugged at his hair. Judging from the weird clumps, he must do that a lot, Miranda thought. "It's kind of a long story. Can I get you ladies anything to drink? We've got some booze."

"It's not even noon," Miranda said.

Carmine shrugged. "Like I know what time it is. Here. Sit." He picked up his chair and offered it to Romi.

After Carmine finished telling them about keeping Marius in the tube of goo, how it failed, and he had to be removed, and how Viers had given him a chance to help stabilize the Enlightened, he wrapped up with, "So, he took the fuck off down the river. We sent some scouts after him, but there was a lot of his blood in the water, so they couldn't track him directly. By the time they found his trail again, he was gone. Probably got in a car and vamoosed."

Miranda and Romi exchanged glances.

"Anyway, I can show you girls where to drop your bags," Carmine started to stand, but Miranda held up a hand in a Stop gesture.

"We're not gonna stay here," she said. "We'll find a place in that little town down the road."

"What does your dad think about that?" Carmine asked.

"My dad lost any rights to boss me around when he left me in Portland," Miranda said. "You remember that, Carmine. You were there."

"I didn't know he was going to leave you," Carmine said, hands up with palms out.

"Really?" Miranda stood up and lifted her hands, letting the tentacles and tendrils from the ceiling drop and wind around her head and shoulders. She pinned Carmine with a hard stare. "It was a small helicopter. There was only room for my dad and one more. I don't remember you offering to give up your seat." Around her the tentacles lifted, moving in wavering, undulating patterns as they turned their attention toward Carmine.

He backed up, knocking his chair over again, and fumbling to right it.

"Miranda, you can't ..." His hands clenched around the chair, holding it up as if he were a lion tamer and she the lioness.

"Can't I?" She leaned forward and the tentacles shot out, catching Carmine before he could make a sound.

"I don't like what you did to Carmine," Albert said.

"I don't like a lot of things you've done," Miranda said.

"Why did you come here if all you wanted to do was

make things more difficult for me?" Her father rocked back on his tentacles, observing her from his one remaining good eye.

"Believe it or not, Daddy, not everything is actually about you," Miranda said. "Besides, Carmine will be fine in a few days. Considering how much he's managed to royally screw things up, it's the least he deserves, don't you think?"

"Meaning what?" Albert's communication tentacles started to reach back to touch the biofilm behind him even as he kept his gaze on Miranda.

"Meaning letting Marius go," Miranda said. Secretly, she was glad Marius had escaped if only because it caused problems for her father and his lackey. Also, she still cared about Marius and John, maybe even about Torres and the rest of the people in New Avalon. She wasn't a monster.

"Why did you come?" Albert leaned forward, for once paying more attention to his daughter than to his work.

"Why did you want me here?" Miranda countered.

"Not to play childish guessing games," Albert said.

"Did you feel bad about leaving me in Portland? Because I sure did," Miranda said. "I could have been killed."

"I knew you were in no danger from the Infected. At the time, I had considerable control over the entire network. Even when you refused to communicate with us, we weren't threatening you. We would never hurt you."

"The Infected aren't the only ones out there capable of hurting people," Miranda said.

"I did what I could to protect you," Albert said. "Part

of protecting you was making sure someone was here to control the network. Do you know what would happen if there were no Enlightened to keep the Infected in line? If there was no one like me, with a clear vision to make sure all of the Enlightened were working together towards the same goal? Chaos. The Infected would rampage, killing and eating. They wouldn't manage their resources. They wouldn't set up hives to nurture the newly formed as they metamorphosize. They would all be dead of starvation sooner rather than later."

"And all the Infected dying off is bad how?" Miranda said.

"Self-preservation for one thing. The Infected would turn on each other in a heartbeat if the Enlightened weren't constantly keeping them in line. Then where would we be, Mandy?"

"I don't like that name, and you know it." Miranda didn't want to be part of her father's 'we' but she couldn't be part of anyone else's 'we', so she might as well be the top of whatever heap she found herself a part of.

"Secondly," Albert continued as if she hadn't said anything. "We have a chance to build a better world. Sure, things are difficult and, dare I say, ugly now, but give it some time. Give us time to learn to control and channel the virus. We have an opportunity to guide humanity through millions of years' worth of evolution by speeding up the rate of mutations."

Miranda rolled her eyes. "Spare me the sales pitch. I'm not one of your golf buddies."

"What you are is an ungrateful little girl who is scorning a once in an epoch opportunity to put your own hand on the tiller of a species and choose where that species will end up."

"What I am is tired." In a million ways, she was tired. Too tired to even try to deal with her father's god complex. She wanted a hot bath and a cozy bed. Romi was back in town, fixing up their house, which meant scavenging the area as if the whole town was a huge rummage sale. Miranda wondered if they could find any tacky yard ornaments. Am I really considering settling down and living here? She needed to think about that more when she wasn't so annoyed with her father.

"Go get some rest," Albert said, dismissing her from his attention as he settled his tentacles back into the biofilm. "I have the herds to deal with."

That caught Miranda's attention. She sat back down.

"What herds?" She didn't mention the ones she and Romi had seen on their journey. Let her father explain.

"We need resources," Albert said as if that should clear everything up for Miranda. She said nothing, waiting him out.

"The uninfected, especially the humans, need to be managed," he said. "Since Portland, we've been losing Enlightened. They devolve."

"Carmine told me. Marius put something in the mold, right?" Miranda said, as if she didn't know all about the mold from Marius himself.

"We were able to use his strain to stabilize the Enlightened while he was here, but now we're reliant on bringing in new Enlightened, untainted by his corruption ..."

Abomination.

I know, I know. Let Albert the Enlightened speak.

"... if not, the Infected will simply overrun all the

human preserves, devour everything, and die off. The virus will burn out when there are no longer enough new vectors available. We'll lose our chance to create a better future for all life on the planet."

Miranda's brain rushed to catch up after the Infected's interruption. It was weird her father hadn't seemed to notice their little side conversation. What if the Infected didn't communicate with him the way they did with her? What if they couldn't?

"All the human preserves? How many are there besides the one in Great Falls?"

Albert rubbed the bridge of his nose, a habit left over from when he wore glasses. "Thousands. Any collection of humans larger than a wandering band of barbarians has been hemmed in. We manage them so they'll have enough resources to live and reproduce but keep them isolated from each other and especially from the groups near Great Falls."

The groups most likely to have or know about the inhibitor-laced mold.

"Are you, like, farming people?" Miranda had always known her father was utterly ruthless and entirely unscrupulous when it came to achieving his business goals, but still she found it hard to believe he could be so callous. She needed to hear him put form to her fears and bring them into the world as words.

"I suppose if you want to be reductive, yes," Albert said. He peered at his daughter, judging her reaction. "Why else would we have agreed to create a human preserve in Great Falls?"

"To capture Marius?" Saying it aloud, she realized how silly that sounded. The Infected had never needed to bargain for Marius. They could have taken him at any point. She knew that now, knew their strengths and their capabilities as well as she knew her own.

"A happy byproduct," Albert said. "Classic two-for-one deal for us. Remove him as a threat and give the uninfected of Great Falls the illusion that they're ruggedly independent Spartans holding off the Persians at Thermopylae. No need to pen them in when they'll stay in their zoo enclosures of their own free will."

"Wow," Miranda said. She couldn't tell if she was stunned at her father's cunning or his cruelty or both.

"Indeed," Albert allowed himself a small smile, proud, but dignified. Or that's probably how he intended it. The white scars twisted his face, tugged his lips off at odd angles.

"I'm going to go ..." Miranda stood up, desperate to be gone from this place with this thing that had once been her father.

He'd always been distant, preferring to outsource his parental duties, but she'd believed that somewhere beneath all his business savvy and scientific detachment, that he truly was trying to make the world a better place in his own profiteering way. Maybe he still was. Maybe he really thought he was doing something good by keeping people in human zoos and farming them for potential Enlightened.

How long before he decided free-range humans were too resource intensive and corralled them into industrial farm buildings like livestock? She tried not to picture Torres and Percy chained in stalls with big heavy bellies producing the next generation of breeders.

But not her. She would be spared, set apart, sanctified

by whatever her father had given her back at Chrysalis. Not the same vaccine John and Torres got from Marius, but something else. Whatever it was had turned her into something other, like the Infected but still able to be herself, mostly. She remembered a book she'd had to read for English Lit about Satan getting kicked out of Heaven. She paused at the door to her father's lair and considered the tag line from the book: "Better to reign in Hell than serve in Heaven."

The house Romi picked out could not have been cuter. It was a log cabin style building with a stone fireplace inside and a stone chimney that went up the back wall. There was a garden patch in the side yard and in the front was a bird bath with a little statue of a fairy peering into the water, while a little statue of mermaid peeked out of it.

When Miranda arrived, Romi was twisting a thick I-bolt into one of the columns that held up the front porch. On the floor, a hammock waited to be strung up.

"Dang, look at you, Suzy Homemaker," Miranda said, standing at the edge of the porch.

"I believe if you're going to be stuck somewhere, you should make yourself as comfortable as possible," Romi said with a grunt as she heaved on the wrench she was using to twist the bolt the final few turns.

Miranda helped her hang the hammock. Romi gingerly backed into it, lifting first one, then both feet. The women waited, listening to the rustle of fabric and netting from the hammock. The bolts and columns held.

"Move over," Miranda said and Romi half-rolled onto her side, so Miranda could climb in beside her.

They listened again, watched the bolts. Everything held.

Romi grinned and held out her arms as if inviting applause.

Miranda golf clapped for her.

She leaned back in the hammock, which Romi gently pushed with one leg. Watching the green leaves, the sky and its birds, it was easy to imagine the world would go on forever just as it had always done. Marius had said something like that. Said that humans were a blink in what he called deep time and that they would barely leave a dent on the world. She didn't like that idea. Didn't like the idea of leaving no trace on existence.

"What are you frowning over?" Romi asked. Miranda turned her head to find the other woman studying her face.

"My dad," Miranda put an arm across her eyes. It was easier to talk in the dark.

"Not exactly a joyous family reunion," Romi observed. "Do you want to tell me about it?"

"No," said Miranda and then she did. Once she started everything just seemed to pour out of her. How he'd left her in Portland, which to be honest, wasn't much of a surprise as she'd only ever been an afterthought to him, which brought her to John and how he'd practically raised her, but she'd turned her back on him, abandoned New Avalon and now she was here, with her father who wanted to kill the ones who actually cared about her or farm them for more people, which seemed totally worse, and …

Romi hugged her. "Let's go inside."

It was like a real house, like a place that had never even heard of HHV or the Enlightened or inhibitor mold. There was even a tablecloth on the table and potholders on the counter beside the stove, as if they might make and serve a holiday meal. It made Miranda start crying for real.

Romi walked her to one of the bedrooms and sat beside her, gently rubbing her back until she had cried herself to sleep.

Miranda had been up for hours by the time Romi wandered into the kitchen. Her long hair was loose, and she was wearing only a baggy T-shirt with a heavy metal band's picture on it and a pair of boyshort panties.

"Hello," she said, rubbing sleepily at her eyes. "Who are you and where's Miranda who never gets up before the crack of 10:30?"

"I need your help," Miranda said. She turned the stove on — where had Romi found bottle gas for it? — and heated up the water for coffee. One thing the Mammoth Cave hive had in abundance was basic supplies. The Infected and Enlightened didn't like coffee and neither did most of their adolescent human slaves.

When she was done detailing her plan, Romi sat back and blew out a long breath.

"So?" Miranda refilled her cup. After so long without real coffee she luxuriated in it, regardless of the consequences she would likely suffer later in the bathroom.

"It's ambitious," Romi said.

"And?"

"If we get caught, your dad will kill me." She smiled at Miranda. "And not for the reasons women's dads usually want to kill me."

"But is it doable, like from a super-secret special forces kind of perspective?"

"Anything's doable from a super-secret special forces kind of perspective," Romi said.

"Are you teasing me?"

"Yes."

"This is serious." Miranda tried to glare but Romi made faces until she laughed.

"Okay." Romi stood up, stretching. Her T-shirt rode up, giving Miranda a view of her toned abs, lower ribs, and the top of her panties. "Let me get dressed and then we'll go sabotage your father."

Step one was to convince Albert that Miranda was a true convert to the doctrine of evolution by Enlightenment. That meant helping out around the hive, while keeping some of her capabilities hidden from him. After a few days of careful observation, Miranda was pretty sure that while her father had a much more instinctive connection to and control over the hives and networks, he didn't communicate with the Infected or the Enlightened the way she did. The best way she could think of it was that when he wanted an Infected to do something, they just did it, the same way if Miranda wanted to scratch her nose, her hand just did it.

For Miranda, there was a distance or a distinction between her and the rest of the network. She was an individual, not part of the collective consciousness. As such, she had to talk to and listen to the Infected and Enlightened to figure out what was going on in the hives and networks.

"How will we know when he trusts me?" Miranda asked Romi one night over dinner. Romi had been gone for a few days hunting outside the hive's territory to find uninfected game. Miranda was surprised how much she missed Romi. Not just the usual loneliness of being on her own, but really missed Romi - her silliness, her attention to Miranda, her gentle curiosity and willingness to listen. No one had ever really wanted to listen to Miranda before. Marius was too busy explaining all his science stuff, Torres didn't care about anyone who wasn't sniper qualified, and John would forever see her as a child he had to protect. But Romi didn't see her that way.

"He'll start giving you small tasks, then bigger ones, letting you prove yourself," Romi said. She slowly turned the rabbits she was roasting on a spit over a fire in the yard neighboring their house. They had cleaned out the yard and used it as their fire pit on cooler evenings. There was no lack of burnable stuff. Miranda checked the foil-wrapped fingerling potatoes baking at the edge of the fire. The apples on the trees in the town's riverside park were reddening up and soon they could add those to their feasts.

"This is nice," Miranda said without thinking.

"Yeah," Romi said and came to sit next to her. She took Miranda's hand and lifted it to her lips, not breaking eye contact the whole time. Miranda leaned forward and kissed her on the lips. Romi put her hands on either side of Miranda's face and slowly drew them down Miranda's neck, over her chest, gentle squeezing Miranda's breasts, down her sides and settling on her hips with Romi's fingertips tucked into the tops of Miranda's pants.

"I missed you," she said.

"I missed you, too." Miranda kissed her again.

After a few minutes of making out, Romi sat up and turned the rabbits over. "They're almost done," she said. "We shouldn't waste the meat."

They ate slowly, savoring the rarity of fresh protein and the chill of the autumn air. Romi reported that where she'd been up north the leaves were starting to change color, which made Miranda wonder how the people of New Avalon were doing. Would they be able to last another winter with little electricity and less gas?

Romi bumped her shoulder with her hip. She had collected all their dishes into a plastic tub and tipped her head at their house. Inside, they washed the dishes by candlelight, not really talking, but kissing and touching a lot. After, Romi took Miranda's hand and led her into Romi's room.

Miranda stood in the heart of the hive, listening to the

great steady thrum of it. Around her the Infected carried on doing whatever it was their Enlightened set them to doing, while the Enlightened in turn looked to her father for guidance. She had been experimenting with commanding them herself. In the hive, it was easier than it had ever been before. The main difficulty for her was still the need to find and connect to individuals, rather than sending out hive-wide commands.

But today was her chance to prove to her father that she was capable of helping him run the show. One of the Infected scouts was back from Wyoming, of all places. Miranda felt the shiver through the hive as it returned, brimming with information.

"I got it," she told her father, who was busy dealing with the devolving Enlightened in the Miami hive who needed to be replaced. The Infected were bringing the Miami Enlightened to Mammoth Cave in hopes Carmine could stabilize it using some of the remainder of the original strain. The hive collective was careful to always think of it as 'the original strain'. Never 'Marius's strain'.

Miranda ordered the scout to meet her in the Star Chamber. She had mostly gotten over her squeamishness about touching and being touched by the Infected. Their communication tentacles made things faster and easier for her to understand. It was easier for her to command them if she was touching them.

The scout showed her traveling west with a swarm. Here and there along the way, scouts would break off to investigate things, while the Littles hunted for things to eat. The swarm came to a place where the air smelled rotten all the time. They didn't like it and they really didn't like the water and steam that shot out of the ground. They found a group of uninfected humans, bigger than many other groups the Infected had encountered.

"Dad," Miranda said, letting herself into Albert's lair after dismissing the scout. "What do we know about a community near Yellowstone? Are there any hives nearby?" She had already checked the network and knew there weren't but her father liked to know more than everyone else.

Albert held up a finger and Miranda waited, studying her fingernails. She needed to repaint them. Something in the hive made the teal polish chip and crack off. On the plus side, the effect looked very industrial chic.

"Now," Albert said after nearly twenty minutes. "What was the problem with Yellowstone?" Miranda explained what she had learned from the scout and repeated her question about the hives.

"No, there aren't any nearby. We've been careful in that area, but it seems we need to establish a hive." He rubbed the bridge of his nose. "This is terrible timing. We're already short Enlightened. I can't send one out to supervise the most basic task of bioforming a suitable location."

"I could go," Miranda said. "The helicopter still flies, right?" Her father squinted at her with his good eye.

"I can control the Infected. I'm experienced traveling around," she hastened to add. This could be her chance to test how much control she had over the Infected and monitor how far the hive's reach could really extend.

"That won't be necessary, Mandy," Albert said. "It's best you stay here where it's safe."

For a moment Miranda's mouth swung open, ready

to skewer her father on his previous abandonments, but then she remembered the long-term plan. Gain his trust. Play the good daughter. Don't give him a reason to more closely supervise her activities.

"But you're still sending a swarm back to Yellowstone?" she asked in what she hoped was a sweet, even submissive tone. Gross.

"I will. I'll have to move some resources around."

"Well, I still want to help, Daddy." Too perky? No, he was nodding. "How about I do some local recruiting, see if I can find any uninfected humans who would like a safe place?"

"Don't have too much fun," he said, waving her away as if she was going out for a night of clubbing and bar hopping.

"I'll try not to!" Definitely too perky that time. She hurried out, sending a command to the scout to meet her outside the cave in the morning. One way or another, she was going to Yellowstone. It was too close to New Avalon for her to pass up the chance to check it out. Besides, mindlessly obeying her father was not a habit she ever intended to have.

Chapter 17 - Marius

Marius rode ahead of Torres so she could watch their back trail. Layton acted as their good-natured tour guide, pointing out a jetty under construction to make fishing easier.

Security seemed good with armed guards on horseback patrolling while the workers moved rocks to set the foundations for the jetty. There were a few garden patches among the pines that covered the hillsides that sloped gently down to the lake, as well as small pens for livestock.

The trail wound up from the lake shore, crossing several roads that paralleled the shore or curved eastward into the pine forests. Occasionally, Marius saw people working in the gardens, but most of the people they passed were felling trees, moving rocks or loads of dirt. Whatever was going on appeared to be a major infrastructure project.

The Yellowstone town hall had started as a collection of long, low buildings intended as gathering places for the surrounding RV park on the eastern shore of Jackson Lake. The spaces between the buildings had been enclosed and roofed over, creating a big, rambling compound. Behind the building were several small wooden water towers and a cluster of sheds with steam coming from pipes in their roofs.

Layton showed Marius and Torres where they could hitch their horses and led them inside. The main room resembled some kind of medieval throne room in that it was a rectangular space with benches and chairs along the side walls. A large table took up most of the space at the far end of the room. A small group of people were clustered around the table. At the center of the group was a white man in his late fifties or early sixties. He had the physique and posture that Marius associated with former military types like John.

When he saw them, he held up a hand, silencing the low buzz of conversation in the room.

"Welcome," he boomed as he came around the table, hand extended. When he shook Marius's hand, he looked him in the eye, squeezing just short of pain and holding for a moment or two longer than necessary. "I'm George Sebald. I hear you're from up north a bit. Helena, wasn't it? I thought Helena was mostly evacuated."

"It was," Marius said, refusing to wince or flex his hand. "New Avalon's further north, on up towards Great Falls. I'm Marius. This is Torres. We're Rangers. Our job is to scout out the territory and where possible establish communications with other communities."

"To boldly go," Sebald said with a wink. To the others gathered around he said, "Why don't we take a break and reconvene tomorrow. Tonight, we're gonna have a good old fashioned pig roast and try to impress our new friends and trading partners."

As the group drifted away, talking quietly amongst themselves, Sebald turned his full attention back on Marius and Torres. "Have I got a surprise for you. C'mon." He strode out of the hall, leading them onto a newly made gravel path that led through the trees.

"First things first," he said as they walked. "Are you part of the Great Falls preserve? We had some folks come in a few months ago from up there. I'll tell you, they've got their work cut out for them keeping their human capital from flying the coop, to mix some metaphors."

"No, New Avalon's independent of Great Falls," Torres said. "We do some trading with the PDF."

"Liam, right?" Sebald said. "Irish fellow?"

"You're pretty well informed," Torres said and Sebald tipped an imaginary hat to her.

As they passed the last of the pines into a clearing, both Marius and Torres stopped.

"It's a runway," Torres said. Marius was staring at the switchbacking tower that rose above the tallest of the trees. It was modeled on Forest Service fire watch towers, but with reinforced legs. The observation platform on one side was about three times as wide as the others.

"Close, but no cigarillo," Sebald said.

"It's an air tower," Marius said. "For zeppelins."

"Ding, ding, ding." Sebald clapped a hand on

Marius's shoulder. "Want to take a closer look? If we're gonna be trading partners you'll need to see what we have to offer, right?"

"Sounds good to me." Marius's mind was already racing with all the possibilities that air travel could open up. Instead of long and dangerous overland journeys like he and Akeem and later Torres had made, they could fly to their destination. It took the possibility of going to Detroit to investigate a potential government holdout site from a mission that would take months, to one that might take only days. Aside from a few flying Infected, who they wouldn't have to worry about much, it seemed very unlikely any other aircraft were functional. Marius couldn't remember the last time he'd seen one aside from the helicopter Viers had sent to fetch him from Great Falls.

"I'd like to see your security measures," Torres said.

"Oh." Sebald glanced at Marius, who made a point of being interested in the tower's bracing. The wooden pegs were nearly the same design they were using at New Avalon.

"Unless that's like a state secret or something," Torres said, filling the over long pause in conversation.

"No, no," Sebald said. He put his hands on his hips as he looked around. "Tell you what, señorita, I'll get Layton over here. He can show you what you're looking for. I've been outsourcing a lot of the day-to-day stuff. One of the things you learn in the Academy is the importance of delegation as a leadership tool."

While Sebald used his walkie-talkie to contact Layton, Torres muttered, "Gotta be FBI. The CIA people call their training site 'The Farm'."

"Alrighty then." Sebald clicked the walkie-talkie back onto his vest. "Layton's on his way. You're welcome to come on up with us or wait down here. Just don't wander off or he won't know where to look for you. No need to call out the guard for one stray, am I right? You understand. You've got that steely-eyed killer look."

"We've all been through a lot," Torres said. "I'll wait down here." To Marius she added. "I'm sure you're more than capable of giving me a full report when I get back."

He nodded. Something wasn't sitting right with her, but she wasn't saying, and he wasn't picking it up, whatever it was. He trusted her training and her instincts though. She started to reach to take his hand but turned the motion into brushing some wood shavings off the banister. Okay, she was really spooked. Maybe they shouldn't separate, but he had no way to ask her with Sebald smiling amiably and waiting right there to escort him up into the tower. Besides, she'd said she would wait below. Whatever was worrying her, she wasn't concerned about his immediate safety or hers.

Marius climbed the spiral staircase that wound up into the middle of the tower from below. Heavy beams extended from the legs and central supports. It looked like they were planning to add a stairway or ramp to the outside of the structure. That would make it easier to move heavy cargo up and down from the zeppelin.

Inside the top of the tower was one big room. Spread across the floor was a huge pile of fabric. Marius picked up a corner and rubbed it between finger and thumb. Silk? Nylon? Something strong and light. Would that be enough to hold the weight of a passenger compartment and keep the air inside? He didn't know a lot about aeronautics.

"As it turns out, we've got a genius in our midst," Sebald said, startling Marius with the strangeness of his comment.

"We do?" Marius said, playing for time. How does he know about me, he wondered.

"Former astronaut. Didn't go to the Moon or anything like that, but she did go into space a couple times. Speaks Russian and all that, but we don't hold it against her." He grinned like they shared a particularly good joke. "She's in charge of our flight project. Gotta get Lady Liberty into the air sooner rather than later. Anyway, Ionna's a certified big brain."

"Wow, I'd like to meet her," Marius said.

"Oh, she'll be at dinner tonight. All the cream of the crop will want to meet you."

As night fell, Sebald brought Marius down to the lake shore where a trench had been dug out to roast the pig in the ground. He seemed to relish the chance to parade Marius around while showing off Yellowstone's accomplishments. They had a mill up on the Yellowstone River, which provided flour for the community. They also had a school and a doctor's office, a general store with a credit system, and a bank.

"It's still a little, you know, socialist," Sebald said, watching some of the other people dragging logs down to the beach to set up a bonfire. "But we're gonna be back on the gold standard in no time. No more of this funny money stuff. That's part of the issue."

"Money?" Marius said. He scanned the growing crowd for Torres.

"Not exactly, but money not being tied to anything, not being real. A man should be able to trust that if he gets a bill from the bank that bill is backed by more than wishful thinking."

"Here I thought not getting ripped to pieces by the Infected would be a bigger issue," Marius said more acerbically than he intended. It was nearly full dark and he still hadn't seen Torres or Layton.

"We've got that mostly handled," Sebald said. "But I hear tell you might have something on the more permanent side?"

"Yes, we do actually." Marius gave himself a little shake. Torres, of all people, could take care of herself. He was fretting for no reason. He needed to stay on mission. Part of that mission was to disseminate the mold far and wide to whomever seemed even slightly interested in taking it.

While the final preparations for the dinner were underway, Marius and Sebald sat at the head table. Marius took the mold samples out of his satchel and explained how to plant and cultivate it.

"How's this work against the Infected?" Sebald lifted one of the plastic bags, holding it up to the waning light over the western mountains.

"It keeps them from mutating," Marius said. Sebald didn't look convinced, so he elaborated. "One of the main characteristics of HHV is that it's highly mutagenic. Every time one of our cells divides, there's a chance it'll miscopy our DNA and cause a mutation.

Most of the time if that happens, the mutation is minor and doesn't spread throughout the individual. The mutant cells just die, no harm done. Sometimes, mutations cause things like cancer. That's more like what HHV does. It causes unchecked growth and mutation."

"But the mold stops it from mutating," Sebald said. "So, the Infected have to settle for only five eyes instead of eight or twenty-seven. I'm still not seeing how that helps us."

"What HHV does is coordinates the mutations so growing those extra eyes or adding tentacles or losing a kidney doesn't kill the Infected." He didn't mention that most of the victims infected with HHV didn't survive their initial system-wide mutation. Their immune systems fought valiantly enough to take HHV out, but the resulting collateral damage killed the patient.

"The mold interrupts the virus's ability to keep all the cells working together," Marius added. "Without that, the Infected's mutations start fighting each other for resources. Their organs shut down and they die."

"Well, that's a nifty trick, isn't it?" Sebald grinned. "How long does this usually take to work?"

"It depends," Marius said. At the edge of the tree line, he caught a glimpse of Torres and Layton. They had stopped and were talking. Marius felt a surge of relief at seeing Torres alive and well. Rationally, he knew they were safe enough, but he couldn't help the anxiety that filled him whenever she was out of sight. It echoed to a lesser degree the anxiety he felt about everyone in New Avalon and about humanity in general. If he could just see them, he would know they were all right, would be able to protect them from danger, and failing that would be able to stand in their place long enough to let them escape. That, he knew full well, wasn't rational at all, but it didn't change the way he felt.

"On?" Sebald tracked Marius's gaze and gave a short nod as if to acknowledge his concerns.

"Depends on the speed of the Infected's mutation," Marius said. Normally, he would have loved to chat with someone about all the ins and outs of HHV infection and how it might be mitigated or eliminated. Right at this moment, he needed to go to Torres, to touch her and know she was alive and strong.

"Excuse me." He stood up and left the table, threading his way through the crowd gathered for the meal. The workers who set everything up had gone, maybe to get washed up and changed as the people sitting on benches and at picnic tables around the bonfire looked a lot cleaner and had on nicer clothes.

Layton was gone by the time he arrived at the edge of the fire's glow where Torres waited. She had her hands in her pockets, a sure sign of distress for her.

Wordlessly, Marius wrapped his arms around her, telling her with his body that she was safe, that he was there, that he would protect her. For a moment, he believed it, too. But then the realities of the world came crashing back, the weight of all the people he'd failed to protect. The burden of all the people who had died horribly while their bodies tried to fight off the virus his immune system had made possible. He buried his face in Torres's hair, already smelling slightly of campfire, and took as much comfort as he gave.

She leaned against him, slightly, not enough to throw

off her balance. He could feel the tension in her muscles, the hunch and set of her ready-for-a-fight shoulders.

"What?" he murmured into her hair. No one was close enough to overhear them, but discretion seemed the better part of valor.

"Don't look now, but we're in a hostage situation."

Dinner was served. Marius and Torres were invited to sit at the head table with Sebald, his wife, Vanessa, and a group of people Sebald introduced as 'The Bosses'.

"Eventually, we'll get back to a real system of government," Sebald said, his voice carrying easily out across the water. Lanterns sat at regular intervals on the table as well as handmade citronella candles to keep the bugs at bay. Here and there around the edges of the gathering, Marius caught flashes of light reflecting off the armed guards who patrolled the area.

"For now, we're just trying to keep the lights on and the trains on time, as they say," Sebald said. "I think our goals are pretty close to yours. Get civilization back up and running."

"You seem to be doing well enough," Torres said, poking at her fresh green salad.

"We work hard and we're careful about who we add to our community," Sebald said.

"What kind of requirements do you have?" Marius asked. He reached under the table and patted Torres's thigh. He trusted her to not endanger them, but her tone was a little aggressive for a dinner where they were playing the part of honored guests.

"Pretty standard in this day and age," Sebald said. "Able-bodied. You've got to bring something of value to the community. We haven't had to turn a lot of people away. One thing the pandemic was good for — clearing out the layabouts and welfare people. Nowadays, you wanna live, you've got to work."

"If a man doesn't work, neither should he eat," Vanessa said. A few of the bosses nodded.

"What if people can't work?" Torres said. "If they're old or sick or something, do you just send them away to die in the hills alone?"

"That's a little too harsh," Sebald said, an amused smile on his face. "We have a sponsorship system. Full members of the community can sponsor new people. If you don't have a sponsor, you can earn your place here. Plenty of work to go around."

"We hear you have contact with the military," Vanessa said.

"We did," Marius said. "The Air Force base in Great Falls is mostly empty now."

"But we still have radio contact with the squadron," Torres added. "It's really nice knowing that Captain McCormick is there to back us up if we need her and her pilots."

Marius took a deep drink to cover his surprise. To his knowledge, the last New Avalon had heard from the squadron formerly stationed at Maelstrom Air Base had been nearly a year ago when they had bombed the quarry in case Miranda's attack on the Enlightened there wasn't enough to destroy it.

"We've got our own little Air Force here," Vanessa

said with a proud smile. "George has been experimenting with alternatives to helium. Hard to find that these days, but we do have a couple of possible sources of gas right here."

"Plus, the tanker," Torres said.

"That was a lucky find," Sebald said. To Marius he added, "One of our members used to be a long-haul trucker. It's amazing the kind of things we can find and salvage off the highways, like a whole truckload of propane."

The conversation drifted to concerns about the coming winter. Like New Avalon, Yellowstone was facing a year where most of the shelf-stable food items had already been eaten. They would have to hope their crops would be enough.

Eventually, Vanessa announced she was tired and left to go to bed. Sebald waved and Layton got up from one of the other tables and came over.

"Why don't you see our friends to the guesthouse?" Sebald said. "You folks will have to excuse me. The bosses and I still have few things to discuss."

"We understand," Torres said, very agreeably all of a sudden.

"Good night," Marius said. He and Torres followed Layton along a winding trail that led to one of the cabins close to the main compound of buildings.

"Let me get you settled in," Layton said. He held the door open and they stepped in. As Marius's eyes adjusted to the gloom, he made out a person sitting on one of the cots by the small window. He froze, holding out a hand to stop Torres.

"That's Oakley," Layton said. "She's my fiancée."

Oakley lit a candle and a lamp and stood up. She was a little taller than Layton, sturdy where he was wiry with darker skin and a mass of dark curls tied up under a bandana. She glanced out the window before she said, "Last patrol went past about ten minutes ago so we've got about an hour."

"What's going on?" Marius burst out. His curiosity had been roiling through him all night and he could barely stand the suspense a moment longer.

"Sebald knows who you are," Layton explained. "He means to keep you and you, ma'am," to Torres, "as hostages."

"Why?" Marius shook his head. They had come to Yellowstone of their own accord, had brought life-saving mold, and were potential trading partners.

"Yellowstone's going to be expanding soon," Layton said. "We can't grow a lot of our own food here, so we're moving east to get more grain and corn and north to get cattle and horses. Sebald wants to make sure New Avalon is in a cooperative mood when we get there next spring."

"Why are you telling us?" Marius asked.

"Because we want asylum," Oakley said. "We came here with my parents, but my dad died of heart attack and my mom passed during the winter, probably pneumonia. Even when she was coughing out her lungs, they said she had to show up for work or they would kick her out."

"Things are a lot harder here if you're not exactly the right complexion," Layton said.

"What happened to 'We accept anyone who's able-bodied and adds value'?" Marius quoted Sebald.

"We do," Layton said. "But rules are much more strictly enforced on some than on others. The number of times one of the bosses mentioned that I might want to marry one of their relatives instead of burdening myself with Oakley and her whole 'tribe' — their word, not mine."

"They're happy enough for a Latina to work in their fields, but draw the line at miscegenation," Oakley said. Layton patted her shoulder.

"Seriously?"

"Seriously," Torres said. "You didn't notice how eighty-five to ninety percent of people here are white? Plus, anyone who doesn't have skin the color of mayonnaise is doing manual labor. I sure did."

Marius shook his head. How was race an issue during the apocalypse? Of all the stupidly small-minded reasons to exclude uninfected people.

"If you're asking for asylum, you must think we can protect you," Torres said, turning her attention to Layton and Oakley. "So, you don't think Yellowstone can annex New Avalon. What about this blimp or whatever? That's a pretty big tactical advantage."

"Sebald tested a small one, using helium, but he doesn't have lot of it. He's got to rely on hot air if he's going to make a bigger zeppelin or look for more compressed helium, which is not common or easy to find," Layton said.

"Can't just order off the internet anymore," Oakley said.

"So, what's your plan?" Torres said. "Are you leaving with us tonight?"

"Can we?" Oakley took Layton's hand, squeezing it

tightly as she searched Torres and Marius's faces.

"Of course," Marius said before Torres could point out they might be spies. He knew they might be, but given everything he knew about their situation, they might also be his and Torres's only chance to escape the Yellowstone territory without alerting Sebald to the fact they knew he intended to hold them. For the moment, Sebald seemed happy with the charade that they were guests, but that would only last a few days until they told him they were leaving.

Creeping through a dry pine forest at night was a louder, itchier process than Marius imagined. He followed Torres, who followed Layton. Oakley brought up the rear of their little group. Through the trees, he could still see the faint orange-red glow of the dying bonfire by the lakeshore and hear the echo of muted voices carrying over the still water.

They edged around the main compound, avoiding the pools of lamplight from the windows, before following a narrow track up into the hills behind the buildings. A few minutes' hard hiking brought them to a small plateau where Layton whispered they should rest.

"Where are our horses?" Torres asked.

"I took them to our place," Oakley said. "That one's kinda mean. He nipped my arm. I've got a big bruise."

"Yeah, Gany's an asshole," Torres said, but Marius could hear the grudging affection in her voice.

He turned in a slow circle, studying the layout of the

Yellowstone community. At night, it was easier to get a sense for the scope and size of the place because the lights picked out where the humans were. There were a lot of smaller lights at regular intervals near the lakeshore. Probably more of the log cabins they'd seen during the day. Inland and up the slope were two dark patches with several lights. As he watched, the light brightened and darkened a few times from one, but not the other. A door being opened and closed?

"What's over there?" he asked, pointing.

"That's the guards," Layton said.

"Guards is a loaded word," Torres said.

"They're guards," Oakley said. "They work for the bosses. The bosses got here first and are the original full members. Everyone else has to earn a place. But everything you do puts you in debt to the community."

"It's like those company stores in mining towns in Appalachia," Layton said.

"Sounds a lot more like feudalism than democracy," Torres said.

"Sebald says it's modeled on the original republic, Rome," Oakley said.

How much time, energy, and lives might be lost if New Avalon had to fight human invaders in addition to worrying about the Infected? Marius wondered. The odd raiding party now and then was bad enough, but what Sebald was contemplating was as close to an actual war as anyone was able to come these days.

"We need to destroy that air tower," Marius said.

"What?" Oakley said.

"We don't have time," Layton added.

"I agree with Marius," Torres said.

"They'll catch us!" Layton hissed. "We risked our lives to help you. Sebald believes in capital punishment. If they find out ..." He pulled off his baseball cap and twisted it in both hands.

"You two should go on ahead," Torres said. "We'll be right behind you."

"Famous last words before you get killed by monsters," Oakley said.

"We can show you were New Avalon is," Marius said. "Listen, you did risk a lot to help us. We're not discounting that, but we have to try to stop Sebald now, when there's a chance to do something without getting a bunch of people killed."

"I'll go with you to the horses. Our maps are still in our packs," Torres said.

"I'll start working on the air tower," Marius said.

"Okay, okay, yes, that could work," Layton said, taking some deep calming breaths while Oakley rubbed his back.

"This way," she said, starting down off the plateau. Torres started to follow, then stopped. She came back to Marius and kissed him thoroughly.

"I love you," she said.

"I love you, too," he said. "Be careful."

She paused once more before disappearing into the dark forest and Marius waved, telling himself this wasn't the last time he would see her. It wasn't like Great Falls.

Memory served him well enough as he made his cautious way down the hillside to the runway or landing strip or whatever they were constructing. He climbed halfway up the tower, trying to figure out the best way to sabotage it. Sadly, he had no handy pack full of C4 to do the work for him. But thinking of explosives made him think of other things that could explode. Like canisters of pressurized helium. Sure, it wouldn't burn, like hydrogen, but it still might do enough damage to set back Sebald's imperial aspirations long enough for New Avalon to get better prepared.

It took a long time for him to find the canisters in a nearby shed and even longer to haul them one-by-one to the base of the tower. Finally, sweating and exhausted, he leaned back against one of the tower legs to catch his breath.

"Marius," someone whispered. He looked around until he saw Torres. She stepped out into the moonlight that partially illuminated the open space around the tower.

"I found the fuel truck," she said. "I've got it rigged. All we gotta do is light the fuse and run like hell."

"Where did you find a fuse?" He lifted his hair off his neck and considered the wisdom of his mother's advice that he should get haircut.

"Not a real fuse," Torres said. "Just a really long rope I soaked in gas."

"That sounds safe," Marius said.

"The safest sabotaging I've ever done. This way." She led him back into the forest. The truck was parked on a paved two-lane road.

"Do you know how to drive one of these?" Torres patted the front bumper.

"No," Marius said. "Why would I know how to drive a semi?"

"You're a genius, remember?" He couldn't see her expression, but he could hear the teasing in her tone.

"Do you?" he challenged.

"Not exactly, but I did drive some big ole trucks in the Corps." She walked around to the driver's side and swung up into the cab.

Marius stepped back as the truck rumbled to life. With much hiccupping and grinding of gears, it started rolling down the road at a pace he could easily jog to keep up with.

Except for the gun pressing against his temple.

Chapter 18 - Torres

No point in keeping the headlights off, considering how much noise the semi's engine was making. Torres swung wide, crunching over a few unlucky seedlings that grew close to the edge of the road. She wasn't confident that she could maneuver the semi, so she needed to line it up correctly on the first try. She hauled on the wheel, focused on the wide base of the air tower. There.

Marius stepped into the beams of light. One of the bosses, Torres remembered his name was Walter, had a hand on Marius's shoulder and gun to his head.

Torres stopped, foot ready to mash down on the accelerator. Her tactical mind did a quick calculation. The biggest threat to New Avalon, outside the Infected, was Yellowstone. They wanted Marius alive as hostage, so it seemed unlikely Walter would shoot him. He was too valuable. Unless Walter didn't know who Marius was, both in terms of his relationship to the leaders of New Avalon and his role in creating the inhibitor mold.

Marius's life against the lives of everyone in New Avalon, including Elfy's.

She held up her hands, hoping Walter could see them against the glare of the semi's headlights.

"Come on out of there, missy," the man said. Behind him, nearly concealed in the trees, she could see two or three more figures. Backup.

"Okay, okay," she said. "I can't figure out how to put this thing in Park."

"Shit's sake, woman," Walter said. He pushed Marius toward the side of the semi.

Torres waited until he was in front of the bumper to duck down and wedge her go-bag onto the accelerator. She kept her foot on the clutch, but the engine roared, trying to engage.

The door latch clicked as Walter tried to open the door.

"Just a second," Torres called. She snapped open her Zippo and lit it, popped the glove compartment, which according to the laws of the universe, was filled with fast food napkins, old paper receipts, and snack food wrappers. She dropped the Zippo into the mass, then in one motion, she pushed the door open, swung herself out, and took her foot off the clutch.

The semi bucked and jerked forward. Torres lost her grip on the door handle and tumbled to the ground. Without looking up, she rolled away, hoping that semi wouldn't skew toward her. What a crap way to go: crushed by her own attempt at sabotage.

People were yelling. Someone grabbed for her. She

kicked out hard, sending them falling onto their butt. She jumped up and looked around. Walter had Marius on his knees, pistol between his shoulder blades. Damn Walter and his halfway competence.

The person who had tried to wrestle her was getting up, too. Not one of the bosses, but a younger man, fit and grinning as he dropped into a ready crouch to lunge at her.

The semi hadn't gotten up a lot of speed and rolled anticlimactically to a stop at the base of the tower, not even bumping it enough to rattle the windows.

Freaking perfect.

"I got her," said a woman's voice from behind Torres. She half expected a movie-style buttstroke to the head, but the woman snapped a pair of handcuffs on her and pushed her, sending her stumble-walking into the pool of light surrounding the grumbling semi.

"Get that turned off and put away," Walter said to the younger man.

Torres caught Marius's eye. She felt stupid for letting them get caught. She should have done a better job scouting the area, but she'd let Marius's enthusiasm carry her along. It wasn't his fault. He didn't have the kind of training she did. His main concern was protecting New Avalon. Her concern should have been protecting him.

The younger man hopped onto the running board and yanked open the door. A whoosh of air rushed into the cab like a giant in-drawn breath. Then fire burst out, the flames singing off the younger man's eyebrows before he could leap to the relative safety of the ground.

"You bitch," the woman said. She kicked Torres in the

back, and without the use of her hands, the best she could do was land on her shoulder rather than flat on her face.

"What the heck is going on here?" Sebald's voice boomed over the growing chaos.

"We caught them, sir," the young man said. "But that one tried to ram the tower and set the truck on fire."

"Well," Sebald said, voice soft and conversational. "You got any ideas about what you should do about that?"

"Put out the fire?"

"Oh, I don't know," Sebald said. "We could just let it burn and see what happens."

"Sir?" The young man looked from Sebald to Walter as if hoping for confirmation.

"Steve, go get a crew over here to put out the fire," the woman said.

Steve dashed off into the darkness as Sebald shook his head.

"You've got a soft heart, Flo," he said. "Take them to the brig. I'll be along once I get this mess sorted out."

Flo frog marched Torres through the forest. She could hear Marius and Walter behind them. They came to another watch tower. This one was smaller and taller. Flo did a pat-down on Torres, making her grateful that Jimmy's HK was still with the horses. Whatever else happened, she wouldn't have to see it captured by the enemy.

Flo uncuffed Torres's hands and re-cuffed them in front of her so she could climb the ladder, which led to a trap door set in the middle of the tower's floor. Torres noted the heavy bolt on the outside of the hatch. It swung down and locked from the outside. No chance for prisoners to barricade themselves in.

Once she and Marius were both inside, the hatch was closed and locked, leaving them in complete darkness with their hands still cuffed.

"That could have gone better," Marius said.

In the morning, the hatch was opened. Torres got her first good look at Flo and Walter. She had seen both the previous evening but hadn't paid a lot of attention. Her mind was too busy with the information Layton had given her about Sebald's plan to hold Marius hostage.

Flo was a white woman with leathery skin that spoke of too much time in tanning beds or under the sun with no thought of sunscreen. She had blue eyes and long brown hair that was bleached blond at the tips showing what color she used to dye it. Walter's skin was very pale in the parts normally covered by his clothes and sunburned everywhere else. He carried a compound bow, which had Torres's attention from the jump.

While Walter stayed back and covered them, Flo removed their handcuffs. Someone passed up a bag of food, two bottles of water and a bucket, which Flo left in a corner before she and Walter wordlessly departed.

"Seems like they don't intend to kill us," Torres said. She sipped the water, which tasted and smelled like nothing other than water. "They wouldn't feed us if they were going to shoot us."

She and Marius picked at the food. Neither had much

of an appetite, but they both knew they should eat when they had the chance. They speculated on what might have happened after they were captured. Considering they hadn't seen a big, fiery explosion, or smelled smoke, Torres didn't hold out much hope that they had succeeded in disabling the semi or destroying the fuel.

By nightfall, Torres started planning their escape. Frustratingly, the tower was a very effective prison. She had to assume there were guards watching from the ground and there was no way to escape without climbing down the ladder.

The next several days passed with both Torres and Marius growing more bored and frustrated. Marius slept a lot, but Torres couldn't find a way to be comfortable for more than short bursts of time when exhaustion helped her sleep. Other than food, water, and the bucket, they weren't given anything.

It was late morning on the fifth day of captivity, when Walter and Flo returned.

"It's time," Flo said, beckoning for them to follow her down the ladder. Walter waited with his bow at the ready, but Torres couldn't think of any situation where rushing him for the weapon would end up with her and Marius free and uninjured, so she ignored Flo's wrinkled nose as she swung onto the ladder above the other woman. If their captors didn't like their smell, they could allow them to wash.

A few other people waited around the clearing at the base of the brig while Torres and Marius climbed down the ladder. They were led back to the main hall. This time, Sebald and Vanessa sat at the high table, flanked by the other bosses, aside from Walter and Flo who stood behind Torres and Marius. The rest of the tables and benches were cleared away, the walls lined with people come to see the show.

"We're met here today to consider the case against Marius and Torres, both scouts from the New Avalon community in Montana," Sebald said. "As you know, we welcomed them into our community. We believed their claims that they were diplomats trying to establish trade and communications with us. But they attempted to blow up our air tower and set fire to our fuel truck, which we were able to save, but not without losing two of our own. Layton and Oakley were killed, probably by these two in an attempt to cover their tracks."

"What?" Marius said. "We didn't kill anyone."

"Quiet," Sebald said. "You'll get your turn to speak. We still believe in the rule of law around here."

"Last time I checked, the law says we're innocent until proven guilty," Torres said.

"Plenty enough witnesses saw you trying to destroy the tower and the truck," Vanessa said.

"Yeah, I did that." Torres glared at Sebald. "But I didn't harm a hair on either of your people's heads. Neither did Marius. Go ahead and prove we did. This should be fun."

She wasn't sure what the point of this whole sham trial was, other than Sebald getting to flaunt his despotism. She still didn't understand the instinct for kangaroo courts, but it seemed like the less the rule of law actually applied, the more eager autocrats were to wrap themselves in the trappings of legality.

"We'll get to that," Sebald said. "As to the matter of your terrorism, since you've just admitted to your guilt, there's no need to continue that part of the trial. Walter, take the one," he pointed to Marius, "back to the brig while we determine her sentence."

Torres looked at Marius, seeing the same realization in his eyes as she must have in hers. This had been the point all along. To separate them. To get rid of her but keep him — the valuable hostage — alive. Of course, they would want a pretext to kill her. She was the one who had asked about security, the one who had military experience, the dangerous one who wasn't the beloved eldest son of the leaders of New Avalon.

Marius took her hand and squeezed.

"I killed Layton and Oakley," he said. The room filled with gasps, hisses, and mutters. Torres felt a surge of grim glee. Sebald had trumped up a murder charge, planning to use it to justify her execution, but instead Marius had called his bluff. He couldn't kill her for terrorism but not Marius for murder, and he wouldn't kill Marius because he needed a hostage.

Sebald sat back, his face not betraying any emotions other than mild curiosity.

"Did you?" he said. "When? How?"

Torres squeezed Marius's hand back. It had been a good idea and she appreciated it, but looking at Sebald, at the other bosses, at the collection of armed guards and surly spectators, she knew they were determined to get the outcome they had planned for. They wanted her dead. That feeling was different from the visceral terror of an Infected attack. The Infected had no personal agenda. They were trying to kill and to feed. That they were trying to kill Torres and feed on her was incidental. These people had premeditated her murder specifically.

"I'd like to make a full confession," Marius said. Torres glanced at him, trying to figure out why he was playing for time. No one was coming to rescue them. It wasn't like the old days of Chrysalis where they could rely on John to show up and snatch their blistered behinds out of whatever inferno they'd fallen into.

Vanessa frowned and leaned to whisper into her husband's ear. He gave a curt nod and stood up.

"I don't know how they do things in New Avalon," he said. "Here in Yellowstone, we're trying to keep our people alive, get ready for the winter, and now, deal with terrorists. If you feel the need to confess, you can write everything down in the brig. We'll review it tomorrow."

Marius gave Torres an encouraging smile. They had another day.

"Take him back to the brig," Sebald said, and two young men moved forward to grab Marius's arms and pull him a few steps away from Torres. She watched his face, memorizing the way hope lit up his green eyes, smoothed away the worry lines on his forehead, seeing the moment when he understood that throwing himself on the grenade of Layton and Oakley's murders wasn't working out the way he intended.

"No!" He twisted, trying to break free, trying to reach her. She wanted to say something to comfort him. It was easier to worry about him than it was to face the fact of her own death.

The main door to the hall burst open and a young woman dressed in close-fitting leather clothes burst in. She pointed a shaking hand out the door toward the sky.

"There's a helicopter!"

Chapter 19 - Miranda

Miranda smiled as the helicopter skimmed over the scraggly pines. At first, having to stop for refueling annoyed her, but as they crossed the country, she realized that it gave her the chance to recruit more and more Infected. It didn't take a lot to push them westward instead of towards her father's control in Kentucky.

Romi watched her but didn't say anything whenever she descended from the helicopter to wander through the towns and fields reaching out to tap into local hives and networks. Carmine whined about the delays. He hadn't left the cave since arriving from Portland. He missed his easy life there. As long as he did whatever Albert told him, he was pampered, the hive's noninfected teens and its Infected both striving to meet his every need and most of his whims.

Miranda wouldn't have brought him if not for the fact

that they needed a pilot and he had more experience than Romi. Lying to him about the mission didn't bother her for a moment. Sure, Albert had commanded them to go to Yellowstone.

"I'm pretty confident I can fly this bitch myself," Romi said softly as the women stood together in a parking lot outside some small town in Nebraska.

"So, you're saying we can push him out over the Grand Canyon?" Miranda kept her eyes on the swarm of Infected churning through the town. There wasn't much left for them, mostly feral pets and a lot of alpacas — who knew Nebraska was good for that kind of thing?

"I'm not not saying that," Romi said. "If he asks to watch us one more time ..." She kissed Miranda's shoulder.

"I'm not shy and I know you're not." Miranda smiled mischievously.

"Not at all, but not gonna perform for that wanker."

"Fair." Miranda heaved a sigh as she turned back to the helicopter. Carmine peered out the windscreen at them, tapping an imaginary wristwatch.

It was early afternoon when Romi reported that they were officially flying over Yellowstone National Park. From their vantage point, they could see small figures of people on horseback, patrolling the edges of the area. Miranda wished she could connect with the Infected to get more information from the scouts, but being airborne had its disadvantages.

"There, over there," Romi said. She pointed to a compound of buildings that had obviously been fixed up recently. "Go around."

"We don't have an endless supply of fuel," Carmine

said.

"Too bad we can't use excuses and bullshit," Romi said.

"Too bad no one asked you, honey."

"Shut up, Carmine," Miranda said. "Take us up. Those people have guns."

Carmine glared but wasn't reckless enough to keep them near the treetops just to prove some point of pride. The longer they were away from the Mammoth Cave hive, the less Miranda bothered to pretend he was her supervisor. Let him tattle to her father that she'd been mean to him. Albert wouldn't care and even if he did, there was nothing he could do about her behavior. Not without risking a divide in the leadership of the Infected. Sure, he ruled in the hive, but Miranda had spent a lot more time out among the actual Infected. She knew them in a way her father never would.

As they circled around — wider than Miranda would have liked but let Carmine stage his little hissy fit — she watched the ground. None of the Infected moved inside the Yellowstone perimeter that she could sense. Maybe some Littles but they didn't have the strength of will to communicate with her at such a distance. What she did see was a faint haze along the horizon to the north.

"What's that?" She patted Carmine's shoulder and pointed. "Get us closer."

"Sure. We'll just fly back on thoughts and prayers." But the helicopter arched away to the west and north.

Romi handed Miranda the binoculars and she peered down. It was a band of riders, going south. There were two groups, moving together, but staying slightly separate. Miranda focused in and froze.

"What's he doing here?" she muttered.

"Who?" Romi held out a hand for the binos.

"John," Miranda said.

There was no place to land near the main compound. By the time Carmine got the helicopter around, the crowd was bigger. They were building some structure near the lakeshore. A short way away, in a clearing in the forest, stood a scorched tower with a fuel tanker parked near its base. Weird.

"Follow that road," Miranda said. "There's got to be a parking lot around here. It's a touristy area."

"It was," Carmine said sourly.

"We're touring it now," Romi chirped. She winked at Miranda, delighting in annoying Carmine.

Once on the ground, Carmine cut the helicopter's motor. Romi hopped out, rifle at the ready, checking all around them. Miranda climbed out more slowly, sending tendrils of awareness out in case there were any Infected nearby. As she'd suspected, a few Littles who passed under the notice of the humans in the area. She sent them east to find the swarms she brought with her.

Show them the hidden ways in. Bring them here, but quietly. She wanted the Infected close to hand in case she needed them but didn't want to be seen with them. It was one thing for the people of New Avalon to accuse her of being in league with the enemy; it was another for her to show John they'd been right. Somehow, she still wasn't ready for him to know that about her. She still wanted him to ... what? Like her? Care about her? Be proud of her?

"Hey, you okay?" Romi's hand on her shoulder brought her back to the present moment.

"Yeah, just organizing the troops," Miranda said with a hard smile. This time, she wasn't alone. This time they couldn't throw her out. Her smile widened as she pictured the look on Mr. Noland's face. You want to burn me as a witch? Fine, I'll be your witch and I'll bring my demons with me.

"C'mon," Miranda said to Romi. "Let's go see what's what. Carmine, keep the engines hot in case we need to get out of here fast."

"That's not how helicopters work."

"Don't care." She blew him a kiss. Romi laughed, shouldering her rifle and waving her fingers toodeloo at Carmine, left in the helicopter like a toddler waiting in the car.

With the help of the few Littles still in the area, Miranda guided Romi out and around the people at the main compound. She didn't know or care who they were. She wanted to see John, wanted to show him that she was okay, that she had survived, had thrived on her own. I'm a big kid now. As if that wasn't pathetic. But she was honest enough with herself to know she needed it, needed a proper goodbye, some kind of closure before she could move on, before she could do what had to be done back at the Mammoth Cave hive.

A rider came out of the trees, following the same narrow trail Miranda and Romi were. She wore a PDF patch on her shoulder, but close beside her was Percy.

All four women stopped and stared. The PDF woman

fumbled for the bow that was hooked to her saddle horn.

"Wait!" Percy said. She climbed carefully off her horse, holding up a hand to stop the PDF woman from firing as she crossed the short distance to Miranda. She held out both arms and, with an eye roll, Miranda nodded, agreeing to the hug Percy was dying to give her.

"This is amazing!" Percy pulled back and looked her up and down, glanced at Romi and back to Miranda. "I'm so glad you're okay. John will be thrilled. He's been so worried about you."

"What are you doing here?" Miranda let Percy lead her back the way the other women had come.

"Marius," Percy said theatrically widening her eyes, but not enough to hide the genuine concern there.

"What happened?" Miranda said. She was beginning to think that the scientist's main genius was for getting himself into awful situations and needing to be rescued like an eternal video game princess.

"We're not completely sure," Percy said. She filled Miranda in on what they did know. A few days ago, a pair of riders had come to New Avalon, claiming to have run away from Yellowstone. They said the leader of Yellowstone planned to keep Marius as a hostage and wanted to annex New Avalon.

"Oakley said they want us to be their vassal state, like dark ages Europe," Percy said. She waved at the hillside and two more people poked their heads out of the underbrush. One was John. On seeing Miranda, he hurried forward, the relief plain on his face. Just before he reached her, he stopped awkwardly, his faded blue eyes searching her for signs of injury or illness.

Miranda held out her hands and did a little pirouette.

"I'm fine," she said, trying to sound both tough and cool, not like a kid trying to impress a grown up.

"Miranda Panda," John said, a smile spreading across his face. "I have so many questions, but right now our priority is a rescue mission. Will you promise not to leave again before we can talk?"

"I promise," she said, her own smile answering his. Impulsively, she threw herself into his arms, causing him to stagger on his bad leg. He didn't seem to mind, hugging her back fiercely.

"I missed you," he said.

"Torres was always the better sniper," she mumbled into his chest. He laughed and held her out for a final inspection before signaling to the rest of the Rangers and PDF people to continue their stealthy march.

"The prodigal returns." Liam's Irish accent was unmistakable, but instead of the usual hostility she felt for the mercenary, Miranda grinned.

"What are you doing here?" she demanded.

"Someone's got to show you lot how to conduct a proper raid," he said. John held up a finger to his lips, to which Liam gave a dramatic salute. It was hard for Miranda to believe with all the noise of their footsteps and their gear and weapons that talking would make them that much more noticeable.

As they neared the edge of the forest, keeping low behind the underbrush, the voices of the Yellowstone people grew louder, if not clearer.

Peeking out from around a pine tree, Miranda saw a man, their leader given the way the others watched him, shouting commands. A few men were dragging Marius away down a track that led east, away from the lake.

More men stood around Torres, holding onto her upper arms even though she had her hands tied and wasn't struggling. Behind her loomed a structure made up of thick beams. Four beams, in sets of two, stood up making a pair of elongated X shapes. Across the top of the Xs was another beam. Two teens shimmied up the Xs and tied the cross beam in place.

"What's the word on the helicopter?" the leader boomed.

Miranda looked over at John and mouthed, "Mine." She pointed to herself and back at Romi crouched next to her. John gave her a thumbs-up 'Got it' sign.

One of the teens balanced on the crossbeam and walked to the middle where he waited until a woman threw him a rope, which he tied in place.

The end of the rope was a noose.

Chapter 20 - Marius

Yellowstone, Wyoming, USA — Autumn, Year 2

Marius had no idea what the arrival of a helicopter might mean, other than that Viers had finally tracked him down. Part of him acknowledged that there were hundreds, if not thousands, of privately owned helicopters in the US. What were the odds that this was the same helicopter that had taken him from Great Falls? Pretty small. Another part of him knew underestimating Viers was a mistake he'd already paid dearly for on multiple occasions.

Even falling victim to a mutagenic virus had only ever minorly inconvenienced Viers.

Regardless of whose helicopter had arrived, from where, or to what purpose, Marius's first and only concern was Torres.

As guards wrestled him away, he tried to find a smart way out. He wanted there to be a perfect intellectual argument that would show them the error of their ways, could induce them to deviate from the ritualized murder they were so intent on committing.

If only he could get a few minutes to think.

The gallows loomed on the lakeshore. Torres stood in the eye of a storm of people who seemed only too eager to let Sebald whip them into a violent mob. How could they be this way? His brain helpfully produced a slew of psychological profiles and social pressures that would set the conditions for even the most mild-mannered pacifist to cheer for the torture and death of someone Other. Someone like Torres, who could be painted with the colors of everything they feared and hated. A target for their Two Minute Hate.

The men who dragged Marius down the trail stopped at the foot of the brig's ladder. Neither of the men was strong enough to haul him up by themselves. Probably both working together wouldn't have been able to do the job. Unexpectedly, their prison's particular structure turned from a benefit to a major obstacle.

Liam pushed through the trees, pointing a pistol at the guards. They had weapons of their own but had them holstered while they were dealing with Marius.

"I'm not keen on pointless murder but I'm not strongly opposed to it," Liam said. "Let the fellow go and I'll give you lads a five second head start."

The guards exchanged glances, but before they could make up their minds, Miranda stepped into the clearing from the left and Percy from the right. Percy had a bow with arrow nocked. Miranda was empty handed, but the threat in her smile was enough to send a thrill of fear through even Marius. He hadn't seen her use her connection to the Infected, but he didn't doubt what Torres and John had said about her growing powers. Much as he was grateful for the rescue, he didn't want to see anyone else torn apart by the Infected.

The guards let Marius go and put up their hands. John followed Percy into the clearing.

"That's their brig," Marius said. Better to lock them in than let Miranda have her way with them. The gleam in her eyes unsettled Marius deeply.

"Go on then." Liam waved his pistol, and the guards climbed the ladder.

As soon as they were safely secured, Percy hurried to Marius and hugged him.

"They've got Torres," he said, squeezing her back. Why was she there in her condition? No time to lecture, not that she would have listened to him.

"We know," Miranda said. "That's why we're here."

When Marius turned to her, they both paused, an unwelcome awkwardness between them. Marius knew that her connection to the Infected was as unwanted as his own, but he couldn't deny the instinctive revulsion he felt. Knowing that the Infected watched him through Miranda's eyes made him feel like he'd never escaped the Mammoth Cave hive.

Miranda's face fell, her shoulders rounding as if preparing for his rejection.

But she was his friend and more. They had saved each other's lives more than once. They understood the Infected in ways no one else could. They shared a wretched bond.

Marius took a step towards her, arms coming up and Miranda met him halfway. He wanted to thank her, to ask for some kind of absolution, but there wasn't time to hash that all out now.

"We have to hurry," Marius said, squeezing Miranda before they separated. He hoped she heard his implied, "We'll talk later."

As he fell into step with John, he patted the soldier's back. "Thanks, John. I owe you. Again. How many more times you going to save me?"

"Old habits die hard, like old soldiers," John said.

"Not that old." Marius elbowed him and waggled his eyebrows. Despite everything that had gone wrong with their trip, seeing John filled him with confidence, the sense that things would work out. John always saved the day.

Liam stayed behind to guard the guards and Miranda took up the rear, her eyes occasionally glazing as she communicated with the Infected. Torres had told him that was something she could do but he hadn't seen it before. Not like this, up close and unabashed. She filled him with an instinctive dread that not even the deadliest of Category Four viruses could. A virus was a living machine. It wanted nothing other than to continue its existence. To infect, consume, replicate, and infect again. Viruses, for all their ills, were not malicious. Miranda, in contrast, had a human's capacity for cruelty and long-term planning. How much like her father was she?

Marius bit his lip, trying to banish the unwelcome suspicions.

John turned off the main trail toward the lake, heading south.

"Wrong way," Marius said. He wasn't great with

directions at the best of times, but he knew this path as it was the one the guards had so recently dragged him down.

"We can't take them in a frontal assault," John said. "There's too many and they have the advantage of knowing the area far better than we do."

"I'm not leaving her." Marius stopped, studying John, remembering another time the soldier had insisted they retreat. The ghost of Otto still hovered between them. Marius determined he would die or kill before letting Torres's ghost join the boy's.

"I know," John said. He glanced at Percy. "We won't, but we need something to level the odds."

"We need helicopters for this kind of work," Miranda said. She grinned, holding out a hand to invite them down the faint track. "I happen to have brought one. You're welcome."

It was the same helicopter. Carmine was in the same seat.

Marius was back in Great Falls. The air was choked with smoke. The sky was full of flying Infected. Screams, roars, and shrieks filled the afternoon. He couldn't tell which sounds were human-made and which were the Infected hunting, catching, killing, consuming their prey. He stood in front of the helicopter and knew that it was death of a kind, and it was the best of all the bad choices. He would do this so the ones he loved could be safe. But below the heroic notions of martyrdom was the primal impulse to survive, the fear of dangers known and unknown, the desire to strike a defiant blow against the forces that made him small and helpless.

Someone touched his arm.

Percy.

Behind her John.

Next to the helicopter Miranda.

Marius wasn't alone. It wasn't Great Falls. This time the flight would be to save someone, not damn them to — He stopped, shutting away the memory of the tube of blue goo. He was shaking already, heart hammering in his ears, his stomach roiling, and bowels threatening imminent rebellion.

"Breathe," John said. "We're here. We're all here with you, Marius."

Percy took his hand, laced her fingers through his and squeezed. "We love you. You're safe."

"Liar, liar, pants on fire." Marius smiled shakily. "We're not safe at all."

"Well, we do love you, even though you're adopted," she said, nudging him with her shoulder. Had their parents told her? Maybe, but that was a question for another time. Still, he was grateful for her teasing. It was an anchor he could cling onto in the face of the storm of fear, rage, and regret swirling through him.

"We can't fit everyone in here," said a woman. Marius had noticed her near Miranda but hadn't paid any particular attention until she opened the door and peered into the helicopter. He'd assumed she was a member of the PDF, but given her familiarity with the chopper, that seemed less likely.

"Here's the plan," John said. He quickly divided the

group, sending the majority back along the lakeshore under the cover of the thicker forest to the south, while a few joined up with Liam to create a diversion.

"If anyone can cause chaos and confusion, it's him," Percy said.

Marius told them about the fuel truck, which Miranda confirmed was still parked where Torres had left it. Setting it on fire would definitely create a diversion.

"I'll go with Liam and Romi to handle the truck," Miranda said. "I can work with the Infected better from the ground anyway."

"Marius, you're with me and Percy," John said. He fixed Carmine with a look. "Let's get moving."

"I'm not a combat pilot, Captain," Carmine said.

"But you can get us to the lake and circle the crowd, right?" John said, with far more patience than Marius possessed. Carmine nodded and slumped sulkily into the pilot's seat. John started to climb in, winced and rubbed his leg before limping up to the co-pilot's seat. Marius sat behind Carmine and Percy took the other seat.

The helicopter lifted off in a wash of wind, pine needles, and sandy soil. Carmine took it on a wide curve toward the lake that glinted and sparkled to the west. In minutes, they were over the crowd gathered around the gallows. Someone had put the noose around Torres's neck and she stood on a chair.

Marius didn't think. He unbuckled and lifted Percy's hunting rifle. He didn't bother to aim, just leaned out and started shooting at the people milling around Torres. No one there was innocent. They were trying to murder her.

And they were shooting back.

The helicopter bucked and swerved as Carmine tried to maneuver it, the rotors screaming in protest at the sudden changes in altitude and direction. Marius nearly lost his footing, but clung onto the door frame with one hand, the rifle with the other.

"Take us back around," he yelled.

Carmine was blathering about damage to something. Red and amber lights danced across the control panel, but none of it mattered.

I'm going to save her or die trying, Marius thought. He wrapped the seatbelt around his bicep and leaned out again, spraying bullets at the scattering crowd below.

"Marius!" Percy was yelling, but he ignored her.

Alarms blared.

Marius glanced up, looked at John, saw his face, the way his gaze moved to Percy, still in her seat, but fumbling with her buckle as she shouted for her brother to sit down and strap in. Smoke rose from somewhere on the side of helicopter.

John and Marius shared a moment of recognition. They'd been in a helicopter crash before, years ago, near Harrow Hall. Just like then, Marius hadn't been in his seat. Just like then, John was faster than the scientist, already moving even as Marius's brain fumbled through the data, coming to the too-late conclusion that he was well and truly doomed. He was going to be thrown out of a flying object into a grove of really pointy trees.

The world tilted sideways, the sunlight pouring in to bathe the interior of the helicopter in a golden glow that was nothing short of heavenly. Percy was radiant, her eyes wide, one hand still working her buckles, the other reaching for John as she shouted against the wind and the rumbling whine of the dying engine.

The helicopter jagged. Marius was thrown free, floating for one weightless instant like the astronaut he'd always wanted to be.

Then John was there. John yanked him back in and down, shoving him ungently into his seat.

The splintering, ripping crash of the helicopter through the trees was too familiar.

Marius clutched his seat with one hand, his other arm around John's waist until John was gone, thrown out like a man-sized rag doll.

The helicopter came to a stop with its nose submerged in the lake, the tail lifting toward the sky even as the rotors clattered to a discordant stop.

Marius stumbled out, fell into the lake, staggered up, and plowed through the water to the shore. John was already up, his face paler than Marius could ever remember it apart from the time the soldier nearly bled to death at Harrow Hall.

"Go!" John stumbled. Probably his bad knee giving out. He pointed and Marius looked.

The crowd around the gallows had mostly scattered, but Sebald stood in front of the chair Torres balanced on. He met Marius's eyes, put out his foot, and kicked.

The beach was a combination of small pebbles and sand. Every step seemed to bring Marius only inches closer to Torres, who seemed to be miles away. He couldn't force his body to move faster, could only focus on her, how she jerked at the end of the rope, feet flailing, hands bound behind her back, her face turning purple. She got a toe on the overturned chair. Sebald had knocked it over, but not away.

Marius pushed past people. Distantly, he heard their screams and yells, the sounds of gunfire, but he only cared about one sound: the gurgling rasp of Torres's labored breathing.

He grabbed her by the thighs and hoisted, trying to lift her enough to create slack in the rope, but the noose itself was already tight. It didn't seem to help. He tried to reach the rope, but it was too high. If he pulled on it at all, he risked snapping her neck.

All he could do was lift and hope, listen for the wheezing inhalations and sputtering exhalations.

"Hold her steady." Liam was in front of him. Percy and Romi were behind the mercenary, keeping the crowd back, but something else was happening. People were screaming, fleeing. Small shapes with numerous and twisting limbs bolted among the Yellowstone residents.

Marius pushed, straining to hold Torres, trying to guess if the shudders he felt were a sign she was still fighting or her death throes. Liam jumped, the knife in his hand glittering against the light reflecting off the lake. The rope, a slender climbing rope, started to unravel.

"One more go." Liam leaped again. This time, Marius could see the final strands fraying out into a starburst of fibers. Torres fell against his shoulder and he staggered.

Liam caught her as she fell forward, bending at the waist over Marius's back.

The two men laid her down on the beach. Her face was mottled, her eyes wide and pink with burst capillaries. Marius held out a hand and Liam put the knife in it. He slipped the blade down Torres's neck, fighting against the rapid swelling to get the point between her skin and rope, the cut the noose away.

When it was gone, she started flopping and for a moment Marius froze, his mind locked up at the reality of staring into her eyes as she died. Then Liam took the knife from him and used it to cut Torres's hands free. She thrashed, pushing the tattered remains of the rope off her, and sucking down air by the lungful.

Marius was crying, sobbing, desperate to hug her but knowing she needed only to breathe. She was alive. For once, he had saved someone. Unlike Otto, unlike Toby, unlike the millions, probably billions of people who'd died from HHV, Torres survived.

"Shite," Liam said. The mercenary fell back onto his heels, looking away up the beach toward the crashed helicopter. Marius glanced in that direction.

The Infected had done a fine job of tearing through the Yellowstone people, and the strand was nearly empty apart from the New Avalon Rangers and the members of Liam's own PDF.

Miranda stood with her head thrown back, her hands out, fingers moving as she swayed in time to a current none of the other humans perceived. Her eyes snapped open, her head turning to follow the direction of Marius and Liam's gaze.

Then Marius saw what Liam was looking at.

Percy knelt in the sand. John lay on his back, his head in her lap. One hand reached up, touching her face, then fell away.

Miranda howled.

Around her the Infected echoed her cry, setting up a blood curdling cacophony. They broke in all directions, attacking anyone at random, not differentiating between the Yellowstone people and anyone else.

"We're just after saving her." Liam pointed to Torres. "Let's get her moving."

Marius felt his head nodding up and down. Yes, they should get moving. John would tell them to go. He would sit up, groaning about how he was too tired and too old for their shenanigans, and he would get them moving. Any minute now.

Percy bent forward, her lips brushing John's forehead.

Liam was helping Torres to stagger to her feet, still wheezing painfully. Her eyes were also on the two people huddled together near the crashed helicopter.

"Marius." Liam toed the scientist. "Get up and get your girl out of this feck up."

"Not." Torres's voice was a low rattle. "Girl." She held out a shaking hand to Marius, who climbed to his feet.

A small Infected charged him but veered off at the last second to leap onto the back of someone else. Whether they were from Yellowstone, New Avalon, or Great Falls he had no idea.

He moved then, keeping his body parts going while his mind stayed on the beach and waited for John to get up.

But there was only Percy, her shoulders shaking,

hands cradling her belly, and Miranda, curled into herself so tightly she couldn't stand upright. There was only Torres, who could barely walk, and Liam who might abandon them at any moment. And Marius, whose blood could keep the Infected away until they could leave the beach, until Miranda could get the swarm under control.

Romi ran to Miranda and held her, letting her keen against her shoulder as they staggered off the beach, following whatever trail they found first.

"Can't." Torres pulled free of Liam and Marius. She pointed a trembling hand and Marius understood.

We can't leave a fallen soldier behind.

Chapter 21 - Torres

New Avalon, MT, USA — Autumn, Year 2

The funeral was held at dusk. John always advised using the liminal hours to conduct any major military operation. What could be more tactical than entering the Afterlife?

Throughout the day, people arrived at the ranch, a steady stream of mourners, most from Crossroads, but many from the other New Avalon communities: Anoheka, Point Zebulon, and Esmerelda. There was even a contingent of PDF members and some Great Falls civilians who came south either to join their leader, bid farewell to John, or both.

Torres stood near the bottom left corner of the pyre. Around her, the grass had been carefully burned away to reduce the ever-present risk of a prairie fire. John had wanted to be cremated, not buried, so the pyre was built of salvaged lumber, gathered sticks, and a powder

Marius promised would burn hot enough and fast enough to do the job.

He waited near the top left corner of the pyre, looking a little ridiculous in the suit he'd last worn at some high school science competition. Across from him, near the bottom right corner, Miranda waited, staring out over the rolling plains toward the east, watching the night reach over the sky to steal the light.

Percy cleared her throat. She was at the top right corner of the pyre, a lighter in hand. She wore a black dress and over it, John's Army blouse. The bottom button was undone, allowing her belly the room it needed.

"We owe John for our survival," she said. "Many of us directly. All of us indirectly. I trust you all. I trust that in the days and nights ahead you will do what you can to be worthy of the chances that he gave you."

In the gloaming stillness, her words carried far, but the crowd was so big that soft echoes told of where people repeated her message for those farther back.

"But I don't want to talk about what John did."

She paused, her eyes moving slowly over the flag-draped body on the pyre. When Erica and Cassy had brought the oversized American flag from the Malmstrom Air Base, Annette had asked, "Will it be right to burn it with ... to burn it?"

Torres looked up from the Ranger roster. It still hurt her neck to move, and she wasn't confident her voice would ever come back.

"There's nothing in the flag code against burning a flag," she said. If she kept her speech low and slow her throat was less likely to threaten to close up on her. "He's probably the last true patriot. Let him have it."

John had somehow outlasted the nation he'd sworn to protect and defend, and she'd outlasted him. It seemed fitting to send the American flag to the afterlife with him. He'd earned that.

"What I do want to talk about," said Percy, her voice gathering strength, "is what we will miss. We will miss John holding his child, miss seeing him be a father. We will miss John's mentorship and his retirement. We will miss John growing old. We will miss his birthdays - which is still classified." She nodded to Marius, acknowledging his very old joke with John. "We will miss his unbearable energy in the mornings and the way he loved us, all of us, not with words, but always with deeds. To John, love was a verb."

Percy held out the lighter to Marius, who took it. He studied it in the cradle of his cupped palms then looked out over the crowd.

"John once told me that we save the ones we can," he said. "Whenever something happened, he ran toward danger. He was strong, one of the most powerful men I ever met. He used that power to help us, to help me. I agree with Percy: none of us would be alive today if it weren't for John. I wish ..." He trailed away, tears falling unchecked as he stared at John's body.

"I wish —" he tried again, then simply held out the lighter to Torres.

She took it, kicking herself for not remembering all the words that had crowded her brain during the darkest night of her life. She should have written them down. She should have crafted a perfect memorial for John.

Instead, what she said was, "John made me want to

be better."

She handed the lighter to Miranda.

"We didn't deserve him," Miranda said. "None of us." She glared around with narrowed eyes but stopped when her gaze met Percy's. "Okay, like, almost none of us. But that's why John worked. He didn't need us to be perfect, to be worthy. John's love wasn't based on us, it was based on him. Once he decided you were in, you were just in, forever. There wasn't anything he wouldn't do for you."

She looked at Marius. "I know what I wish," she said. "I wish John had been my dad. I wish I had learned to use power to protect, not to punish. But I didn't. None of us had John for a dad." She glanced at Percy's belly, this time with the ghost of a smile. "Okay, like, almost none of us. So, the question is what are we gonna do about it? Are we gonna whine forever because things weren't handed to us the way we wanted them? I did. See how that worked out." She waved a hand around at the ranch, aglow with candles in every window even as the shadows from the mountains slunk over them, bringing a chill breeze with them.

"I don't know about you all," Miranda said, "But if I don't do better, if I don't change, and like right fucking now, John won't have made a difference for all the nice things we say here."

A murmur swept through the gathering at her disrespectful tone, the sulky pout, the defiant tilt of her head, but Torres just waited. Miranda had more to say.

"I'm not gonna make you any promises," Miranda said.

The murmur was turning into gasps, a low hum of

fear building as eyes gleamed from the edges of the gathering. Hundreds, maybe thousands of Infected eyes, luminous as they reflected the last of the sun's dying rays, surrounded the mourners.

Miranda handed the lighter to Percy.

"I'm going back to Kentucky." She stalked forward and the crowd parted around her, or more accurately, shrank away from her.

For several long moments, no one dared move, but as Miranda's silhouette joined the greater darkness, and the many eyes blinked and vanished several at a time, people relaxed.

Percy beckoned and Anatole and two young women stepped forward. They held out a card with lyrics on it and began to sing.

> Of all the money that e'er I had
> I have spent it in good company
> Oh and all the harm I've ever done
> Alas, it was to none but me
>
> And all I've done for want of wit
> To memory now I can't recall
> So fill to me the parting glass
> Good night and joy be to you all
>
> So fill to me the parting glass
> And drink a health whate'er befalls
> Then gently rise and softly call
> Good night and joy be to you all
>
> Of all the comrades that e'er I had

They're sorry for my going away
And all the sweethearts that e'er I had
They would wish me one more day to stay

But since it fell unto my lot
That I should rise and you should not
I'll gently rise and softly call
Good night and joy be to you all

So fill to me the parting glass
And drink a health whate'er befalls
Then gently rise and softly call
Good night and joy be to you all

Good night and joy be to you all

Torres wasn't sure which was worse: clearing John's things out of the Rangers' headquarters in the barn or leaving them as a daily reminder. She studied the maps and rosters, ignoring the empty recliner with the tangle of unfinished knitting next to it. John had been making a blanket for his child.

Torres lifted her mug of tea, warming her hands against the early chill. Autumn, which had been creeping down the mountains, had given up stealth and pounced with three mornings of frost that had people in a panic about the yet unharvested crops. Torres didn't know anything about farming, but she did know that they needed food, especially in the winter when traveling to scavenge would be difficult. Plus, this year there would be less to scavenge. Either things would have gone bad, or they would have already been taken by others.

New Avalon was facing its first winter of near total self-reliance and she didn't know if they were prepared. Percy and her parents, along with Mayor Flynn and the leaders of the other New Avalon communities met twice a week, going over tallies from gathered supplies, harvested crops, slaughtered animals, and scavenged items collected by the Rangers.

Which brought Torres to the barn at the freaking crack of dawn. They needed to send some Rangers to Point Zebulon to bring in a load of feed for Crossroads. They also needed to send a patrol up the mountains to winterize the radio repeater. Great Falls wanted to set up a market day and Samhain celebration — thanks, Liam — which was a wonderful idea, but would mean not only did they need a lot of security, but they would have to coordinate transportation for crafters and artisans who wanted to attend.

"I thought I'd find you here." Marius came up behind her, put his forehead against her shoulder and wrapped his arms around her waist. He was still warm from sleep, and she leaned into him, nestling. Since the funeral, he had alternated between spending long hours alone, either in the mold shed or on short-range patrols, and seeming to want near-constant physical contact. Torres didn't mind that. She needed closeness herself, but she worried about his times alone. John's armchair diagnosis of depression seemed accurate, at least to her non-expert understanding.

"Trying to figure out how to staff twenty-five

Rangers-worth of missions with fifteen available Rangers," she said.

"Can I help? I'm good at math." He nosed into the fluffy hairs at the nape of her neck, his breath tickling as it warmed her skin.

"This is practical math," she said. Her body stirred at his closeness, but the specter of John's forever-empty chair quieted her desire. If John had been alive, it might have been fun and naughty to have sex in his office, but she couldn't imagine doing so now. "Not that fancy math you do with letters, which is just spelling."

"What are we going to do about Yellowstone?" Marius asked. It was the question that had been on everyone's minds since they'd returned, but so far, no one seemed to have a clear idea either what the problem was or what the solution might be. Layton and Oakley insisted that Sebald wouldn't give up. There had been other communities, much smaller than New Avalon, that Yellowstone had already 'invited' to join at the barrel of a gun.

"People know it's wrong," Oakley had said, standing in the kitchen, where most of the serious business of the ranch still got decided. "But when the other choice is watching your kids starve, a little light tyranny seems more reasonable."

Torres couldn't fault the logic. Everyone had done hard things, sometimes horrible things, in the name of survival. She wasn't judging, only trying to get a sense for her enemy's motivations. Knowing what Sebald ultimately wanted would help her guess the strategies and tactics he might use to achieve mission success.

So, not only did she have to figure out the regular

roster and missions, she also needed to do something about Yellowstone. Being second-in-command was a role she was comfortable with. John told her the objective and then she put her brain, her will, and her Rangers to work. Actually making the objectives herself was far harder than she'd ever imagined. What if she prioritized the wrong thing? What if she set the Rangers a task they couldn't complete? What if …?

She walked her fingers down the map, covering the space between the Morning Star ranch and Yellowstone in seconds. Too bad the helicopter was out of commission. One good bombing run and they could all but guarantee that Sebald wouldn't be able to come after them until spring at the earliest.

"I don't know," she confessed. "Send a scouting mission." She meant it as a statement, but it sounded like a question — not to Marius, but to the ghost of John sitting in his empty chair just beyond the edge of her sight.

"Makes sense," Marius said. "We have to know what we're dealing with before we can deal with them, right?"

Torres nodded, trying to seem confident. Had John ever worried this much? Ever questioned himself like this? Did he share those fears with Percy? Or did he try to protect her from them?

She looked at Marius, noting the dark crescents under his eyes. Considering how much he slept, he never seemed well rested. No, she couldn't put more onto him. He already carried the weight of the HHV pandemic and everything that had happened after, regardless of how illogical that was.

"Are you up for another all-expenses paid trip to

sunny Wyoming?" she asked brightly, beaming a fake infomercial smile.

"I had another destination in mind, actually," he said. He joined her at the map, touching Crossroads and then tracing his own route south and east to Kentucky. When his finger stopped on a point south of Louisville near the middle of the state, he looked over at Torres.

"No," she said, already seeing the determination in his eyes and hating how much she loved that about him. Whatever faults Marius had, inertia wasn't one of them. But she wasn't convinced he was trying to solve the right problem. He probably wanted to do something, anything, to feel like he was honoring John's memory. She understood the instinct.

"Winter's going to be here soon," Marius said. "When it hits, the mold will either die off or go into a dormant state — probably die off mostly. Regardless, it means we lose our biodefense against the Infected, who are also going to be hungry and desperate as their primary food source decreases with every season."

"That's nothing to do with Viers," Torres said.

"We don't have the resources to fight Yellowstone and the Infected," Marius said.

"I know," Torres said. Better than most, she knew.

"If I go back, I can bring enough mold to eliminate the hive."

"You said the reason you worked with Viers and Carmine before was because without the hive, the Infected would kill us all," Torres said.

"But now we have the mold."

"We had it before," Torres said, trying to keep the frustration out of her voice. "You just said it would probably all die off in the winter, so we don't really have it now."

"What do you think Viers is going to do when he finds out John is dead and we are under attack?"

Torres frowned. She wanted to tell him that it was ridiculous to think Viers would go out of his way, halfway across a continent, to attack them. She didn't, because it wasn't. Viers knew how valuable Marius was. The only possible outcomes were eliminating Viers or Viers eliminating Marius. Or capturing him, which was basically the same thing.

"I think Viers has got plenty enough problems of his own and I think we do, too. There's no reason to go jump on that particular landmine."

"Lourdes," he said. "It's not like that. I'm not going off on some dumb hero quest, okay?" He held out his arms, but she was furious. She could see the leaving in his eyes. He hadn't been asking for her input, only telling her about his decision.

"That's exactly what it's like, because that's what it is." She held up a hand to stop him from touching her. In her current mood, she might break his arm.

"This needs to be handled," he said. "I'm the best one to go. I've been there before. I'm immune. I can pack and transport the mold so it'll be viable when I arrive."

"Those are all good reasons for you to be the one to go," she said. "But there's still no good reason for anyone to go. Not right now. We need to focus on Yellowstone and surviving the winter."

"This is a hundred percent about surviving," Marius said, dropping his hands to his sides. He shook his head. "I'm sorry about John. He meant a lot to me, too. You know that. But we can't hunker down here forever because we're afraid to lose someone else. If we don't take care of the people we love, they'll die anyway. They'll starve, or the Infected will kill them, or some band of raiders will come through. If it's not Yellowstone now, it'll be someone like them next year. We have to get back out there."

For a moment Torres could only stare. Part of her was immensely glad to hear him say they needed to take action. It was a welcome change from his withdrawal and lethargy. Part of her was deeply offended that he would suggest she was being too timid. And she was deeply hurt that he would believe she might ever neglect protecting the ones she cared about.

"Fine," she said. "Get back out there."

"Lourdes." He held out a hand to her again.

"No," she said. "I can't do this with you again. I can't wait here, wondering when you'll come back, if you'll come back, imagining all the ways you died or worse. You are determined to go, so go. But don't try to dress up your suicide-by-Viers as anything else."

She started to storm away but stopped at the door. In a calmer voice she said, "I am staying here not because I'm scared or I'm sad about John or I don't think the Infected are a problem. I'm staying because the ones I care about are here and if I can't protect them, because I'm not a one-woman SF team, I want to be with them when the end comes."

She opened the door and stepped out, turned back to look at him, half shadowed by the office door, his long hair loose around his shoulders. Experience had made him alert, thinner, stronger, harder. He was still the movie star hottie from the first time she'd flown with him all those years ago at Chrysalis but missing the carefree optimism.

"I want to be with them," she said. "Because I love them."

Chapter 22 - Miranda

Mammoth Cave, KY, USA — Autumn, Year 2

Miranda didn't expect a warm welcome when she returned to the Mammoth Cave hive. The trip back took a few days or weeks. She wasn't paying attention. Most of the time, she stared out the window. Romi handled the day-to-day of travel, finding food and vehicles, and scouting out places to sleep. She gave up talking to Miranda somewhere in the Dakotas. They stopped on the outskirts of Minneapolis so Miranda could send some Infected scouts in to see what had survived the great fire. Not a lot, her Littles reported. Most of the fires were out, the cities smeared with ash and debris and dusted with the first flurries of early winter. Miranda was glad when Romi turned their current car south and they left the snow behind.

The hive was full of its usual bustle, with the Infected eager to catch her up on what she had missed, trying to cram information in with the enthusiasm of a three-year-old reporting on her favorite dinosaur. Miranda put up her walls and marched to her father's office-lair.

"We need to talk," she said. Albert hunched over his desk. He looked up, and she froze. His skin looked greasy, his remaining good eye clouded. His mouth looked slack as if he was missing teeth.

"Yes." He waved a minor tentacle at one of the mismatched chairs that faced his desk. She sat.

"Where is my helicopter?" he said, his speech slurring slightly. "Where is my scientist?"

"Marius?"

"No!" Albert erupted, lunging forward, his tentacles yanking free from the bioformations behind and around his chair. Miranda flinched, sure he was going to hit her. He didn't, stopping with his tentacles quivering alongside her face, the fury burning in his eyes like she'd never seen before.

With a visible effort, he pulled himself back, slumping into his chair. He sagged as his tentacles reattached to the wall and ceiling. He rubbed the bridge of his nose and shook his head.

"Carmine," he said in a deeply weary tone. "Where is Carmine?" He fixed Miranda with his milky eyed stare. "Do you have any idea how demeaning it is to have to rely on that ... frat boy? Half the time, I'm fixing his mistakes. But at least I know he's not actively trying to kill me. It would be nice if I could say the same of my own daughter."

"I wasn't trying to kill you," Miranda said. "I wanted to get out of here, to find out what was happening in the rest of the world."

"We don't have to leave to do that," Albert said. "We have the network. Every hive reports it. It's all centralized. From here, I can touch anywhere on the continent."

Miranda shivered. She had suspected that the Infected controlled the whole country and more, but it was still shocking to hear her father admit it so casually. What did that mean for the little pockets of civilization like New Avalon, Great Falls, and even Yellowstone? How long could they hold out while the Infected kept getting stronger and more numerous with each person they bit?

"Mandy, I don't know why things have to be so hard between us," Albert said, sounding almost wistful. "We're on the same side. We're trying to build something here. I know you had a crush on him, but it's time to grow up. Personal loyalties don't count for anything when the stakes are this high. People get hurt. The weak fall behind. We continue on."

"Personal loyalties like John's?"

"John who?"

It was worse than if he had hit her. All the air left her body.

John, the man who basically raised me because you and Mom were too busy with your conferences and parties, your business meetings and your charity auctions. John, the one who cared if I lived or died. John, who will never see his child born. John, who never left anyone behind.

Out loud she said, "Captain John Courage."

"Oh, from Chrysalis? Didn't we replace him with that other fellow after what happened at your school? What's he got to do with any of this?"

"Never mind," Miranda said. She felt hollow as if she was only now realizing John was gone - again. It hurt every time. "I'm going home." She meant the house Romi had made up for them.

"I want you to think of this as your home," Albert said, his tone more businessy than fatherly.

"I do," she said, her smile as real as the plastic plants that used to be in Albert's Chrysalis office.

"Good, good." He nodded and relaxed back into the bioformation wall with a deep, gurgling sigh.

"What's wrong with you?" Miranda tried for a sympathetic tone.

"I'm devolving," Albert said as casually as if he were announcing this quarter's earnings had been a bit under par. "Carmine was using some of the base sample we stored to counter the effect, but he's gone now, isn't he?"

Miranda resisted the urge to cringe under her father's displeasure. She sat up straight and looked him in the eyes, the way John had taught her. His words seemed to echo in her mind. "Take responsibility for your actions."

"The helicopter Carmine was piloting crashed," she said, matching Albert's matter-of-fact tone. Don't think of who else died in that crash, she whispered to herself.

"Which means we are left with a very significant issue. If we can't control the hives, the Infected will exhaust their food sources within a few months and die off. Which brings us to how we can best apply your new strategy."

"My strategy?"

"Moving the Infected en masse. It worked brilliantly to disrupt the settlement in Wyoming." Albert offered an approving smile. "Most of the noninfected were either killed, scattered or added to our number."

"How does that fix the devolution problem?" Miranda was annoyed that Albert was making her tease out the information. She recognized one of his favorite power moves from the many business meetings she had sat in on back when her father was grooming her for a career in finance.

"It makes putting a hive there much easier, which makes it much easier to screen and process the noninfected to determine who has the potential to join us and who might have the base strain." He meant Marius and anyone who had gotten a direct infusion from him, like — not thinking of him — John.

"That's the new strategy?" Miranda wrinkled her nose. "Active genocide?"

"Mandy," Albert tisked. "Let's not use emotional rhetoric. People can't survive without civilization and civilization is gone. You know better than I about the kinds of violence that are going on out there, and it's being done to people, by people. Even with the external threat of the Infected, they're still more interested in killing each other than they are in their own survival."

Miranda squirmed, frustrated she couldn't argue with her father's point. Between the raiders who'd tried to kill them and worse on their way from Portland to Montana and the people in Yellowstone trying to enslave the people in New Avalon, humanity was really not sending its best.

After all, it hadn't been the Infected who'd killed John.

It had been people.

Air.

That's what she needed.

Fresh air.

Miranda fumbled her way out of the hive, climbed the many, many stairs to the main entrance and stood heaving under the twilight sky. Even in late autumn the humidity lingered past sunset. Miranda felt feverish, sticky with sweat, slimy, as if she would forever be coated with a thin film of bioformations.

In the back of her mind, the Infected buzzed with urgent requests and numerous trifling demands.

We need more nesting material.

We want fresher food.

Why can't we eat all the noninfected in this valley?

Our Enlightened devolved. We need another.

"Miranda." Romi stepped away from the car parked at the far end of the otherwise vacant lot. Another person skulked in the shadows behind her. Miranda narrowed her eyes. It wasn't like Romi to let anyone sneak up on her, which meant she probably knew the person — a man, judging from the size and stance.

Romi's head turned to follow Miranda's gaze. She gave the 'All Good' signal and waved Miranda over.

Under the heavy branches of the untrimmed trees surrounding the parking lot, it was nearly full dark, but Miranda didn't have any trouble recognizing Eli. His gear was different, better. Nothing was patched or mended. All shiny and new.

"Are we clear to talk here?" Eli asked.

"You mean, am I reporting our conversation to my dad like a good spy?" Miranda raised an eyebrow, probably invisible to Eli in the gloom.

He started to nod, but Romi said, "We know you're not a spy."

"Now you're 'we' with him?" Miranda knew she was being unfair, but that didn't stop the doubt from gushing through her, reminding her of all the people who saw her as nothing but a means to an end.

Romi didn't say anything long enough for Eli to shift uncomfortably and cough softly.

"This is kind of time sensitive," he muttered.

"Oh, I didn't realize we were on your schedule," Miranda drizzled her words with enough snark to sink a snark liner in the middle of the snark ocean.

"Let's go talk somewhere else," Romi said.

Miranda almost refused out of spite, but Romi held out her hand and Miranda decided not to be so childish as to ignore it. I'm an adult, having an adult relationship with another adult, she reminded herself. This sucks.

They left the car. No reason to waste the limited fuel driving wherever Romi wanted to go to talk. They walked down the road, now an overgrown track. An owl swooped past on silent wings. Miranda knew there used to be lots of bats in the cave, but since the Infected moved in, they'd either been eaten or mutated.

"Okay, this should be far enough," Romi said when they crossed the bridge and were in the town proper. She put her head on Miranda's shoulder and whispered into her neck, "Wither thou goest, I shall go and wither thou diest, I shall die and there will I be buried."

"You're so weird." Miranda laid her head against Romi's and let the anger flow out of her muscles until she could fit her body to Romi's as easily as sleeping late fit a Saturday morning.

"I went to Detroit," Eli said. "It's a whole thing. Government, military, labs, the works. They've been tracking this mold that's damaging the Infected."

"We know about that," Miranda said. She didn't tell him how. Protecting Marius's secrets turned out to be a hard habit to break.

"Good, that makes things easier," Eli said. "They pinpointed this area as the likely epicenter of Infected activity by tagging and following some of the swarms. When we got close enough, I contacted Romi."

"Who's 'we'?"

"The 10th Mountain, or what's left of them," Eli said. "Mostly it's a collection of anyone with any kind of military training from some Eagle Scouts to National Guard to Coast Guard."

"Which will really help with all the blow the Infected are smuggling in," Miranda said.

"What?" Eli stared at her.

"She's messing with you," Romi said. "Go on."

"You told us about how you destroyed the hive in the quarry. Our commander thinks that solution can work again. We just need to get enough of the mold into the heart of the hive here and —" Eli swiped a finger across his throat.

"How are you planning on doing that?" Miranda asked. "The hive is full of Infected. There are Enlightened, and devolved in there, too. It's not small, like the one in the quarry."

"Some help from our friends." Eli held up a radio.

"That's not going to work!" Miranda waved at the radio and back toward the cave. "There are thousands in there. Any bite is basically lethal."

"It'll work," Eli said. "Because we have you."

Chapter 23 - Marius

Everything in the room reeked of failure. From the faint scent of new paint and freshly milled wood that made up the replaced interior wall, to the lingering scorch smell coming from the ceiling and outer wall. The closet had a musty smell as if it had never fully dried out from all the water used to battle the house fire.

Marius yanked his rucksack out and set it on the bed. He pointedly didn't look at the paperback open face down on the crate Torres used as a bedside table. It was easy to pack following the checklist John had drilled into his head since the early Chrysalis days. His hands moved without much thought, which was good since keeping his overly busy brain quiet was his only defense against

...

Someone knocked on the door.

"Come in." He tucked the last of his clothes in and

cinched the bag closed.

Percy opened the door. She looked around, probably noting the absence of Torres, and came in, closing the door behind her.

"Mom and Dad are worried about you," she said.

"They're more worried about you," Marius said.

"They're worried differently about me," Percy said. She leaned against the bed frame and studied her brother. "They understand what's going on with me. They've dealt with pregnancies before." She ran a hand over her barely bulging belly.

"I mean John," Marius said. They hadn't talked about her loss since returning from Yellowstone. Marius didn't know where to even begin the conversation. The terror and helplessness he'd felt when Torres was nearly hanged still woke him in a cold sweat at night. If things went differently, if she were the one who'd died ...

"I know," Percy said. She tugged at the ruck's strap. "Where are you going this time?"

"South." He didn't want to admit where he was really going. Percy would just argue with him and he was too tired to deal with her. "Got to see what the Yellowstone people are up to."

"There are other Rangers," Percy said.

"We all have to do our share," Marius said.

"Okay. I'll go with you."

"No."

"Why not?" Percy raised her chin. "Because I'm pregnant? I'm not *that* pregnant yet."

"No, this has nothing to do with that." Marius knew she was baiting him and he still couldn't resist.

"Doesn't it? So, why can't I go?"

"Because Mom and Dad need you here."

"And they don't need you? Bull pucky, Marius. They're desperate for their best beloved son to hang around for more than a day or two and you know it."

"I'm not and I don't," Marius said.

Percy frowned at him. "What's that supposed to mean?"

"Didn't they tell you?"

"Tell me what? Honestly, whatever game you think you're playing is going way over my head."

Marius studied his sister. It surprised him how hard it was to say the truth out loud, but she deserved to know, deserved to be able to contextualize their parents' behavior and understand her place in their family.

"I'm not their son. Dad found me." Without thinking, he added, "If he'd left me there, none of this would have happened." It was a mantra that went through his head so often it seemed inevitable.

"You don't know that," Percy said.

"I do."

"How?" She folded her arms over her belly and squinted at him in a near perfect imitation of Annette.

"Because Rasmussen was tracking me. I was one of his test subjects when I was a baby. Dad found me in an abandoned lab."

"So?"

"So? What do you mean, 'So?'? This is a big deal, Perc."

"So, I mean if Rasmussen was experimenting on the virus for twenty years between the time Dad found you and the time you went to Miranda's school and met him, don't you think he had other subjects? Did other experiments? For flip's sake, Marius, not everything is about you."

He stared at her, but she went on as if she'd been saving all this up to tell him for years. Maybe she had.

"I think we were lucky."

"Lucky?" Marius managed to croak, waving around him at his smoke-damaged room and beyond.

"Yes," Percy said. "Lucky. If it had been someone else, someone less, well, I'll say it, less good — shut up, you dork! If it had been someone less stupidly altruistic or who hadn't studied viruses, what do you think would have happened? Do you think we'd have a retrovirus spreading mold to give us a chance? Do you think someone else would have bled themself over and over like a weird self-vampire to save other people?"

Marius sat down on the edge of his bed.

Percy sat next to him and put an arm around his shoulders.

"So, yes, I do think we all got extremely lucky that the ring came to you, Mr. Frodo."

It was Marius's turn to narrow his eyes, fighting off the smile at her clumsy and extremely effective attempt to cheer him up.

"Who's the dork now?"

"Pft." She snorted and stood up. "You're adopted." She ruffled his hair.

"Too soon!" But he was smiling as he stood up.

Percy hugged him. "I love you, big brother."

On his way to the barn, Marius practiced his apology.

"Lourdes, I'm sorry I didn't listen to you about the hive." No. They both agreed the hive was a problem, so he wasn't wrong about that.

"Lourdes, I'm sorry I undertook a solo mission, which I know is against the Ranger code." No. Torres herself had gone on a solo mission to find him, so she would understand that.

"Lourdes, I'm sorry I left you before and before that and before that. I want to be with you, no matter where that is or how long we have left." Yes. He would tuck Torres against his chest, bury his face in her hair, know that even if they weren't safe, they were together.

The barn bustled with activity. Rangers were laying out their gear or packing supplies, joking and smack-talking as they prepared to leave on missions to Great Falls and Point Zebulon. Nestor and Dawn stood together near the wall map. Nestor was carefully copying down a series of grid coordinates onto slips of paper. Dawn was braiding her hair back into two long plaits while reading a checklist written in Percy's curling letters.

"Hey, where's the boss?" Marius asked, maneuvering his way through the controlled chaos.

"Left this morning." Dawn looked surprised. "We thought you went with her."

"Where's she going?" Marius glanced at the map, his gaze following the southerly path Torres's fingers had walked only hours ago.

As if reading Marius's mind, Nestor tapped the red pin on the map indicating a dangerous area. Yellowstone.

"I have to go," Marius said. If he hurried, he could catch up. He had to catch up. If he wasn't with Torres when she got to Yellowstone ... The creak of the hanging rope, her faint choking gurgle echoed in his mind. His heart seized then galloped.

He was down the driveway and out the gate before he thought to say goodbye to his family. He stopped, pulling Chaldene in a tight, dancing circle as he considered riding back. No. He was already hours behind. His family would have to understand. Percy would tell them.

Marius tugged the reins and pressed his knees into Chaldene's flanks. She eagerly sprang into a trot, shaking her head as if happy to feel the crisp autumn wind in her mane. Out here, away from the ranch and the people, away from the shed and the mold, the vials that never had enough of his blood and the needles that left his arms looking like a junky's, he could breathe, could simply exist in a space where there was only the thrumming cadence of Chaldene's hoofbeats, the cool air carrying the scents of browning grasses and impending snow, and the piercingly blue and cloudless sky.

He turned his face up and closed his eyes, letting the weakened autumn sunlight touch his cheeks. The Flash hadn't caused an unending winter. The mold would be back next spring, stronger than ever. He would catch up with Torres, would apologize, would stay because she needed him to stay even if she never admitted it. He would try to believe she and Percy and so many others were right when they said the HHV pandemic wasn't his fault.

Something passed between him and the sun.

He opened his eyes.

A lumpy oblong sailed through the air above him, like a poorly made balloon animal that had come undone. Hanging below the main balloon was a large basket. Dangling under the balloon were people. They were low enough that Marius could see they had weapons — bows, guns, even spears and machetes — strapped to them.

The balloon was coming from the direction of Yellowstone, heading northwest, towards Crossroads.

Marius held up a hand, cupping it over the visor of his Army cap as he squinted south. His heart lurched. There was a faint haze on the horizon. Dust. Whatever was coming was moving in force and with enough bodies to raise a big cloud as they crossed the plains.

He needed to warn Crossroads. Torres would understand.

Chapter 24 - Torres

Crossroads, Montana, USA — Autumn, Year 2

Torres led a three-person team consisting of herself, Seung, and Annie. She couldn't spare even that many Rangers, but she couldn't ignore the potential threat from Yellowstone. Besides, Annie needed some experience, and this way Torres could supervise her on her first official mission outside of patrolling the Morning Star's perimeter.

They swung east, giving Crossroads a miss. If they stopped, the townsfolk would want to know all the latest news and gossip. They didn't have the time, and frankly, Torres didn't have the patience. After her fight with Marius, she was as raw and hostile as a singed tiger. How dare he imply she was a coward when he was running away himself? It wasn't ruggedly glorious to stay and do the everyday work of keeping the Rangers running, but it was necessary. Why didn't he see that? He was smart so he must know. He was choosing to leave because whatever was wrong in him hurt more than being with her helped.

Summed up: She wasn't enough.

The realization ate away at her, like a cancer, hollowing out her bones, until she felt nothing but emptiness. She hadn't been enough for her own mother to choose her over Cynty. She hadn't been enough to protect the Morning Star ranch from the Infected or to escape from Yellowstone. She wasn't enough to fight off the darkness that was drowning Marius in guilt and self-loathing.

Another part of her scoffed at the oh-woe-is-me self-pity. She was furious at Marius and his rejection. She was a badass Marine who kept a lot of people safe and alive against really big odds. If he didn't want to be with her, that was his loss. If Marius wanted to court Death instead of her, let him. She had too much self-respect to be anyone's backup plan or second choice.

"What's that?" Annie pointed west, towards the low dark mass of the town of Crossroads on the horizon. There was something in the air above the town. A big lumpy something.

A zeppelin.

Torres yanked on Ganymede's reins. He stuttered to a stop, laying his ears back and humping his spine in protest.

Torres's tactical brain kicked in, assessing the situation, listing their assets and liabilities. She looked at the other two Rangers. Seung had more experience, but Annie was lighter. She would probably be faster on a breakaway.

"Annie, get back to the ranch. Let them know Crossroads is under attack. Make sure Bailey radios the rest of New Avalon, then get every Ranger not on home defense and come to town. Got it?"

Annie nodded, her eyes wide, frightened and excited.

"Go!" Torres waved, and Gany jerked his head. Annie got her own mount turned around and shot off, bouncing nearly out of her saddle, but clinging on. Torres had to trust that she would make it.

She turned to Seung. "Let's go fuck up their invasion."

To his credit, Seung didn't waste time with questions, which was good because she had nothing even resembling a plan. All she knew was that she would die before losing someone else. No one else. Not after Miranda ran away, John died, and Marius left her.

They turned their mounts and raced west, nearly lying on the horses' necks to stay on.

As they thundered into town, Torres noted a few of the locals already standing out in their yards or the street, looking southeast. Torres slowed enough to find out that Mayor Flynn was at the diner across from the post office and they were off again.

Grieg's Hall had transformed from sleepy cafe to a popular spot where people gathered to share news and socialize. It didn't hurt that it was an easy place to find Flynn and often a Ranger or two who was passing through Crossroads.

Torres pulled Gany to a stop and jumped off, nearly catching her foot in the stirrup and hopping for a few steps while her horse blew and stamped. No time to see to him. She burst into the diner and looked around. Flynn was seated at the big table in the back corner with the blacksmith from Esmeralda and her brother, the glassblower.

"They're coming," Torres said. She pointed towards the southwestern sky. "Yellowstone. They're using their zeppelin."

Flynn stood up and hurried to meet the Ranger. Already a knot of concerned people was forming outside the diner, pummeling Seung with questions as he took care of the horses.

"We know they're probably not coming in peace, right?" Flynn asked. She barely came up to Torres's armpit, but that never seemed to slow her down in the least.

"No, probably not. I sent a Ranger back to alert the ranch. They'll put out the word to the other towns, but no telling how soon we can get anyone here to reinforce us. We have to act like we're alone."

A good day to die.

As Torres stood behind the hastily constructed roadblock on the southern edge of Crossroads, she thought of all the days she might have died. At least this day was bright and breezy. She wasn't soaked from rain, freezing from snow, or hot and sweaty.

The civilian defenders were doing well. So far no one had started firing wildly or tried to run away. One of the scouts on the water tower reported that there were ground troops massing on the south bank of the river. Torres considered sending Seung to blow up the bridge but scrapped the idea. It would only harm Crossroads in the long run, assuming they survived the day. Besides, it might take him a long time to find explosives, assuming there were any to be found in Crossroads.

Torres pushed her hair back from her forehead and sighted through her scope, recounting the number of people in the zeppelin as if knowing there were thirty-three instead of thirty-five would change the odds in some way. One of the balloonists ran out away from the airship on a beam and cut a line. A tarp that had been secured against the balloon's underside flapped open. Liquid cascaded down splattering rooftops, gardens, and even a few defenders.

Gasoline.

The smell was unmistakable.

Crossroads nestled in a wide river valley between the last of the swells of the Great Plains and the first foothills of the Rocky Mountains. East of the town stubbly fields or wild stretches of prairie grasslands and meadows baked in the early afternoon sunshine. North, a narrow strip of trees pretended to be a forest. To the south, the riverbed was mostly dry this time of year, leaving a wide boggy patch of land with a thin stream twisting through its heart. In the west, the land was rocky, covered with scrub brush and a few scattered pines.

Torres unclipped the walkie-talkie Mayor Flynn had given her and keyed the microphone. "Flynn, get your fire department ready. Wildfire drill."

Behind her, a wave a frightened murmurs rippled through the defenders. Torres ignored them, studying the zeppelin. Would Sebald risk destroying the whole town to conquer it? What would be the use of another burnt out town? No. He needed the people, at least most of them. So, the fire had to be a calculated strike meant to break the fighting spirit of the defenders. It was a smart move with a good chance of success at very little cost to the Yellowstoners.

"Pull back," she ordered. "Seung, get them set up by E&E's." The park across the street from the grocery store had been used as an open-air market during the summer and had almost no grass left. Nothing too flammable.

While the other Ranger led the rearward advance, Torres pulled aside a few of the townies who she knew to be reliable in a crisis. She set them up in obvious defensive positions, keeping an eye on the zeppelin. It swung wide, arching north and west to cross the center of town before turning back south. Scouting. Fine. That gave her time to set up fake resistance while Seung got the real defenders in place.

Her job would be to keep the zeppelin focused on her for as long as possible. That meant not just acting like a credible threat but being one.

"Flynn, I need a bear-hunting gun," she said over the radio. "Fast as possible."

By the time a man thrust a hunting rifle into the former Marine's hand, the zeppelin had almost finished its slow circle. Torres sprinted to the laundromat, the only building in Crossroads with a New York style exterior fire escape. She clambered up and looked around. No cover or concealment.

"When they get closer, light the gas by the car wash," Torres called down to the defenders below. The car wash was surrounded by a wide lawn of very dead grass and had been splashed by the zeppelin's first pass. Outside the yard, was a country road on two sides and parking lots on the other. Torres hoped that the fire wouldn't jump.

"The firefighters aren't here yet," one of the defenders called back.

"I know. I just need a few shots at the balloon," Torres said. "After you set the fire, fall back into town."

She could hear the defenders discussing, but she didn't have time to convince them. She would have one chance and she wasn't even sure this would work. What if the hunting rifle weren't strong enough to pierce the zeppelin's balloon? She had no idea what the material was. Regardless, she was determined to keep fighting until she couldn't.

Chapter 25 - Miranda

If Miranda never had to be part of another military operation, she would die happy. Eli led the main group towards the wide stairs leading into the cave system. Two other groups moved in from other entrances. Miranda worked quickly to put her plan in motion.

Over the past few months, she had gathered more control over the Mammoth Cave Infected, especially the scouts. The Enlightened still reported directly to her father over the bioformation network, but without the scouts, they had little outside information to report. Miranda sent her scouts away on busy work trips.

Go check how low the river is. Go find ten uninfected deer. Go find a place with a lot of cans of food.

Once the 10th Mountain got inside the cave itself, hiding them would be more a matter of luck than skill. She warned them to avoid touching the bioformations or letting the sensory tendrils reach them, but she wasn't hopeful they would make it far in.

Sure enough, as she, Eli, and Romi stepped off the stairs into the wide room the uninfected teens used to screen newcomers and later to sort their discarded gear, one of the soldiers tripped. He fell hard into the wall, flailing at the soft, grabby tendrils trying to get a bite of him.

Eli whipped out a tube filled with ground up mold and spores. Before he could throw it at the wall Miranda put a hand on the wall. She sank in to the wrist as she reassured the bioformation that what it had sensed was simply a new prospect for Enlightenment.

Nothing to worry about. I'm here. I have everything under control. She didn't know if the network had fired off an alert to her father, but too late to stop it now.

"I told you," she hissed.

"Let's just get this done." Eli shouldered past her.

"You're welcome," she muttered, pulling her hand free of the meat wall with a moist slurping sound.

They wound down, past tunnel openings and the cell-like spaces the teenagers used as their dormitory. As the last of Eli's troops crept away, Miranda caught Romi's hand and pulled her close.

"Get the kids out," she whispered into the other woman's ear. "Don't come back in. This is going to go really bad. I'll find you when it's done."

"What part of 'I stay with you' wasn't clear to you?" Romi laced her fingers through Miranda's and squeezed.

But Miranda couldn't accept her promise as much as she would have liked to. She had to keep Romi safe, even from herself.

This is what it's like, Miranda realized. This is what it's like for Marius and Torres when they leave the rest of us behind. It's more important to them to keep us safe than to be with us.

She felt a rush of altruistic pride at her own instinct to self-sacrifice. But, no, that wasn't what she planned to do. Nothing so noble as Marius and his quest for martyrdom or Torres and her watchdog loyalty.

"I'll be fine. My dad's not going to hurt me, and Eli knows they need me or none of them are getting out alive," Miranda said. "Please. Those kids will probably get killed in the crossfire or whatever is about to happen in here."

"I'm not leaving you," Romi started forward, tugging Miranda with her, but the other woman held her ground.

"Romi," she said and something in her voice stopped the former commando in her tracks. "I need to do this alone. You're not leaving me. I know it's not like before. I'm leaving you. Is that an okay way to think of it?"

"No. That's never an okay way to think of it. We go together."

"We'll be together after this."

"Promise?"

"Promise."

Their kiss was deep as if each were trying to find reassurance in the other's lips.

Romi started to leave but stopped and held out her pistol. Miranda shook her head.

"Hey!" Eli whisper-shouted from down the passage. Miranda could see the cluster of nervous soldiers waiting for her.

"Moving, sir!" she whisper-shouted back in her best

faux military voice.

"Where's Romi going?" Eli asked when she caught up.

"I need her to distract some of the Infected. They already know her, so she'll be fine." Miranda hoped, but she had no way to know for sure how the Infected would react when everything started happening for real.

"We shouldn't split up," Eli said.

"We shouldn't be down here at all," Miranda said. "Every minute you stand here whining because no one asked your opinion makes it more likely the Infected will notice you and I won't be able to cover for everyone."

Without waiting for Eli's response, she brushed past the soldiers and continued down the winding tunnel that led to her father's chamber. At each major junction, she told Eli to station one of his soldiers with their mold ready for her signal. Those intersections were controlled by Enlightened who reported directly to her father, their messages fast and clear over the network at such short distances.

Outside her father's office, Miranda stopped. There was no going back from here. She closed her eyes and pictured John the way he'd looked the last time she'd seen him alive. He and Marius had joked about him fathering a child at his age. She remembered the contented pride on his face. It was a look she'd never seen her own father have when considering her. After everything John had done for her, had meant to her, Albert didn't even remember who he was.

Miranda opened her eyes and gave the signal. Less than a minute later, the first howls and shrieks began rising through the hive.

"Don't come in here," Miranda said to Eli.

She strode into Albert's office. He was twitching and rolling as his sensory tentacles buffeted him with frantic input from throughout the hive.

"Miranda," he said. His gaze moved past her, out the door to where Eli waited, a canister of mold in his hand.

Miranda snatched the mold. She took two light running steps and jumped up onto her father's desk.

Albert shrank back, the Infected's instinctive fear of the mold greater than any outrage he might be feeling. "What are you doing?"

"Succeeding you, father." She yanked the lid off and doused him in the shimmering black powder.

Miranda stumbled through the cave, trying to re-establish control over the Infected. The network, once a seemingly infallible source of information, was down. Tatters of bioformations hung from ceilings and walls or mushed underfoot. As bad as the overly warm sweet-meaty smell of the Infected usually was, it seemed a million times worse. Plus, there was the disgusting charred hair smell and the lingering odor of whatever chemical grenades the 10th Mountain had cooked up.

Every time she brushed against a bioformation, the surge of information was overwhelming. Panicked Enlightened reached out for instructions, demanded reassurance, or screamed out their final moments of pain and rage.

The mold! The Abomination's mold is here. Albert, do something. Albert?

The mold killed Albert, Miranda told them. *I'm here. I'm in charge now.*

A few resisted, but most didn't question her claim to the throne. They were grateful to have someone coordinating the hive again and the wider network.

Exhausted, Miranda sat on a wide, flat-topped stalagmite in the egg-shaped chamber that once held a tube of blue goo and its insensible prisoner. She didn't particularly want to be in Marius's former cell, but it was the only other place in the cave system that had hive-wide connections. A few levels above her, Albert's remains smeared the walls, floor, and ceiling of his former office. Under no circumstances could Miranda concentrate enough to get anything done while staring at the puddle of purplish red on the floor, or the still-twitching sensory tentacles that were embedded in the meatwall.

What she wanted more than anything else was a long, hot bath. She settled for dousing her hands in the mineral rich water that ran in the underground river inside the cave. Even so, she kept rubbing her hands against her shirt, trying to wipe off the spatters of her father.

Kill the noninfected? They meant the teenagers. The hive had always been about a minute away from eating the wannabe Enlightened. Without Albert's constant reminder to leave them alone, the Infected turned their attention to the closest ready source of food and nesting material.

Maybe later. Cleanse the hive first, Miranda instructed.

She tried to believe that Romi would get the kids out

safely or have the sense to leave them if that wasn't possible. If Miranda admitted to the hive that she was trying to protect the kids from them, she would likely face a full-scale rebellion. The only option was to lie. But it was hard to keep her true thoughts separated from the hive as more and more tendrils dropped from the ceiling or reached out from the walls, seeking instructions and information.

The Infected, unable to connect with the Enlightened, were either clustering around the bits of the bioformation that remained or were rampaging through the cave and out into the surrounding countryside in an orgy of destruction. They gleefully attacked anything they found, venting the aggression that the Enlightened had forced them to keep pent up. Miranda didn't bother to try to slow them down once they were out of the cave. She didn't have that kind of control.

As the network broke down inside the cave, thanks to Eli and his busy soldiers, it was harder and harder for Miranda to get any sense of what was happening. She fought the remaining Enlightened to keep the main passageway clear. If Romi or any of the teenagers were still inside, she wanted them to have an escape route.

To add to the confusion, Enlightened from distant hives pummeled Miranda with questions.

What's happening? Should we attack the human preserves? Should we send reinforcements?

Should we attack the Abomination's hive instead of the humans in Crossroads?

Wait! Miranda pushed aside the other questions, letting her subconscious deal with them as best it could as she focused on the Enlightened's question. She could tell from the signal strength that it was far away, somewhere in Idaho or Montana.

Who's attacking Crossroads? Technically, the town was part of New Avalon so not protected by the Great Falls human preserve arrangement, but since the last attack on the Morning Star ranch, the Infected had been wary of the area. There were a lot of easier meals to be had elsewhere.

Carmine, like Albert told him. The Enlightened seemed indignant.

He's not dead?

No. He is leading the Infected to help the attack. Let the noninfected weaken Crossroads and then we take it.

Tell them to stop. Miranda pushed all the authority she could muster into the order.

I can't. The Enlightened cringed back from the force of her command. *They're gone. There are no hives, no networks near the Abomination's territory.*

Miranda's mind whirled. There was too much to do. She needed to find Romi, to make sure she was all right. She also needed to check on Eli and his troops. Even if Eli wasn't her favorite mistake, she wished him and the 10th Mountain all the best. More immediately, the hive was screaming for her attention in a thousand thousand different ways. Albert using the Enlightened as middle managers was beginning to make a lot more sense.

"We're on our own." A man's voice echoed through the nearby tunnels, jerking Miranda out of her spiral. "She wouldn't help us if she could."

"I'm not leaving without her." Romi's voice, tired and monotone as if she'd already repeated herself a dozen times.

"She's probably — ouch, fuck — dead." Miranda recognized Eli's voice.

"I'm not dead," Miranda said. "I'm busy."

A clatter of footsteps and Romi burst into the chamber and flung herself into Miranda's arms.

"You were supposed to leave." Miranda didn't know whether to shake Romi or kiss her.

"You really believed I would?" Romi settled Miranda's internal debate by kissing her. Eli leaned against the chamber's opening. The front half of his uniform was smeared with dark slime, black mold, and blood. His arm hung uselessly, the sleeve in tatters.

"Speaking of leaving," Eli said. "This place is coming apart at the seams. Could we —?" He waved down the tunnel.

"I can't," Miranda said. In only the few minutes she'd been distracted the bioformation was buzzing with messages from the other hives and local Infected. If she left, went where she couldn't tap directly into the network, she wouldn't be able to control the chaos. To be honest, she wasn't doing a great job of that anyway, but things would get a lot worse without her there to at least channel the chaos in some way.

"I said I would help you get out, but I can barely do that right now. I'm keeping this together by my fingernails, so if you're gonna go, you better do it now."

"We're all going," Romi said. "That was the plan, right? Destroy the hive and get out."

"But if I leave ..." Miranda didn't know how to explain the weight, the complication, the obligation that she felt. The Infected were a part of her and she a part of them.

Leaving the cave wouldn't free her from the Infected any more than leaving Harrow Hall had freed Marius from the virus he carried in his blood.

"You can't leave," Romi said. She always seemed to understand what Miranda couldn't put into words. The relief of not having to explain herself was enormous.

"And he can't stay," Romi added, nodding to Eli. "I'll get him out and come back. Can you hold on that long?"

"Yes, but before he goes, we need to talk about how things are gonna work now," Miranda said. She patted the stalagmite beside hers. "Have a seat, Eli. Let's talk about what kinds of jets you have access to."

Chapter 26 - Torres

Crossroads, Montana, USA – Autumn, Year 2

The zeppelin circled lazily over the outskirts of Crossroads. Torres braced against the metal struts that held up the laundromat's signage. She sighted, half laughing at the ridiculousness of taking time to aim. The zeppelin was huge, impossible to miss. The old pray-and-spray method all but guaranteed that she would hit some part of it.

The problem was that she only had four rounds and she needed to hit something critical. Would peppering the balloon itself do the job? Or should she try for something like steering? Did it have a rudder?

The crew was moving around the bottom of the balloon. There was a basket carrying a few people and what looked like weapons, ammunition, and gear. Most of the people stood on planks holding onto rope railings with harnesses tethering them to the airship.

One of the crew raised a bow and sighted in on Torres, making her decision for her. She took out the archer and took two shots at the balloon. The crew scrambled and trampled to get away from her line of fire. She grinned savagely as one fell off the walkway to flutter along below the zeppelin like a streamer.

An arrow struck the roof near Torres. She jerked back. Two archers on the far end of the walkway were shooting at her. The second arrow tore through the laundromat sign and nearly hit Torres. No more time to play around. She started to retreat across the roof to the fire escape but paused. The zeppelin turned enough for her to see there were two motors on the back of it, rigged up to propel it forward and steer it.

Another arrow bounced off the metal strut near her head. Now or never. She shot at the nearest motor, aiming for what she hoped was its gas tank. Sadly, no Hollywood-style ball of fire. An arrow grazed her shoulder. She ran, dodging in a zig-zagging pattern, thankful that the fire escape was around the corner from the zeppelin. Once she was on it, she was effectively out of sight and out of range of the airborne archers.

Torres didn't know how quickly they could get the airship turned around or if they would bother to come back for her, but she didn't wait to find out. As she hit the ground, fire flared up from the carwash. In a few minutes, the smoke would screen the defenders from view.

But there were no defenders. They had followed her orders and retreated. Good.

She ran, keeping close to the buildings, glancing over her shoulder from time to time, trying to gauge where the zeppelin was and where they might be going.

"Torres!" Seung's voice rang out. The Ranger stood in the doorway of a house and waved her in. She ducked inside and they both ran through the living room to peer out the windows, necks craned as they searched the sky for the zeppelin.

It was descending.

"Too much to hope for that it's crashing," Torres said.

"What's the plan?" Seung asked. The plan had always been a John problem. Torres executed the plan. But she didn't have time to rage again at the unfairness of his death or consider all the ways she missed him. She needed a plan.

"We get back to the rest of the townies and get up high. Our advantage is that we know the area and we're defending." There. That was the plan.

She radioed Flynn to let the mayor know they were coming and not to shoot them. More running. How far had the townies retreated? Torres didn't want to admit how much she missed Gany as she and Seung trotted down the empty streets, taking turns carrying the hunting rifle. Even without bullets, it was too valuable to leave, especially since the people from Yellowstone probably had rounds they could use in it.

Flynn had organized a hastily constructed barricade by having the townspeople push several cars across Main Street. Torres sent defenders up into the buildings overlooking the two parallel streets, thankful that Crossroads wasn't a big town. Sure, the Yellowstone people could flank them, but they would have to go out of the town itself and then come back in, splitting their forces and providing the defenders the opportunity to shoot at them from cover the whole time. If Torres were making plans for Yellowstone, she wouldn't choose that one.

"The balloon's crashing!" someone yelled. Torres climbed on top of one of the cars in the barricade and stood on tiptoes, cupping her hand over her eyes. The zeppelin was definitely going down. Puffs of black smoke billowed from the rear. Had she really shot them down? Or were they simply landing as per plan?

"Hold positions." Torres was pleased to hear the command echoed back through the town's defenders. "Ranged, ready," she called, knowing that in upper floors and on rooftops the defenders would be readying their guns, bows, and whatever else they had.

The Yellowstone forces charged up the two side streets. They must have seen the barricade and decided to run the gantlet.

"Fire!" Torres shouted as she hopped down off the car. Shots rang out and the smokey tang of gunpowder filled the air, cutting through the reek of gas drifting in from the southern edge of Crossroads. Arrows flashed downward. Torres saw one bounce off the body armor of one of the invaders. Another caught one of the Yellowstone men in the neck.

For a few crazed moments Torres watched the assault, but then she realized what was happening. It was too easy. The attackers weren't pushing forward, weren't digging in, weren't retreating. They were simply keeping the defenders busy. They were well armed with enough ammunition to keep the defenders pinned in place for hours, at least until dark, when the whole battle would change. The defenders had the luxury of choosing their targets with care and not wasting a shot. They could easily keep the invaders at bay for hours. This battle was a stalemate; anyone could see that.

The question was why commit the zeppelin crew to this when they could have landed and attacked anywhere?

Despite the danger of making herself a lone and obvious target, she climbed back up onto the car. She turned in a slow circle, looking out past the battle, past the balloon wallowing in a parking lot, past the edge of the town.

There.

Movement, low to the ground, but she caught the flash of metal glinting in the sunlight as someone low-crawled through the prairie grasses toward the lightly defended north part of town.

"Freaking Sebald," Torres muttered.

Torres took a deep swig of water and stared out the second story window of an abandoned house at the street below. Nothing moved. Nothing had moved since the last invader had tried her luck sprinting. The corpse lay on the sidewalk, soaking in a puddle of congealing blood.

It was early evening, the sun's last rays spiking behind the mountains. The past few hours had been a marathon. Torres and Seung had run back and forth rallying the retreating defenders in the south and organizing the mostly unarmed and terrified townies in the north. For the moment, they held off the attackers, but night was falling fast.

"Torres," Flynn's muffled voice crackled over the radio. "They're waving a white flag over by the hardware store on Ivy."

"On my way," Torres said, trying to keep the exhaustion from her voice. She just wanted to sit for five continuous minutes. She levered herself up and stretched, trying to unknot her muscles and get her joints warmed up. Everything snapped and popped. When had that started happening?

"Here." She handed Seung the walkie-talkie. "You're the boss while I'm seeing what this is about."

"I'll try not to let the power go to my head," Seung said, his voice sounding as weary as Torres felt.

She trudged down the stairs and out the door. She was halfway across the street when she froze. She hadn't checked the area. Anyone could have been lying in wait. Quickly, she scanned the surrounding houses, noting the three that had Crossroads defenders posted were the only ones that seemed occupied. Still, she kept to the shadows, making her way through the town at a shuffling run.

Mayor Flynn waited behind the car barricade. She had a big thermos that smelled like it had mostly real coffee in it and a basket of pasties. Torres's stomach rumbled, reminding her that war was hungry work and she hadn't eaten since her pre-dawn planning session in the barn.

Where was Marius now? Assuming he'd ridden all day, he would probably be just east of White Sulfur Springs, setting up a quick campsite. No, she wasn't thinking of him. That led to the aching and angry void in her heart. She didn't have time for that.

"What's going on?" Torres asked, kneeling behind the barricade as she looked around. No movement on Main Street other than a pair of Yellowstone people, holding up a white flag.

"That's it," Flynn said. She shoved a pastie into Torres's hand.

"Missus Flynn," one of the dark figures called. Torres recognized Walter's voice. "We're still waiting for your answer."

"Not patiently," Flynn shouted back. "And it's Mayor Flynn to you, sonny Jim."

"Yes, ma'am," Walter said.

"Where's your boss?" Torres called.

"Is that the hanged woman?" Walter sounded smug.

"Your boss is as good at hangings as he is at invasions," Torres snapped, resisting the instinct to rub her neck. The skin was still very tender and shouting made her throat burn.

"This isn't an invasion," Walter called.

"Could fool us," Flynn shouted.

"Can we talk?" Walter waved the white flag up and down.

"We are talking," Flynn yelled.

"We're yelling."

"I'll go," Torres said. She didn't trust her voice to hold out much longer. "Seung's got the walkie and he knows what to do." He didn't really, but no reason to scare the civilians. Torres didn't know what to do either, to be fair to her fellow Ranger. All she knew was Yellowstone wouldn't take Crossroads while she was alive.

Flynn squeezed Torres's arm as she clambered up and over the cars. The street was strangely empty and quiet. To the south the faint orange glow showed the car wash fire had mostly died down. No shots rang out in the night, but there weren't the normal sounds of evening life like neighbors talking, animals being tended, or safety patrols moving around.

Torres took a deep breath and started walking.

"Now!" Walter yelled. The other person with him threw something. In the gloom, Torres couldn't see it, but she heard the metallic clank as it hit the street, landing only a few feet from her. She'd spent enough time on training ranges to know the sound of a grenade.

There was nowhere to go, so she dropped to her knees, head tucked, arms up to protect the sides of her head and hands over her neck.

The grenade went off, shattering the darkness with a flash and a scream of metal. The grenade spit hot, twisted fragments everywhere. Some sliced across Torres, tearing bloody furrows in her scalp, her arms, hands, and back. A big shard buried itself in her upper thigh, just below the curve of her hip. That would make walking difficult, running impossible, assuming it hadn't hit a major vein and she didn't bleed to death first.

Rough hands grabbed her, pushing her onto her stomach as someone tried to pull her arms behind her back. She twisted, posting on one foot and shoulder, trying to get back up, but her attacker had the advantage of height and weight. He put his knee between her shoulders and leaned down, crushing her to the cold asphalt.

"I got her!" Steve sounded triumphant. And premature. Sure, he'd been able to push her down, but keeping her there was a different story. She still had one arm free. She drew her knife and stabbed up and back, catching Steve's leg. She could feel that the cut wasn't deep, barely more than a flesh wound, but he howled and jerked back, giving her enough space to get both arms free and push up to her knees.

Steve lunged for her barehanded and she slashed, nearly taking out his eyes. Her knife opened a line across his forehead.

"Hold her steady," Walter said, his voice sounding much closer. He must have come up to help Steve capture her.

"What kind of truce is this?" Flynn demanded, but Torres didn't have the time or focus to spare in answering her. Torres staggered to her feet; the knife pointed out menacingly. She kept her attention on Steve, who was looking for an opening.

Walter stopped and lifted his pistol.

"Drop it," he said.

What would he do if she didn't? Would he shoot her and risk being taken down by the Crossroads defenders?

But if she was dead, she would have exactly zero chance of salvaging the situation.

Unclenching her fingers from around her knife was one of the hardest things Torres had ever done.

"Steve, lead the way," Walter said. "Don't try anything," he added to Torres.

"What's going on?" Flynn called. Torres pictured the older woman squinting at their indistinct dark shapes moving around in the gloom.

"It's fine." Torres tried to sound confident and reassuring. "I'm going with them to negotiate. If I'm not back in fifteen minutes, assume they killed me and show them no mercy."

"Enough." Walter pushed her forward. "Move."

Torres moved, following the faint light from Steve's flashlight, hoping that Sebald really did want to negotiate, not simply finish what he'd started on the lake shore in Yellowstone.

Chapter 27 - Marius

Marius took the Old Line gully north, keeping out of sight of both the zeppelin and the ground troops coming behind it. If he could get into Crossroads, he could warn Mayor Flynn. Chances were good Torres had taken a radio with her. Flynn could contact her, let her know to turn back if she hadn't already seen the zeppelin.

As he rode up out of the gully on the northern outskirts of town, Marius realized that the attackers from Yellowstone weren't the only threat. A swarm of Infected rushed down the mountains from the west. A week or two earlier and Marius might not have seen them, but now the rocky slopes were mostly bare, the leaves gone with winter coming on.

Marius yanked Chaldene to a halt so hard the poor horse nearly sat down. The last time he'd seen this many Infected was at Mammoth Cave and even there, he mostly only saw a few at a time, not all together like this swarm. No, the last time he'd seen this many Infected was in Great Falls right before he gave himself up to Carmine.

He suppressed a shudder, wrenched his mind away from the tube and everything that followed. What did John always say? Work the problem. The problem, in this case, was a hive's worth of Infected seemed to have sprouted from the mountainside and were on an avalanche's course to destroy Crossroads.

Options. He needed options. He could go back to the ranch, a good two-hour ride now, and raise the alarm, round up whichever Rangers were still around to defend the town, but by the time they got back there probably wouldn't be a town to defend, so no. He could warn the town, but what could they do? Realistically, they couldn't fight both Yellowstone and the Infected. They would have to abandon Crossroads and go ... where? To the ranch? Try to get to Anoheka, the next closest town? Thirty-seven miles on foot was more than a day's walking, assuming they weren't attacked along the way, which they probably would be.

The only things Marius had with him to fight against the Infected were the inhibitor infused mold, which was part of every Ranger's kit, and his blood. He had to be smart about how he used them. The mold would cover almost a mile if he laid it down in very thin lines. Looking at the edge of Crossroads, he figured he could channel the Infected toward the east side of town. That would give the defenders the most time to see them and respond.

And when the Infected reach the end of the mold line,

Marius thought, they'll meet me and my abominable blood.

It wasn't a great plan, or even a good one, but as he coaxed Chaldene into a reluctant trot and then a gallop, he knew it was the best one he had.

The Infected were fast. Marius knew that from experience, but it seemed that they were even faster than usual. Or he misjudged how close they were. Whatever the reason, every time he glanced up from spreading the mold, they seemed to have jumped across wider gaps of the foothills and prairie than he could have imagined.

Afternoon vanished into evening. Marius strained to pick out the dark patches of mold against the gloom-shrouded ground. He didn't have enough to double up anywhere. The work was painstaking, methodical, and backbreaking.

Finally, with a long popping creak of his spine, Marius stood upright. His supply of mold was depleted.

The Infected were barely a half mile away from town. Chaldene caught their scent and her head jerked up as she snorted, ears pinned back, eyes rolling. Marius patted her neck before taking off her saddlebags, saddle, and bridle. The mare's best chance was on her own. He trusted she had the good sense to keep well away from the Infected.

Now it was time to get to Crossroads. Marius took his go-bag out of the saddlebags and turned back toward town.

Two Littles, former rabbits from the look of their bedraggled ears, stared at him. He didn't think, the knife already in his hand, slicing across his palm as his brain registered what the creatures were. The blood welled and he squeezed, flicking a handful of red droplets across both the Infected. He didn't wait to watch them die. Their shrieks and screams were enough. He didn't need to see it, didn't need to watch their organs liquify or pressurize or turn inside out.

If he was lucky, those were scouts, not linked into the Infected network. If he wasn't lucky, he'd just alerted the whole Infected hoard to his location. Either way, he needed to put some distance between himself and the rapidly dying Littles.

Scattered along the north end of Crossroads were a row of McMansions, a development that some investment company from the East Coast started in hopes of cornering the real estate market on all the work-from-homers who were destined to move to Montana for the fresh air and low rent. The arrival of HHV ensured no one would ever cash in on their speculating. The houses loomed, empty, dead-eyed hulks, too big for anyone to live in without central heating.

Marius slipped between the houses, using them as cover from the Littles and any other Infected that might be close by. As he sprinted across a narrow alley, an arrow whizzed by barely a foot over his head. He dropped, rolled, and came up in a crouch, flattened against one of the houses. In the twilight, it was impossible to see where the shot came from.

"That's right, you Yellowstone piece of shit," hissed a

voice. It sounded higher up, probably in a second-floor room or on a roof. "Try sneaking up somewhere else."

"I'm not from Yellowstone," Marius snapped. His hand smarted from the cut but he didn't want to bandage it considering there were definitely other Infected in the vicinity.

"Prove it," came the voice again.

Something blocked the faint glimmer of light still visible above the jagged black peaks of the Rockies. Marius looked up. A pair of flying Infected about the size of very large eagles, soared silently over the prairie, moving directly towards where the scientist crouched in the alley.

"Hey." The archer didn't seem to have noticed the Infected.

"Get inside," Marius whisper-shouted. "The Infected are coming."

"What kind of lame attempt is that? Go inside or the Infected will get you and oh, by the way, thanks for letting me waltz down the str —"

Marius didn't need to hear the screaming or the visceral crushing, squishing sounds to know what was happening. The mold might slow or redirect the Infected on the ground, but it was irrelevant to the flyers. All he could do was hope there weren't many of them.

No point staying. Marius tucked his rifle under his arm, wrapped his scarf around his hand, and scuttled away from the lookout post. He didn't know how far around the eastern end of town the Infected might go, so he kept moving, sprinting from shadow to shadow, hoping the lookouts were more interested in the screams from the north end of town than in one person running down the road.

He dashed around a corner and skidded to a stop. An Infected stood at the end of the street, its bulk blocking the intersection. Once it had been a bear, a grizzly. The bear Infected lumbered down the street, smacking its jaws, a trail of slobber glinting in the fading light. Marius stumbled back, tugging the makeshift bandage off his hand. The Infected reared up, nose twitching, multiple small eyes searching the gloom as its sensory tentacles flailed toward the scientist.

The bear Infected roared and bluff charged but skidded to a stop well away from Marius. It swiped a paw in his direction. Most of its fur had fallen out. Patches of the bear's skull gleamed white against a few matted tufts of hair.

"I don't think she likes you, bro," said a voice that chilled Marius.

Carmine stepped into view from behind the bear. Shuffling behind him, came an Enlightened. It hunched, using several thick tentacles to hold itself upright. The bear growled again, drawing back its lips to show several rows of crooked teeth.

"We thought you died in the crash," Marius said, playing for time.

"How many times have you tried to kill me?" Carmine asked. He reached over and caressed the bear's shoulder the way a gunslinger might stroke their holster before a shootout. "I'm gonna miss you, bro."

The Infected charged.

Marius flung out his hand, spattering the creature with his blood, even as it crashed into him. They rolled and slid across the street and smashed into a parked car.

Marius kicked free, half-crawling, half-running to escape. The bear Infected wrapped its tentacles around his legs and yanked. Down and back, his lacerated hand grating across the asphalt.

The bear Infected flipped Marius over, onto his back. For a moment, it glared down at him, its milky eyes rolling in its bleached skull. The remaining skin around the muzzle was starting to blacken and slough off — his blood at work.

It wouldn't be fast enough. The bear Infected would kill him before the inhibitor could kill it.

Carmine loomed above, a triumphant smile on his face.

"Not sure Viers will be happy about you being dead but say la fee. You speak French, right, bro?" Absently, Carmine tangled his hand in the shuffling Enlightened's communication tentacles. "Anyway, there's a cost to everything."

"There's a cost to everything," John had said. They were sitting on the sofas in the Level 3 observation area at Chrysalis. Outside, the violent reds, oranges, and yellows of a desert sunset streaked the sky. Christmas was only two weeks away and John, Marius, and Miranda were enjoying their recently granted freedom from the Submarine quarantine.

"I'm still thinking professional assassin would be an awesome internship," Miranda said. She cuddled against Marius's arm, hands wrapped tightly around a mug of coffee. "I could definitely get access to anyone. I'd act all sweet and innocent and like I needed help or whatever and they would let me in."

"Getting access isn't the problem," John had said.

"Anyone can kill someone else, as long as they're prepared to trade their life for the mark's."

Marius could try to escape, could squirm away from the bear Infected and run. He might hide in the town until other people were able to react.

Or.

He flicked open his pocketknife. The bear Infected lay down, pinning his legs under its massive body. Marius lifted his right arm and sliced, not across, but up.

There's a cost to everything. Killing the bear, spreading the inhibitor to the Enlightened, igniting a Flash that might save Crossroads from the swarm. If he was willing to trade his life for the mark's.

Marius shoved his arm, fountaining blood, into the bear's maw. With his left hand, he bashed the road flare from his go-bag on the street.

He smiled as he watched the sparkling shimmer of the inhibitor crackle over the bear's back, up the tentacles, across Carmine who was touching both the Infected and the Enlightened.

"Thanks, Anino," Marius said. "I couldn't have done this without you, bro."

The Enlightened screamed, incandescent for a moment and then gone as the Flash rolled outwards with it as epicenter.

Chapter 28 - Torres

Torres didn't know whether to be insulted or glad her captors didn't bother to blindfold her as they hustled her through Crossroads. Her mind scrabbled for a plan, an escape, any way to salvage the situation.

The only bright spot was that Marius's stubborn martyr complex had, for once, taken him out of the path of danger. He would be relatively safe for the weeks the trip to Kentucky would take. She would be lucky to survive the night.

The Yellowstone invaders' temporary headquarters was inside the Dairy Dollar, an abandoned gas station and convenience store near the southeastern corner of town. Rifles and bows were stacked in a corner. In another corner, a bundle of duffel bags waited. Sebald himself was holding court from behind the long disused counter. Paper maps in plastic protectors were spread out in front of him. They were marked up with wax pencil showing the Yellowstone forces' positions and where they believed the Crossroads defenders were dug in.

"Any problems?" Sebald asked, barely glancing up as Walter shoved Torres forward. About two dozen people milled around, sorting weapons and ammunition, packing small parcels of food and supplies. A few treated others with wounds.

"She fucked my face up," Steve said. He pressed a wad of cloth over the slice on his forehead. Torres tried not to smirk, imagining Frankenstein-esque stitches across his face.

Sebald glanced up. "Language," he said flatly before returning his attention to the maps.

"You've lost your tactical advantage," Torres said. "Unless you have NODs, you're not doing anything with that blimp tonight."

"How do you think this ends?" Sebald said.

"With you dead."

"There you go, getting all emotional." He shook his head and smiled. "I should have asked to talk to the man in charge. Walter, where's that scientist fellow?"

"Haven't seen him, boss," Walter said.

"Guess we're stuck dealing with you, then," Sebald said.

"We're not dealing," Torres said. "We're accepting your surrender."

"You don't dictate terms, señorita. You listen."

Torres shoved her hands into her pockets to keep from lunging at the man. Her pride wasn't the only or even the most important thing on the line. Every minute of time she kept him focused on her was time the defenders had to build barricades, get the non-combatants out of harm's way, and maybe allow reinforcements to arrive.

"There's no reason we can't all work together," Sebald said. Torres dug her nails through the thin fabric of the inside of her pocket and into her thigh. Her hip was still bleeding a little and throbbed a bright, sharp pain whenever she moved. She focused on the pain, feeling it wash through her and over and beyond.

"I'm listening." Torres managed to drizzle her voice in sweet compliance. Men like Sebald craved dominance, feared being seen as weak. Torres wasn't in a position of strength, so she would have to be smarter.

"What we're offering is mutually beneficial, win-win. Crossroads comes under the protection of Yellowstone and we get some resources we need."

"What resources did you have in mind?"

"There's a lot of ranches and farms around here," Sebald said. "Don't know if you were paying attention, but not a lot of crops grow around Yellowstone. We'll need food."

"We'll also need the food we've spent all year growing," Torres said.

"And we'll need bodies to help move, process, and guard that food," Sebald continued as if she hadn't spoken.

"What do we get in return for giving up our food and labor?" Torres wanted to know what Sebald envisaged for their joint future. Something like a feudal system in medieval Europe, she suspected. That was the kind of unoriginal scheme he would latch onto.

"Protection, like I said. Clearly, you need it. Look how easy it was for us. What if we had bad intentions like killing everyone and burning this place to the ground? Or just taking every able-bodied person and leaving the rest behind to starve?"

Torres didn't point out that was basically what Yellowstone was trying to do: burn the town, kill people, and enslave those strong enough to be useful while letting the rest fend for themselves.

"Protection," she said, as if actually considering his ridiculous offer.

"Let me put it this way," Sebald said as he folded up one of the maps. "Either you agree to our terms and you become Yellowstone civilians, or you force us to expend a lot of our limited supplies and manpower, which means when we take your little town here, which we will, we'll need to resupply and plus up our numbers. That means not only will you owe the usual tithe, but damages."

"You want us to pay you to cover the costs of you invading us?" Torres used most of her willpower to keep from laughing in Sebald's face.

"Resistance isn't just futile, señorita, it's also expensive."

She stared at him; her mind slammed to a halt by his sheer audacity.

"Now, I'm going to have Walter and Steve take you back so you can let the rest of your men know to stand down. My offer is only good for the next thirty minutes. After that, anyone resisting will be killed and their family will be on the hook for the trouble they caused."

"This way," Steve said and when she hesitated,

staring at Sebald, trying to figure out exactly what kind of megalomaniac she was dealing with, Steve pushed her shoulder.

"Okay, I'm going," Torres said. There was no way Crossroads would accept Sebald's terms and surrender, but half an hour would give them more time. Without reinforcements, she didn't know if they could hold out longer than the night. The zeppelin would likely be up and flying again by morning and it was too big of an advantage. The best they could hope for was to clear everyone out of town during the night and torch it. If they couldn't have Crossroads, no one would.

She had no idea how she would convince Mayor Flynn or the rest of the townies of that logic. They would probably want to make some kind of heroic statement, raised on too many last stand movies like The Magnificent Seven, 300, and Evangelion. Torres valued living to fight another day. Defeat was only permanent if you were dead.

As they exited the gas station, Steve shoved her hard and she stumbled. She felt the wound in her hip reopen and a fresh trickle of warm blood run down her thigh. She pressed her palm against the rip in her jeans, trying to get an idea of how bad the injury was. It had to be just a flesh wound or she wouldn't have been able to keep going this long.

She limped alongside Steve, barely able to see him in the darkness when the sky burst open. A ball of light exploded from somewhere on the north end of town. Flashes raced out from the epicenter, crackling in all directions, most going west where smaller explosions of fire and light followed.

"What the h —" Steve started but stopped with a choking gurgle. Torres spun in time to see him slump to the street, blood pumping from a gash in his neck. A man stepped back from Steve's body, wiping a knife on the sleeve of his jacket.

"So, what's the story, then?" Liam asked. "Need a bit of rescuing, do we?" He smirked and, for once, Torres didn't want to murder him.

"It's a beautiful sight, isn't it?" Liam took out a thin piece of paper and sprinkled in tobacco before carefully rolling a cigarette.

"Don't smoke in here," Mayor Flynn said.

They stood in the Post Office, behind the counter with its pane of bullet proof glass and heavy, locked door. Through the front window, they could see the street and the fleet of motorcycles parked in ranks. Twenty-four by Torres's quick count. Where Liam had found that many functional motorcycles, and how he'd managed to get enough gas to get them all from Great Falls to Crossroads, was a mystery for another time.

At the moment, they needed to use the explosions to their advantage. Yellowstone wouldn't understand what was happening on the northern edge of Crossroads. There was no reason for the defenders to be blowing up their own territory.

"Shit," Torres said, realization twisting around her brain. "Freaking shit."

"What now?" Liam tucked his cigarette in the breast

pocket of his denim jacket.

"The Flash," Torres said.

Liam and Flynn exchanged puzzled glances.

"The Portland Flash." Torres leaned over the counter and peered out the front window, but all she could see was her own dim reflection lunging back at her.

"And that means what, exactly?" Flynn joined her, looking into the darkness beyond the glass.

"Marius said that in Portland the inhibitor went through a city-wide hive. He set one of the Infected on fire and it spread through the Infected network. That caused the Flash."

"Sure that sounds like a good thing," Liam said.

"Yeah, except if we're seeing a Flash —" Torres started.

"There must be a lot of Infected," Flynn finished.

"Feck."

"Indeed," Flynn said drily. "Yellowstone to the south and Infected to the north."

"Or not," Liam said. "If there was a Flash, wouldn't that do for the Infected?"

"Maybe," Torres said. "But we have to assume they're there until we know they're not."

"Me and my lads are gonna leave that mess for you to sort out," Liam said. "We're here for the Yellowstone crew and our share of the spoils." He winked at Flynn as he stepped outside to light his cigarette.

"We need all the friends we can get." Torres shrugged. "I'll go north. You still have contact with Seung and the others?" The mayor nodded. She squeezed Torres's arm briefly and turned back to her own maps. For a moment, Torres hesitated. What did

Flynn know about defending a town under siege?

As much as I do, Torres thought. She shook her head with a rueful grin. No, she would have to trust that Flynn was competent. Much as she wanted to, Torres couldn't be everywhere at once, couldn't fix everything herself.

What she could do was scout out the Infected and figure out exactly how deep in shit they were.

She gave Liam a half-friendly punch on the shoulder as she headed out, thankful for the tight bandage Flynn had helped her apply to her hip. As she suspected, it was a flesh wound, but in a really inconvenient spot for someone who had to do a lot of walking, running, and now skulking.

Although true night had the town in its jaws, there was still enough light for Torres to pick her way along the streets. Avoiding the hulks of the mostly useless cars was easy. The occasional flare spattered the sky with Independence Day hues. Ahead, a flickering wall of fire marked out where the Flash ripped across the north edge of town. Further out, patches of smolder and char shone against the gray dun of the prairie grass. Torres thanked the recent rains once again.

The first of the Infected she found was alive, but barely. Half its body was gone, the stumps of limbs and trails of viscera cauterized and reeking. She stabbed it through the ear, didn't wait for the twitching to die off before she moved on.

As she made her way toward the heart of the Flash, she found fewer intact Infected. At the edges of the Flash's radius, the Infected were mostly all together. Further in, they were smoking husks and chunks, and near the center, piles of ash and stains.

Beside the biggest pile of ash, she found the arm.

His arm.

She was on her knees, fingers scrabbling through the slimy, sooty remnants of some huge Infected, hoping and terrified to find the rest of him. But no. Only his right forearm, the end a blackened snarl of ligaments, strings of muscle, and bloodless veins.

She knew the way her fingers fit through his, the shape of the palm that had cupped her cheek, the soft skin on the underside of his wrist, but she didn't want to know. There was a gash torn up the inside of his arm, from below the wrist up, the skin split open, bloody and burned. She turned the arm over, saw the round pink scars that marred the olive skin on the back, a reminder of the white phosphorus bombing in Wiltz. Final, definitive proof.

It was Marius's arm.

She didn't scream, didn't cry, didn't even groan. There was no sound terrible enough to express her pain. All she could do was rock back and forth, clutching the arm to her chest.

Rain.

Slow and soft. Cold and hissing as it quenched the few small fires left along the Flash's path.

Torres looked up, her eyes tracking the ash as the wind swirled it away. It caught on the bones of the beast that had died on at her feet. Something big, like a bison or a bear. Maybe a moose. Her mind leaped on that puzzle so it didn't have to think about the lifeless arm cradled in her lap.

As the ash blew away, it revealed two bodies. Not Infected bodies. Humans. Two men.

Torres staggered up.

With shaking hands, she rolled the nearest one over. A blackened trail slashed from one arm to the other. The skin of his face had peeled away from the middle of his skull, but she could still recognize him. She'd seen him enough at Chrysalis.

Carmine Anino.

The other man lay on his side, his dark hair powdered gray by the ash. Torres hesitated. In this moment, she didn't have to know that he was dead. As long as she hovered above him, watched the rain caress the soft shell of his ear, trace lines down his throat, she didn't have to face the rest of her life without him. She could stay, exist in this time sheltered by her own willful ignorance.

"Marius." His name, like a prayer filled with all her wishful dreams and couldn't-be's.

She lowered herself, careful not to disturb him as if he was only asleep. His face looked peaceful, happy; almost satisfied. She brushed away the ash and soot on his cheek.

His eye lids fluttered. A sliver of jade green, his pupils wide and shocky.

His hand moved. His one remaining hand, lifting, trying to take hers. She caught it, squeezed his fingers, so cold, but still somehow alive.

"I was wrong. I'm sorry," he murmured, words slurring together as his eyes closed again.

"I don't care," Torres said. All that mattered was the

pulse flickering in his neck, rapid and weak, failing and fading.

She jumped up. "Medic!" There was only her, the wind, the rain, and ashes of the Infected.

And Marius's aid bag. Never leave home without it.

His arm had been severed just below the elbow. The only thing that had saved him from bleeding out was that the Flash had cauterized most of the wound. Torres cleaned and bandaged the stump as best she was able, trying to avoid touching the raw bits of bone she could see.

"Is he ...?"

Torres looked up, startled at Percy's voice. She didn't know how long Marius's sister had been standing there or how she'd known where they were.

"No," Torres said. "Not yet."

"We're not losing him, too." Percy grabbed Torres's arm, stopping her useless rummaging in the aid bag that had given all it had to give.

"Go get Ursula."

"I'm not leaving him." Torres shook her head.

"And I'm not running for a half a mile." Percy swept a hand over her bulging belly. "I'll stay with him. He won't be alone."

Won't be alone when he dies.

No.

Torres rejected the thought. She gave Percy a quick hug, not having the time to find the words she needed and ran.

What Torres remembered most from the night of the Battle of Crossroads wasn't how Mayor Flynn and Seung rallied the frightened townspeople to defend their homes or how Liam and his motorcycle calvary pushed the invaders back from nearly overrunning city hall. She didn't remember the way the rain came in, washing the streets clean of the Infected's ashes. She barely noticed when an F-16 screamed out of the sky, dropping fire and death on a gas station on the south edge of town, nor was she present for Sebald's ignominious capture.

What she remembered most was holding Marius's limp hand, while a grumbling veterinarian and a frantic immunologist struggled to save his life. His O negative blood, so perfect for giving to everyone else, meant no one could give him blood. Sometime in the deepest dark of night, Liam sent one of his bikers to the ranch to raid the stock of blood Marius had set aside for making vaccines.

By morning, chill and rainy, Marius was in a coma. Ursula and Rajiv quietly discussed organ shut down and systemic shock. Flynn radioed to the ranch to send for Philippe, Annette, and Anatole. Percy and Torres took turns at Marius's bedside.

Liam found Torres outside the Crossroads veterinary clinic where Ursula still held office hours even though these days most of her patients were humans.

"Smoke?" He offered one of his hand-rolled cigarettes.

Torres shook her head. She stood under the striped awning over the front door and watched the thin sheets of rain drizzling down.

"Flynn wants you at city hall," Liam said. "They've got the pilot on the radio."

He might as well have been speaking Swahili.

"Come on, old girl." He held out a hand and she allowed herself to be led. Why not? She had found Marius only in time to watch him die. What else could matter now?

Inside city hall, medics tended the wounded, and a soup kitchen was in full swing. The mood was triumphant, celebratory. Torres wanted to scream at them. Didn't they understand the world was ending? Not in the slow, impersonal sense of a pandemic, but in the real sense of a heartbeat faltering to a stop.

"Here." Flynn handed Torres a mic and automatically she took it.

"Torres here."

"Torres, this is Captain Zeller with the Light's Hope Squadron out of Detroit. Your friend Miranda asked me to check in on you. Hope you liked the present I dropped."

"Miranda?"

"Yes, ma'am," the pilot said. "I'll be out of range soon, so anything you want me to pass on to her?"

"Marius is dying." Torres hadn't meant to say that, but the words burst out as if she was vomiting them.

"I don't know who that is, but I can drop my emergency med pack. Got coordinates for me?"

"One mike." Torres handed the radio to Flynn as she flung herself at the maps.

After she relayed the ten-digit grid coordinates to the pilot and signed off, she hurried back to Ursula's clinic. Rajiv dozed in an uncomfortable armchair in a corner of the exam room Marius was in. Percy looked up as Torres entered. The room reeked of disinfectant and smoke.

"They brought this from the shed. Rajiv said it might help." She pointed to a bag of blood hanging from the IV stand. "I need to eat."

Torres pulled up the wheeled exam stool and leaned on the bed. She pillowed her head on her arms on the bed, watched the slow rise and fall of Marius's chest. Under his eyelids, she could see the flicker of movement. Was he dreaming?

She closed her eyes, pressed her face against his good hand, his only hand. Wouldn't it be nice if they could just fall asleep together and never wake up?

Voices.

Torres jerked awake. She sat up, wiped the drool off her cheek and off the back of Marius's hand. His still warm hand that was attached to his still breathing body.

Annette and Percy peeked in, the request clear in Percy's face and the desperation just as clear in Annette's.

"I need a walk." Torres stood and stretched. As she passed, Annette pulled her into a hug that nearly sent her into a crying fit. No one had hugged her like that since Mamá.

Outside she wandered. The town, so empty the previous day, seemed full of defenders, Rangers, and fighters from the other New Avalon communities. They mixed freely with the PDF members from Great Falls. The only people Torres didn't see were the unfamiliar

Yellowstone faces with their little badges on the sleeves.

She found the survivors of the bombing evacuated to a used car lot. Liam was supervising a few guards, but from the dispirited look of the prisoners, Torres didn't judge they were likely to cause any trouble.

Except Sebald.

After everything that had happened, he was unscathed.

"Come to gloat?" he said, standing up. One of the guards started forward, but Torres held up a hand to stop her.

"Do you remember what you asked me?"

"I asked you lots of things," Sebald said. "What I'm wondering right now, señorita, is where the heck did you find that fighter jet? Talk about an ace up your sleeve!"

"You asked me how I thought this would end."

"It would be a mistake to think this is over." Sebald waved at the other prisoners. "The better part of valor and all that. Live to fight another day."

"Do you remember what I said?" Torres tilted her head, watched the strong pulse in Sebald's neck, hated the way he took it for granted. Hated what he had brought to Crossroads and that he would do it again in an instant if no one stopped him.

People like Sebald were the uninfected personification of HHV. They consumed and consumed and consumed, twisting and warping everything they touched with no regard to any will but their own design. There were no draws, no ties, no win-wins, or amicable negotiations. Only winning however they defined that goal.

"You said something about my surrender." Sebald

didn't bother to hide his sneer. Torres understood him in that moment because she was like him in this one regard. Neither of them would ever surrender. They might be defeated, but they would never give up, never stop fighting. She might be able to admire him or at least respect the reflection of herself she caught in the mirror of him.

But no.

"I said, it would end with you dead." She jammed her knife up through the soft patch under his chin and into his skull. His eyes crossed and blood spattered out his nose. She wrenched the knife out and watched him fall.

People were yelling. She studied Sebald's body. He was still, more still than Marius. She smiled, wiped the blood over her face like a warrior of ancient days.

Hands on her, pulling her away. Torres let herself be taken. She had done what she meant to do. She killed monsters.

When she looked around again, really looked, it was late morning. She was sitting on a porch between Nestor and Dawn. Nestor held out an MRE poundcake and she scarfed it down like a starving vegetarian wolf.

"Flynn said when you were sensible again it would be okay to let you go back to Ursula's," Dawn said. She put an arm around Torres's shoulders. "I'll go with you. You're not alone."

Epilogue

Miranda — Mammoth Cave, Kentucky, USA —
Autumn, Year 7

It had been a long time since they'd had visitors. Uninfected visitors, that is.

Miranda double checked that all the Enlightened had their instructions. They accepted her commands easily after all these years, but she had learned the hard way to make them repeat things back to her. They occasionally got creative in their interpretations. Today was not the day for surprises.

Or rather, any more surprises.

Miranda wound her way out of the complex of the Mammoth Cave hive. At regular intervals, glowing patches of biofilm provided a pale blueish light, enough to see easily for most humans. It had been Romi's idea to ask the Enlightened to incorporate luciferins into the meat walls. Little built-in lamps so her girlfriend didn't have to risk losing her way in the labyrinth of her lair.

Romi waited for her with the golf cart in the one parking space they kept clear of the plants that had eagerly swallowed up most of the visitors' center. Her long hair was twisted into a fancy updo and she wore her favorite leather jacket with the asymmetrical collar.

"Eli sent a scout," Romi said as Miranda climbed into the cart. "Hey." She turned her face, lips puckered, towards Miranda.

"Hay is for horses," Miranda said, quoting one of John's old lines, but she kissed Romi anyway. They drove in silence back through the town, now mostly greenish humps where the buildings had been. The strangest graveyard, Miranda thought.

No bodies. We looked.

The Infected were always hungry. And angry. Miranda blew out a breath, puffing up her bangs, and tried to ignore the concerned eyes Romi was giving her. But the other woman simply stared harder, twisting her neck to lay her head on Miranda's shoulder and peer up at her, pouting out her lower lip.

"OMG, you're so weird. Stop." Miranda pushed her off. "Watch where you're driving, crazy woman."

"But what's wrong?" Romi corrected the cart's drift to keep them out of the soft ground where the roots of the sycamores gnawed away the asphalt.

"Nothing."

"Right," Romi said. "You heave big dramatic 'something's wrong' sighs because everything's going so well."

"Fine." Miranda tried to grump, but Romi's antics

were too much. "I just feel like I'm the mom of a bunch of teenagers. The Infected are so whiny and needy and angsty. It's exhausting."

"Good thing they're not drama queens," Romi said.

Miranda narrowed her eyes.

"Seriously, ahuvati. I know you're nervous about seeing them after all this time." She patted Miranda's leg. "It's going to be okay. And if it's not, you can just have the Infected murder everyone, right?"

"When you say it like that you make me sound like a crazy dictator or something." It was Miranda's turn to pout.

"You do have a bit of an authoritarian streak." Romi parked the cart in the clear space they kept in front of their house. She hopped out and stood for a moment, hands on hips, studying the porch with a critical eye. Twinkle lights wound up the columns and hung under the eaves. The six rocking chairs, collected over the past five years, gleamed from a fresh coat of lacquer. Homemade citronella candles waited at regular intervals on the porch railing.

"I don't have an authoritarian streak. Take that back." Miranda climbed the stairs and checked the cooler. Plenty of sun tea and clean water.

"There it is," Romi said, joining her. "That's the one."

Miranda checked her watch. 6:32. They were late.

"They'll be here," Romi said, lacing her fingers through Miranda's. "Since when were any of them ever on time?"

"Hey there!" A man's voice. When was the last time a man had been here? Not since Marius and Akeem's escape. Or did Carmine have the distinction of being the last uninfected man to live near the hive? No, it had to have been Eli and his 10th Mountain pals. After Miranda took over, she sent all the teenagers north with them. Let whatever remnants of the government that existed in Detroit deal with them. Or they could try for New Avalon if they felt particularly lucky and adventurous. Either way, not her problem. She had enough to deal with between managing the devolving Enlightened and disbanding the hives. Keeping the Infected under control was a full-time job plus three or four side hustles.

A rustle of feet scuffing through half a decade's worth of unraked leaves. Miranda looked up from her musing.

Eli led the group. They walked down the road single file. Miranda did a quick headcount. Ten people as they'd agreed.

Romi waved and shouted something in Hebrew. Eli grinned and waved back. He'd gone grey at the temples, even though he couldn't be more than mid-thirties. Hard years.

Romi kissed Miranda's cheek and skipped off the porch to hug Eli. They hung back with the other escorts while four people stepped forward.

Torres's hair was still short. Percy's was still in a long ponytail. Standing between the women was a little girl. She had her mother's cleft chin and sandy blonde hair, the same shade as John's. The girl held Percy's hand tightly, leaning back against the man who stood behind her.

He was every bit as handsome as he'd ever been, even short half an arm. He smiled his old, crooked grin.

"The Survivors' Club missed you, Miranda."

Marius — Detroit, Michigan, USA – Summer, Year 7

Months gone. Missing or more accurately taken in a feverish haze.

When Marius finally woke up enough to stay awake for more than a few minutes, winter had slipped in and disguised the world in snow. Crossroads was rebuilding, this time with an eye to defensibility. Torres convinced some construction workers and the blacksmith from Esmeralda to help her build an air tower. She spent the rest of the winter getting the zeppelin functioning again when she wasn't nursing Marius back to health or supervising his physical therapy. Learning to get through life one handed was one of the most annoying and frustrating challenges Marius had ever faced. At least it was his right hand he lost. Small mercies.

Hectra Courage-Tenartier was born on a stormy night in late April. Reggie assisted Percy through labor and delivery, with Rajiv hovering the background, determined to learn more what he called hands-on doctoring. Annette and Philippe seemed intent on drowning their grandbaby in crochet blankets, knitted booties and sweaters, most of which she only wore once before outgrowing them.

By summer, Marius was ready to join the Rangers on their patrols. In the autumn, nearly a year after losing his hand, he and Torres led a long-range patrol south to scout out what remained of Yellowstone. The Infected had found the community first. It took three trips to eliminate the hive that had taken root in the lakeside community center. By then the snow was back and worse than before.

Three years of bad winters followed. No one knew where the clouds came from. Volcanic eruptions, Flashes, nukes. They had nothing but rumors and short summers, which sent them bustling like manic squirrels to store up food for the winter. Every year, usually around January or February, the New Avalon council heard proposals about moving south in the spring, and every spring when the lambs and calves and colts wobbled through new green fields, people forgot they ever wanted to leave.

"It'll take more than a few unprecedented disasters to pry us from our homes," Percy said, summing up the general feeling.

A year ago, they made contact with the Air Force squadron that had left Great Falls for Duluth. That spring, they received the first relayed message from Jada Hallis, acting President of the United States. She had been the Speaker of the House. When everything fell apart in Washington D.C. she evacuated to a bunker in Detroit. To the best of her knowledge, she was the ranking member of the last duly elected government.

"I understand that many Americans rightly feel our government failed them," she said in her recording. "It is my intent, along with surviving members of the Joint Chiefs of Staff, to reestablish your faith and trust in the government, which is necessary to reconstitute our United States of America. To do that, we are reaching out to survivors. Whether you are alone or part of a community, you are welcome. We are currently based in Detroit and are working hard every day to reestablish contact with the rest of the nation. You are not alone. For those in need of assistance, we are able to offer housing, medical aid, including HHV vaccines, and protection. I am looking forward to getting a chance to meet you. Until then, stay safe and may God bless America."

"Well," Torres said, turning off the radio broadcast. "She certainly sounds like a politician."

"Detroit again," Marius said. The winter hadn't been as bad as the previous two, a sign of better days to come according to Philippe and his weather eye. After nearly four years of perimeter patrols with the occasional trip to Running Rabbit, Great Falls or Yellowstone, Marius was ready for something more challenging. Something worthy of the title Ranger. Something with the possibility of an actual laboratory at the end of the long, dusty, and dangerous trip.

"I know that look," Torres said. She leaned her head against his shoulder, and he knew she would go with him. Her restless heart needed space just like his. In the summer, Torres deputized Nestor to lead the Rangers in her absence and they packed their gear and headed east. They avoided the Remnant in Minot and the burned out remains of the Twin Cities in Minnesota. Parts of Chicago were underwater, and the aquatic Infected there were particularly troublesome. The inhibitor mold was better, but still not exactly fast acting. They fought their way clear, marked Chicago as a no-go zone, and continued their trip.

The morning they arrived in Detroit was overcast with a prickly heat in the air that promised a storm later. The main streets of the city were clear. No rusting cars or piles of leaves. Solar panels graced many roofs and windmills stood sentinel on hills. Freshly painted signs advertised a weekly farmers' market and gear swap. And there were soldiers. Actual soldiers. Not militia. Not mercenaries or raiders. Professionally trained people who had vowed to protect the idea of America with their lives.

They were stopped and searched by scouts before too long, which seemed to make Torres feel better. Marius objected when they confiscated Isaac Mendelsen's badge.

"Next step to enter Detroit for free trading is medical quarantine," the young sergeant on duty informed them.

"They want us to quarantine," Torres said, with a barely concealed smirk. "In case we're infected."

"Yep." Marius didn't think it was nearly as funny. To be so close and stopped for this nonsense. His missing arm ached, which it often did when he was stressed.

"What else can we do?" Torres said. She shot him that 'Don't you dare' look in case he might be tempted to reveal his identity.

"Nothing," Marius said.

They spent a few hours in the quarantine cabin, which other than having a lock on the outside, was very comfortable. Even so, Marius couldn't stop his pacing. Torres flopped onto one of the cots, pulled out the paperback she was reading, and ignored him.

A knock on the door, quick and soft. Torres slid off the bed and in between Marius and the door before the bolt was unlocked.

The door opened.

The man who stood before them had a monk's fringe of hair around a mostly bald head. He wore wire rimmed glasses and a button up shirt that not only had recently been washed but also ironed.

"Dr. Tenartier," he said and held out a hand to shake.

Marius took the other man's hand with his left, a huge grin on his face.

"Dr. Mendelsen. Sorry it took us so long to accept your invitation. There was this pandemic ..."

Torres studied the New Avalon charter and the Ranger creed. She stood in the barn, beside the cracked La-Z-Boy. After all this time, John's scent was very gone, but she still came here to ask his advice, as if he haunted the Ranger's headquarters benevolently dispensing insight as needed.

"The question is," she said. "Do we formally accept citizenship in Hallis's America or do we maintain our independence?"

It was hard to believe that was the question. What would John make of a former Marine who didn't jump at the chance to serve and defend her nation? But was the reforming collection of communities based in Detroit a nation? And if it was, that didn't make it hers.

True, over the past year, New Avalon benefited a lot from their trade relationship with the reconstituted United States. Marius made two more trips to bring mold and follow up with Dr. Mendelsen on Detroit's own growing operation as well as share more of his base strain blood.

"Ah, here you are," Soraya said as she walked into the barn. "I assured the happy couple you would not be late today of all days."

Torres nodded, carefully re-rolling the papers and putting them away in their plastic document protectors.

"You're not nervous?"

"Not about the wedding," Torres said.

"About the offer from Detroit?"

"Yeah. It feels too much like Yellowstone. Would we be under their protection? What would that mean? Marius is so happy to get into a real lab again, he's not looking at the strings."

Soraya took Torres's arm and hooked it through her elbow, drawing the other woman out of the barn. The Morning Star ranch was nearly unrecognizable from the family operation it started as. A rambling two story bunkhouse served as a home base for Rangers not on long range missions. Three windmills graced different hilltops, providing electricity, as did the solar panels on every southerly facing roof. A large tent fluttered on the front lawn, hung with colorful bundles of autumn leaves and pine boughs. Streamers of gauzy material waved from the tent's corners. A banner proclaimed: Congratulations, Mirzha & Washington!

"I can't believe I have to get all dressed up to walk twenty feet," Torres grumbled. She tugged at the sky-blue vest she wore over a creamy yellow button-up shirt.

"You look wonderful," Soraya said. "I would expect nothing less of my daughter's co-parent."

"How are you calmer than me?" Torres said. "You're the mother of the bride."

"I don't think of it as losing a daughter, but rather, that I am gaining a son."

The tent was packed. Torres hardly recognized most of the guests. She would bet all the coffee she had that most of these people didn't know either the bride or groom personally. These days, folks seized any excuse to celebrate.

Torres and Soraya waited beside the tent. Inside, a low hum of voices as the guests caught up on what was going on in their respective communities. Torres peeked in at Washington, standing beside Mayor Flynn who was officiating. Freshly washed, brushed, and shaved, he looked more eager than nervous. He beamed at her and waved.

The front door of the main house opened and Annette stepped aside to let Mirzha out. Torres had to admit the New Avalon tailors had done themselves proud. The dress was pale yellow with blue accents that perfectly set off Mirzha's complexion. Her dark hair was loose and curling around her shoulders, a crown of late season wildflowers atop her head. She looked around and smiled as her eyes met Soraya's.

"Don't cry," Torres said as Mirzha lifted her long skirt and made her way, with dainty steps, down the porch stairs.

"I am not one of your Rangers," Soraya said. "I do as I please." She wiped her cheeks and smiled at her daughter.

Torres tapped the side of the tent to signal Elfy. Her niece and Wahida were co-ring bearers. The tweens paced down the aisle, the picture of solemnity. Hectra and Asha were co-flower girls. With a whoop they set off, flinging handfuls of leaves and dried flower petals at the assembly. Elfy and Wahida started giggling while they tried to glare the younger children into better behavior. Washington shook his head but winked at Torres.

Soraya hugged Mirzha.

"Thank you," Mirzha whispered. "I love you both."

"We love you, too," Torres said. She held out her arm and Mirzha took it.

After the ceremony, came the food. Everyone had

brought something, eager to show off what their community had to offer. Point Zebulon was shamelessly courting Ursula as their own doctor had recently died. They made a show of giving her jars of fresh honey, kombucha flavored with blueberries and ginger, and mittens lined with rabbit's fur.

Marius came to find Torres as she sat on the hill behind the main house, watching the bonfire and listening to musicians tuning up for what Liam called 'a proper session'. Marius carried two bottles of beer, tucked under his left arm. He handed her one and lowered himself carefully so as not to jiggle the other too much.

"That's life," he said as she opened the bottles for them. They clinked and lifted their beers in silent toast to the newlyweds, who were being earnestly serenaded by a trio of singers and a fiddler.

"That's what we've been fighting for all these years," he added.

Torres leaned against him and he wrapped his half arm around her, pulled her tight, and rested his cheek against her head.

"So, when's our happy ending?" Torres said. The offer from Detroit still buzzed in her brain. It would be nice to retire, to leave the endless, exhausting, heartbreaking job of security to someone else.

"Who said we get one?" Marius said. She turned to look up at the underside of his chin, the sharp sweep of his jaw, his dark hair pulled back for the occasion, although she preferred it loose so she could get a handful of it.

"Who said we wanted one?" she mused. She would

never be able to trust someone else to take care of those she loved like she did. They would never be willing to make the sacrifices necessary to allow studious Mirzha and thoughtful, poetic Washington the luxury of this night.

Every scar was a token of her commitment, every long hour scouting for Infected or cold night on patrol for raiders were her love letters to her family, her community, to John's memory and to the future of his child and the other children likely to come soon.

Elfy strolled around the house and waved.

"Tia Lourdie, Nestor said to tell you there's someone at the gate for you. Tio Marius, your mama said to get your butt back down there and show her you've got two working dance feet."

"Debatable," Marius said, clambering up.

"Ha!" Torres said, pushing him a little with her hip. "At least I don't have to dance."

"But you'll come save me, right?"

"Always."

She kissed him and poked Elfy. "Wanna go with, mi sobrina favorita?"

"Nah," Elfy said. "Me and Wahida are spying on the kids from Great Falls." She put a hand on her hip, watching the festivities. For a second, she looked exactly like Cynty. She's growing up, Torres thought with an unexpected pang.

"Have fun, Elfy."

"Elfreda." Her niece rolled her eyes. Where had she learned that? Miranda had only visited once. She'd been invited to the wedding but she declined, saying she didn't really know the couple and she understood how distracting she was.

"Got it. Sorry, Elfreda," Torres said. She caught the girl in a hug, wandering how much longer until she was too mature for such things. Hopefully, never.

The gatehouse had been much improved, but the original sign with the original letters and star symbol remained. Torres waved to the guards on watch. She could see a small group of refugees waiting in the designated screening area. Over the years, the number of people coming to the Morning Star ranch itself had dropped. Most people couldn't travel long distances, especially not during the years of the bad winters. Unless they had very good reason for leaving whatever community they were in, they stayed put.

As she approached the gate, two women detached themselves from the others and started towards her. They stopped short of the gate, uncertain of their welcome.

"Open the gate," Torres said. She was surprised her voice was steady because she was shaking all over.

The gate swung easily on well-greased hinges. Nothing but air stood between Torres and her sister and her mother. She ran to them.

The End

About the Author

M. K. Martin is an author and editor. Her work appears in literary journals, in several anthologies, and in her novels *Survivors' Club* and *Ashfall*.

Martin is a restless world traveler who started writing young. She was an exchange student to Paraguay, joined the US Army, got deployed to Afghanistan and to Iraq, and currently lives in Ireland, where she indulges her deep love of tea.

Find out more at mkmartinwriter.com

Special Thanks

To the Gullkistan Center for Creativity, located in picturesque Laugarvatn, Iceland. If not for spending a month there, I never would have finished this book. Okay, probably I would have, but not any time soon.

To my Irish writers' group:

- Diana "Pom" Lorenz - who effortlessly writes witty and whimsical stories, full of twists and humor. I'm honored to be a part of your writing journey.
- Abi Montgomery - whose searingly honest and deliciously insightful food memoir pieces inspire both creativity and hunger. I can't wait to read the finished book!
- Rebekah Phelan - who beguiles language and makes words dance to her tune. I can only hope to read more of your fantasies.
- Lucy Varanius - who sees the profound in the everyday details of life and has somehow mastered

the art of the short story. Would that all writers were so gifted.

To my dedicated beta readers: Katie & Ciarán McKenna - I'm sorry there weren't more nipples. 'Tis a shameful lack and I deeply regret failing you in such a fashion.

To Soňa Dowds, Helena NíGabhadubh, Conchobhar Ó Súilleabháin, Walter Montague, Kieran "Noodles" Barry, and the rest of the reenactors for welcoming a Yank blow-in and teaching me what bits of Irish history I have.

To my stalwart editor, Karen Eisenbrey. Thanks for sticking with the series, for your keen eye in spotting mistakes, and your tactful suggestions for improvement.

And finally, to Aaron, my muse, and to Varya, my ~~raisin~~...*raison d'être*. I hope I make you proud.